Jenny Eclair is one of the UK's most successful and popular comedians and actors. She is the author of two previous critically acclaimed novels. She is one of only two female comedians to have won the prestigious Perrier Award.

LIFE, DEATH AND VANILLA SLICES

Jenny Eclair

SPHERE

First published in Great Britain as a paperback original in 2012 by Sphere
Reprinted 2012 (twice)

A CIP catalogue record for this book
is available from the British Library.

ISBN 978-1-8474-4493-6

Typeset in Bembo by Palimpsest Book Production Ltd, Falkirk, Stirlingshire
Printed and bound in Great Britain by
Clays Ltd, St Ives plc

Papers used by Sphere are from well-managed forests
and other responsible sources.

MIX
Paper from
responsible sources
FSC® C104740

Sphere
An imprint of
Little, Brown Book Group
100 Victoria Embankment
London EC4Y 0DY

An Hachette UK Company
www.hachette.co.uk

www.littlebrown.co.uk

For June, Sara and Phoebe, and for mothers,
sisters, daughters everywhere

Acknowledgements

I'd like to thank my parents for supplying me with northern roots and London for letting me re-root.

Many thanks also to my editor, the ever-patient Antonia Hodgson, and to Avalon for occasionally cracking the whip; cheers too to Geof who is always there, even if he's just pretending to listen.

Anne

Busy, Busy, Busy

Anne has had a busy day. This morning she queued for thirty-five minutes outside the organic butcher's on Lordship Lane, only for them to be 'fresh out of partridge breasts. Would some nice fillets of pork do?'

The fillets sit glistening on Anne's black marble kitchen work surface, fleshy and pink in their white paper wrapping.

What on earth had she been thinking? No one likes pork, not really, but she'd chosen the fillets and now she must do something with the wretched things, and not just throw them at the wall.

Anne Armitage is forty-eight and peri-menopausal. This shouldn't be a big deal, it's nature. It's what happens to women: they are ruled by their hormones. Anne has been dealing with her ovaries ever since she started her periods during a compulsory Wednesday morning game of hockey when she was fourteen. 'Come on, Collins, run faster.' But she couldn't; blood was trickling down her thighs.

Since then there have been thirty-four years of cramps and bloating, tampons and pads. Some days she can almost feel the wear and tear. Really, the whole rigmarole is getting to be quite unnecessary. After all, it isn't as if she is going to have any more babies.

Ah, babies. This morning in the butcher's shop the woman in front of her had been pushing twins, glorious matching blue-eyed babies in a buggy that could have been designed by NASA. The mother had been one of those yummy mummies, all cashmere, blond hair and beige suede boots, the sort of woman a butcher would keep partridge breasts under the counter for.

The babies smacked of IVF – there was a lot of it about these days. In The World According to Anne Armitage, smartly dressed, slightly over-anxious women in their late thirties pushing multiple-occupancy prams in newly gentrified areas of London scream 'Private Fertility Treatment'.

Obviously she'd done the cooing thing. When one is a woman approaching middle age society expects one to acknowledge cute babies. So you cluck and make goo-goo noises, even when there is a part of you that wants to scream into the mother's smug face, 'They will disappoint and upset you. You think this bit is hard? Just you wait until the school reports start making a mockery of the fees that you pay and there is a pool of dried sick on the glass roof of your kitchen-diner extension, courtesy of your eldest puking up through his bedroom window.'

She should have taken Mrs IVF to the park, sat her down and bought her a cup of coffee. She could have broken the news gently.

'Listen, I'm so sorry but you know those twins you've spent twenty-five grand conceiving? Well, how can I put this? There will be days when you will wish you'd put the money towards something else, a really nice convertible or a few decent holidays, because you know what? Kids don't come with a guarantee and, however faulty the goods, you don't get your money back.'

Anne looks up recipes for pork on the internet. She uses the PC in Paul's study and browses through ideas involving red cabbage and cider, or apricots and couscous.

Why on earth is she having this dinner party?

Because, she reminds herself, it's what she is meant to do, given her age, occupation, marital status and the cost of her recently installed Smallbone of Devizes kitchen.

You can't really justify spending over fifty grand on new handmade oak units and a powder blue Aga if you're not going to invite a constant stream of envious guests round. What would be the point?

Hmm, baked pork with pears, potatoes, onions and Roquefort butter, as demonstrated by Diana Henry on *Saturday Kitchen*. Anne likes *Saturday Kitchen*; she likes it best when Paul is playing golf and the boys are out, and she can curl up on the sofa in what she laughably calls her 'jogging' bottoms and thrill to James Martin and his cooking cronies.

Anne is a good cook but sometimes she gets anxious and makes silly mistakes. She is forever burning herself or slicing the tips of her fingers. She would like her family to notice these wounds and offer sympathy, but they don't.

There is too much testosterone in this house, thinks Anne. How nice it would be to have had a girl, a nice, sensible, dutiful girl, a girl a bit like herself, bookish and willing, keen to do her best, a girl who would leave the toilet seat down, sit at the kitchen table and just *chat*.

Instead she has two boys, Nathaniel Dominic and Julian William, Nat and Jools as their friends call them. Nathaniel and Julian don't chat to their parents, they grunt and huff.

Anne tenses at the computer. Should she open the file marked Family Photos and revisit her children as they used to be? Freckle-faced little chaps in cricket whites; toddlers in towelling robes all ready for cuddling and bedtime stories; pyjama-clad boys under glittering Christmas trees holding up *The Guinness Book of Records* or a new Playmobil pirate ship. She can envisage the once-upon-a-time summer-holiday snaps – her skinny sons in their baggy swimming trunks diving into shimmering blue water, ice-cream faces smiling.

When did her sons stop smiling?

Stop wallowing, Anne tells herself, children grow up and that's that; but there is an insistent voice in her head: yes, children grow up and yours have turned nasty, they are selfish and they smirk at you as if to say, 'Are you just stupid or *really* stupid?'

Anne swallows hard and mutters, 'Well this won't buy the baby a new bonnet' under her breath. 'Diana Henry's cheesy pork bake it is.'

She presses print and closes her eyes. Anne is a technophobe and believes that computers and printers stand more chance of working if she's not watching them. The printer whirrs reassuringly and by the time she opens her eyes the recipe will be printed out, all nice and neat. Slowly she counts to ten for luck.

She opens her eyes. The paper that has emerged from the printer is bare. The printer has run out of ink, of course it has.

Anne strides into the kitchen, picks up the pork fillets and feeds them into the waste disposal unit. She feels like a murderer, like one of those serial killers that has chopped up a victim and then must dispose of the corpse.

'Fuck it, I shall order a takeaway.'

Twenty minutes later she is parking her car in the supermarket car park half a mile away. She can't justify a takeaway, not with the economy in the state that it's in, not with the vet's bills. Poor Galaxy, the chocolate-button-coloured Labrador, so riddled with tumours she looked like she was wearing a string of turnips around her throat. The vet had put her down – 'She won't feel a thing, Mrs Armitage' – and as he pressed the syringe into poor old Galaxy's jaw it was all Anne could do not to roll the dog off the slab and offer her own neck instead.

'I am tired and fat and old and sometimes I suffer from stress incontinence and my tights smell of wee when I put them in the laundry basket.' And, as if she needed to feel any worse, she adds, 'And nobody loves me.'

As she manoeuvres the car into a space that looked the right size but obviously isn't (a bit like the skirt she tried on in Hobbs last week), she feels herself flush. It starts round the back of her neck and travels down her spine. Hormones or temper? She can never really tell.

Before she takes the paintwork off a rather smart people carrier, Anne reverses and finds a bigger space down at the far end of the car park, a nice roomy size-18 space. 'That's better.' Talking to herself has become an occupational hazard.

As she walks towards the supermarket she tries to pull her stomach in and swing her arms. She'd like people to think she is the type of woman for whom brisk walking and plenty of exercise is the norm. It's only once the glass doors have slid open that she remembers she has left her selection of Bags for Life in the car. Anne allows herself a whimper of frustration and pinches herself on the inside of her fleshy left forearm. This is what Anne does: she doesn't cut, that's for teenagers, she pinches. Occasionally, when she has the screaming ab-dabs, she has attempted to aim punches at her own face, but it's never terribly successful.

'Just a basket,' she instructs herself, keep it simple, some lovely salmon steaks with watercress and new potatoes, but habit makes her reach for a trolley. While she's here she might as well pick up a few bits and bobs.

Forty-five minutes later the bill has come to £126.42 and her Nectar card is not in her purse.

Anne drives home convinced that she can smell stale sweat from her armpits. 'Memo to self,' she murmurs, 'no more polo-neck jumpers.' Cardigans are the way forward, something she can easily take off should her temperature continue to yo-yo.

She parks her car in the gravel driveway. There's easily room for two other vehicles and if Nat had his way there would be three cars on the drive, but Anne has put her foot down. There is no way she is going to buy her eighteen-year-old son a car!

If he was that interested in learning to drive he'd have passed his theory test by now. She bought him a special DVD online, to help him revise the Highway Code, but it's still in its Amazon sleeve on the stairs.

Anyway, he keeps being silly, wanting this, wanting that, a Ford Mustang if you please. He sneers at her Honda Jazz, informing her that he wouldn't be seen dead learning to drive in that 'heap of crap'.

Anne puts her key in the lock. 'Nathaniel,' she bellows. It's four o'clock in the afternoon, surely he should be up by now?

'Nathaniel, I could do with some help with the shopping.'

He doesn't reply. He's in her en suite, hers and Paul's, she can hear the power shower. He will be using all of Paul's birthday Acqua di Parma. 'You utter shit,' she seethes through clenched teeth.

The Armitages live in a red-brick five-bedroomed thirties semi. The hallway is wide, the staircase solid oak, and the front door sports an original stained-glass panel featuring a tulip design.

Anne is proud to live in Dulwich Village. She may not inhabit one of the flashier Georgian properties, but hers is a fine example of the Arts and Crafts style and anyway, most Georgian houses tend to be all stairs and not much else.

She breathes deeply and carries her Sainsbury's bags through into the kitchen-diner. The extension, despite being three years old, still gives her a thrill, especially now that the rain has worn away the halo of puke Nat deposited on the glass roof back in the summer. There is so much space, such a wonderful family room.

Of course the family spend very little time in it these days. The boys have their own bedrooms and a games room in the attic.

Years ago the attic room was awash with toys, and with each passing phase nothing seemed to get thrown away: toy cars and wooden Brio trains, Meccano and bits of broken-up Scalextric track, tiny Warhammer figurines and desiccated pots of enamel paint.

A couple of years ago they'd had a big clear out, the boys dry-eyed as their childhood was boxed up and distributed around various charity shops.

'Don't you even want to keep an Action Man each?' Anne

had pleaded. In the end she'd kept a small box of favourite toys, some Lego and a few books, including *The Tiger Who Came to Tea*, *The Jolly Postman* and *Where the Wild Things Are*.

'What the fuck for? In case either of us gets brain-damaged and ends up in nappies with a mental age of three?' Jools had sniggered.

Now the games room smells of dope, the floor is a viper's nest of computer and Xbox cables and the walls are plastered with cheap-looking girls with no tops on, perma-tanned blondes with ridiculous breasts.

Who would pay to have big bosoms, wonders Anne. Hers have been the bane of her life, costing her a fortune in scaffolding disguised as lingerie. They're forever getting in the way, she's sick of leaning over the table to pick up her glasses only for her bosoms to brush the butter dish. Lurpak on her cashmere sweater, what a palaver.

She unpacks the food into the honey-coloured oak cupboards and American-style fridge. One of the boys has broken the ice dispenser and neither of them will own up. Each would rather blame the other than tell the truth. Anne tuts unconsciously.

Julian should be home soon, although he probably won't. He likes to go to the park and 'cotch' with like-minded boys and unsuitable girls, girls whose parents don't ask them what they've been up to and why aren't they at home doing their geography homework?

Julian is in Year 12 or, as Anne prefers to call it, the Lower Sixth, and he's coasting.

Anne realises she is talking to herself out loud, itemising the contents of her Sainsbury's bags in a dull monotone she finds comforting. 'Avocados, spinach, pine nuts, cereal, cereal, cereal.'

Three boxes. The men in her life have different breakfast requirements: Paul wants oats, Nat likes Dorset Cereal with berries and cherries – 'the purple box Mum, you mong' – and Julian, despite being almost six foot and therefore taller than both his brother and his father, likes Sugar Puffs.

What about me? thinks Anne and her conscience replies, 'And for you, Special K because you are getting very fat.'

At this point Nat wanders into the kitchen. He is wearing a towel around his hips and although Anne has seen it before she is still shocked by the tunnel of dark hair that reaches his navel. Casually he rips open a packet of pitta bread and slots four into the family-sized Dualit toaster.

'Lunch?' asks Anne, trying to keep things light. Sometimes talking to her sons is the verbal equivalent of lighting the blue touch-paper. She never knows if they are going to explode in her face.

'Snack,' he yawns back.

She watches him heap hummus and tzatziki on to a plate, but as he reaches for the marinated olives she slaps his hand.

'They're for tonight. The Robinsons are coming.'

Nat rolls his eyes and gives a theatrical shudder. 'Ergh the Robinsons, Jesus fuck.'

The pittas leap like salmon from the toaster. He catches two of them in mid-air (Nat could have been sporty) and saunters back upstairs.

He won't bring the plate back down. Anne or Loretta, the cleaner, will eventually unearth it.

I have brought my children up to expect women to do everything. I pity their future wives, thinks Anne. Most mothers think their sons' future brides are not worthy. Anne has reached the stage where she is thinking the poor bitches, whoever they might be, are welcome to these two.

Julian rings the doorbell at ten to six. He has forgotten his keys and 'some cunt' has stolen his iPod Nano.

'The Robinsons are coming for supper,' Anne repeats.

'For fuck's sake,' responds her youngest as he bounds up the stairs two at a time, as if fleeing from the impending guests.

'They won't be here till eightish,' yells Anne. 'I'll do you and Nat a pizza in an hour.'

They used to like the Robinsons, so much so they went on

holiday together. The Robinson children are shuffled in with her children in the Family Photos file. Anne met Melanie Robinson when they shared antenatal classes in Herne Hill almost nineteen years ago. Nathaniel and Piggy attended the same nursery school; they were both in the yellow class, as were Julian and then Hannah a few years later.

We don't see them very much these days, thinks Anne as she runs herself a bath. Nat has left three Peter Jones towels twisted and wet in the corner of the bathroom, and as she bends down to pick them up Anne finds herself stuffing one of them into her mouth. Her mouth is full of navy blue towelling and she bites down hard. She's not sure why she does this. Maybe it's to stop herself screaming.

Jean

Touch and Go

Jean Collins lies flat on her back. This isn't my bed, she thinks. She opens her eyes but she can't see anything, she can't hear anything either. It's quite nice, peaceful and quiet. Now where was she?

She was outside and it was raining, she hasn't got her umbrella and her tights are soggy. Someone's taken those off. Maybe she's been drugged and raped?

Oh well, she'll check for bruises later.

Maybe she should spend a penny? When you get to her age it's sensible to go even if you don't really need to, just in case.

Jean attempts to move her legs but she's not quite sure what she's done with them. It's like she left them on the bus.

They worked perfectly well this morning, carrying her around as normal, bedroom to bathroom, stairs down to the kitchen. Her feet had hurt but then they always do, she needs to see the chiropodist. Strange what's happened to her feet, they used to be so lovely, but that was before the bunions.

What a funny dream this is. Perhaps she's fainted, it's happened before – now when was that? Maybe when she comes round she should have a biscuit and a glass of milk, but she's not hungry or thirsty, not cold or hot, she's not anything, she doesn't need anything! It's quite relaxing being like this. She hasn't even got heartburn, there's nothing she has to do, nothing she can do. It's a bit like being a baby, only babies don't have memories and Jean's head is full of memories, which is good, at least that's something she can do. She might not feel like knitting for a while and she's no idea when she'll be up to posting her LoveFilm DVDs back, but until then, at least she can remember.

It's a bit like having a television in her head: 'Ladies and Gentlemen, it's *The Jean Collins Show.*' At the moment she's watching herself leave the house, almost forgetting she still has her slippers on, checking in her handbag for her keys and her purse. Jean watches herself go back into the sitting room, kick off her slippers and change into her slip-on leather shoes. Then she buttons her coat and shuts the front door. Should she bother to double lock it? No, she'll be home in an hour. She pops the keys back her bag and the picture on the keyring makes her smile, the little devils!

Now where on earth is her handbag?

Jean's handbag lay in the road with Jean on top of it. For a second everyone stopped like musical statues on the street then, just like a DVD that had been paused for a moment, the action starts up again, people shouting, pulling mobile phones out of bags and pockets. 'STOP,' someone yells but the motorbike roars into the distance.

Mothers turn their children's faces away: 'Don't look, it's rude to stare,' but at least one of them adds, 'See that's what happens if you're not careful. What do I tell you?'

Around Jean's head is a big red stain as sticky as jam. 'Fucking hell,' someone breathes.

A woman in a pink tabard runs out of the cake shop and kneels in the road. She holds the old lady's hand and puts her ear close to her mouth. She can't be dead if she's still talking.

The ambulance wails around the corner, just like in *Casualty.* Gently, gently they carry her away. Poor old thing.

11

'I could see her pants,' a small boy crows.

Jean's handbag has fallen open, her Rimmel Peach Sundae lipstick rolls into the gutter.

Jean can't remember any of this. All she can remember is leaving the house – was she going to the post office or to the fishmonger's? If only she knew what day it was, that would give her a clue. Friday would be fish. It's frustrating not being able to see what happened next.

Oh well, if she can't look forward at least she can look back. There are seventy-two years of memory tape looped around Jean's brain, reams of the stuff. Some of it has got jumbled up, all higgledy-piggledy. She can see herself watching *This Morning* last week, the picture is so clear she can see the patterns on Phillip Schofield's tie and now she can see herself feeding a rabbit when she was nine. Benji the rabbit who turned out to be a girl.

Her head is like a big airing cupboard, all these bits need sorting out. It's time to have a good tidy, put things into drawers. It's a bit like filing: memories should slot into neatly labelled compartments, Births, Marriages, Deaths, Happy, Sad.

When the important milestones are sorted perhaps she could fill a box marked Too Boring to Remember. Which, when she gets her legs back, she can take down to the charity shop to sell to people who haven't had enough experiences of their own.

But for now she's not going to do anything. Jean turns off the television in her head and floats back into blackness. Maybe when she switches it back on she'll get *Coronation Street*.

'D'you think she'll come round?'
    'Dunno. Have you ever tried anal sex?'
    'Yeah. Doesn't really work, does it?'
    'Nah. You've got to give it a go, though.'
    'Why?'
    'I dunno.'
Karen and Mai-Lin are the nurses on duty. Coma patients are

a doddle, you don't have to remind them to take their teeth out or struggle to lift their withered arses over bed pans, everything's done by tube and drip and they don't cry out in the night. Ideally, all patients should be put into comas on arrival, it would make nursing so much easier.

'I bought a lovely top from Next the other day.'

'Have they informed the next of kin?'

'Not sure. Apparently, when they picked her up she was still conscious and covered in cake!'

'What do you mean, *covered in cake*?'

'Vanilla slices, right mess. Splattered all over the road.'

'Blimey!'

'Yeah, the woman in the cake shop saw it happen, said the old lady came in all confused, ordered the cakes and then just walked out of the shop and straight into the road. She sat with her till the ambulance came, said she was talking gibberish, kept repeating the same thing: "Who'd have thought I wouldn't recognise . . .?" over and over again.'

'Who?'

'The old woman, when she got knocked down. Kept going on about someone she didn't recognise.'

'Lost it, probably. My Auntie Brenda went like that in the end, talking utter rubbish, couldn't understand why my cousin Nigel looked so old. "He's only twelve and he's got grey hair," she kept saying. Thing is, he wasn't twelve, he was fifty-two! Nothing worse, poor cow. If you've not got your marbles you're best off dead.'

Fortunately Jean has got all her marbles, it's just some of them aren't where she left them. Her marbles are scattered, they need time to settle. After all, she has just had a terrible bang to the head.

Anne

Explanations

Anne lies in the bath and gives herself a hard time. These bosoms of hers are getting out of hand: she has always been a 'big girl upstairs', 'well upholstered', 'stacked', but now as fifty looms her breasts are bigger than they have ever been.

She has spent three hundred pounds on new bras over the past six months. Three hundred pounds! She remembers buying her first car for less than that.

Anne worries about money – according to Paul, it's one of her less attractive traits. Paul, because he comes from money, finds talking about money unspeakably vulgar or, as he would pronounce it, 'unspickablih vulgah'. Paul talks in the same way a comedian talks when he's taking the piss out of posh people and is so posh he can't see what's wrong with wearing slightly too short orange corduroy trousers. Paul strides around Dulwich in his orange cords, bushman hat and Barbour as if it was a small country estate and not a bizarre London village, which, despite looking like a *Miss Marple* location (complete with pointed-finger road signs) lies no more than two miles away from Brixton.

Really, thinks Anne, Dulwich is for people who want to live in the country but can't be arsed with the inconvenience of living in the country. Of course, many of the Armitages' friends and neighbours have rural or seaside second homes and at six o'clock on Friday evenings, particularly in the summer, there is a mass exodus of estate cars. Mercedes and Audis mostly, although there are a worrying number of four-by-fours that no one really approves of, with their boots bulging and back seats full of bickering children, determined to play with their Game Boys even though 'the beeping, darling, drives Mummy mad'.

The Armitages, bucking the usual Holt, Rock or Cotswolds trend, have a share in a little place in north Majorca. Paul's parents bought it in the seventies and it still has the original orange kitchen tiles, macramé plant-pot holders and avocado bathroom suite.

Paul's mother Ellen refuses to have it refurbished. It reminds her of when Paul's father was alive and her children were small, and it was 'such fun' eating paella and drinking sangria for the very first time.

Ellen refers to what is ostensibly a small bungalow as 'that darling little place up in the hills above Alcúdia'; when she says Alcúdia she pronounces it Catalan-style — *Al-koo-thea*.

Anne thinks it could do with some air-con, a properly functioning cooker and a new bathroom. The boys think it could do with a decent-sized pool and Sky telly — according to Julian, family holidays are 'sad' unless they are somewhere 'sick' like the Maldives.

There had been a time when it hadn't mattered, about ten years ago when they went with the Robinsons and spent a fortnight fighting lilo wars and lighting barbecues. But Nat refuses ever to go again. 'It's in the middle of fucking nowhere,' he sneers, and it is: when Anne and Paul popped over last year they realised that, if they wanted to eat out, one of them couldn't drink — and that's always me, thinks Anne, scraping a blunt razor along her bristly shins.

Anne is feeling nostalgic: why does everything have to change?

The holiday with Paul had been difficult. She had wanted room service and spa facilities, and Paul had wanted sleep.

He works hard, she reminds herself, but then so do I and I do all the domestic crap. The only time Paul ever has to decide what to eat is when he's sitting in a restaurant and a waiter has handed him a menu.

She covers her enormous breasts with lime green flannels. She is sick of the sight of them. There's something rather barmaidy about her breasts; they seem to contradict the rest of her. After all, Anne is a bright woman with a 2.1 in English and French and twenty-five years' teaching experience.

At the moment she teaches French part-time to the juniors of a local fee-paying girls' school.

It's not hard, and the children are willing. Some are even a little too keen, begging for extra homework and competing in the classroom as to who can get their hand up fastest. To be honest, a few of them are priggy and annoying, but then their parents tend to be priggy and annoying too.

At Christmas and before the summer holidays Anne is inundated with 'charming gifts' and has to remember to bring a large carrier bag in to school so that she can transport her swag home. Sometimes she feels guilty receiving yet another potted plant or box of Swiss chocolates from the mother of a seven-year-old who is hoping for more than a C on her daughter's school report.

Anne understands these parents; she remembers when she was forever waylaying primary teachers, eager for some optimistic feedback about her sons' progress.

These days she has learnt to take a back seat where the boys' education is concerned. Nat is dyslexic and therefore didn't pass the entrance exam for the College (as in Dulwich) down the road. He ended up at a boarding school where Anne has a horrible feeling the staff colluded with the pupils and very little of what was on the curriculum ever got done.

Certainly Nat got himself into plenty of scrapes. There were incidents involving drink, incidents involving girls, incidents involving inappropriate nudity and an incident involving the words 'wank maestro' written on the frosted-up car window of the homosexual head of music.

Nat once said they could never expel him because he had a picture on his phone of said music teacher sucking off a boy in Year 11. Anne presumes he was joking but can never be entirely sure.

After seven years and over a hundred thousand pounds of fees, my eighteen-year-old son has five GCSEs (but not maths) and one A level (sociology), despairs Anne, dunking her head under the water. He plays neither rugby nor cricket, cannot paint or play a musical instrument and seems to be content to spend the rest of his life sponging off his parents, rolling joints and necking vast quantities of vodka and Red Bull. He doesn't read, refuses to go to art galleries and thinks classical music 'sucks'. In fact most things, according to Nat, suck; the only things that don't are clubbing (drum and bass), fit blondes and caning it.

Julian, at least, is quite clever. He is at the College, but he is supercilious and superior. He knows he is bright and takes pride in doing as little as possible in order to get by. Julian is not a team player – in fact, quite the opposite. Julian sees nothing wrong with cheating, he has no moral compass. At least Nat is too stupid to be devious.

Paul doesn't worry so much about the boys, because he was a boy and he knows how boys tick. That's what he says, but deep down Anne suspects he is anxious. Paul is a well-respected ear, nose and throat man, who works for both the NHS and a private hospital in Kensington – although these days, it has to be said, most of his work is done privately.

Anne doesn't like to think about Paul's work. She knows that skin is sliced, lifted and pulled back, that is it bloody and occasionally smelly: 'An extraordinary fungus, Anne, had eaten through all the soft tissue and was beginning to nibble at the brain.'

What Paul can't contemplate is that anything should go wrong with either of his sons. Nat's dyslexia was something that he needed convincing of, insisting for a good eighteen months that he'd grow out of it. Honestly, thinks Anne, how can someone as bright as Paul be so thick?

Paul has not been raised to expect anything but success. He went to a good prep school, followed by a well-known public school, followed by a good university (not, however, Oxford – much to his mother's consternation). His father was a neuro-surgeon, his uncle a QC, his family tree is peppered with politicians and fighter pilots and jolly good sports. His sons will come good in the end; they have to, they come from decent stock. Any bad blood will have come from Anne's side.

This is what bothers Anne as she lies in the bath: her mother-in-law has never thought she was good enough. There are certain things Ellen expected of a daughter-in-law that Anne fell spectacularly short of: the ability to saddle and ride a horse, make a soufflé, mix a proper gin and tonic, know 'people', eat kippers for breakfast without gagging, have confidence with dogs, and possess a quality rope of pearls, a set of sterling silver fish knives and forks and a decent pair of ankles.

Actually Anne's ankles just about pass scrutiny but only because, compared to her thick calves, they are positively dainty.

Since becoming Mrs Armitage she has learnt to cook, love dogs, fix a really good gin and tonic and wear the pearls her husband bought for her twenty-fifth birthday. She still can't ride or eat kippers, and there isn't an operation in the world that can really sort out her washerwoman legs.

'Coooeee.' Paul is home – he has been consulting today. Thursdays are gore-free and he has mostly been sending remote-controlled cameras around patients' sinuses, checking to see what can be killed off by drugs and what needs to be put under the knife.

Most of Paul's patients are terrified that they have cancer. Most of them haven't; not yet, anyway.

Today was easy, a couple of cases of vocal nodes, a pair of

rotting tonsils and a nasty bacterial infection. He also had a few post-operative cases to check up on, a rugby player's ruptured nasal cartilage, nicely stitched and on the mend, and a nine-year-old chorister whose adenoids had been privately and swiftly removed courtesy of Westminster Cathedral Choir School.

All done and dusted, Paul pours himself a drink — a creature of habit, he likes a small sherry — before having a shower and changing. Paul likes sherry from a decanter, he likes cut glass, he likes things done properly.

Anne heaves herself out of the bath and quickly wraps herself in a towel before she catches sight of her reflection in the mean mirror.

It's seven o'clock and the Robinsons will be here in an hour, no need to panic, but she feels slightly anxious. It's your nerves, she reminds herself, that's what doctors would have said twenty years ago, 'nerves' having been a euphemism for 'hormones'.

She talcs herself with Crabtree and Evelyn's Lavender dusting powder courtesy of little Katy Trepass (Katy is capable of good work but is occasionally distracted and careless) and pulls her favourite navy linen trousers out of the wardrobe. If she wears them with that long Boden shirt thingy she won't have to iron.

Paul doesn't really like this sort of ensemble: he thinks his wife looks untidy, like a laundry basket on legs. He prefers a more tailored look: his mother, for example, resembles Margaret Thatcher at the height of her powers, while his sister Gilly is the spit of Princess Anne.

'Aren't you going to iron those?' he ventures.

'They're linen,' Anne snaps back. Paul is confused, his mother used to use linen napkins and they were very well ironed.

Anne is setting the table. They are having fish but not using the fish canteen; this is because fish canteens are deemed naff these days and anyway, as she keeps insisting, it's 'only a kitchen supper'.

The fish canteen lies tarnished in its blue velvet nest. Anne has decided that life is too short to polish silver. Paul's mother would find this both slovenly and disturbing.

19

Jean

Jim's Whopper

That's it! She was going to have a nice pork chop for her tea, a pork chop with a little bit of apple sauce. She always did have a sweet tooth. Ooh, and some lovely mash. Of course nowadays she does the packet mix, it's not the same but it's a heck of a palaver to mash potatoes for one.

How long has that chop been sitting on the draining board?

She got it out of the freezer just after the *Jeremy Kyle Show*, dreadful people, but she can't resist the live paternity test results: 'Course, if it's mine I want to be involved. If it's mine I'll apologise live on national telly for calling her a slag, for accusing her of going with other fellas behind my back. If I was wrong I'll admit it.'

Jeremy opened the envelope: 'And the results prove you are . . . not the father'. The lad's face crumpled, the girl looked shocked too, gobsmacked in fact, thought she'd got away with it. You never do, love, stuff catches up with you in the end, doesn't do to go round telling fibs.

Jim told a fib, he told a whopper that time he first came round to her house. Skinny bloke, Jim, big ears, nothing to write home about, not her type, not that she was old enough to have a type. He came round on his pushbike, she should have known then he wouldn't amount to much. He never did learn to drive, though there were reasons for that and it wasn't his fault. Anyway, better a pushbike than a motorbike, considering what had happened.

It was the Wednesday after the accident, all the curtains were drawn, the whole house in deep shadow, cards of condolence propped up on the mantelpiece. 'Deepest sympathy for your loss.' Sentiments expressed in curly gold lettering. 'Thinking of you.'

Jean had answered the door, her mother was 'in no fit state' and neither, presumably, was her father; Victor Whittaker had barely drawn a sober breath since the police had rung their doorbell three days ago.

'Mrs Whittaker, may we come indoors? You might want to sit down. Is there someone who might be able to put the kettle on?'

'Jean, Jean, come here, I need you. The police, Jean, the police are here.'

Wednesday 14th March 1956. The story was on the front page of the *Gazette*:

Tragic Local Man Killed in Moss Side

Brian Whittaker, aged 23, died in the early hours of Sunday morning as a result of a motorbike accident. No other vehicle is thought to be involved. Eyewitness Jim Collins described how he had been cycling through Moss Side just after midnight when he came across the scene of the accident: 'There was nothing I could do, I held the young man until he passed away in my arms.'

And here he was, the eyewitness, nervously turning his hat in his bony hands. 'I came to offer, my, my, my . . .' Jean almost finished the sentence for him, 'my hat, my condolences, my love, my hand in marriage, just spit it out man.'

He was so slow. Later, of course, she came to realise that Jim stuttered when he was nervous, which unfortunately turned out to be most of the time.

Her mother was inconsolable, a bundle of misery dressed in black. When she realised who Jim was she clutched at him, red-eyed and sour from not washing. 'Did he say anything, my boy, my baby boy, did he say anything?'

'He, he, he,' stuttered Jim, 'he said, I love, tell my family I love them and I'm very sorry.' Jean's mother howled at that point and then fell to her knees, wrapping her arms tightly around Jim's ankles.

I thought he might topple over, recalls Jean, and then she remembers how some years later Jim had admitted that her brother's dying words had in fact been, 'Shit, that's me fucked then.'

Naughty Brian, he was always a cheeky lad, pockets full of frog spawn, pulling up girls' skirts in the playground. 'He'll be the death of me,' her mother had said, and he was.

Fifty-six years ago now; he'd have been seventy-nine had he lived, goosing grannies and still thinking itching powder was funny, he was that kind of a boy – and Jim, how old would Jim have been? But it's no good, she needs a piece of paper and a pencil to work that one out, she was never very good at mental arithmetic, that was Jim's job, Jim did sums with . . . But she's gone.

Anne

Wine on Whine

Something is not right with this evening. The food is good, the wine is flowing, but even so there is a stilted quality to the proceedings, the conversation keeps stalling, perfectly serviceable topics are steered into dreary culs-de-sac.

What's wrong?

Anne frets and feels flustered, she drops cutlery and every time she moves her chair it makes a vile screeching noise on the tiles. The Robinsons are our oldest friends, she acknowledges, but tonight I wish they'd just fuck off and go home.

For starters they were late and Anne loathes lateness, it's the teacher in her. It's bad enough when it happens at school, but at least she can dish out lines and detentions. Really, if she'd had her way she'd have made them stand outside for twenty minutes just to teach them a lesson.

But of course Paul had opened the door and the first person she'd seen was Hannah! She didn't recall inviting the children, surely they weren't expecting Nat and Jools to join them at the dinner table. Polite chitchat was hardly the boys' forte and anyway, she'd already done them a pizza.

'Hannah,' she'd almost screamed, 'how lovely to see you!' Did she imagine it or did the girl wince?

'She's brought some homework,' Melanie interjected. 'I thought maybe she could do it in the living room. It's a bit lonely for her at home, what with Theo away.'

For a second Anne was stumped. Who the hell was Theo? Then she remembered: Theo was Piggy's real name, it's just everyone called him Piggy.

'Not any more,' smirked Melanie. 'He didn't want to start college with "Piggy" hanging round his neck and, let's face it, he's hardly porcine these days.'

'Of course not, no, of course not,' Anne repeated, knowing full well it was Nat who had bestowed the moniker on the child back at nursery.

'So how's it going, you know, at uni?'

'At Oxford,' Melanie corrected. 'Oh you know, a lot of hard work but lots of fun − he's started rowing.'

'How super,' trilled Anne. 'I'll just shout the boys down.

'Naaaaat, Juliaaan,' she bellowed up the stairs.

By the time the boys made an appearance Anne had accidentally downed two gin and tonics before joining Paul on the white wine, Christopher Robinson (yes really, his mother hadn't thought) was training for a marathon, 'so really Paul, mate, just water' and Melanie was rather smugly mixing her white wine with Badoit.

'And here they are,' Anne trumpeted theatrically as her sons mooched silently into the kitchen-diner. 'Well come on boys, aren't you going to say something?' she asked, which both her sons correctly interpreted to mean 'Why can't you just make a fucking effort for once?'

Hannah, Anne noticed, went purple at the sight of them, poor little thing, sitting there in her school uniform, all puppy-fattish, her mother's 'difficult' gingery hair frizzing around her spotty face.

At least my sons are good-looking, Anne noted peevishly as Melanie and Christopher went into interrogation mode: what were Nat's gap year plans, exactly, and as for Julian, was he disappointed by his GCSE results? Nat and Jools weren't exactly rude, they were just ever so slightly bored and detached. They answered in monosyllables and exchanged sly grins.

What on earth gave them the right to be so bloody superior, Anne fumed as she lifted the tinfoil off the salmon steaks and shoved them back in the Aga for 'just another two minutes'.

Nat hoisted himself up on to the kitchen island and Julian slumped against the fridge.

'Gosh,' twittered Anne, 'do you remember when you were little and we used to go to Majorca together and you'd all run around with no clothes on?'

Why on earth had she said that?

Hannah went aubergine and because her embarrassment was so acute, so all encompassing, that without wanting to everyone immediately imagined her naked and running around, fat, white and embarrassed, right there in the kitchen.

'I've got loads of geog to do,' the girl muttered and she beat a clumsy retreat into the living room.

Melanie whispered conspiratorially, 'They're predicting straight A*s for her GCSEs,' and it was all Anne could do not to hit her in the face with the fish slice.

But now it was just the four of them. Clever, ugly Hannah was doing her geography in the living room (she hadn't even put the telly on, what was wrong with her?); Nat had gone to the Dog, she couldn't stop him, she couldn't exactly say, 'No pub tonight Nat, it's a school night' because he'd left school; and Julian had retired to the upper reaches of the house to do some work, which was, of course, a euphemism for contacting his friends on Facebook.

Julian is very popular, he has over four hundred friends. Anne knows this for a fact. She has joined Facebook as an anonymous fifteen-year-old Notting Hill clubber (Star van Hoff), all the better to keep tabs on her sons. Nat has two hundred and sixty friends because, he insists, he's choosier than Julian.

And I've got about six, reckons Anne, and the ones I've got around my kitchen table tonight are getting on my nerves.

Anne can't relax, she feels tired and bored and drunk. She is horribly tempted to just leave the table, go upstairs, put on her nightie and go to sleep.

The men aren't helping: Christopher is being dreary about running, Paul is being dull about buying a track bike and doing some serious training at the local velodrome. And all the while Melanie drones on about the wonderful opportunities that Oxford has to offer, and when she isn't banging on about the Dreaming Spires she's droning on about Hannah deciding to do Greek at A level even though 'very few girls are given the option'.

Anne thinks about the number of alcohol units she has drunk this week. She really should cut down, start doing pilates. In the meantime, she should really be getting the pudding out. But somehow her legs seem to have lost the will to walk to the fridge, they are as heavy as sandbags and about as much use.

I am tired, she realises, not just of tonight but of everything, tired of trying to be good enough for Paul so that his mother can't say 'I told you so', tired of wearing glasses that don't really suit me because I am too mean to buy some more. But mostly I am tired of being such a middle-aged female cliché. Book club – check; Eastern European cleaner – check; thinking about getting a wormery – check; overweight – check.

Difficult teenage sons – check. Boring friends – check. Distant husband – check.

Anne glances at Paul. He loves me, she thinks, but he never actually looks at me and he makes love to me as if I were a family pet that needs the exercise.

It's at this point Anne makes the mistake of switching over to red wine.

Jean

For Better, For Worse

Jim was old even before he was old, that was the trouble with Jim. Jean sighs but the respirator is noisy and no one hears her.

'What level is she?'

The cleaner has come barging into Jean's room; she's heard about the new girl, Coma Nan as the nurses have nicknamed her. They sang a song yesterday as they changed her catheter: 'Coma Nan, Coma Nan, does whatever a Coma Nan can . . . Nothing.'

'About a nine on the Glasgow Scale.'

(This is not a great score: as comas go, fifteen is good, anything below a ten is worrying.)

'She won't mind if I don't mop under her bed then.'

Jean has been examined: she has incurred a massive head trauma, the wound has been stitched up so her brain can no longer fall out but it has been bruised and shaken and she responds to neither sight nor sound.

Who knows how long she will be like this? No one can really tell. They have scanned her on machines that cost hundreds of thousands of pounds and shone battery-operated torches into her eyes, but only Jean really knows what's going on inside that bandaged head.

That pork chop will just have to go in the bin, there's no way she's cooking today. Anyway, she's not hungry, she's got enough on her plate putting all these memories in order. Maybe she'll have a sandwich or some cereal with hot milk later.

Right now she's got to sort out Jim. My *husband* Jim, she reminds herself. Of course I am a widow now, but once upon a time I had a husband and he was called Jim.

She tries to recall his face and not just his sticky-out ears. Up in the attic there's a suitcase of photos, Jim used to be very keen, took a Box Brownie with them on honeymoon, all those snaps of her when she was young and had a skirt as round as the moon, a red skirt covered in white spots, polka dots like the china service they had, now what was that called? Cream plates with a red polka-dot trim, came with a gravy boat and every-thing, a wedding gift from her mother.

The 8th September 1956.

'Do you, Jean Elizabeth Whittaker, take Jim Collins to be your lawful wedded husband?' For a moment Jean thought the regis-trar said 'awful wedded husband'.

It was a quiet wedding, what with it only being six months since Brian had passed away. Her mother wasn't up to a big do and Jim's family weren't the type to help out.

So they opted for the registry office, but she had a pricey new outfit and for once her hair did what it was told.

After the ceremony they went for a nice meal in one of the smart hotels along the front, the Grand was it? The Grand Hotel with its patterned carpet, a vivid swirl of red and blue paisley all the way to the shiny chrome lift. 'Come on Jean, follow me.' Her knees are weak and she's not steady, she never should have followed him, she should have known better, if only she hadn't gone up in that lift.

But the lift doesn't belong in her wedding-day memories. It's the wrong hotel, wrong year, wrong everything. She steps away from the chrome doors and to take her mind off the sickening swirls of the carpet, she concentrates instead on what she wore when she and Jim were pronounced 'man and wife', a heavy dove grey crêpe two-piece with a pleated skirt, which she wore with a cream silk blouse. Jim wore a navy suit. She got sick of the sight of that suit, he wore it every time he went for a job interview. 'It's my lucky suit,' he'd say. 'Must be – I wore it when I married you.'

She felt guilty when he said things like that; she always knew he loved her more than she loved him, but what was she meant to do?

She had to leave home: she couldn't bear her mother's cloying unhappiness any longer, the suffocating grief that hung around the house like a fog, her father spending more time in the pub, weeping on the shoulders of strangers, her mother wailing through the night. No one in their right mind would blame her for marrying Jim and getting away.

They went to the Lake District for their honeymoon and ate Kendal mint cake; fifty years on she can still taste its sharp fresh-air sweetness.

They stayed in a boarding house and the handwritten rules in the hallway stated that all guests should vacate the premises by 10 a.m. and not come back until 5 p.m. They hired bicycles and Jim rowed her across Lake Windermere, which took it out of him. He was the colour of a church candle for the rest of the day, he never did have much puff.

'Whooping cough as a kiddie, lungs weak for life,' the doctor said. Course, he was never properly looked after, his mother was no better than she should have been.

The Collins family were rough – his brothers were the type of men who brawled in the street – so really it was both of them that were getting away from where they came from.

Jim wanted respectability and the Whittakers were a cut above the Collinses. After all, Jean had been at secretarial school, she could have been a secretary. Only as it turned out she couldn't. Oh her hands were quick enough, it was just her brain couldn't keep up!

Dyslexia, that's what they called it, a daft name for a condition that means you can't spell.

Ah but she could draw, and nowadays she'd go to art school, be a painter, splashing colour over great big canvases. As it was she used to draw her shopping lists; it was easier to draw a chicken than write the word.

'The quak broon fax.' Jean recalls her Pitman's exercises. Who on earth was going to employ a secretary that couldn't arrange letters in the right order?

Good job Jim came along when he did, all polite and apologetic, a man determined to do his best, a man who polished his shoes every day, only to tread in dog shit. What was it with poor Jim? His feet were a magnet for dog shit.

He didn't want her to work, but she got bored. The flat wasn't big enough to clean all day, it was only a titchy thing above a haberdashery shop. Now what were they called, the two sisters who owned The Stitch in Time? Val and Mo, they taught her to embroider. She'd always been handy with a needle but once she learnt to embroider she couldn't stop, tablecloths with cherries all over and matching napkins, sunflowers and forget-me-nots on the collars of her blouses.

She needed something to keep her occupied in the afternoon, something quiet while Jim sat in an armchair and slept off his early morning postman shift.

All that walking made him even thinner. She tried to fatten him up, but eating too much just gave him indigestion. He was always on the Epsom salts and at night she would lie awake listening to his digestive tract compete with the flat's botched plumbing and wondering whether she should have held out for a bit longer and found someone a bit more exciting. Like Gregory Peck.

Anne

Croc Attack

Anne cannot remember going to bed, she cannot remember finishing the claret or saying goodbye to Melanie or Christopher. She vaguely remembers getting into a mess serving the pudding and having to remove a large dollop of gooseberry fool from Christopher's lap. He hadn't wanted her to help, but she'd attacked his groin with a damp tea towel and insisted the Robinsons should go home with one of the Stain Devils that she keeps under the sink.

Anne pictures herself on her hands and knees, rooting around in the cupboard under the sink like a massive pig sniffing for truffles, and blushes in the dark. She has made a fool of herself and, what's more, she has an awful feeling that she didn't stack the dishwasher before she staggered up the stairs.

Her breath feels hamstery. According to the luminous dials on her watch it is two o'clock in the morning and she has no idea whether her eldest son has come home from the pub. This means she doesn't know whether the burglar alarm is on.

Being burgled is one of Anne's phobias: she has had her car radio stolen three times (shattered glass turning the gravel drive diamanté) and both Nat and Julian have been mugged for their bikes in local parks. Anne would like to see the perpetrators have their hands cut off, she'd do it herself if necessary. Anne has a large selection of kitchen knives, any number of which could hack through the sinews of a man's wrists.

Theft happens all the time, especially where they live. If I were a burglar, thinks Anne, suddenly realising that she is sprawled naked on top of the bed while Paul is hunched like a neat corpse under the sheet.

If I were a burglar, she repeats in her head, I would cruise around here in the wee small hours, in black leather gloves. I would check the side gates and back entrances. After all, this is where the good stuff is, this is where the spoilt girls and boys live with their laptops and computer games and digital cameras, where the men keep thousands of pounds' worth of golf clubs in garages that one day they will forget to secure and Mercedes car keys glint in the moonlight on kitchen tables just beyond French windows that may or may not have been properly bolted.

It's no good, Anne Armitage has a vivid imagination, has done ever since she first started writing stories in Miss Ferris's class back in 1968. 'Anne, that's a super story, shall we put it up on the wall? Listen everyone, Anne's written a story about coming face to face with a giant octopus.' Octopus/burglar – you can kill an octopus by punching it in the eye, but a burglar? Burglars must be prevented, they must be kept out, she must keep her family safe.

God knows what would happen if anyone did break in. She's not sure what lengths her family would go to protect her. Would they punch a burglar in the eye?

She will not be able to sleep again until she has made sure that the house has been Fort Knoxed. Anyway, she needs to get a drink of water, unless she remembered to bring some up last night. There is a glass on her bedside table. Oh God, she can smell it. Brandy, what the hell?

Anne hefts herself off the bed. It's too hot, someone must have overridden the central heating, it's meant to be on a timer.

Some paracetamol might be a good idea. There's a medicine box in the cupboard above the microwave. Anne was a Girl Guide, she is conscientious about things like bandages and small tubes of ointment for conjunctivitis, and when you are the mother of boys you get used to reaching for the plasters.

She liked that, a boy with a grazed knee needing TCP and a cuddle. Not any more: now they are big her sons keep their lumps and bumps to themselves, and anyway these days bruises tend to be around the neck. Anne shudders. Her sons' sexuality is something that makes her feel queasy. From whom, for example, did Nat pick up the cold sore virus that flares up on his bottom lip every so often? Anne keeps a stash of Zovirax handy for these occurrences and she knows Julian occasionally helps himself to her Buscopan. IBS runs (or rather doesn't) in the family, not that Julian would ever admit it.

Anne creeps down the stairs. She is naked but all she needs to do is check the front door and make sure the alarm is on. As she reaches the bottom step there is a noise outside on the porch. Instinctively she reaches for the light switch and in the newly cast bright yellow light looks around for a weapon. A pair of size 9 red Crocs have been carelessly discarded on the welcome mat – hers. Big feet are just one of the many banes of her life; her mother-in-law refuses to believe that it is physically possible to be female and have feet that are anything bigger than a six.

Well Ellen, thinks Anne, reaching for one of her colossal Crocs, my big feet just might save my family's life. If she has to kill with a plastic shoe, then that's what she will do. She jumps back on to the stairs, Croc raised above her head. The front door swings open and there is her eldest son, a bottle of Budweiser in one hand and a pretty girl in the other.

'Jesus fucking Christ!'

Anne drops the Croc and runs as fast as she can back up the stairs. Maybe it's the first time the girl has seen cellulite in motion, maybe she is the nervous type, but Anne is not the only one to turn and flee: the blonde is out of the door like a peroxide eel and Nat is left wobbling in the hallway, looking like he might be sick.

Back in the bedroom, Anne reaches for the un-drunk glass of brandy and throws it down her neck. This pushes her total of alcohol units well into binge figures, but at least it means she can slide gratefully into unconsciousness.

Deep in the dark black of her booze-induced slumber Anne has a nightmare about not being able to find her passport and turning up at Gatwick naked apart from an enormous pair of red Crocs. She looks ridiculous, like a clown, and even though Anne feels embarrassed in her dream it is nothing compared to the humiliation she will feel when she wakes and remembers the previous evening's sequence of events.

Meanwhile, down in the kitchen Nat runs the cold tap and splashes his face in the kitchen sink. Normally, coming in late at night, Nat would raid the fridge, sticking his stinky nicotine-stained fingers into anything his mother had carefully put cling film over and swigging milk from a carton he'd leave on the draining board to go sour.

However, the sight of his bare-bottomed mother has diminished his appetite, not to mention his erection. Nat picks up a bottle of brandy – odd, his mother usually only gets the brandy out when she's making Christmas cake – unlocks the French windows and lights a cigarette in the garden. He'd been on a promise with Zoe Carpenter: she was easy, everyone knew it; he'd already had a feel of her tits and he hadn't even bought her a drink. Oh well, plenty more fish. His house is ideally located for totty, the Village is awash with fanny. Nat, for whom maths has never been a strong point, does a rough calculation: there are probably around a hundred shaggable girls currently attending the two 'good' schools locally, maybe more if he counts the pre-GSCE chicks. He has his whole gap year to get through as many as possible. His aim, he decides, is to be the Russell Brand of SE21.

34

An ancient fox stares at him. Her fur, once amber, has turned the grey of his mother's ghastly pubic thatch. Shit, his horrible ugly fat mum.

He should sue her. What if he has flashbacks, what if he can never get it up again?

Nat shivers and comes inside, inevitably forgetting to lock the French windows. He pours an inch of brandy into a Bart Simpson mug that once upon a time came complete with a big purple shiny Easter egg. How many years ago was that?

Two.

Bloody hell! His mother just can't seem to cope with the fact that he and Jools have grown up. They don't need her any more. Anne's handbag is hanging off one of the kitchen chairs, unzipped and gaping, her purse clearly visible. Casually Nat reaches for the purse and helps himself to a twenty-pound note.

His mother is tight, she wants him to get a job – and he will, but in his own time. That's what she doesn't seem to understand, that the more she nags the less inclined he feels like doing anything. Quietly the boy tiptoes up the stairs. He might need something to blot the image of his mother out of his subconscious before it scars him for life. Nat has a collection of pornography under his bed, and there's a pretty decent centre-spread in this month's *Nuts* magazine. With any luck the twin charms of a couple of pouting nineteen-year-olds from County Durham will eradicate the dreadful sight of his suet-fleshed mother.

Anne snores; next to her Paul seethes. It is four o'clock in the morning and he has a busy day ahead of him. He's operating from 11 a.m., starting with a nasty set of adenoids. Thinking of which, judging by the hog-like sounds that his wife is emitting Anne's are also in dire need of whipping out. He'd do it right now if someone passed him a scalpel.

There is something rather masculine about Anne's snoring. My wife is not delicate, rues Paul. She has big hands and big feet, something he'd first noticed with any clarity on the day they got married. Even in a wedding dress there was something of the female impersonator about her as she strode down the aisle. In the photos she is stooping and his mother looks cross.

'She's such a sporty-looking thing, Paul, are you sure she doesn't play tennis?'

Anne has crashed out like a large tree, not surprising considering how much she had to drink. He'd been shocked: drinking to excess is not like Anne. Throughout their marriage she has been the one in control: as she always said, you never know when you're going to need to drive to A and E.

Recently she has been irrationally moody. Being a medical man, Paul knows that it will be her hormones. That, and the fact that her domestic status is under threat: the boys don't really need her any more, they resent her interference, the way she expects them to eat breakfast together, her fury at their lack of gratitude, their barely concealed ambivalence to her maternal needs.

Poor Anne. Paul feels a rush of tenderness. She has been a good and faithful wife. She could do with more affection, but if he goes to hug her she automatically thinks he wants sex and starts to squirm around in what she mistakenly thinks is a sexual manner, which embarrasses him.

Many of his friends' wives are much better-looking; that's because they are second or even third wives. Anne is like an old sofa, gone saggy but no need to take her down to the tip quite yet. There are still a few more years in her and really, she asks for very little.

Jean

Sex and Epilepsy

Whose bed is this, wonders Jean. It's certainly not her own.

I do hope no one is expecting me to have sexual intercourse, she frets, I'm not a big fan, never really have been . . . apart from . . . no that doesn't belong here, that goes in a drawer marked Much, Much Later. Let's get this story right.

Let's go back to the honeymoon. Honeymoon, what a lovely word! A moon made of honey. She was twenty-two years old and a virgin. A virgin complete with a hymen. Jean has a horrible feeling Jim had been one too, he was a bit useless.

All they'd done before they got married was a bit of kissing and that was enough of a shock, his tongue poking about her cavities like an inquisitive slug.

She remembers the wedding night, how she shivered with nerves in that little pale blue nightie with the ribbons round the neckline, waiting for him to come out of the bathroom, waiting and waiting. In the end she'd fallen asleep.

The sound of someone shouting and banging a door outside in the corridor woke her up: 'I'm not having drunks in here, this is a respectable boarding house. I'm not having you crashed out like a tramp on my lino.'

Jean had put the bedside light on; a yellow light flooded the room sickly as typhus. It was nearly midnight and Jim wasn't in the bed. She'd poked her nose out of the bedroom door. The landlady was in her dressing gown, rattling the bathroom doorknob. 'It's locked,' she explained to Jean, 'but he's not answering. I can see he's on the floor. Did you bring liquor in with you?'

'No,' protested Jean, even though they had. They'd smuggled in a bottle of cherry brandy. The next thing she knew, she'd put her fist through the frosted glass of the bathroom door and opened it from the inside.

He was lying on the cork tiles, foaming at the mouth.

All she could do was kneel down next to him and repeat over and over again, 'There now Jim, it's all right, I'm here.'

'Petit mal,' he explained to her when he could speak again, that's why he wasn't allowed to drive. He'd had a horrible feeling it might happen.

'Overexcitement,' she'd said, trying to be the understanding wife and running her hand under the cold tap. Oddly enough, there was only one tiny cut, on the knuckle of her right hand.

'Epileptic?' said the landlady, sweeping up the broken glass with a dustpan and brush. 'I'd never have given you house room if I'd known.'

Over the years she got used to the signs, his sudden vagueness, the way he'd complain about having a funny taste in his mouth and then the strange absence in his eyes, followed by the little jerky spasms.

It wasn't often he'd end up on the floor, just that first night and once in the foyer of the Blackpool Opera House when they'd paid to see Dickie Henderson.

To be honest, she decided, the sex was more trouble than the brain seizures. He'd never had the coordination for it, nothing ever slotted easily into the right place and the harder he tried the more embarrassed she became. In the end she'd just let him get on with it, lain back and thought about nice fabrics for cushions and curtains while he shoved and grunted and stuck his elbows into her ribs.

Lord knows how she managed to get pregnant. They'd not discussed it, it wasn't planned, it was just assumed they'd one day start a family. Otherwise, she supposed, he would have used johnnies, that's what they called them. She'd found one once when she was a little girl, in her father's drawer. It was in a tin and all covered in powder like a misshapen piece of Turkish delight.

Of course nowadays condoms are advertised on the telly and girls are encouraged to keep them in their handbags, just like Parma Violets in the old days!

She could have asked him to wear one – he was always very amenable to any suggestion she might make – but she hadn't and now she was pregnant.

The doctor confirmed her suspicions: 'Congratulations, Mrs Collins.' Congratulations, she thought, what for? She'd not really done anything to deserve any congratulations.

Not like when she was at school and she'd done that collage of a horse made out of crushed eggshells and yellow raffia, and her teacher had said, 'Congratulations, Jean, that's a splendid piece of work' and Jean had felt like her insides had turned to treacle.

Jim was over the moon. He said, 'I've never really won anything before,' and she'd snapped back, 'You've not won anything now.'

'But I feel like I've won the pools,' he said, all wet around the eyes. He could be terribly sentimental could Jim, he could cry at anything.

Him being pleased just made her feel cross about it, like he'd got one over on her, she didn't know why.

They had to tell the parents. 'I hope it's a boy,' her mother wept. 'A little boy, you could call him Brian.'

Her father wasn't in, he was in the pub, but he sent her a postcard from Fleetwood telling her how pleased he was. What on earth was he doing in Fleetwood?

Telling Jim's family was much more of a palaver. For starters the Collinses didn't have a phone, so this meant catching two buses to the back end of Blackpool on the off chance they were in.

They went on a Saturday, but all the menfolk were at a football match – of course they were – and as for Ma Collins, she wasn't that fussed. All she had in was a tin of luncheon meat, but when they asked her to accompany them to the chippy for a celebratory dinner she said she wasn't particularly hungry and that luncheon meat was perfectly adequate for her, and she didn't know where Jim got his airs and graces from.

He said it was the vinegar on the fish that made him cry.

Anne

In No Fit State for Bad News

As soon as Anne comes round she knows she has a hangover. She lies quiet and still, wishing the day ahead was already over. She is already slightly ashamed. What must the Robinsons think?

Then she remembers the naked Croc incident on the stairs. Oh sweet Jesus no! The flashback is mercifully silent but in full Technicolor: once again she sees her son's appalled face, the comedy drop of his jaw, the flash of a disappearing blonde.

I wouldn't mind dying right now, thinks Anne, there is nothing to look forward to in my life except more humiliation.

Paul is still asleep, he has barely moved all night – he rarely does, his pyjamas remain uncrumpled.

Anne's right arm has gone to sleep under her right breast. Absent-mindedly she feels herself for lumps, thinking, At least if I was terminally ill then my family might be kinder to me. And, she adds as an afterthought, maybe I would lose some weight.

She doesn't mean this, she is just feeling sorry for herself, bloated with last night's alcohol, her belly a queasy saddlebag of booze. Ergh.

But if I did die, she perseveres, would Paul and the children miss me?

Anne toys with the idea of pretending to be dead, just for a minute, just to see if Paul panics, to see if he calls their sons: 'Nat, Julian, it's your mother, I can't seem to wake her. I think . . . Oh Christ . . .'

Anne allows herself a tiny fantasy. Her husband and sons standing by her open grave, it's raining, there are umbrellas, their faces are etched in misery. It looks like a rather classy BBC 1 Dickens adaptation: Anne loves a bonnet drama. Just as she is about to imagine her husband throwing a single scarlet rose on to her oak casket (on second thoughts make that a cardboard coffin, she would prefer to be eco-friendly in death) the phone rings and automatically she lifts the receiver.

'Hello, this is Blackpool Victoria Hospital, we've got your mother.'

For a second it sounds like a hostage scenario. Who on earth would want to kidnap her mother?

'She was brought in last night, RTA.'

'RTA,' parrots Anne, desperately attempting to decode the acronym. What on earth is RTA? Is it some band?

'Road traffic accident. She was run over. By a motorbike. Your mother . . .' The person on the other end of the phone enunciates slowly and clearly, as if Anne might have a learning difficulty, which, judging by the severity of her hangover, she sort of has.

'The police have only just brought in her handbag. They talked to her neighbours and we found your number in your mum's phone.'

Anne is reeling. Paul is hovering at the end of the bed, his pyjamas looking like a smart/casual summer suit. He could wear a tie with his pyjamas and look better dressed than most men, thinks Anne. Her brain is spinning.

'Is she all right?'

The woman on the other end of the phone doesn't really have time for this. What part of road traffic accident does this

42

silly cow not understand? Why would she bother to ring if the old lady was all right?

She takes a deep breath. 'Your mother is in intensive care. She was run over by a motorbike doing forty-five miles an hour in a twenty zone. She has a number of broken bones and a head injury; actually, your mother is in a coma.'

'A coma,' repeats Anne.

'Yes, a coma.'

Paul is offering her a pen and a piece of paper. Why on earth is he doing that? This is no time to be writing a shopping list.

'Ask which ward,' he instructs.

Of course, this is stuff he knows about: patients, hospitals, concerned relatives.

I am a concerned relative, thinks Anne. I am the daughter of a woman who has been run over and is in intensive care.

Paul takes the phone off her. 'My wife is very upset,' he explains in his posh don't-mess-with-me voice and he scribbles 'Hamilton' on the piece of paper.

Anne walks by remote control to the bathroom. She is unsteady, as if a small child is operating her movements. She is jerky, bumping into the bath, crashing down on to the toilet, standing up, wobbling, turning round and throwing up into the bowl.

Behind her Paul closes the door of the en suite. He has always been squeamish about sick. He can deal with blood and tissue, sinew and bone, but sick and shit have never been his thing.

Anne cleans her teeth and her gums bleed a little – damned gingivitis on top of everything else. She feels dreadful; obviously she is going to have to go north and she will have to go right now. She can't possibly drive, though. Anne knows she is too hungover for the M1. She can take a train, a train direct from Euston. Euston to Blackpool and a cab from the train station to the hospital.

She will need an overnight bag, she will have to call school, she has a class this afternoon, they will need to arrange cover, how long will she be away?

Anne steps into the shower. She needs to get organised. My mother has been run over, she reminds herself. Should I take two skirts and a pair of trousers or two pairs of trousers and a skirt?

It is October and the autumn term is in full swing so this is all very inconvenient. The weather has been lovely in the south but it will be colder up north, she'll probably need tights.

She toys with trying to exterminate the hangover by turning the shower dial to freezing but worries the shock might just kill her, and then she'd be 'neither use nor ornament', as her mother would say.

Poor Jean, how on earth could it have happened? Her mother was a stickler for waiting for the green man. She'd always been taught as a child: look right, look left, look right again. What on earth had she been thinking? For a moment Anne is transported back to her childhood. She is standing by the kerb, one hand in her mother's while the other holds a smaller hand, a hand that is always pulling away. She would weep if she had the time, she would sit on the floor of this shower unit and howl.

All the suitcases are up in the loft. Paul's family has proper luggage, inherited leather suitcases too heavy to carry, relics of a time when porters hovered on station platforms, but there are other bags up there, roll bags, overnighters, Nat's old school trunk, festival rucksacks. She will need someone to help her get the loft ladder down, she can't do it by herself, not with a hangover. She can't ask Paul, Paul has to be very careful of doing that sort of thing. He mustn't trap his hands, he can't change a car tyre, it's not worth the risk.

Forget Paul and his hands, Anne instructs herself as she tries to scrub last night's booze out of her pores with a papaya body gel, I should get one of the boys to help.

Anne steps dripping out of the shower. It is half-past seven, time Julian was getting up for school. She wants her sons to sympathise with her – would it be too much to ask for a cup of tea and a hug? If only Nat could actually drive, he could take

44

her north. It would be a bonding experience but no, she will have to do this alone. Maybe that's what's upsetting her.

'I have no one to hold my hand,' she mutters. 'Who is going to help me?' And then she starts to shout, 'Julian! Julian!' at the top of her very loud voice.

Jean

Expecting

Jean can't remember when she last had something to eat but she's not that fussed. It's been a long time since she last sat at a table with a knife and fork, you don't tend to bother when you're on your own. These days she eats off a tray in front of the telly and rarely cleans her plate.

Mind you, she was never a big eater. Neither she nor Jim had much of an appetite and it didn't take much to put her off her food: sometimes just watching Jim chewing his breakfast was enough to make her put her cutlery down. There was something of the scrawny donkey about her husband, the knobbly joints, the long ears and the slowness.

He used to worry about her. 'You're such a skinny minnie,' he'd say, like he had room to talk. 'Come on now Jean, love, you're eating for two.'

Trouble was, at this stage in her first pregnancy she knew the more she ate, the longer she'd be with her head over the lavatory bringing it all back up again. Even the doctor was concerned.

'You've got to try, Mrs Collins. That baby is relying on you, it won't grow big and strong if you're not taking in enough nutriment.' He gave her a pamphlet, 'Healthy Eating for the Mother-to-Be'.

Joan chuckles silently. Healthy eating, my bum. The only thing that didn't have her heaving was Bird's Angel Delight.

Packets of it she went though. She liked it best raw. Strawberry flavour was her favourite, tipped straight from the packet and into her mouth, yum. Afterwards she'd rip the packet open and lick it clean.

Her mother would have been horrified. Poor Margaret Whittaker, she'd always been a stickler for table manners. Jim's side of the family had appalled her at the wedding: they ate like pigs. And the language! Well, she could see that even the waiters thought they were common.

Really it was too bad, she'd had such hopes for Jean, and now look at her, married to a man with a disability and a baby on the way. If only Brian had lived.

Jean cannot decide whether her mother died of shame or grief, but early in the January of 1962 Margaret went to bed, as she always did, with a mug of hot milk and a ginger biscuit and never woke up. On the death certificate it said 'coronary'. So that was one grandma down before the baby was even born.

The second one went in a more dramatic fashion, two weeks after Margaret's funeral (very quiet). Ma Collins fell off a tram and never got up again. An embolism, they said, might have been pressing on her brain for months. No wonder she said such nasty things.

After the grandmas-to-be had died the grandpas sort of faded into the background. Grandpas weren't very hands-on in those days, not like today, thinks Jean. These days the local parks are full of grey-haired men pushing toddlers on swings, feeding the ducks.

Some say it's cheap labour, all those mums and dads that can't afford childcare but want to work so they can have foreign holidays and Wiis, fobbing their kids off on pensioners.

Jean thinks it's nice, be lovely to have her grandkiddies nearer. She's not seem them for . . .

Best not think about that. If she starts thinking about things that are happening now she'll get confused about what was happening then, and everything will get all upside down and back to front.

Jean pulls herself back to January 1962.

My father, she recalls, went straight from my mother's funeral in St Annes to Fleetwood, where he'd been wooing a widow on a bench overlooking the sea. Rumour had it, he took her a piece of fruitcake from the wake (which Margaret had actually made for the christening of her future grandchild) and he never came home again. The bungalow was sold and Jean received her share in the post.

A cheque for fifteen hundred pounds, it was better than winning the pools!

She would have liked to have gone on a cruise but Jim said, 'Let's be sensible Jean,' and so they bought the little house in Marton, just past the mushroom farm and diagonally opposite the playing fields. It was a funny place to live, neither here nor there, people usually passed it on the way to somewhere else.

'It'll do for us,' said Jim. There was a pub down the road, a big yellow-brick thirties job, with crenellations like a castle; a primary school just a five-minute walk away; and a parade of shops complete with a chippy bang slap opposite.

Of course later on the local takeaways got more adventurous. Alongside the chippy there are two Chinese now and a Thai called Wok-u-Like. Jean has become quite a convert to chicken pad thai.

Not that she needs her usual number 42 on the Wok-u-Like menu. For the time being all Jean needs by way of nutriment is being delivered 'chew free' via the tube up her nose and the drip in her arm, directly into her system. It's all very convenient and there's no washing up to do either.

113 Marton Edge Road. Jean was a bit superstitious about the 13 and of course as things turned out she was right, but at the time Jim just laughed. He said, 'Everyone has their ups and

downs.' And it was true, it's just Jim seemed to have more downs than ups.

Poor Jim, he just couldn't help it, he wasn't a lucky man. For all the pigeon shit that rained upon his head, fate conspired against him. Inexplicable punctures erupted in his bike tyres, clumps of his hair fell out for no reason whatsoever and scaly patches of skin itched all along his arms and down behind his knees.

But of course back then people didn't expect so much, they were just relieved bombs weren't dropping on their heads and that young men weren't going overseas and never coming back.

That's the trouble with young people today, reflects Jean, they don't know how it feels to be truly scared.

Now that's just the *Daily Mail* reader in you, argues Jean's conscience. Young people today have got plenty of other things to be scared about, there's drugs and not being able to get a job and obesity for starters.

Well, hark at me, she marvels. I might not know where I am or what's happened, but I'm still capable of rational thought. I've not gone gaga. I might not know what day it is and as for the time, well that's anybody's guess.

But judging by how tired she suddenly feels, she reckons it must be night-time. She can't be bothered with cleaning her teeth, all that can wait, but before she drifts off into the deep black again she'd like to get to the bit where she has the baby. The first one. What was her name?

Anne

Getting Ready to Go

Anne knows she should knock before entering her son's bedroom. He is sixteen years old and therefore entitled to some privacy.

Not really, Anne corrects herself. He can have privacy when he has bought his own house. Then he can have as much privacy as he likes.

Right now he is under her roof and if she feels like barging into his bedroom at seven-thirty in the morning then she has every right. Only she doesn't. She is scared these days of what she might see. Boys are so genitally obsessed, the last thing she wants to do is walk in on her son and find him masturbating.

This sort of thing is regaled with much laughter at her book club. Helen Trent seems to find her seventeen-year-old son's masturbatory prowess something to gloat over: 'I tell you, girls, he'll have a right arm as big as Popeye's if he doesn't stop wanking.'

'Hahaha' laughs everyone except Anne, who feels queasy.

Anne doesn't really like it when the book club meetings get side-tracked into what she calls gossipathons. One joins a book club for intellectual stimulus, not for hours of chitchat about sex and men and sex and children and sex and schools.

What's odd, thinks Anne, is how some parents collude in their children's sex lives, actively encouraging them, allowing girlfriends or boyfriends to sleep over, offering condoms and turning a deaf ear to squeaking bedsprings. Well not in my house, she resolves.

Just because 'everyone else does' doesn't mean that 'we do'.

Anne knocks and composes her face into an expression of 'very worried indeed'. She has used this face a lot over the years, in particular when the boys brought home their school reports.

'Wha'? Wha' you wan'?' moans Jools. It's a shame people don't approve of elocution lessons any more, thinks Anne. Once upon a time, if you wanted to get on in the world you aped the ruling classes, but no longer. Anne's sons sound exactly the same as the teenage scaffolder who worked on the extension a few years ago. They know their glottal stops and carefully adopted Alan Sugar-esque grammatical errors drive their mother mad – maybe that's why they do it. 'Innit,' she adds under her breath before raising her voice and braying, 'Darling I need to come in. I need to ask you something.' She hears him mutter 'Fuck's sake' as she inches the door open.

Jools's bedroom is not like his brother's. Nat's room is a typically squalid Lynx-drenched sty. Nat is a slob but Jools is tidy, his bedroom has the air of a boutique hotel crossed with a Bond lair. There is something about her younger son's bedroom that unnerves Anne, the clinical precision with which everything is displayed, the thick creamy candles on the mantelpiece, the expensive bottle of aftershave. Jools will not wear anything from the high street behind his ears: he's got that from his father, thinks Anne.

Jools has a touch of the playboy about him and he is only just sixteen. Last Christmas he asked for a wolfskin throw for his bed. His paternal grandmother gave him the money and he bought one off the internet. Anne thought it rather strange: in contrast to his older brother's lurid pin-up walls, Jools has just one framed poster, advertising Kubrick's *A Clockwork Orange*. A book I have not read and a film I have not seen, Anne admits.

Jools has propped himself up in bed. He is lean, his chest

golden and hairless. How come Jools, who is so blond, can retain a summer tan for so long? He has grown his hair so that a thick forelock covers half his face. Anne has to resist the urge to snip at this curtain of hair with the bacon scissors. He can't see out of one eye, he could do with a hairband, he deserves to get spots. But he doesn't. Jools is languid and confident and his lip curls when his mother parks her large backside on his silvery throw.

'It's your grandmother . . .'

The eye that isn't hidden by a thick wave of yellow hair widens, he looks anxious. Anne is momentarily pleased, until she realises he thinks something might have happened to Ellen. Ellen is Paul's mother, Jools is her favourite, she likes him because he is handsome and charming – she likes Nathaniel too but he doesn't try as hard as Julian does to flatter her. Ellen is forever palming little treats into her youngest grandson's hand: a pair of cufflinks his grandfather wore, a silver tie pin, a twenty-pound note.

She starts again. 'My mother, your Nanna Jean, has had an accident. She's been run over.'

Even as she says it she can sense the ridiculousness of the statement and she sees Jools's mouth twitch. If he laughs, even in a nervous, hysterical kind of way, she will have to hit him.

'My mother is in a coma in hospital; please can you get the medium navy suitcase with the wheels down from the attic for me.'

'Yeah, course, no sweat.'

She doesn't know what else to say. The door to the attic is in the ceiling on the landing immediately outside Julian's room.

'Would you bring it down to my bedroom, I need to pack.'

'Yeah' and he gives her a look as if to say, 'Well fuck off then.'

Of course! She has to leave the bedroom before he can get out of bed, it's been a long time since Jools wore pyjamas. He is naked under the wolfskin.

Once upon a time it wouldn't have mattered. For heaven's

sake, this is the boy who used to curl up on her knee after a bath, whose toes she would play 'This little piggy' with.

Anne misses the sons she used to have, the ones who wore stripy pyjamas and matching towelling dressing gowns. She misses the way they could all move around the house together, brush against each other without flinching. How long is it since she has been able to touch either Nat or Julian? Life for the mothers of sons starts to get difficult when their boys are around eight and old enough to go to the men's changing rooms by themselves at the swimming pool. This, decides Anne, is when you start to lose control.

She should knock on Nathaniel's door next and tell him what's going on, but she can't quite face him. Paul can fill him in later.

No doubt he will react with the same nonchalance as Jools, not that her younger son's reaction surprised her. They have seen so little of their grandmother over the past few years that there are probably school dinner ladies that the boy feels closer to. 'That's my fault,' Anne whispers to herself, 'it's all my fucking fault.'

Jean

Cauliflowers and Contractions

Jean has no idea how long she has been down at the bottom
of the deep dark well, but now she has emerged again and
although everything is a bit fuzzy round the edges she has just
about managed to get back to where she left off.

She is remembering being pregnant. She would like to give
her tummy a comforting rub, it would be nice to reassure herself
that she still has a stomach, but unfortunately she can't get her
hands to obey the order. Wouldn't it be awful if she were just
a floating head?

Jean imagines herself tutting and saying, 'Now you're just
talking silly.'

She found being with child a bit embarrassing, especially as
her condition became more obvious with every passing month:
the big lump of it sticking out of her coat, everyone knowing.
She may as well have had a sign above her head saying, 'My
husband puts his penis into my vagina.'

Not that Jean has ever used those words, it's always been his
thingy and her china.

China was the word her mother had used. Maybe it was to
make her doo-dah sound more precious, only to be used on

very special occasions, and suddenly Jean imagines her downstairs area all dusty, like an ornament that's not been taken off the shelf and given a good seeing to for years. But now she's getting fanciful again.

Anyway, it was a good job for Jean that her china wasn't made of china, it would have smashed into a million bits the day the baby came.

It was a windy day in April and Jim was on his round, delivering letters courtesy of the Royal Mail, which made him sound like he worked for the Queen! They still wore hats in those days. Poor Jim, he tried to keep himself tidy but he always looked as if he was coming undone, a button hanging off, a shoelace trailing, an accident waiting to happen.

Anyway, he was working and she was in the back yard, they'd not been in Marton long and the garden wasn't much to write home about. She wanted rose bushes, flowers running all over, but Jim got hay fever, he liked a shrub and a tidy border. But he'd put her a washing line up and promised her a little rockery in the corner, maybe some crazy paving.

She still felt a bit shy when she pegged out his underwear. Jim wore aertex undershorts while she wore a white or beige-coloured panty. There was something so intimate and revealing about their underwear hanging out on the line for everyone to see; the sight of her bras made her blush. Sheets were less embarrassing, but they were heavy and you were forever having to run out of the house to fetch them in when it started raining.

Jean squinted. The sun was a squirt of lemon yellow in her eye but there were clouds moving in. She reached down to pick up Jim's Sunday shirt and when she tried to straighten herself up, she found she couldn't.

'Oof.' She staggered backwards and, wouldn't you know it, fell into the wide plastic laundry basket. There she sat, on top of sopping tea towels and wringing wet pinnies.

Your waters had broken, old coma Jean tells the young Jean, who continues to sit in the laundry basket. She cannot get up, she is stuck there with a pain like a horse has kicked her low down in her guts, folding her in two.

I was that scared, Jean remembers, I didn't know what to do. So I started throwing pegs into next door's garden. I thought if I could just get my next-door neighbour's attention . . .

Old Jean is enjoying listening to young Jean tell this story, but occasionally she interrupts her younger self: 'It was a good job everyone did their washing on the same day back then. Of course these days people don't have to rely on neighbours, they've got mobile phones to get them out of sticky situations.'

Jean even has one herself, a little Nokia that requires her reading glasses to see the tiny numbers on the buttons. But in 1962, if her next-door neighbour hadn't been doing more or less the same as she'd been doing on the other side of the wall, then God knows that baby would have been born in a laundry basket and what kind of a start in life would that be?

As it was Mrs Kane, alerted by the shower of wooden pegs, popped her head round the back gate, clocked the situation and immediately tick-tacked on her slingbacks down to the phone box on the corner and rang for an ambulance.

When she let herself back into the Collinses' back yard she asked Jean for the tuppence it had cost her. 'I thought the emergency services were free,' Jean said between contractions.

She was sly, was Mrs Kane, always popping round for a pat of butter or an onion and never paying you back. Mind you, she was a better bet than Mrs Gaga who lived on the other side: you wouldn't want her bending over you when you were in labour, all covered in cat hair, with her sardine breath and moustaches. At least Mrs Kane was compos and clean. 'You might be best taking your knickknacks off,' she said as Jean moaned from the laundry basket. 'The ambulance won't be long and you might feel embarrassed having a stranger remove your undergarments.'

Mrs Kane turned her back and lit a cigarette from the packet in her apron pocket while Jean wriggled out of her panties. She then patted her beehive; a zipper of kirby grips kept her liquorice-coloured hair in a precarious mound on top of her head.

'Now listen, love, I've not had kiddies myself – me and Mr Kane decided we'd rather have a Ford Consul – but my sister had a lad and she wouldn't let them cut her. Let the boy tear her to shreds, said you could hear it, like a pair of old curtains. Take my advice, love: if they offer to cut you then just say "yes". She's had trouble ever since, has my sister.'

'Can you get my bag?' panted Jean. 'I've an overnight bag packed by the bed, and my handbag.' Mrs Kane disappeared through the back door. She took her time, and when she came back she'd got both bags and a cauliflower that Jean had put out on the side ready to make cauliflower cheese for her and Jim's tea.

'You'll not be wanting to bother with this, pet. Can I just have a borrow? I'll pay you back, eh, what are neighbours for?'

But at least she locked everything up and promised to write a note for Jim and push it through the front door, and then she sat and held Jean's hand and tried to take her mind off everything by singing Cliff Richard songs. Ever since that day Jean has never been able to listen to 'Living Doll' without thinking she might need to bear down.

Audrey Kane, she wonders, whatever happened to her? Jean tries to imagine Audrey's beehive gone grey, but she can't. The last thought she has before she falls back down to the bottom of the well is that Audrey never repaid her for that cauliflower.

Anne

Family Planning

Anne should eat, after all she has a long journey ahead of her. She should have a nice sensible boiled egg, but she realises she might vomit again if she does. Instead, she resigns herself to eating at the train station even though it's a monstrous waste of money.

Into the blue suitcase Anne packs five pairs of knickers, two skirts, one pair of trousers, several pairs of tights, a combination of short- and long-sleeved T-shirts, a couple of cardis, her wash bag (containing her special gingivitis mouth care preparation) and a selection of carefully chosen jaunty scarves. As she attempts to roll her giant bras into unobtrusive bundles she hears her mother-in-law's voice in her head: 'It's nice to be able to coordinate, it shows one's made an effort. Sometimes a little scarf tied *just so* can make all the difference.'

She has managed to have a serious, if snatched, conversation with Paul. It has been decided (or rather Anne has suggested and Paul has agreed) that his mother should come up and spend a few days to keep an eye on things.

Ellen is a very well-equipped woman. She might be in her eighties, but she still has all her faculties and is certainly not the kind of woman to cross a road without looking right then left then right again. What's more, Ellen is such a stickler for things being just so that, with any luck, by the time Anne returns all the silver will have been cleaned and her mother-in-law will have done the insides of the windows with newspaper and vinegar. Done properly or, in other words, better than either Anne or Loretta could possibly manage.

She asks Jools to order her a cab before he leaves for school; she is pretending to be too upset to pick up the phone but in reality she is too hungover to remember the number.

'Yah, Dulwich Village,' her younger son barks, and for a second she marvels at how assured he sounds, as if he's been ordering cabs for years. Come to think of it, he probably has.

Paul has an account, and no doubt Jools helps himself to a taxi courtesy of his father whenever he feels like it. Jools is not one for the night bus.

The cab is ordered for nine-fifteen; there's no point Anne setting off any earlier. Any train leaving Euston before half-past nine is astronomically expensive.

'It really doesn't matter darling,' says Paul.

But it does, it's the principle.

Anne might not be many things, she may not be a woman who can polish silver or clean the insides of her own windows properly but she is a woman of principle. Her mother might be dying and it is her duty to be by her bedside, but there's no need to get financially mugged by Virgin Trains in doing so. She is not a fool.

Paul has to leave before she does, he has a full morning of ENT ahead of him. His steady pink hands are scalpel-ready. It's unfortunate that his mother-in-law should have had this accident, but with any luck she will be dead by the time Anne arrives and his wife can return on the next available train. He really doesn't want to drag his mother away from her bridge cronies, she finds London really rather ghastly and he's worried that she might get upset by the boys.

Not that there's anything untoward about Julian and Nathaniel, they're just very typical of young men today. It's fine when Ellen comes for Christmas and everyone's on their best behaviour, but it wouldn't do to expose his mother to some of his sons' less salubrious habits: all that swigging milk straight from the carton nonsense, not wearing a shirt to the table and generally being a tad uncouth.

Anne wouldn't bother alerting Ellen either, but Paul is due to leave on a week's golf jolly tomorrow evening – he and his Dulwich Golf Club buddies are heading for the Algarve. Normally they go to St Andrews but it's Justin Entwhistle's fiftieth and they've decided to push the boat out.

'I'm just not sure how long I'm going to be there for,' bleats Anne. Ideally she would like to hear Paul say, 'Don't worry, I'll cancel the golfing holiday. I'll stay here and hold the fort,' but he doesn't. He mutters, 'Really, this is all very inconvenient' under his breath.

Unfortunately Anne hears every word and, had she the energy, she would rise to the bait: 'Oh, it's *inconvenient* is it? My mother getting run over? Well I'm terribly sorry to put you out, only, um, hang on a second, I'm not putting you out, I'm not asking you to do sodding anything. That's how *inconvenient* it is for you.'

The words are all lined up ready to come out of her mouth. She would quite like to turn this into a full-blown row, secure in the knowledge that in this instance the moral high ground is rightfully hers, the selfish bastard.

Only she can't be bothered. Anne cannot bring herself to challenge her husband because the simple truth is it *is* inconvenient.

Her mother has always been inconvenient. She has never been a bitch or a cow or a nightmare, just a nagging guilt-stinging barb her conscience will always get hooked on, like a woollen jumper on a barbed-wire fence.

Anne knows that she is lucky, an inconvenient mother is not a psychopath like Maggie Reynolds's mother, or undermining like Claire Winterbottom's. Jean has really been no trouble, she has kept herself to herself, unlike Erin Nesbit's mother who came for Christmas last year and refused to get in the car when it was time for her to go home.

On the contrary, Jean hasn't visited Anne and Paul for five years and it's been at least eighteen months since Anne ventured north. Her mother has never complained – 'You're very busy, love' – and Anne has always been grateful, grateful that her busy life should provide such a perfect excuse and grateful to her mother for conspiring in this excuse.

I am not a bad person, Anne reminds herself. Every year she and Paul invite her mother on holiday with them. Jean could have gone skiing with them to Courchevel last year.

Fortunately she turned them down – 'Oh I don't think so dear, but have a lovely time' – which was a relief really: Courchevel was prohibitively expensive.

But she phones once a week, on a Sunday, or at least every other Sunday, and at Christmas they send a Fortnum's hamper, and not a cheap one: it costs five hundred pounds and arrives in a wooden box with leather handles.

'You shouldn't have,' says Jean who, unbeknown to Anne, means it. After all, there's only so much game terrine a woman in her seventies can stomach.

Of course, maybe she should have made the boys visit more often. But it's difficult, what with Nat spending the last three summers with a boarding-school friend whose family rent a villa in Corfu for the duration of the holidays and Jools dividing his time between cricket camp and (more recently) various music festivals.

Paul is itching to leave, he needs to catch the 8:26 to London Bridge. Obviously it would be nice to stay and see Anne into the taxi but she's a big girl and parents die, that's the order of things. Paul knows this for a fact: his father died ten years ago, keeled over in one of his greenhouses, dead before he hit the floor, a proper, decisive kind of death, none of this dithering around.

Paul doesn't know Jean very well. Anne has told him that he intimidates her. He doesn't do it on purpose, she just isn't the sort of person he would expect to find himself related to. He suspects she's not very bright. Jean has always struck him as the type of woman who, when asked if she wants a tea or coffee, will reply, 'Whatever's easiest.' He has a feeling he might have snapped at her in the past, 'They're both as easy as each other. It's not a brainteaser, it's a simple question: which would you rather have? Tea or coffee?'

Life or death?

Just choose, woman.

Jean

The Baby

Jean is back in 1962 once more. Two fully grown men are pulling her out of the laundry basket: 'One, two, three and ups-a-daisy.'

The ambulance men were very nice, even if one of them did have a look under her skirt. He was only doing his job and he did say she was 'coming on very nicely'. He was called Derek (odd what pops into your head almost fifty years down the line), he had curly grey hair and he held her hand all the way to the hospital.

She doesn't remember much about getting from the ambulance into the maternity ward, just the colours: all that green and white, white tiles, green paint, green uniforms, white aprons. These days they slop around in funny trouser suits like something out of *Star Trek*. Back then, it was still little cardboard caps for nurses and silver upside-down watches on a little chain above their bosoms.

They called her Mrs Collins, she was a married woman after all. There was nothing shameful about what she was doing, she'd committed no crime. Women did this every day all over the world, it was normal and natural, but even so, Jean remembers being very embarrassed.

It was all so messy. She'd been sick for starters, they'd barely managed to get the bowl under her nose before some of the sick hit the lino and splashed a black lace-up shoe. 'I'm sorry,' she said.

It was never like this in the movies, you never saw this bit. You just saw the bit after, with the baby all clean and bundled up in its adoring mother's arms, the mother supported by plumped-up pillows, her hair all tidy with just a little bit of lipstick on her ecstatic face.

She thought of all the little white matinee jackets she'd knitted, the booties threaded through with little satin ribbons, all so dainty, kept pristine. None of that stuff belonged in here with all the sick and the blood and the shit.

She could smell it, it was like being in the butcher's, but worse. It was like being in a butcher's that also dealt in fish, a meat-monger's, maybe? It wasn't very nice.

You were only twenty-four, she reminds herself, but if the sex had been a bit uncomfortable she should have known that giving birth was going to be even worse.

It was worse than anything she'd ever known, worse than sea sickness, vertigo and food poisoning all rolled into one.

Even though she was lying down, when a contraction came along she felt like she'd been knocked off her feet and dragged into a tidal wave of pain, there was no centre to her any more, she couldn't tell which way was up and which way was down. That's why she kept moving, she thought it might help but they told her to stop thrashing about.

They wanted her to calm down. They said she might fall off the bed. They wanted her on her back with her legs in the stir-rups. Her husband was here now, he was outside in the corridor, think how pleased he'd be if she could just be a good girl and slip her feet into these stirrups now.

She was cold. She remembers shivering between contractions; she'd always been the chilly type, always needed a cardi even in the summer, and she goose-bumped very easily.

That's what she remembers about having a baby. She can't conjure up the pain any more, but she still remembers the embarrassment and the shivering cold of it.

She was relieved Jim hadn't see her do it. She was glad they'd tidied the baby up and let her put a comb through her hair before they let him in.

He was the most thrilled she'd ever seen him, it was better than Blackpool winning the cup, he said. 'You don't mind then,' she'd asked, 'that she's not a boy?'

'I'd not swap her for all the tea in China,' he replied and he held the baby like she was a new puppy. He was gentle with her, but he wasn't scared, not like Jean. Even though the baby was a healthy eight-pounder Jean held her as if she were made of spun sugar.

Still, it was nice to see Jim looking so happy. It took a lot to make his face look enthusiastic; he had to be proper beaming not to look like a miserable sod. Hangdog, that was his natural expression, but there was nothing hangdog about him holding that baby. It was a relief: at least the kiddie had one parent who loved her.

Now then, old Jean admonishes young Jean, what do you mean by that?

'You know,' her younger self sighs back, 'they'd call it bonding nowadays. I just didn't really take to her, not for a while. Even when they'd wiped her down I could still see bits of me behind her ears, in all the nooks and crannies. Every time I closed my eyes I saw her covered in my blood, dangling by her ankles, a silent scream on her face, so wide her mouth seemed like a great knife-gash in her face.'

She didn't breastfeed; you could if you wanted but it wasn't considered either nice or necessary. Anyway, there were advantages to the powdered milk: you knew exactly how much nutriment your baby was getting, it was all measured out for you. 'Mother Nature is a clever old thing,' said the midwife, 'but there's not a pair of bosoms in the world that can guarantee the right

65

balance of protein, fat, carbohydrate, minerals and vitamins that a bottle can.'

So a bottle it was, which meant that once they got home Jim could give the baby her milk. 'It's like being a proper family,' he kept saying. 'It's like being a proper family.' And it was, sort of, but there was always a bit of Jean that felt that she was playing house, that at any moment she could put the baby away and go and play another game. She always referred to the baby as 'the baby', even Jim noticed. 'You always call her "the baby",' he said. She didn't like to tell him that sometimes she couldn't for the life of her remember what they'd decided to call her. What was it again?

Anne

Notes

Anne decides to leave a note for Nat. It takes her some time to find a working pen, which makes her sob and stamp on her own toe with frustration. Eventually she finds one in the fruit bowl.

NAT, she writes in capitals,

Emergency!! Nanna Jean has had a terrible accident and is in a coma in Blackpool Hospital. Your father is still going to Portugal but Grandma Ellen is coming to stay as of tomorrow. Not sure how long I will be. Am leaving twenty pounds, please buy supper for the three of you.
  Love Mum

Anne reaches for her purse. Damn, she was sure there had been at least three twenty-pound notes in there, now there are just two.

She removes a purple note and anchors the Queen's face to the table with the butter dish. It's a relief not to have to confront Nat, and by the time she is back the whole Croc incident will have been forgotten.

Before the taxi comes she needs to tidy the kitchen. There

are splodges of gooseberry fool all over the Yorkstone floor. Damn, Loretta comes on a Monday: can she trust Paul to leave her some money? No, he won't remember.

Anne feels herself heat up and a tiny bit of sick rises into her mouth. She is frozen between the table and the dishwasher with the remnants of last night's dinner party in her hands. 'Just drop them,' whispers a small voice behind her ear. 'Just drop everything and go.'

So she does. Anne drops a pile of plates and the soufflé dish she's had since she got married, the one with the crimped sides and lemon motif. Not everything breaks, but the soufflé dish shatters. There is now gooseberry fool splattered like ectoplasm up the sides of the kitchen units. Anne reaches for the pen: 'If I'm not back, remind your father to leave money for Loretta,' she scrawls, and without bending down to pick up a single shard of broken china she grabs her handbag and exits the kitchen. Woe betide Nat if he walks in there with bare feet.

Julian has gone to school. He didn't say goodbye, he didn't wish her luck or tell her he hoped his grandma would pull through, he just left. At least he's gone, she comforts herself, plenty of them don't: they just sit around the house watching *Jeremy Kyle* in their underwear, so she must be thankful for small mercies. Anyway, she can't worry about her sons now, it's her mother's turn. She must concentrate on the job in hand, phone the school secretary when she is in the cab and alert them to the situation. There won't be any problem. In fact, when Deirdre Kingsley's mother died last term they all had a whip-round and got her a lovely orchid in a pot and an evening at the Sanctuary Spa in Covent Garden.

Anne hadn't been too sure about the Sanctuary voucher. 'Is it an appropriate way to deal with grief,' she had asked, 'to go and have your eyebrows reshaped?'

'Yes,' Wendy Gilpin (history) had snapped. When *her* mother died she'd treated herself to a red rinse: 'It was a sort of tribute, she never did like me being mousy.'

Some teachers can be very stroppy, concludes Anne.

The minicab driver sounds his horn. Why can't he get out of his seat and ring the doorbell, really? Anne screams, 'Coming' out of the bedroom window. A neighbour walking past with a dog shouts back, 'Lucky for some!'

'Actually,' rallies Anne, 'my mother is dying and I am talking to the cab driver.'

Sometimes she has no sense of humour. She can feel it drain out of her.

'Sorry,' responds the neighbour and Anne feels guilty. It's that nice gay bloke, the one who helped her find Galaxy that time. Blushing, she shuts the window and rather than carry the suitcase she drags it down the stairs. It thuds on every step, maybe Nat will hear and wonder what is happening, maybe he will stick his head around the bedroom door and offer to help. But he doesn't.

The driver doesn't get out of the car to open the boot either. Really, thinks Anne, what is it with men these days?

All of a sudden she remembers her father, how gentlemanly he was, how he treated her mother like a lady, always walking on the outside of the pavement even if he spent half his time falling off the kerb and into the road, helping her on with her coat but totally missing her arms. Most of the time his efforts backfired and Jean just got infuriated.

There's no getting it right really, they're either slobs or subservient idiots, she concludes before reminding the driver that she needs to get to Euston.

'I know,' he smart-alecs back. 'It's in the system.' Anne notices he is using a sat nav. There was a time when a cab driver would be expected to know the way from Dulwich Village to Euston off by heart. Anne believes in knowing things off by heart: it's all very well to Google information, but you can't do that in an exam. A good memory is very important.

Gosh, that reminds her, she needs to phone the office. Simultaneously, the driver passes the lower school where Anne works part time, a seventies red-brick appendage to the much more gracious upper school.

She digs in her bag for her mobile, the school secretary's number is stored to the phone's memory – good job too. Anne presses the requisite buttons and gets the answer machine. Of course, they'll be filing into assembly, all those high-pitched little voices. 'Girls, keep it down, no talking in the corridors.'

You can't let them talk all the time, thinks Anne, they sound like parakeets in a horribly cheap cartoon.

Anne moderates her voice into one of calm composure. 'Anne Armitage here. I'm terribly sorry, but I won't be in today: it's my mother.' She allows her voice to crack on the word 'mother'. 'She's had a terrible accident and I'm going to see her in hospital.'

For some reason Anne doesn't want to mention Blackpool. There is something about the word 'Blackpool' that reduces everything to a seaside postcard; instantly Anne conjures up an image of people sitting up in their hospital beds, the women with their big pink breasts on display and the men with lumps sticking up under bed sheets, lumps that may be broken legs but might well be erections.

She ends the call and shuts her eyes. She feels dreadful: how much is hangover and how much is shock?

Oh come on, she reminds herself, you knew this day would come sooner or later.

The car crawls down the Walworth Road towards Elephant and Castle. Paul despises this area, with its acrylic nail salons and betting shops. He's a terrible snob, admits Anne, hence the infrequent visits to see her mother. Anne's roots have become very deeply buried, her Lancashire accent barely detectable. The past is another country . . . now who said that? As the minicab negotiates some roadworks Anne retrieves her BlackBerry and types 'who said the past is another country?' into the Google search engine.

Back in his pit, Nathaniel stirs. Something is going on, he's been hearing noises all morning and it's only ten. There's no reason why he should be awake at ten, it's too early to even bother having a wank. Nat turns the TV on, Jeremy Kyle is in full flow. There's no such thing as a normal family, thinks Nat, doesn't matter where you live or how much money you've got, everyone's fucked, and once again he recalls the sight of his mother's wobbling derrière.

As if to reassure himself that not all arses are dimpled and grey, Nat checks out the array of firm-fleshed totty that adorns his bedroom walls, orange-skinned nineteen-year-old girls poking out their tongues and sticking their nipples into his face, but his penis remains resolutely limp. Oh Christ, what if he needs to buy Viagra to get it up? His mother will have to give him an allowance for it; after all, it's her fault.

Furious now, Nat pulls on a T-shirt that carries the slogan 'Angelina Adopt Me?' and heads downstairs. 'Mum?' he yells. 'Dad, Jools?' There is no reply. Good, Nat likes having the house to himself. He can fry himself a full English and wash it down with a bottle of lager; he can then open the patio doors and roll a nice fat joint before going back to bed. Into the kitchen strides Nat, with his big bare hairy feet.

'Fuck, shit, cunt, wank.'

Nat has cut his left foot and as he hops away from the broken china he cuts his right foot. Both Nat's feet are bleeding; he actually doesn't know what to do. He calls out to his mother, she should be here, she should be here to pick these jagged shards out of his feet, stupid bitch. What the fuck is going on?

Nat sits on the floor and tends to his feet. He has to be quite brave: one of the broken pieces has buried itself deeply into his left sole and pulling it out hurts. Blood oozes dramatically, so Nat reaches into the tea-towel drawer and wraps a tea towel round each foot; one features the faded hand-drawn face of his brother. He must have done it when he was about six, it's titled Rosedean Primary, Yellow Class 2001. It's crap, why can't his mother ever throw anything away? It's quite satisfying watching Julian's face turn red with his older brother's blood. His mother

71

would have something to say about that, she'd say it was symbolic or some such bollocks.

Nat feels a little shocked: unlike his father, the sight of blood makes him feel faint. Good job he's not going to be a doctor then! The brandy is still on the kitchen table: medicinal, reasons Nat, hobbling over and spying the note – both notes, the twenty-pound note and the handwritten one from his mother about his northern grandma being in a coma. Big deal, she might as well have been in a coma for the past ten years considering the crap Christmas presents she sends. Twenty quid for dinner? Bollocks, his dad can order a takeaway and put it on his card. Nat tucks the note into the waistband of his Calvin Klein underpants. Honestly, his mother can be thick sometimes. If she wants him to get a job so badly then she shouldn't leave so much money lying around. Silly cow.

Jean

Name That Baby

Primrose, Marina, Leonora: these were just some of the names that Jean had discussed with Jim.

'They're a bit fancy aren't they, love?'

And when you looked at the baby he was right, there was nothing frivolous about her, nothing to suggest she might grow up to be in the least bit flighty or exotic.

'How about Anne, Anne Margaret, after your mother?'

'Yes,' agreed Jean, though even to this day she doesn't know why.

I never liked either of those names, she recalls, but once the ink's dry on the birth certificate you can't keeping chopping and changing.

She can still see the registrar's loopy handwriting: mother's maiden name Whittaker.

Father's occupation? Ooh, now let me think, ponders Jean, who is physically incapable of doing anything else. Her organs are being pumped pneumatically, only her memory floats free from the coloured wires that tether her to various bits of whirring machinery.

A postman, that's what Jim was, and lucky to be one too

considering his medical history: flat feet, weak chest and prone to sudden fits – no wonder he couldn't join the army. However, on the plus side, he was conscientious and punctual and he never minded going out whatever the weather. He took the job ever so seriously.

'You never know what folk are waiting for, love,' he told his wife. She thought he was being a bit soft. Letters were letters. The brown ones were bills and anything else was probably a birthday card.

'Do you read the postcards?' she enquired quite casually one day. She should have known better: he was furious that she should doubt his 'professional integrity', as he called it.

'I would,' acknowledged Jean. 'I've always had a streak of nosy in me.' What was it her teacher had written on her school report? 'Jean needs to concentrate on her own work and not other people's. However, her needlework this term has been exemplary.'

Somewhere back in the house where a pork chop is turning rotten there is a christening gown. I made that, smirks Jean, without moving a single muscle in her face.

She can see the white satin gown as clear as daylight, but she can't for the life of her remember where it is.

Just a simple Butterick pattern she put together using her mother's old Singer sewing machine – not a patch on the electric one she got later but it did the trick – and then she added lace by hand and embroidered daisies all over the bodice.

That was the beginning of it all, thinks Jean, but then she corrects herself. No it wasn't! The sewing business started later, she mustn't rush herself. This mind-tidy needs to be done properly, no point shoving bits of memory just anywhere. If a job's worth doing, it's worth doing well.

Now, where was I?

That's it, the christening. It was a small do, what with so many dead relatives there weren't very many people to invite. We didn't have so many friends in those days, muses Jean. Nowadays everyone has so many friends.

Her father came with his fancy woman, wearing a fox tippet that matched the colour of her hair. Jim's dad and brothers were invited but only the one brother turned up, the others were all at a football match. Vince was the one that showed his face – funny little man, got done for flashing schoolgirls in Stanley Park about ten years later. She was glad they'd lost touch.

Who else? Jim had his friend Malcolm Braithwaite, who brought his wife Shirley. Big girl was Shirley, but very nice, only she had twins and so she knew it all.

Of course Barbara was there. Barbara was Jean's best friend from school; she'd not been able to come to the wedding because she'd contracted scarlet fever the week before, but she was there at the christening.

I always wished Barbara had lived next door to me, instead of three bus rides away, reminisces Jean, but then again you can't blame her, she did marry ever so well and Southport was very smart back then. She arrived with Harry in a very flash car, a Vauxhall something, all ivory paintwork and red leather interior.

'Do you not drive, Jim?'

'No Harry, I don't.'

Barbara had been very complimentary about the christening gown. In fact, she'd had more to say about the gown than the baby, who really wasn't looking her best that day. 'Is that a lazy eye?' asked her Uncle Vince.

'Really Jean, you could be a professional dressmaker,' Barbara had gushed, and she should know, she wore labels now. Harry was very generous.

Shame the cake had been a bit dry, but never mind, Fat Shirley had enjoyed it.

She tried the idea out for size on Jim a couple of nights later: 'Barbara said I could be a dressmaker.'

He didn't say she couldn't, but to be honest Jim didn't want her to work at all. He wanted a wife at home, like Malcolm.

'But Fat Shirley's got twins,' Jean argued. 'No one but a mother wants to look after twins, but you can get a minder for one kiddie.'

75

I just needed to get out of the house, she admits to herself almost fifty years on. She can still recall the boredom of being stuck at home with a small baby.

Anyway, I wanted to buy nice things, I wanted an astrakhan coat like Barbara's and a handbag that matched my shoes. I didn't want to have to rely on Jim for every last penny.

So she got a part-time job in a grocer's just a ten-minute walk away, three afternoons a week and as much bruised fruit as she could carry home.

With Jim doing the early morning postal round it worked out well. He'd come home and she'd pass him the baby faster than an athlete passing the baton in an Olympic relay race and then she'd be out of that door before you could say 'rabbit'.

E. R. Pemberton's, the lettering was curly and gold on a shiny dark blue background, 'Purveyors of the Finest Fruit and Vegetables'. Ernest Pemberton took a shine to Jean, she was small and neat, and smilier in the shop than she was back at home with the baby.

'You're an asset to me, Jean Collins. Tell you what: come and work for me a couple of mornings and I'll make it worth your while.'

Jim wasn't keen. 'What about Anne?'

'Who?'

'What if I'm carrying her and I have a you-know-what . . .'

He meant a fit but he'd never say it out loud, as if voicing the possibility would inevitably bring on a turn.

Privately Jean thought the baby was pretty solid and that, unless she took a direct hit to the head, she'd be fine. She was well padded for falls.

But she could see his point, it was an accident waiting to happen. Fortunately she had a solution and she smiled at Jim like she smiled at her customers.

'I've got it all worked out. My friend Brenda at the shop has a sister-in-law, Marie Boothroyd, never had kiddies but she's mad for them. Lives on the next street on from the shop and she'd be happy to have her. You don't need to worry, she was at my school, Jim, only she's a bit older than me, her husband's a plumber. The baby will be as right as rain. Marie's got a parrot and an Alsatian, so she'll have plenty of company. Bren says she used to look after hers but now they're at school, well, she's twiddling her thumbs.'

'Anne,' he said. 'The baby is called Anne.'

Anne

Emergency Services

Anne alights at Euston station; the fare comes to twenty-three pounds and seventy pence. Anne scrabbles in her purse to find the requisite loose change; she doesn't tip the driver, but she does tell him why not. She says, 'Here's a little tip for you: a gratuity is more likely to be forthcoming if you actually get out of the car and ring your passenger's doorbell rather sitting on your backside and blasting the horn. You might also think about helping said passenger with her luggage. Good day to you.'

The taxi driver tells Anne to fuck off.

I need breakfast, she reminds herself. She knows from experience that she can turn very nasty on an empty stomach: she'd come very close to taking a swing at nine-year-old Lulu Wong last year, for the precise reason that she'd left the house without so much as a bowl of cereal or a slice of toast. Unfortunately there isn't a single governor on a board of school directors who will sympathise with a teacher hitting a child simply because she was hungry.

Anne withdraws a hundred pounds from a cash machine then pays for her train ticket, shoving her credit card into the maw of yet another machine. 'Machines, machines,' she tuts to herself, 'there's no such thing as service any more,' and then she marches off to pick up some breakfast before she either faints or punches someone.

Anne goes to Marks and buys a cheese, ham and pickle sandwich, a strawberry smoothie, a packet of chocolate muffins, some dried apricots and a bag of cashew nuts. There might be a lot of waiting around at the hospital and just to be on the safe side she pops a microwave chilli con carne into the basket. She'll need something for her supper and she can't be sure her mother will have much in.

The girl on the till scans Anne's items and then asks if she'd like a bag.

'No,' Anne retorts, 'I will carry this lot on my head.' The sarcasm is lost on the girl, who looks blankly at Anne until she has to explain that she'd been joking and yes, she would like to pay five pence for a carrier.

It's a shame she hasn't got time to pick up some paracetamol and a nice latte, but the train leaves in six minutes. Anne trots to platform 13. Her bosoms hurt and her ankles feel like they could crack at any moment. My mother is in a coma, she reminds herself. I could be on the verge of becoming an orphan.

As she settles herself into her Virgin pendolino seat, another thought strikes Anne. What if her mother doesn't die? What if she lives but is permanently disabled? What if she can no longer walk or look after herself? What on earth would she do?

She'd have to go into a home. She couldn't come and live with them in London, it would be very distracting for Jools, who needs to be able to concentrate on his A levels. She can't get Julian through his A levels and look after an invalid. A home is the only solution, she will just have to sell her mother's house and use the equity to pay for it. Shame really, she'd quite like to flog the house and put the money into her own bank account, but that's the way the cookie crumbles. We all have to make sacrifices, concludes Anne, though she can't help wondering how much her mother's house is worth (even in the current market) and how much a good residential care home might cost. How long before one cancels the other out?

The train is relatively quiet, apart from a young man sitting diagonally opposite Anne whose earphones are leaking terrible rap music. Anne tries glaring at him, but he is oblivious. At least her sons don't have silly pierced eyebrows.

God, her head is killing her. Anne roots in the Marks bag for her sandwich; hopefully she will feel better once she's eaten. Yes, breakfast first, then she can get on with reading this month's book club choice. Linda Mayer has chosen David Mitchell's *The Thousand Autumns of Jacob de Zoet*, which is just showing off really.

It's not an easy book to read with a hangover. In fact, the thought of opening it makes Anne feel queasy. The words are very small and crowded on the page. It's no good: she makes her way to the buffet car, where she buys a dreadful cup of coffee and this week's *Hello!* magazine.

It's easier to concentrate on some girl from *Coronation Street* than on a historic battle between the Dutch and the British, but even so Anne's mind wanders.

What do you do when you visit someone in a coma?

What do you talk about?

Should she play her some music?

A dollop of pickle falls out of the sandwich and on to Anne's shirt.

Oh well, it's not going to upset her mother. You could turn up to visit a coma patient in your vest and pants and they'd be none the wiser. Anne thinks about the footballers and pop stars who visit poorly kids in hospital and coax them out of vegetative states. Who would bring her mother round?

She used to like Val Doonican and Engelbert Humperdinck; Tom Jones, of course, her mother would come round for Tom Jones. Inexplicably, her mother also likes *Emmerdale*, and it would be a damn sight easier to get one of the cast of *Emmerdale* to pop by than Tom Jones. After all, it can't be too far from Yorkshire, where the series is filmed, to her mother's bedside in Blackpool Victoria Hospital.

Anne is worried about talking to her mother. She knows instinctively that she will be encouraged to talk to her about familiar things, anecdotes from the past.

I have spent most of my adult life escaping from my past, Anne admits to herself. From the moment I knew I could go away to university I've never really been back.

Anyway, there are certain subjects that need avoiding: names not to be mentioned, secrets that have stayed secret for so long that the original secret is too deeply buried to bother digging up. The scars are there, they always will be, but they have faded. Sometimes it's almost possible to forget about them, but not quite. Every day something will happen to make her remember. It must be even worse for her mother.

While Anne attempts to distract herself from the past by eating chocolate muffins, Paul snatches a moment between operations to call his mother. The cleaning woman answers. 'Channing House, Wanda speaking,' she singsongs down the line. His mother trains her cleaners to answer the phone *properly*. They are also trained to wear indoor shoes and a housecoat. Anne lets their cleaner wear whatever she likes and Loretta's English is certainly not good enough to ferry important messages.

Paul feels a rise of impatience in his chest. Anne likes to think she is efficient, but she can be very sloppy at times.

'It's all in the detail,' his mother would say, and she is certainly very particular. Ellen would never forget to heat the plates before serving a meal, and while it took years for her to come round to ready-sliced bread, she still insists on using loose tea leaves and a little silver strainer. Anne, on the other hand, throws bags into tannin-stained mugs and has never really got to grips with the concept of a tray cloth.

His mother comes to the phone. Throughout most of his childhood Paul played second fiddle to his younger brother, but since Nigel moved to South Africa with his surgically enhanced wife, Paul has taken pole position.

'Hello darling, anything wrong? I'm playing bridge with Minty Greenhalgh and some of the girls this afternoon so I'm thinking early lunch.'

In other words, his mother was about to sit down, at the dining table, with a bowl of homemade soup, two Jacob's crackers and 'just a smidge' of cheese and/or pâté. On the side of her plate she will have a little pile of salt into which she will dip a stick of celery. Occasionally she will also have a tomato.

Ellen is very disciplined about food: she hasn't eaten a pudding apart from at dinner parties, when it would be rude not to, since 1989.

Paul is suddenly embarrassed to ask his mother what Anne expects him to ask: that an eighty-two-year-old woman should drop everything, bridge rubbers and silver tea strainers, to come and look after a couple of hulking teenage boys for a few days, possibly longer.

He braces himself. It wouldn't be so bad if the golfing trip wasn't being extended by a three-day ENT conference in Faro; now that's something he really can't wriggle out of.

He could always cancel the golf.

But he doesn't want to.

'Ma, thing is, got a real spanner-in-the-works situation. Anne's mother—'

'The woman who lives in Blackpool?'

'Yes, Jean.'

'That's it, Jean.'

'She's been run over.'

'Not a tram?' (Ellen has seen *Coronation Street*.)

'No, a motorbike, we think. Anyway, she's in a coma.'

'How extraordinary. What a peculiar thing to do.'

'I don't think she did it on purpose.'

'Well was she not looking where she was going, or did the motorcyclist mount the pavement?'

Ellen likes to apportion blame. It's so much easier when it's someone's fault.

Paul checks his watch. He has precisely seven minutes before he needs to scrub up and get his hands on a putrid tonsil.

'Anyway Ma, Anne's had to make a mercy dash.'

'To Blackpool?'

'Yes and the thing is, I'm off to Portugal tomorrow to play golf.'

'On the Algarve?'

'Yes.'

'Bits of it are very common, you know, darling. The Jacksons came home early last year, lots of ghastly families in nylon football shirts, apparently.'

'It's a very smart hotel . . . anyway . . . the thing is, we don't like leaving the boys.'

There is a silence as the penny drops.

'And you'd like me to come up and be *in loco parentis*, as it were?'

'Yes.'

'Well I can, but I'm not going to come right this minute. I shall come up tomorrow lunchtime. Tell the boys I will arrive around three. You can look after yourselves for one night, surely. You can have a pizza.'

His mother pronounces it 'pitsa', she always has.

Jean

Fruits of Labour

Lunch is being served on the Hamilton Ward. A whiff of shepherd's pie and tuna bake (for the vegetarians) cuts through the smell of piss and shit, adding a topnote of gravy and tinned fish to the heady scent of disinfectant.

Jean won't be eating, she's nil by mouth. She's not fussed, what's the odd meal missed as long as she doesn't lose too much weight?

I've always been slight, Jean reminds herself, all that bending, filling shelves at Pemberton's, and then there was the dancing every Wednesday night at the social club. Jim wasn't keen but she was: I was a mover, everyone said so, and she recalls the strappy silver ballroom-dancing shoes that she kept in a green felt drawstring bag.

Jim would change his shoes too – his dancing pumps were black leather, shiny as earwigs – but most of the time he wouldn't be dancing, he'd be sat on a red leatherette banquette, smoking and sipping a pint.

Everyone smoked back then; course, it's gone out of fashion now but the ballroom dancing has come back in. Funny how things go in circles. She loves *Strictly Come Dancing*, even though watching it makes her heart twist, stabbing pains that

84

burn in her chest, like a stiletto heel putting out a fag.

It's nice when they do the shows from the ballroom in the tower. If she does die and go to heaven, she'd like heaven to have an organ and a nice dance floor. In fact, if heaven was just like the Tower Ballroom she'd be quite happy.

She wouldn't even mind dancing with another girl; be nice to see Barbara again. She died of breast cancer when she was only fifty-two. A crying shame, that's what it was. She had plenty more life in her, only as it turned out she hadn't, poor Barbara.

'I should have gone to the doctor sooner,' she'd written, her familiar spiky blue handwriting on a piece of Basildon Bond.

I've still got that letter somewhere, thinks Jean. It's in the tin with the chrysanthemums on.

But that's not until later. She needs to go back to E. R. Pemberton's, she's not up to Barbara dying, that's not for ages. Right now they're still in their twenties and it'll be years until she even buys the chrysanthemum tin.

I was a young working mum, recalls Jean, not without pride.

The Marie Boothroyd solution was working out quite well, though Jean always got the impression that her daughter's child-minder didn't really approve of her.

She was a bit jealous, was Marie. She'd always wanted kiddies of her own and maybe she didn't like the way Jean found her own child so easy to leave.

But I was a better mother for it, reasons Jean. She liked working in the shop, she liked the friendship of the other girls, the harmless flirting with the delivery men, the customers and their gossip. She dreaded Wednesdays with its half-day closing, the long afternoons stretched out in front of her, just her and the baby, with Jim snoring on the bed upstairs.

Mind you, Anne was an easy baby and she grew into an easy toddler. The only demands she made were on her clothes: she grew out of everything. It was good job Jean was a fast knitter. No sooner had she knitted one little cardigan than it was time to knit another, only this time a bit bigger.

She took the cast-offs into work. 'Are you sure you'll not be keeping them for the next one?' they all chorused, snatching at the little matinee jackets and tartan pinafore dresses. 'Ooh Jean, you are clever.'

'The next one? Oh no,' she told them. 'I'm not thinking of having any more.'

I was very naïve back then, she admits. Not wanting another baby isn't a particularly reliable form of contraception, though, oddly enough, for a number of years it seemed to work, not that they had sex very often.

Jim was very patient about that. The other girls would talk about their husbands' demands in the shop. One of them, a woman in her fifties with a bosom that went from her throat to her waist, said her old man wanted it every night and if she wasn't happy to roll over and spread her legs he'd give her what for and then have his way whether she liked it or not.

Jim was never like that. If he put his hand on her breast and she moved away, then that would be that. Sometimes she'd wonder what it was like to have a man whose urges were more animal, who wouldn't be shrugged off, who would tear at her nightie and bite at her breasts.

It wasn't just the men who were sex mad: some of the women couldn't get enough. What was her name? The one that left a lipstick stain wherever she went, on the towel in the girls' toilets, smeared across the china cups in the little kitchen out the back. Sandra! She wasn't even married and she did it in the back of cars with strangers.

Mr Pemberton got rid of her in the end. She came in one day with a fat lip and a black eye; he said her sort lowered the tone.

It was a relief when she'd gone; there was something too wild about her, a scent of something dangerous. Common, some of the other women said, but somehow the word 'common' didn't do Sandra justice. She was something more than common. Sandra was the first female that Jean had ever heard use the word 'tits'.

Maybe if Barbara hadn't been so coy about her tits she might have gone to the doctor's earlier. But the fact was, even years after Sandra was sacked from E. R. Pemberton's, women were still hiding their bits away, turning their backs to each other in the swimming pool and worrying should the curtain not quite meet in the department-store changing room.

Times change, concludes Jean, remembering how E. R. Pemberton's had kept up with every new-fangled invention, 'whilst still taking pride in old-fashioned customer service.'

She remembers when they still had delivery boys with wicker baskets on their handlebars and she also remembers the first time they served salami on the deli counter. A lot of people thought it was foreign muck. Jim never liked it, he thought it was 'a bit much', but then that was Jim. He was the type to check inside a sandwich before he took a bite. It drove her mad, he didn't like surprises and putting piccalilli in with his ham rather than a smear of Colman's mustard unnerved him.

Jim didn't like change, he was happy with things the way they were, just him, Jean and three-year-old Anne, the apple of his eye. His little girl could do no wrong and if he'd earned more money he'd have spoilt her rotten. Because he didn't have money, he spent time with her instead.

He was endlessly patient, happy to tell the little girl story after story. It suited Jean down to the ground. She'd give Anne her bath and pop her into bed in one of her flower-sprigged nighties, then Jim would take over: Topsy and Tim, Beatrix Potter and all the Grimm Brothers' fairy tales. He never did funny voices, never tried to be a wicked witch or a funny elf, he just droned on and on. No wonder the child fell asleep.

Sleep, that's what she could do with now. It's been a busy day putting all these memories in order and there's still a lot to sort out, some of the past needs careful attention, like a tangle of fine gold chains in a jewellery box. It'll take time, she'll need to concentrate, but not now. Not now that she's sinking into a thick black darkness as deep as the sea.

Anne

'Hello Mum'

Anne tiptoes up to her mother's bedside. She doesn't know why, it's not as if she's going to wake her up. There's a big difference between being in a coma and having an afternoon nap.

'Mum, it's me. It's Anne.'

At least they have put Jean in a room by herself. A tiny sliver of a room, but she has privacy, not that she needs it. For the first time in her life Jean Collins could accidentally bare her bum for all the world to see and she wouldn't even blush.

She'd taken a taxi from Blackpool North train station. The cab driver had been slightly over-familiar in that northern-male way that she finds annoying and simultaneously reassuring:

'Ooh Blackpool Vic, is it a relative?'

'Yes, my mother.'

'And you don't live up here, more as likely you've come from London, changed at Preston?'

'Yes.'

'Is she poorly then?'

'Of course she's poorly, it's a hospital not a hotel.' Only she didn't say that.

'Yes, she's in a coma. She was run over.'
'Oh, I'm very sorry to hear that.'

The hospital had changed, she realised this as soon as she arrived. The entrance wasn't where it used to be and modern low-rise extensions had been tacked on to every corner. Once upon a time it was a fine Victorian red-brick building, now it had all the flimsiness of a child's Playmobil set-up.

She was nervous, she didn't know why, and by the time she reached her mother's bedside there were sweat patches under her arms and her hair was damp against her brow.

Her mother actually looked better than she did, that was her first impression. Only as she moved closer did she realise that while the right-hand side of Jean's face was completely normal, the left was a mass of bruising, brown and yellow, as dark as tortoiseshell. It was a shock, but the nurse who had accompanied her into the room simply stated, 'Yes she's a bit of a mess, your old mum. She must have landed on that side of her head with a right old smack. Probably best you sit this side of her, no need to upset yourself.'

Anne drops into the chair. Her mother makes such a small shape under the regulation sheet and blanket that if it weren't for the grey hair you could easily mistake her for an eleven-year-old girl.

'Apparently I take after my paternal grandfather,' Anne mutters to herself, confused as to how she ever, even as a baby, managed to emerge from the tiny bundle on the bed.

'Yes, well, I'll leave you to it,' answers the nurse, backing out of the door. She looks about seventeen. 'If you want to know anything, it's probably best you ask someone who knows,' she adds, smiling vaguely, as if what she has just said makes total sense – which it does, logically.

Anne suddenly wishes Paul could be with her. How is she meant to handle this? Where are the grown-ups? Surely, she thinks, there must be a man in a white coat, preferably with horn-rimmed glasses, a knowledgeable air and a stethoscope around his neck, who will explain everything to her.

But no, Anne and Jean are alone together and Anne is stuck for words. After introducing herself she doesn't really know what to say. 'How are you?' would be silly and 'I've brought you some dried apricots' ridiculous.

Her mother's little hands, piped with purple veins, have various cannulas attached. Anne is slightly squeamish and despite Paul's job her hospital visits have been minimal. She delivered her sons at King's College (NHS, but a recovery room all to herself both times – Paul insisted) but before that she had never so much as broken a bone. As a child she had been neither sickly nor particularly accident-prone, no fits, no choking emergencies, no strange allergic reactions.

In some respects, thinks Anne, apart from a nasty bout of eczema I was very little trouble. Just the usual childhood illnesses, measles and chicken pox, neither of which necessitated more than a week or so in bed.

Her own children have been slightly less fortunate. Between them they have broken a collarbone, a wrist and an ankle, but then again as a girl she never went skiing. Most of Jools and Nat's fractures occurred on the slopes of the French Alps.

'Of course I came to see Daddy here,' she says, speaking aloud, trying out her voice for size. What sort of decibel level is suitable? Her mother is slightly deaf, maybe if she's to have a chance of getting through to her she should position her mouth close to the old lady's ear and yell.

Anne opts for the sort of tone Jenni Murray uses on *Woman's Hour*, quiet but authoritative.

'Remember, he had that heart attack?' But perhaps her mother doesn't want to remember her dead husband. Maybe it's best to keep things light, no need to go digging up old bones. Not now, not when she's just arrived.

Anne begins again, this time she attempts the cheery voice she uses when her Year 5s need geeing up. 'Well what a silly old

90

sausage you are Mum, fancy getting run over by a motorcycle! Well never mind, you're in the best possible place, they've got you tucked up all cosy, snug as a bug in a rug. I tell you, I wouldn't mind a little lie down after the journey I've had.'

Anne is indeed exhausted, the hangover has subsided into a grimy lethargy and just for a second she wonders if she could gently roll her mother to the edge of the bed and lie down next to her.

As soon as she has formed this thought she dismisses it. It has been a long time since she has shared a bed with her mother and within a single blink she has a brief vision of a green satin eiderdown and a pink candlewick bedspread.

Of course her own boys used to come under the duvet with her and Paul, every Saturday and Sunday morning, the four of them like sardines. Obviously as they got older she had to be careful that her nightie covered all her bits.

'The boys were very upset when I told them. Nat and Jools, they send their love, and of course Paul does too,' she continues.

It isn't strictly true. Paul might have mumbled something about it being a shame but her sons really couldn't care less. In some respects she should have forced Nat to accompany her. There was no reason why not: it's not as if he has anything else to do. So why hadn't she?

'Nat wanted to come,' she hears herself saying, 'but he's got a job, Mum. He's on his gap year, he'll be applying for universities soon, but before that he wants to go travelling so he's working in the local garden centre and apparently he's a bit of a hit.'

Where on earth had that come from?

Oh well, no harm done. It was quite comforting, in fact. Odd how a few fictional sentences made Anne feel better about her eldest child, as if by saying these things they could quite easily come true.

'Of course he's always loved nature,' she adds, and suddenly she sees her oldest son, smiling in jeans and a T-shirt, cheerfully

91

mowing a lawn. 'He's been doing some work with a landscape gardener as well, seems to have a real feel for it. As for Jools, well, it's nose to the grindstone for him. He's doing very well and there's talk of him trying for Oxbridge.'

Well that was a whopper! No one has mentioned either Oxford or Cambridge. In fact, if her younger son continues to coast like he is at the moment then he'll be lucky to get into somewhere like Loughborough.

Her mother doesn't flicker, nothing registers. It doesn't matter what she tells her, she can tell her anything. All of a sudden Anne is quite convinced that even if her mother can hear she's not listening. It's as if she's a million miles away.

Anne reaches into her bag. There's just one chocolate muffin left and it's not as if her mother's going to eat it.

Jean

Whoops

Chocolate, she can smell chocolate. Well, she can take it or leave it: liquorice was always her thing, Bassett's Allsorts. She liked the ones with the little blue seeds all over. Jim was a toffee eater, toffees and mints; he was quite happy to sit in front of the television and chew his way through a whole bag of caramels. He liked those lime and chocolate stripy sweets too, the ones that splintered and then stuck your teeth together. Back then you'd choose your sweets from big glass jars in the newsagent's: a quarter of dolly mixture and a quarter of pear drops please. It was nice to have a little treat while they watched the telly after tea. Back then they ate early.

I wasn't a very adventurous cook, thinks Jean, but then Jim didn't like to experiment. He liked a hotpot and a roast, and they had fish from the chippy every Friday, most people did. Apart from that he was happy with egg and chips.

He didn't like seafood but she did. Prawn cocktail, that's what she would have when she went out for dinner. Not that they ever did – a couple of times a year, perhaps, birthdays and anniversaries. Jim would have the soup, Brown Windsor – what was all that about?

In December Mr Pemberton took all his girls out, treated them to a slap-up dinner in one of the big hotels along the seafront and they all had a drink before dinner and wine with the meal. Dubonnet and lemonade, that was her tipple. She was never much of a drinker back then, what she liked best was sucking the sweet chemical-tasting maraschino cherry that accompanied the drink.

Jim like a half of bitter or a pint of Guinness but he never woke up with a head, she never saw him out of sorts. Not like Mr Pemberton: every December at the works do his face would go all pink and shiny like a glazed ham and his eyes would bulge, he'd want to dance with them all. 'Dirty old sod,' said Ida who worked on the cold meats counter, but Jean didn't mind. It was quite exciting, the press of him against her, it gave her an ache deep in her belly, made her want to go to the toilet, made her breasts tingle. Why did Jim not make her feel like that?

She'd still been tipsy by the time she got home. Eileen Bradshaw's husband came and picked them up. Mr Pemberton waited with them in the car park, they were the last to leave. As Mr Pemberton helped her into the back seat of the car his fingers brushed her breast. It could have been an accident, but as he waved them off he was licking his lips like a wolf, and all the way home, all she could think was, He touched my tit.

If she could blush, Jean would blush at this point, but it's no good getting silly about it; it's what happened. She was a little bit drunk and the space between her thighs felt slippery and wet. She felt like a stranger, like a foreign woman in a film, and for some reason when she got into bed next to Jim she kept her bra and suspenders on. She wanted him to take them off her, she wanted him to roll her nipples between his fingers, she wanted a hot mouth on hers, she wanted him to be Mr Pemberton with his big hands and what had felt like an enormous penis, as big as a draught excluder. She wanted that stuffed up her, she wanted what that fat woman's husband wanted every night. She wanted to be fucked.

Poor Jim, he tried his best. She was all over him, shoving his hands to the sticky entrance of her vagina, rubbing herself up and down until his cock stiffened, she even told him what she wanted. In no uncertain terms she told him to 'stick it in me'. 'Shh,' he'd said, 'Anne might hear,' but she didn't care about Anne and she liked it when he put his hand over her mouth and when he did finally stick it in her she pushed her thighs up and down and locked her ankles around his waist.

The next morning she threw up and neither she nor Jim could look each other in the eye as they sat facing each other over the breakfast table.

'I think it's something I ate,' she mumbled and she asked Jim to phone in sick for her. 'It might have been the chicken.'

Four weeks later she was sick again. This time 'it might have been the liver', it hadn't tasted right. Then nothing did, everything tasted of cutlery. She was down to sucking on water biscuits before it dawned on her.

She didn't tell Jim, there was still a chance it wouldn't take. Some babies didn't, some of them slid out before they had proper arms or legs, just little flippers. It had happened to Marie Boothroyd four times.

She was forever popping to the lavvy at work to check for a tell-tale red stain in her knickers until Mr Pemberton told her off: 'If you've trouble with your waterworks you might want to go to the doctor,' and he didn't even give her a wink.

In the end it was Marie Boothroyd who guessed. 'You're looking ever so peaky, Jean, are you sure you're not in the family way?

And before Jean could deny it, she was throwing up into the Boothroyds' primrose-coloured lavatory. She'd not even had time to close the bathroom door so between retches she could hear Marie say to Anne, 'Well now young lady, how do you feel about that? Looks like you're going to have a little baby brother or sister.'

Anne was nearly four and she had what Jean called big ears: she was a listener and, like a baby elephant, she didn't forget.

She'd tried to deny it – 'Well that's a load of rubbish, Marie' – and she'd yattered on about how she might be anaemic and that the doctor was thinking of giving her some pills, but all she really needed was a tonic.

'Anaemic, eh?' said Marie. 'Good job you're not having your monthlies then.'

Marie had worked in a chemist's shop once, she knew about menstruation and iron.

'Don't talk daft, Marie,' Jean had snapped, but both of them knew the game was up.

Still, it was a few days until she had to tell Jim. Anne hadn't said anything and Jean thought maybe it hadn't really sunk in, but on the Saturday morning the girl was doing drawing at the kitchen table. 'What's that?' asked Jim, even though to Jean it was as clear as day. It was a picture of Marie, Anne, the parrot, the dog and a little baby.

'When Mummy has the baby then I can bring the baby with me to Marie's house and it mustn't be frightened because the parrot's only joking, he's not really going to peck your face, and anyway, the doggie doesn't bite.'

Jim just put all the crayons neatly back in their box, then he told Anne to go and wash her hands upstairs in the sink like a good girl and off she went.

'Well then?' he asked, and she felt her face burn.

'I'm not sure, Jim, it's early days.'

He wasn't even cross with her, he was as pleased as punch again. 'You've made me the happiest man in the world.' But when he came over to embrace her she shot him such a murderous look he ended up patting her arm like a team coach: 'Well done, old thing.'

Anne

Breaking and Entering

Anne sits in yet another minicab; her old address rolls easily off her tongue. It's raining, the windows are steamed up and the car smells like a chemical toilet set deep within a pine forest.

There'd been a slight altercation as she left the ward. All she'd wanted was her mother's handbag but they wouldn't give it to her.

'We haven't the authority,' the teenage nurse kept repeating. 'Someone in authority would have to give us the authority.'

'I just want the house keys,' Anne had snapped. 'How the fuck am I meant to get in the house?'

Well that hadn't helped. The nurse looked affronted – Anne might just as well have slapped her in the face – and then, as if delivering a poem, the girl parroted, 'With all due respect, may I remind you that hospital staff do not at any time have to put up with violent or threatening behaviour from the general public.' She flushed with triumph when she finished the speech.

'But with all due respect, I'm not the general public,' Anne had argued. 'I'm your coma patient's daughter and I need to get into my mother's house or I shall be spending the night curled up on the front step.'

But there was no persuading her. Anne even described the

keyring, which she'd bought for her mother just the previous Christmas: 'Liberty, floral and tasteful.'

To give the girl some credit, she peered into the bag, poked around its contents and curled her hand possessively around the keyring that she found. 'Sorry, that's not what it looks like.'

Anne felt like snatching the bag out of the girl's hands but she had a horrible feeling the police might get involved.

So now here she is in this stinking cab, about to arrive at her mother's without a key.

Once upon a time, when Anne was at school and her mother was out working, Jean kept a spare house key under a flowerpot in the back garden, but that was back in the seventies when people were stupid about such things. Privately Anne hopes her mother is still just as daft and that there will be a spare key somewhere blindingly obvious. If not, she'll just have to break in.

She pays the driver and gives him a tip, but only because he leapt out of the car and got her case out of the boot. 'Would you like me to take it in for you?' he asks but she declines, she doesn't want him to know that she is keyless. What kind of daughter can't get into her own mother's house?

She makes a big show of searching in her bag for keys she can't possibly find, and as soon as the car has driven off she wheels her case round the corner, where there is access to the back garden via a ginnel. Anne knows instinctively that her sons would pick her up on the word 'ginnel'. 'Why don't you just call it a back alley?'

She lets herself through the back gate. The pale blue painted wood is soggy and rotten at the bottom; it could do with replacing. Anne's eyes scan the garden, looking for places where an ageing mother would hide keys. She upturns old flowerpots and checks in the raffia panniers of a straw donkey. There's nothing under the ceramic tortoise crouched under the laburnum and they are not hidden inside the plastic watering can.

Well I'm not standing here all day like cheese at fourpence, she thinks, shocked to find yet another northern colloquialism popping up so soon after ginnel. She peers through the kitchen window. On the work surface below she can see a big bluebottle walking idly around a pork chop.

She'll have to smash the window. Anne looks around the garden for a suitable implement with which to smash the glass. The clothes prop might do it, but what she really needs is a hammer.

Suddenly Anne notices there is a garden shed clearly visible over next door's boundary wall. Sheds = tools = hammers.

She drags a wrought iron chair from her mother's sorry little patio area over to the wall. It's a good job she's wearing trousers, she thinks, grunting as she hoists herself up and on to the brick divide, squashing her breasts in the process.

As she teeters on the top of the wall, she notices the drop on the other side will deliver her into a children's sandpit. That's good, a nice soft landing and then into the shed for the hammer. Anne rolls and lands, her linen shirt has come undone but she doesn't notice and as quickly as a fourteen-stone woman can she crawls out of the sandpit, the sand sticking muddily to her wet trousers, and enters the shed.

It smells like all sheds should smell, of rotten apples, putty and white spirit. The window panes are thick with cobwebs. Anne's eyes adjust to the gloom and havoc; a limp paddling pool droops down from the ceiling, deckchairs are stacked precariously next to a rusty barbecue and a work bench is littered with what look like the vital organs of an old computer. Finally she spies a hammer hanging between two nails tacked into the back of the door. Sorted!

She removes the hammer and exits the shed, only to encounter a strange man walking down the garden path with a bulging nappy sack in his hand

'Put it down,' the man says. 'Put the hammer down. No one's going to hurt you, just put it down.'

He is very authoritative. Anne drops the hammer and puts her hands up in a mock 'I'm a baddie and you've caught me' stance.

Only when she raises her hands does she realise her shirt is blowing open in the breeze. She is wearing a rather garish raspberry-coloured bra and instantly her face blushes to match. She really needs to stop exposing herself like this.

'Hahahaha,' she laughs as if the two of them are attending some hilarious garden party and someone has just told an amusing anecdote.

'I'm so sorry, what must you think? Hahaha,' she chortles, doing her buttons up. 'I'm Jean's daughter, next door. I need to get into the house – I'm staying whilst she's in hospital, only I don't have a key! I've come all the way from London. I'm a teacher.' At this point she laughs as if 'I'm a teacher' is the punchline to the funniest joke in the world. What the hell is wrong with her?

The man has picked up the hammer. He is standing between her and his back door, where a small child wearing a T-shirt and nothing else is curled around the doorframe, watching her father and the strange lady with wide eyes.

Anne sniggers on, 'Gosh, look at me, I'm filthy!' This time she laughs and simultaneously snorts, which is something that she keeps doing. Even Paul has commented on it.

The man swings the hammer. 'You're Anne?'

'Guilty as charged,' she titters. He's very good-looking, mid-thirties, a sort of tawny look to him, broad shouldered, paint on his combat trousers.

He brushes past her, drops the bulging nappy sack into the bin and says, 'Come in, we've got spare keys. I'm sorry about your mother, it's a terrible thing. She's been good to us.'

Anne follows him into a small kitchen. She's been in this house before, many years ago, but it's almost unrecognisable. Not that she can see what it's really like, not under all the mess.

The house looks like someone has turned it upside down and given it a shake. All the cupboard doors are open, and Anne sidesteps a plastic cereal bowl. The little girl with the naked bottom is running on the spot, shaking her head. 'She likes making herself dizzy,' her father explains, and at that precise moment the child falls over into a tray of cat litter and starts to cry.

Another wail, slightly thinner and coming from somewhere

above Anne's head, echoes the first. The man is rummaging in a kitchen drawer. The work surfaces need wiping down, the sink is full of dirty dishes and the dishwasher gapes, revealing ketchup-smeared plates. On the kitchen table is a changing mat; there are still some balls of shit-covered cotton wool next to a bottle of tomato sauce and an open packet of biscuits.

The stereo wailing becomes more insistent; the child gets up from the cat litter with her moist bottom all gritty and begins her dance again.

Anne's headache nudges her temples.

'Here,' says the man, handing her a set of keys. Anne recognises the fob, it's the one she bought her mother from Liberty. How odd that it should end up on the spare set.

'They're for the front door,' he adds.

'Thank you,' yells Anne above the tiny banshee and she makes her way out of the house through a hallway littered with colouring books and discarded tights.

Maybe his wife has left him. At the top of the stairs a furious, red-faced smaller version of the child in the kitchen is shaking the bars of a staircase.

'Thank you, thank you, so very kind,' she throws over her shoulder. Behind her, a potty bounces down the stairs. Hopefully she won't be able to hear this racket once she's safely ensconced next door. It really is a terrible din.

Twenty minutes later Anne has deposited the rank pork chop in the bin, swatted and killed the bluebottle with a rolled-up copy of the local newspaper, reclaimed her suitcase from the back garden and put the kettle on.

It's strange being here without her mother or her father, or even . . .

She switches on the radio. It's better if Radio 2 drowns out both the silence and the ghosts.

Jean

It's Coming

Marie Boothroyd was a bit triumphant. 'I told you so,' she said when Jean came round wearing a maternity smock.

Jean sighs imperceptibly. In real life she has been unconscious for over twenty-four hours now, but back in the past it is 1966 and summer is coming. In London people were swinging off the rafters, smoking wacky baccy and being all permissive, while up in the north it was still pregnancy smocks with Peter Pan collars designed to avert the eye from the offending bulge.

Even the doctor couldn't say the p word, referring to her *condition* as if it were something nasty.

She was constipated – that much she did know – but of course she never said anything, just swigged from a bottle of prune juice when no one was looking.

She didn't get very big this time. 'It's a small baby, Mrs Collins, but don't let that worry you.'

She wasn't worried, the smaller the better. She didn't really want this baby, it was embarrassing, she felt caught out. One was quite sufficient, thank you.

What if she didn't have enough love? Her reservoirs of affection often ran low with Anne. The child made her impatient, she was physically slow and clumsy, she took for ever to eat her tea and she was already having to wear pink plastic National Health glasses.

'Yes, it is unusual for a four-year-old child to be this short sighted,' the optician declared.

Privately Jean blamed Jim. There was nothing wrong with her eyesight, she had twenty-twenty vision. It was Jim that woke every morning blinking and scrabbling on the bedside table for his tortoiseshell spectacles, unable to even visit the lavatory without shoving them on to his bony nose. Surely no one could be that blind?

Of course, now that she can't read the TV listings without first finding her reading glasses she's a bit more sympathetic, but back then she was convinced that if he tried harder he'd be able to see further.

Anne was intrigued by the prospect of the baby. She was forever putting her waxy yellow ear to her mother's belly, breathing her hot breath through the fabric of Jean's clothes. 'I can hear it,' she crowed. 'The baby wants to come out and play with me.'

'Not yet,' Jean snapped.

'Go easy on her,' Jim said. 'She's just excited.' So was he; he wanted a boy, Jean knew he did, and for that reason alone she wanted another girl.

He was so smug about it, just the sound of him sanding down the old cot and giving it a fresh coat of paint made her want to scream. She knew she was lucky: there were women at work whose husbands more or less ignored their kids. Jim never shouted or raised his hand; he was endlessly patient, always willing to read another story or give the swing just one more push in the park. Jean got bored, she had a short tether.

She never hit Anne, but sometimes she was rough with her. When they were in a hurry, she'd shove her daughter's shoes on her feet without untwisting her socks and frequently thrust shrunken pullovers with tiny neck holes over the girl's cannon-ball head without first removing her glasses.

'Ow,' complained Anne.

'I'll give you "Ow",' echoed her mother.

But even at the time she'd been embarrassed about her behaviour. I always knew when I wasn't being nice, Jean admits to herself, it was just sometimes I couldn't help it.

As her due date approached Jim seemed to grow in cheerfulness. He put her teeth right on edge with his tuneless whistling, his constant gormless grin.

Jean felt herself closing down. She couldn't be bothered with anything; even though she worked in a purveyors of fine produce she barely gave any thought to what they might have for supper. She'd completely gone off food herself and Jim wasn't the type to make a fuss if she just opened a tin of Spam. Really, compared to everyone else's husbands with their demands for sexual intercourse and steak and kidney suet puddings complete with treacle pudding or an egg custard for afters, Jim was an absolute dream. So why did she occasionally fantasise about him dropping down dead?

'I trapped myself,' she whispers to herself. 'I panicked, I should have waited. Something more exciting might have come along.'

Sometimes she wondered what it would be like to go home to a man like Mr Pemberton, a man with enormous polished leather shoes, bigger than a policeman's, whose pinstripe suit could almost be heard groaning at the seams.

Mr Pemberton had a fancy silver cigarette case and an expensive lighter. He smelt of nicotine and geranium-scented pomade.

Jim smoked too, Capstan Full Strength untipped. He often kept one behind his ear. He didn't have a lighter – he used matches – and he favoured Wright's Coal Tar Soap.

Mr Pemberton asked her if she thought she should stop working: she was at least six months gone, did she not want some time at home before the new arrival?

'Not really, what would I do with myself?' She'd already knitted more matinee jackets than a baby could puke on in a month.

Of course these days, muses Jean, you can find out the sex of the baby before it's born. Back then it was a fifty-fifty guess. So, to be on the safe side, she kept her yarns neutral and went for a lot of lemon and white.

Thinking back, she was ready for a break. Sometimes by the end of the day she'd be dead on her puffy feet, but if she wasn't working she couldn't justify the expense of Marie looking after Anne. They'd be at home together, hour after hour after hour.

Anne wanted stories, that was her problem, and such was her appetite that Jean was having to borrow new books from the library every week, which was exhausting. It wasn't that Jean couldn't read, she could read perfectly well, it was just sometimes the sentences seemed to dance backwards on themselves and the words got muddled up.

Jean preferred making stories up, but Anne didn't like that. She liked proper stories that came from proper picture books. Jean tried illustrating her own stories on scraps of paper – she was good at drawing – but it still didn't wash with Anne. She was a methodical child who liked to turn pages.

'Can I just stay on for a few more weeks?' begged Jean and Mr Pemberton relented. He always did have a soft spot for me, reckons Jean.

Anne had been ten days overdue; this one came three weeks early. She was still working in the shop – can you imagine the embarrassment?

She felt a bit queer on the till so she asked Maureen if she could cover her, just for a couple of minutes, but as she walked across the shop floor her waters burst. She was in the tinned goods aisle. She grabbed hold of a shelf and staggered; broad beans, butter beans and baked beans clattered around her sodden ankles.

'Hell's bells,' gasped Edam Andrew from the cheese counter.

'Everybody out of the way!' ordered Mr Pemberton. 'Come on, no gawping.'

He took her to the hospital himself, Mr Pemberton, in his big blue Humber Super Snipe.

'My husband doesn't drive,' she explained, wishing that she

wasn't on the way to the delivery suite, wishing like mad that Mr Pemberton was just taking her out for a nice drive in his swish car. She'd like to go the Lake District, it was a nice day. He'd have a rug in the boot, a tartan rug, and they could lay it out on the shore of Lake Windermere and she'd feed him hard-boiled eggs and a slice of pork pie.

Ooof, a contraction hit hard. 'It's all right,' said Mr Pemberton, 'we'll be there in a jiffy,' and he lit a cigarette and drove like the clappers.

They arrived in no time. Shame, thought Jean. Mr Pemberton didn't park where you were meant to park, he just pulled up right outside the entrance to the hospital, scooped her out of the car and ran into the reception area with her in his arms, as if he'd just rescued her from a burning building.

To be truthful, it wasn't entirely romantic. Mr Pemberton was a bit out of puff and he still had a cigarette clamped between his lips. Can you imagine that nowadays?

They caused a bit of a commotion arriving like that. She remembers her hair getting caught on his enamel Rotary Club badge, and the next thing she remembers is being in a wheel-chair.

'He's a good-looking fella, your husband,' the young nurse said, trotting alongside the hospital porter who was pushing Jean through the corridors.

She was just about to deny he was her husband when a contraction took all the wind out of her.

In the end it was an easy birth. In fact, by the time Mr Pemberton had got back to the shop and young Sally Metcalf had been ordered to mop the floor ('A bit briny,' she said after) and the tinned veg shelf was neatly restacked, Jean had delivered another little girl.

Only this time it was different. For starters, she'd not felt sick, or got chilly during the pushing bit. Somehow her body knew what to do: her bottom half just seemed to open up like a piece of well-worn Tupperware and out popped the baby.

She was only six pounds and had wisps of feather-white hair. For a moment Jean wondered if she could call her Snow White, but then she realised she was just being silly and anyway, Snow White was always a brunette.

Looking back as she is doing now, there had been a fairy-tale quality to the whole day, what with Mr Pemberton playing the knight in a Humber Super Snipe and herself cast as the damsel in distress.

Later, when Jim and Anne turned up, she couldn't help thinking that Jim looked like a poor woodcutter and Anne some kind of troll.

Jean couldn't get over it: compared to her newborn sibling, Anne looked monstrous. Many years later Jean heard a lady talking about this phenomenon on *Woman's Hour* and it made her feel much better, but at the time she was shocked and horrified by the size of her four-year-old.

Anne had spent the day at Marie's with the dog and parrot, so Jean didn't want her touching the baby until she'd washed her hands thoroughly. To be honest she didn't want Anne touching her at all, ever. But Jim picked her up and put her on the bed so she could cuddle Mummy and the baby.

'My sister, my baby sister,' she squealed until Jean begged her to 'put a sock in it'. She wanted Jim to lift the big lump off the bed.

'Jim, can you just get her off?' But Jim was far too busy taking a photo of 'my three girls'.

He said it was better than winning the World Cup and she should have been grateful, she'd given him two daughters and he really didn't mind. He was the nicest man in the world and yet at that moment there was something about him that made her want to kick him in the face.

Anne

'Home'

Her mother had obviously expected to tidy the house when she returned from wherever she'd been before she got herself run over.

It wasn't untidy, not compared to next door's plastic toy and discarded knicker chaos, but there was something slightly unkempt about it, a grubbiness around the edges, finger marks, crumbs and unexpected sticky patches. Jean could do with a cleaner, which was ironic, considering that she used to be one.

Anne can't remember not having a cleaner. She's had one ever since she was married: Irish, Polish, Portuguese and a bad-tempered Russian.

'I have been quite spoilt,' she supposes. Cleaners, gardeners, au pairs, she's never really had to do anything around the house by herself. As for doing any mending beyond sewing a button on, she's always taken her clothes to the dry cleaner's. 'I have never replaced a zip in my life,' she concedes.

Anne pokes around in the kitchen chatting amiably to herself. 'At least I'm a better cook than my mother. In my cupboards I have exotic herbs and spices, I have drawers full of Lakeland goodies, silicon egg poachers and gizmos to core pineapples. I have gourmet graters and pepper mills with different settings, coarse or fine. I have absorbent pads that soak up the grease from a grill pan, disposable piping bags, three oven thermometers, a tagine, a slow cooker and a bread maker. And that's just for starters. I also have decorative gourds and a mounted display of antique jelly moulds.'

In Jean's condiment cupboard there is a stainless steel salt and white pepper cruet set that Anne remembers from the seventies, some Colman's mustard powder, Sarson's vinegar, tomato ketchup and salad cream. No one eats salad cream any more, thinks Anne, removing the offending article and dropping it in the bin. There is also some Worcestershire Sauce and, more surprisingly, a bottle of chilli sauce. Of course, in recent years her mother has become a bit of a fan of the Chinese takeaway over the road. 'It's not real Chinese food,' Anne finds herself muttering, 'just a load of monosodium glutamate muck, but that's the north for you – you can't expect a Hakkasan on your doorstep.'

It's a good job no one can hear her. Not only is she talking to herself, which as everyone knows is the first sign of madness, but she is also being a crashing snob. She can't help it: she has lived in London too long.

She feels like an intruder, a burglar who has accidentally revisited the scene of a previous crime.

In the sitting room her mother's presence is even more acute. There is a bundle of knitting on the armchair, a tangle of blue and yellow wool, and yesterday's *Daily Mail* lies open on the television page. Her mother had ringed the programmes she wanted to watch in biro: *Emmerdale* of course, *Coast* and *Gok's Fashion Fix*.

A pair of battered slippers lie discarded on the carpet. Anne is sure she'd bought her mother some nicer slippers less than a year ago. What has she done with them? You can't lose slippers.

She perches on the edge of the two-seater sofa, like a guest who'd really rather be leaving. Everything about this house is so small, including the television. It's smaller than the one Anne keeps in the spare room back in Dulwich. At least there's a Freeview box, and a bookshelf that sports more ornaments than books. Her mother was never much of a reader: she was dyslexic, of course, before anyone knew what dyslexia was. No wonder Paul refuses to blame his side of the family. Maybe he's right, all the bad blood does comes from her side. But she stops the thought right there.

Her mother buys *Woman's Own*; there's a stash of them down by the side of the sofa. On top of the magazines is a box of Cadbury's Heroes. Anne eats three.

It is nearly six o'clock. She could call home but Paul won't be back for another hour, and she has a horrible feeling the boys won't answer and that will make her worry. The sooner Ellen gets there the better.

Neither Jools nor Nat has the guts to behave badly in front of their grandmother, they're too mercenary. They are very aware that Grandma Ellen is loaded and so the last thing they want to do is blot their copybooks and lose out on the cash.

Anne tries to remember if they've ever stayed here as a family, all four of them, but she knows they never have. The house is too claustrophobic and there isn't a guest en suite. Paul could never have coped, he's funny about his ablutions.

She used to bring the boys up when they were younger but it was never very successful. Blackpool's golden sands can be hard work when it's struggling to reach sixty degrees in July and anyway, Julian developed a phobia of donkeys, which he mani-fested by screaming until he was sick at the sight of one.

Jean has a couple of ancient school photos of her grandsons inserted into silver frames on the sideboard. They look toothy and slightly Canadian for some reason.

Anne wonders if her mother would recognise either of her grandsons if she should come round from her coma and they happened to pop their heads round the door. The photos are half a decade old, her children look like children. Jools is yet to have his brace fitted and Nat is still a virgin. Now where did that thought come from?

She doesn't want to think about that, the boys and their sex lives; that's why she is glad Ellen is coming to stay. Without Ellen the house would be swarming with teenage girls, all those over-confident Ugg-boot-wearing privately educated young ladies with their big hair and bra straps. Anne doesn't trust any of them.

Between the school photos of Nat and Jools there's a photo of Anne on her wedding day. She has to look hard to find her mother: she's right on the edge, looking a little bit cut off. It's usually the bride's family who organise everything, but with Paul's parents having such a massive house and garden in Wiltshire, well, it would have been silly not to have had the wedding down there. After all, you could hardly get a marquee and a string quartet in Jean's back yard.

Anne suddenly feels a pang of embarrassment for her mother. She really hadn't known anyone at the wedding. Ellen's house had been full of real family, so Jean was booked into a room in a local guesthouse. 'A really super place, everyone raves about the food,' Ellen had said, but a quarter of a century on it strikes Anne that she has no idea if anyone had seen her mother safely back to her accommodation that night. Certainly she and Paul had rushed off without saying a proper goodbye, squealing down the drive in Paul's new Golf convertible all covered in shaving-foam hearts, with tin cans clattering from the bumper.

'I was very traditional,' admits Anne, conjuring up a picture of herself in her going-away outfit, a black and cream polka-dot shirtwaister with cream court shoes and a black patent clutch bag. 'I was very Lady Di.'

After a night at the Park Lane Hilton (including a cocktail in the infamous Trader Vic's) they set off on their honeymoon. As they flew to Barbados Anne recalls thinking that she'd finally done it, she'd gone as far away as possible from where she had come from and all she could feel was relief.

'I don't think I even sent her a postcard!'

Dear God, she was doing it again, talking to herself. It was quite unnerving, she might have to put on the television and drown out these random mumblings.

Not that there had been much to write home about. Literally: she'd had terrible prickly heat and Paul ate a dodgy crayfish on the third day which resulted in him spending an entire week in bed. He managed to get up a couple of days before they were due to fly home and sat on the balcony sipping tonic water and eating dry toast, while she sat beside him swathed in a damp sheet, trying not to scratch.

Other people have sent her mother postcards. There's one behind the clock, sent a couple of months back. Something about the handwriting sends Anne reeling back. She can smell damp newspaper and something more acrid catches the back of her throat, she can see herself eating a buttered crumpet and cleaning out a bird cage . . . while under the table a dog runs its damp sandpapery tongue across her bare knees. Of course, it's Marie Boothroyd's handwriting. That licked-knee memory must be over forty years old.

Marie is writing from the Canaries: 'The weather is very pleasant and the hotel has all mod cons and some smashing entertainment.'

She replaces the postcard. She is going to have to be more careful; she might have escaped from her past but that doesn't mean it's gone away. This house is stuffed with it; she will have to watch that she doesn't stumble upon anything that will upset her. She will have to leave drawers unopened and cupboards locked. It's best if things that have been swept under the carpet stay under the carpet. Certainly there is nothing in this room that would merit awkward questions, but Anne knows that while certain things have been hidden from view they have never been thrown away. This house may not be a shrine to the past but Anne can feel herself slipping back. This is the room where she opened her eleven-plus results; this is the room where the policeman stood; this is the room where her mother kept a vigil by the window and watched and waited and hoped.

Anne plays remote-control roulette until she manages to turn on the television. The local news informs her that police are still

112

investigating a hit-and-run incident that has left an elderly local woman in a coma. It takes a couple of seconds for Anne to realise that the picture of the elderly local woman is her mother, and for some reason she blushes and switches the television off.

Her stomach rumbles in the ensuing quiet. Time for that microwaveable chilli con carne.

Jean

Dirty Anne

Jessica, that's what she wanted to call the baby. Jim wasn't sure: 'But does it go with Anne? Anne and Jessica. Would Jane not fit better?'

She barely listened to him. He could blather on all he liked, she'd made up her mind.

She even went to the expense of putting an announcement in the local newspaper: 'To Jim and Jean Collins, the gift of a second beautiful daughter, Jessica Louise, 1.08.1966.' The cutting still exists, carefully pasted into an album, a skinny paper finger nicotine yellow with age.

Jean would have liked to thank the nursing staff and Mr Pemberton for getting her to the hospital, but at so many pennies a word it seemed a bit extravagant.

'It's just an announcement, Jean,' Jim told her. 'You're not writing a book.' He couldn't understand why they were doing it; they hadn't gone to the papers when Anne was born.

'Yes, but this is different,' said Jean, and when he asked her why she couldn't think of an answer.

It was lovely having a summer baby. When Jean thinks back to that first month she can feel the sun heating up the backs of her bare legs as she pushed the pram along the street. It was like being on holiday; they didn't call it maternity leave back then.

Most of the time she had Anne with her as well. Marie Boothroyd was taking a break, she and Arnie had gone abroad. They could afford Spain because they didn't have kiddies, not yet: later on they adopted a little boy, but she mustn't jump ahead, she wants to remember that Indian summer.

It was September and even the Lancashire coast was baking. Blackpool Tower shimmered in the distance and Jean and Anne were taking Jessica to see the girls in E. R. Pemberton's; they were always 'the girls' even though some of them were knocking on fifty and had hairy chins.

Anne was excited because she knew she'd get sweets. She was starting school next week, she was a big girl now, and she was: she'd grown out of all her little summer dresses. The one she was wearing now was a bit tight, the smocking stretched across her broad chest, the elastic of the puffed sleeves leaving dark pink ridges on her fleshy upper arms.

But it didn't matter, she couldn't be small now that she was a big sister.

Jessica was just four weeks old and Jean was already back in her pre-pregnancy frocks. She'd made a special effort today: the dress was a simple little shift, navy cotton covered all over in yellow roses. 'Simple and elegant', that's what it had said on the pattern, and it was.

I was in my prime, thinks Jean, and even though medically she cannot feel, see or hear anything, she is once again clutching the cream plastic pram handle. She is watching the spokes of the wheels cast shadows on the pavement, she can hear cars and birds and the click-clack of her kitten-heeled sandals. She is so alive she could burst.

They made a big fuss of the baby, all the girls, and that soft lad, Andrew, with the spots, who garrotted great rounds of cheese with a special wire. 'Ooh Jean, she's gorgeous. Couldn't you just eat her? What a little sweetheart, oh, doesn't it make you want one?'

She sat Anne on the heavy wooden flap at the back of the shop, the one you had to lift if you wanted to get behind the counter. They caused quite a stir: even the customers in the shop wanted to come over. There's nothing like a new baby, especially one that has the pink and white colouring of a bag of marshmallows.

She pulled the baby out of the pram like a conjuror and let everyone have a hold. Her hair was coming through fast now and spotty Andrew remarked that she was 'blonder than Peroxide Mary'.

'And she doesn't have to burn her scalp off with the bleach every four weeks,' shrieked a woman with a great big yellow beehive. She looked like a fat Dusty Springfield, thought Jean, and all of a sudden she realised this must be Peroxide Mary, her replacement.

She didn't notice Anne take the chocolate. She should never have sat her there, right next to a rack of the stuff, the child just helped herself. It was a hot day, her hands were sticky, there was chocolate all round her face and down her dress. Jean felt herself flush. She thrust the baby into Sally's arms and marched over. 'Anne!' she shouted. The girl looked up and promptly fell backwards off the counter. In the split-second that she saw her daughter's heels disappear over her head Jean couldn't be sure whether she'd done something to make her fall. Had she pushed her?

She braced herself for the screaming. She could see the pool of blood before it even appeared and she was counting stitches before she realised that Mr Pemberton had caught her.

Caught her by an ankle, just as her head was about to hit the floor. 'Ups-a-daisy,' he said, and suddenly Anne was standing the right way round, her glasses dangling off her ear.

Jean was on her knees, shaking her daughter by the shoulders. 'How could you, Anne?'

She shouldn't have done that, it only made matters worse. The shouting scared her, she was only four, and so she piddled. Jean is forcing herself to remember this bit, it's the bit she usually leaves out of the anecdote. The eating of the chocolate and the falling backwards, all that was funny, especially considering how

Mr Pemberton caught her, no damage done, but the yellow puddle on the wooden floor? Jean is still embarrassed by the wee. She could have beaten the child; she'd have liked to have wrenched Anne's knickers off her and rubbed her face into their stinky wetness, but she didn't. She grabbed the pram blanket, one of those ones with the silky edge, and mopped the floor. Then they went home.

That night Jim said she was quiet. She *was* quiet: she was thinking about how she could never show her face in E. R. Pemberton's again, she was that ashamed.

The girl seemed to understand; she was quiet too. She ate her tea nicely and went to bed without asking for a story. Joan threw the cot blanket in the bin: she never wanted to see it again, and she certainly didn't want it anywhere near the baby.

The baby smelt of talcum powder, she was strawberries and cream, she didn't belong under piss-sodden blankets. She was like a princess in a fairy tale. No wonder Anne was jealous. She'd have to watch her: if she was capable of throwing herself backwards off a shop counter to get attention, then what else could she do?

Jean started to get a bit silly after that. She can admit it now, but at the time it didn't feel silly, she couldn't help herself. She started off washing the baby's clothes separately from Anne's; she didn't want her eldest child's grubbiness tainting the sweetness of the baby. Everything about the older girl seemed smelly and ugly; she was clumsy and left dribble patches around the place. Her hands were always filthy, she hadn't to touch the baby with those hands. Jean started to bleach Anne's hands, then it became routine. At first she diluted the bleach but then she began to worry it wasn't strong enough, that it wouldn't kill off all the germs, so she washed Anne's hands in neat bleach and began to drop a capful of Dettol into her bath. After all, it wasn't just her hands that needed to be clean, she really needed to be clean all over, you couldn't be too careful. She kept a separate flannel for her and hid a scrubbing brush in the bathroom cabinet.

Anne didn't like it. She didn't like the smell and her skin became dry and inflamed. Jean soothed her cracked little hands with the cream she put on the baby's nappy rash and it helped for a while, but the child would wake in the night with her skin on fire and she'd cry.

'It looks like eczema,' said Jim, and he wanted to take her to the doctor's. 'We don't want her to be teased at school. You know what kiddies can be like.'

Poor Anne, all she did was scratch and the more she scratched the worse it got, until one day she got a sore around her mouth that went all crusty and purple and started to spread and Jim said he didn't care what Jean thought, this looked bad and if he had to take a day off work to get to the surgery then that's what he would do.

In the end Jean took her. 'Impetigo,' said the doctor, 'a common infection. Is she a picker?'

'Yes,' said Jean, 'she's a picker,' but then she broke down in tears and told the doctor what she'd been doing.

He was very angry, and said that if his own wife did anything so silly with their little boy he'd take a stick to her. He told Jean that she was a useless mother and didn't deserve to have two little girls, and what about all the other ladies who would love to have two little girls and couldn't?

She started to sob then, and he wouldn't even give her a tissue. He told her that he wanted to see Anne again in a month's time and if her skin wasn't back to normal he'd inform the police and the girls would be taken to the local children's home.

Jean didn't doubt he meant it and she knew the children's home existed. Everyone knew Thursby Hall, a dark red-brick building squatting gloomily on the seafront between St Annes and Blackpool. The home was surrounded by high walls and nothing to either side of it but sandhills. Jean was petrified. If they took Anne they would take Jessica, and if they took Jessica her heart would break, it was as simple as that. She had a month to put things right.

Anne

Bedtime Stories

Anne decides to sleep in her mother's bed. It's the only double in the house and once upon a time her father Jim slept next to Jean in this bed.

I loved my father, thinks Anne, and for a moment she can picture his bedside table as it used to be, his tortoiseshell spectacles, amber-coloured pill bottles, glass of water and the plastic-coated library book he changed every Saturday morning.

She used to go with him, it was their special time together and as soon as she was old enough she was given her own card. She loved the way the librarian stamped the return date on the gummed-down 'Property of Fylde County Council' slip and she'd wonder who had borrowed the books before her.

She can still recall some of her favourites: *The Wind in the Willows*, *Stig of the Dump* and just about every Famous Five book Enid Blyton ever wrote. For years when people asked what she wanted to be when she grew up, she had her answer as ready and as firm as that rubber stamp: 'A librarian.'

The bed smells both musty and sweet, as if Jean hasn't changed the sheets for a while and has been keeping wine gums under the pillow. A hand-embroidered cloth covers a cheap white laminated cupboard on her mother's side of the bed; arranged on top of the cloth are a travelling alarm clock (as if she had flights to catch), a weirdly corporate-looking beige eighties telephone and an empty packet of Deflatine. Oh the glamour of old age. Anne can't help wondering whether excessive wind might be hereditary, flatulence being just another thing to worry about, especially when she's walking down the corridor at school. You can't just let rip when you want.

The wallpaper is faded; pale yellow honeysuckle weaves around a broad pink stripe thinly trimmed in gold. At regular intervals a hummingbird buries its beak deep into a well of nectar. Over the mahogany chest of drawers is a Monet print.

Her mother would have made the curtains herself, rose-coloured velvet with a cream cotton lining. If someone were to make a film of her mother's life the soundtrack would mostly be that of a sewing machine.

Anne has a quick bath. The bathroom suite is a strange shade of dark peach and the water chills quickly because the bath is plastic. I am a very fortunate woman, Anne reminds herself again. At home I have a traditional cast-iron slipper bath with brass feet.

She puts her nightie on. It's nearly ten; she should ring home, she can't keep putting it off. Paul will be packing and anyway she wants to make sure that one of the boys puts a towel and some soap in the spare room, shows a bit of effort. It's the sort of thing that Ellen will notice, especially if it's not done.

The battery icon on her BlackBerry is on empty, an orange warning light flashing intermittently. She needs to dig out her charger but she knows before she even looks in her case that she has forgotten it. She can see it right where she left it, plugged into the kitchen wall at home. Shit.

She speed dials home, only to hear her own rather irritating voice echoing back into her ear. 'I'm terribly sorry, but the Armitages are not available at present. Please leave a message.'

'Um, where are you? It's me, Mum, Anne, it's nearly ten

o'clock. I just thought someone would answer. I bet you've got that stupid TV blaring away. Anyway, I'm here and I'm fine.'

She puts the phone down, suddenly realising that no one has bothered to ring her. Neither her husband nor her sons have phoned to ask if she has arrived safely and how is her mother?

Is it just my men, she wonders, or do men in general just not give a flying fuck about anything except themselves?

The Armitage men have popped out for dinner. Despite the vast wealth of many of the Village's inhabitants (including TV comedians and actors whose names will be forever on the tip of your tongue), Dulwich is not overrun with Michelin-starred restaurants. There are a couple of cheerful pizza joints and a trendy new brasserie, but Paul, Nat and Jools opt for the pub and order Cumberland pork and apple sausages with balsamic red onion gravy. 'Better than your mother's,' says Paul, and they all nod in agreement.

It's quite nice, a trio of testosterone. Paul avoids asking Nat what he's going to do for the rest of his life and conveniently forgets when he's buying a round that his younger son is only sixteen.

They drink pints of bitter, play a couple of games on the Trivial Pursuit machine and then Paul leaves to do his packing.

'Will we get anything?' asks Jools.

Nat might not have much general knowledge, as demonstrated by the pub quiz machine (he was stumped by the capital of Australia), but he understands immediately what his brother means

'Nah, just that poxy house in the arse end of Cuntsville.'

Paul gets home in time to hear the tail end of his wife's message. He should call her back; the kindest thing to do would be to pick up the phone and call Anne. He should ask her about the journey, tell her that his mother is happy to come down and that he's just had a nice bonding session over sausages in the pub with his sons.

He should reassure her that her mash and onion gravy is far superior and wish her luck.

But he can't be bothered. Anne is rather needy at the moment, prone to tears, drinking a bit too much – she was hog-whimpering last night and he's still a bit cross with her, to be honest. Paul doesn't like it when women lose control, and a drunken middle-aged woman is a terrible sight.

No, he will contact her in the morning. His flight is mid-afternoon so he'll text her from the airport.

Paul wanders into the kitchen for a nightcap. Putting the light on, he notices that there is broken china all over the floor and that someone has been at the brandy.

Suddenly he is really glad to be going on holiday tomorrow: things are starting to get out of hand here. It's time he had a week away, a week of golf and a few beers with the boys, catch a bit of sun without Anne bleating on about skin cancer.

He roots through the cupboard and finds a broom to clear the mess up. The floor is sticky with gooseberry fool; it could do with mopping but there's no way he's going to mop his own kitchen floor. He'll bribe Nat to do it in the morning: he'll do most things for a tenner, not that he should need paying but that's just the way things have turned out. He hopes that they don't upset his mother. Ellen can forgive most things apart from deceit and laziness and lies and . . . well, all the things his sons are really good at.

Paul pours himself a good measure of Courvoisier. He needs to sleep: Anne was snoring like a warthog all last night, her breath fetid with fish and booze. It'll be a relief to have the bed to himself. With any luck the boys won't come home too late, waking him up by crashing about. They can be quite selfish. Poor Ellen, it's a shame his mother isn't as deaf as most women her age. Oh well, with any luck his mother-in-law will be dead by the morning, Anne will be home pronto and his mother can remain in Wiltshire unscathed.

★   ★   ★

Nat decides to have a last pint. He's yet to break into the twenty-pound note that his mother left for their supper. He could have a pint and buy a gram of coke if he likes, he's noticed the bloke in the baseball cap popping to the gents every two minutes. Nat's got a good nose for drugs. Ha, that's a good one, a good nose for drugs. He should think about doing stand-up.

Jools has just left in a flurry of text messages to visit a mate. Jools has a lot of mates, Nat doesn't ask which one it is – it's not cool to need to know stuff like that – but it's still a bit of a shock to find himself in danger of being outshone socially by his younger brother.

Course that's the thing about being at boarding school, no one lives nearby. It's all right for Jools, he's a day boy and his school is half a mile away from their house. It's easy for him.

Nat is feeling a bit sorry for himself. All the boys that he used to know when he was at the local primary have turned into strangers. Some have turned into the type of high-achieving strangers that bugger off to university; some even know what they want to do with the rest of their lives. Even Piggy Robinson has managed to get away. Fucking Oxford, Jesus.

What would cheer Nat up at this moment, he decides, is some fanny. He picked up that Zoe bird here last night. Course that ended in disaster, but even more reason to get back in the saddle.

He looks around. It's heading for ten-thirty and a couple of sixth-formers, probably from that school hideous Hannah Robinson goes to, are finishing what look suspiciously like lime and lemonades and shrugging into tatty denim jackets. They look arty and intense, not his type, and anyway time is not on his side, it's nearly ten-thirty and they're sober, talking animatedly about Chekhov. He's no chance. One last pint before bed.

There's a fat little dyed redhead in the corner drinking red wine with a blonde and a bloke. She must be about twenty-four. Every time she reaches for a drink she shows a bit more tattoo – it's on her right shoulder – bare legs, denim skirt, roll of belly, slightly bulgy eyes, lips stained Merlot purple.

His cock twitches. Well that's a relief, at least his mother hasn't spoilt everything. Suddenly the redhead rolls to one side and disappears under the table, emerging seconds later waving a packet of cigarettes and a lighter then, stumbling slightly, she weaves off into the garden for a smoke.

Nat follows her, lighter at the ready. His hand is steadier than hers; she's wobbling around, suddenly pissed in the fresh air. His flame ignites her cigarette; she sits down suddenly on a wooden bench and he sits next to her, she's got a funny warty lump on her left knee but her tits are massive.

'Thanks darlin'.'

She's Scottish. 'Glasgow?' he hazards and she nods. Her nostrils expand as she inhales. She's older close up, about twenty-eight; her skin is a bit coarse, the pores open and grimy. It's a shame she's sitting in the bit of the garden that's overly lit. If he could just take her somewhere dark, if he could just turn her to face a brick wall and hold on to her tits and fuck her from behind, then it would be fine.

'My name's Nat,' he begins. For some reason she finds this hilarious. She laughs and coughs and repeats 'My name's Nat' in a stupidly posh voice. 'Oh la di da Natty boy, and what have you come out here for boy? You come for a suck on ma diddies? You want me to rub yer wee cock?'

If his mother had been here she could have informed him that this woman was like something out of an Irvine Welsh novel, *Filth* having been Anne's choice of summer reading a few years ago. As it is Nat knows nothing of Irvine Welsh, he just knows this woman is a common slag and rather than wanting to fuck her, he now wants to punch her stupid face. He would like to see her fat nose bleed. He mutters 'Cunt' under his breath and walks out of the garden, through the pub and home.

Jean

Back to Work

She pulled herself together, it was what you did in those days. After she'd seen the doctor Jean went home and told Jim that Anne's itchy skin was all her fault.

He was very patient, he sat there listening while she owned up and when she'd finished he just said, 'The poor little mite,' and then he marched upstairs and poured the bottle of Dettol down the sink.

'If I catch a whiff of that stuff again, Jean, there'll be trouble.'

She knew he meant it. His eyes were as hard and cold as pebbles behind his specs.

It took a long time to make things normal. She still washed Jessica's clothes separately and it was ages before she could bring herself to put the girls in the bath together, and even when she made herself do it she didn't really like it.

Something shifted between her and Jim. It was like he had one over on her for a change. Of course she was glad he'd been so understanding about the Dettol, but she didn't like feeling grateful for it.

If he'd shouted at her or given her a smack it could all have been done and dusted, but for months she felt like she was being watched all the time. Her own husband was spying on her and who could blame him?

He took Anne off her hands whenever he could; they had special trips out to the library and the train station.

'Where on earth are you thinking of going?' she'd ask, but they didn't go anywhere. They just went to look at the trains.

'You're never too young for a bit of train-spotting,' said Jim, and he was serious. Anne would come home with a little red notebook crammed with numbers.

Jean thought it a bit odd. She'd understand if Anne were a boy, but Jim insisted she was inquisitive and that children should have their eyes opened to anything and everything, and with that he promptly carted the little girl off to stinky old Fleetwood Docks to look at the trawlers.

Still, it was nice to have time alone with baby Jessica; Jean never tired of taking her youngest out on her own. Now that she was toddling she kept her on pink leather reins. You had to watch little Jess, she'd be teetering by Jean's side one moment and the next she'd be dashing off into the road. She thought it was funny. Jean was forever hoiking her away from the kerb, lifting her by the reins out of harm's way, leaving the child swinging in mid-air, laughing her head off.

'You're a danger to yourself,' Jean would gasp, while passers-by said, 'You've a handful there, Mrs. Quite the little madam.'

Secretly Jean liked the fact that Jessica had spirit. Anne was so ploddy by comparison; she was six now, all wobbly teeth and brown pigtails, nothing to write home about looks-wise and a little bit knock-kneed, but she was doing very well at school.

When Jim went to the parent-teacher evening he returned glowing. 'They really think something of her you know, Jean, she's clever and she's conscientious.'

Conscientious meant that she liked doing homework, regardless of the fact that Pickering Road Primary didn't set official homework. Anne liked to sit down at the kitchen table and practise her sums and her spelling.

Jim would set her whole pages of addition and it was Jean's responsibility to check her spelling. It was a good job she was only in the yellow class and still on words like 'bus' and 'then', but it wouldn't be long before Jean knew she wouldn't be able to help.

Anne liked learning. Learning was Anne's thing; she was very careful with her books and pens. Jean had to watch Jess like a hawk, she was having a bit of trouble teething and could often be found with one of Anne's precious books hanging out of her mouth like a cat with a vole.

It was the only time Anne ever got cross with her. For the most part she was endlessly patient with her younger sibling, but then Jessica was Anne's passport to popularity. Not many girls in her class had such an adorable baby sister. They used to crowd round Jess when she and Jean came to meet Anne from school, begging for invitations to tea so they could play with the baby.

And so they came. Jean is struggling to remember names: skinny Elaine; pretty Karen thingy; Debbie Stother, the only girl among five boys, who just liked to watch Jess's nappy being changed: 'I'm that sick of willies,' she said.

Anne was proving to be more popular than Jean expected her to be and, surprisingly, she wasn't bullied. A couple of boys had apparently called her 'speccy four eyes' but she seemed to rise above it. She thought they were idiots and they were, though Jean was still surprised it didn't hurt. But then Anne was mature for her age, everyone said so.

Jim started talking about her going back to work, he never let up. He was sure there would be a vacancy back at E. R. Pemberton's, why didn't she just pop by? Marie Boothroyd would be twiddling her thumbs. After all, Jean had gone back to work by the time Anne was Jess's age, and they could do with the money.

They certainly could. Jim had lost his job; he was almost too embarrassed to tell her. It was the January of 1968 and a happy new year to you, Royal Mail, thought Jean.

He'd had a fit, a big one, fallen badly and his bag came undone. A lot of letters fell into the recently thawed snow, all the inked names and addresses ran in the slush, it was a mess, his bosses said they were very sorry but they had a duty of care to the customer and Jim wasn't able to guarantee that service. He had to go.

'I'm sure I'll get another job,' he said, but he looked worried and as a precaution Jean bought a lot of cheap tinned goods.

'Why don't you just nip up to the shop and ask,' he urged. 'You never know.'

So she did. She left both the girls with Jim: Anne was off school with a bad cold and catarrh.

Jean wasn't looking her best, she was recovering from a similar virus to the one Anne was now snuffling over and her nose was red and sore. It didn't matter how much she kept powdering it, the pinkness shone through.

There were a lot of new faces at Pemberton's. Jean felt a bit shy, which was silly: she'd always felt like one of the family before. She gave spotty Andrew a wave and he mouthed something back but she couldn't make out what he meant, and she caught Sally's eye but she was busy slicing a side of ham so they just gave each other a sly wink.

Jean knocked on Mr Pemberton's office door. She suddenly felt a bit sweaty. Her breasts did that tingling thing, as if someone had rubbed itching powder on her nipples, and she really wished she was wearing something more exciting, something that would show off her figure and make Mr Pemberton whistle and say, 'Well Jean . . . just look at you, girl.'

'Come in.' Jean was momentarily confused. Mr Pemberton's voice sounded like a woman's. She opened the door to see a busty blonde with a cloud of yellow hair perched on Mr Pemberton's desk. It was the fat Dusty Springfield lookalike, the one they called Peroxide Mary.

'I was expecting Mr Pemberton,' stuttered Jean.

'Ernie's out,' explained the yellow-haired one. 'He's business to attend to in Preston, so he's left me in charge.'

She offered Jean a pudgy hand. 'I'm Mary, Mrs Pemberton to be,' and she waggled a big diamond solitaire in front of Jean's astonished eyes.

She had to recover herself fast. 'Congratulations, I'm sure you'll both be very happy.'

Mary filled her in with all the gory details while Jean fixed a 'how thrilling' smile to her face. Apparently he proposed after the works Christmas do, it wasn't very romantic: they were waiting for a taxi in the car park when all of a sudden he got down on one knee!

He'd made her a manager first and now he was making an honest woman of her, what a lucky girl she was!

Jean felt something she'd not felt since her brother had died, like her heart had a small hole in it and some of the happiness that she kept in there was leaking out.

Anyway, Mary went on, they didn't have much going in terms of work at the moment, but if Jean was interested there was always the evening shelf stacking and cleaning shift.

'I don't do cleaning,' Jean heard herself say in a surprisingly haughty fashion.

'No pet,' Mary shot back, 'but you never know, and it's nice to know the offer's there, you know like, should you get desperate.'

She left the shop with her face blazing. It wasn't just her nose that was red, she was the colour of a phone box by the time she got home

'Stuck up cow,' she spat at Jim, who was playing ludo with Anne on the sitting-room floor while Jess looked bored in her high chair.

'Who does she think she is? I'll show her.' And she did.

Jean allows herself a tiny smirk of triumph. Unfortunately the nerves from her brain to the muscles round her mouth are still frozen and the smirk is something that cannot be seen to the naked eye.

The very next day she put on her smart navy woollen two-piece suit and the cream mohair coat that had been her mother's best, plus a fur tippet, and applied for a job in ladies' fashion.

Shirley Lovell's was in St Annes, a half-hour bus ride away, but it was very smart and catered for the cut above. You'd not get the likes of Peroxide Mary in Shirley Lovell's, thought Jean.

It was hard work, though, and the other assistants were a bit snooty. Still, it was nice to work in a shop that was wall to wall carpet, where all you could hear was the rustle of expensive material and the low murmur of sycophantic approval.

Madam was always right, even when Madam wasn't.

Jim was still struggling to find a job, which was a bit embarrassing, and because they didn't want people to know Jean continued to walk Anne to school like she normally did and then caught the bus from opposite the school gates. All she can remember is how her feet were killing her by the time she got home at six.

It was a difficult time. She missed the camaraderie of E. R. Pemberton's but at least now she could afford to shop there again and she took great pleasure in ordering fancy items in front of Peroxide Mary. 'Yes,' she would say in a loud voice, pointing at the vanilla slices, 'four please. I am currently working in ladies' fashions. Shirley Lovell's in St Annes – very exclusive, no riff raff.'

No riff raff and not many laughs either, but she learnt a lot about clothes. She quickly saw how items were constructed; she had an eye for how different shapes suited different women, but she would never really have the confidence to make people listen.

Then, out of the blue, Jim got a job at the bowls club. He started off on shoes, putting the customers' own shoes into a cubbyhole and swapping them for a pair of soft soles. They said if he proved himself worthwhile they'd give him more responsibility. 'It's a start,' he said to Jean, but to be on the safe side they decided it would be best if she stayed on at the frock shop.

This meant calling on Marie Boothroyd again, to mind Jess and pick Anne up from school.

Marie was fine about it. She had a soft spot for Anne and Jess was a poppet, though as she admitted to Jean when she picked them both up on that first Friday night, she was harder work than her older sister.

When she thinks back to that weekend, Jean knew something was wrong as early as Saturday morning. Jess wasn't herself; she even phoned Marie Boothroyd to see how she'd been the day before. 'A bit listless,' came the response, 'but fine.'

Only she wasn't fine, she was floppy and off her food. Jean remembers feeling panicky. Jim was working: they'd offered him a Saturday shift and considering he was still on probation he'd decided to show willing. It was just her stuck in the house with Anne being all bossy about wanting to do some hard sums, and Jess just lying there not eating, not sleeping, just being hot and making little crying noises like a lost kitten.

Jim was a bit concerned when he got home, but not too worried. 'All kids get ill,' he told Jean. 'Apart from my Annie: she's no trouble, strong as an ox,' and he sat down with Anne and made up a page of hard sums with plenty of carry ten and borrow one subtractions.

She can't remember sleeping that night. Jess stayed in their bed, a fetid human hot water bottle damp to the touch, her little chest rattling with each breath.

Sunday was no better. She managed a little water but nothing solid. Even Anne knew she had to keep quiet so as not to upset her mother and made a big effort to tiptoe around the house.

'I'll be up to the doctor's with her first thing,' said Jim, but Jean said, 'No, it'll be too late,' and even though Jim accused her of being dramatic, at ten o'clock on the Sunday night she phoned the emergency doctor.

He arrived at midnight, reeking of red wine and cigars, and within seconds of pressing his stethoscope to the child's bone-white chest declared the case an emergency and summoned an ambulance. 'Hurry!' he cried, suddenly sober, and Jean did all but faint.

That's enough remembering for today, thinks Jean, there's no point rushing things. She mustn't tire herself out, not if she's ever going to get these legs of hers working again. It's not as if she doesn't know what happens next, she can deal with it tomorrow.

Even women in comas need a bit of kip now and again.

Anne

Via Jumping Beans

By the time Anne wakes up, gloriously sans hangover, her BlackBerry battery has completely died, which is a bore but not, she reminds herself, the end of the world.

Instead she reaches for the hideous beige contraption that squats on the bedside table, realising as she lifts the receiver how dusty it is. Her mother obviously doesn't sit in bed chatting on the phone too often. This thought makes her feel guilty. Stop it Anne: you call her once a week, you're here, aren't you?

Within seconds of dialling home Paul answers, babbling as soon as he realises who it is. 'Hello darling, sorry I missed your call last night. I'm afraid I'm in a bit of a rush, bags at the ready, I'm doing a couple of hours at St Thomas' and then my flight's at three. I was going to text you from Heathrow.'

'My phone's out of juice,' she explains. 'Are the boys OK?'

'Not surfaced.'

Anne checks the travel clock. It's twenty-past eight, surely it's time Jools was up for school? She feels a wave of fury rise in her chest, but what can she do? She is two hundred miles away; she can do nothing. It's quite liberating.

'And Ellen, is she OK to come up?'

'Thrilled,' laughs Paul. She can't be sure if he's joking or not, you can never tell with Paul. For years she was never sure whether he was quite funny, but in such an odd way that no one realised it, or whether he was just a bit odd. She has since come to the conclusion that he is just a bit odd and when he is embarrassed or caught out he laughs, it's a nervous thing and right now he is giggling away like a hysterical fool. Oh God, suddenly she has a flashback to her own inane chuckling in next door's garden yesterday, how embarrassing! She must have caught this ridiculous habit almost by osmosis. Yet another downside to having been married for so long.

She interrupts his guffaws: 'Have a good time. I'll call Ellen tonight.'

Paul's chuckles subside. 'Good thinking, and do, you know, keep me posted, if anything dramatic happens . . . hahahahaha.'

He's doing it again. He means if her mother dies.

'Goodbye Paul,' says Anne quite firmly, using her 'it's your own time you're wasting' voice. Sometimes being a teacher is the best training you can have for being a wife and mother.

Anyway Jean isn't dead, she is alive but in limbo. To be honest, thinks Anne, she wouldn't mind being in a coma for a few months, or even a few years, herself.

It would be nice to wake up some time in the future, completely refreshed, to find the boys doing really well, Paul wearing normal-coloured trousers and the mortgage paid off.

Of course the boys *are* doing well . . . suddenly she remembers the hogwash she dripped into her mother's ears yesterday. Oh well, she can put it all right this afternoon, she can confess all.

Anne has never been religious but the idea of having someone completely deaf to the world, to whom she can impart her darkest secrets, is appealing, and cheap too.

There have been times in her life when she's toyed with the idea of therapy. In her early twenties, when the nightmares didn't stop for weeks on end, she even went as far as to look up some phone numbers, but in the end she could never face telling another human being, no matter how professional or sympathetic, the details of those dreams.

She hopes being back in this house won't trigger them again, that's why she must be careful. So far this room, the bathroom, the kitchen and the sitting room are safe. As long as she sticks to the rules and doesn't go poking about she should be all right. The boxes in the attic and the other two bedrooms, however, are out of bounds.

Hunger propels her downstairs. She needs to make a list, possibly pop over to the shops, try to remember which bus will take her to the hospital. She can't fork out for taxis all the time, it's just silly and extravagant. Her mother won't exactly be sitting up and waiting for her. She'll worry about getting a charger for her phone tomorrow; now that she knows that Ellen is coming she can relax about the boys.

A quick check of her mother's fridge reveals a carton of clotted milk, some low-fat spread, two eggs, a jar of marmalade and a pork pie.

Immediately Anne is back in E. R. Pemberton's, 'the best pork pies in the Fylde', the pastry gleaming as if it had been polished, not too much jelly, plenty of pork and the special ingredient, a hard-boiled egg bang slap in the middle of every pie. Suddenly she is four years old and her hand is curled sweatily around a cream plastic pram handle. Anne sways in the midst of this memory. Suddenly she is overwhelmed by the need to wee and she quickly trots to the bathroom before there is a puddle on the kitchen floor. How odd, she thinks as she sits on the lavatory, I am almost fifty, but every bit of my childhood is imprinted into every vital organ.

On closer inspection, the pork pie in the fridge is from the Co-op over the road. A pork pie for breakfast? Anne decides to make the meal healthier by accompanying the pie with a side order of dried apricots and a handful of cashew nuts.

E. R. Pemberton's no longer exists, she knows this for a fact: it closed down in the eighties. There was no car park – people expect a car park – and anyway it couldn't compete with the new Morrisons up the road.

Apparently a London-based architectural salvage company saved all the fixtures and fittings; those Victorian hand painted blue and cream tiles must have been worth a bomb. Poor old Pemberton's, it's a bicycle sales and repair shop now. Oh well, at least the cake shop and the newsagent's are still in operation, though the florist's has gone and when did Bob's pet shop, complete with doggies in the window, disappear?

She got a hamster for her birthday once, but it died of a nosebleed three days later.

God, she's reminiscing. She is already skating on to thin ice, she needs to be careful, she needs to keep to the edges.

Be practical and keep busy, she instructs herself, washing up her breakfast plate and throwing the pork-pie wrapper in the bin. It wasn't very nice.

Fifteen minutes later, with a shopping list in her hand, Anne has decided to tackle Morrisons. It's a twenty-minute walk, which means that if she had her car she'd use it, but as she hasn't it's Shanks's pony. She doesn't know how her parents managed, neither of them ever drove. I spent half of my formative years, Anne calculates, sitting on a bus.

As she turns to lock the front door she is aware that the man next door is mirror-imaging her actions, only his efforts are somewhat hampered by the two small girls hanging off his legs.

'Good morning, I'm off to Morrisons,' says Anne, flashing a friendly smile, which she knows is spoilt by the inordinate amount of gum she reveals whenever she opens her mouth.

'Um, I'm trying to get these two to nursery.' The girl who had been dancing with cat litter on her bottom is scowling and the smaller version has her eyes tightly shut and her arms wrapped around her father's ankles.

'Come on ladies,' commands Anne, clapping her hands. 'Chop chop, let's get to nursery. What fun!'

She sounds so ridiculous the smaller girl opens her eyes and the older one swaps scowling for a look of astonishment. 'If you're going my way,' continues Anne, 'I'll help you out. It's the least I can do after yesterday.'

It takes a little bit of persuasion but eventually the four of them set off in a stunted double crocodile to nursery. The father (or Drew, as he has introduced himself) and the younger girl Coral lead the way, while Anne and three-year-old Amber follow.

It has been a long time since Anne has held a sticky little hand in hers. Amber has Sugar Puffs in her hair and more stuck to the front of her jumper. Progress is slow, largely due to the fact that the gusset of Coral's tights is dangling by her knees.

Gradually, between screaming at 'bitey' dogs (Amber) and 'wanting a carry' (Coral), Drew manages to throw together enough details of his domestic scenario to put Anne in the picture.

His wife Sally is in hospital, awaiting the arrival of their third child. 'An accident, obviously,' he admits over his shoulder. Her waters have broken, it's a stressful time, he's not coping so well, Jean used to come and tidy, Sally's sister picks them up from nursery, but she's feeling put upon, she got two of her own, it's a mess and he has to work.

'What do you do?' yells Anne.

'Builder,' he shouts back. There's a lot of traffic, no wonder her mother never let her cross this road when she was little. An ambulance screams past. It makes her feel sick, it always has. It's a feeling she has never managed to grow out of, which is tricky considering she lives in South London.

'Extensions, attic conversions . . . in fact I'm about to go up into mine. We're running out of space.'

He asks after her mother. He says that as his wife is in the same hospital he will drop by and see her; he's a big fan of Jean: 'She's a good laugh, brilliant with the kids.'

He asks her nothing about her own life and Anne wonders how much her mother has told him. She wonders if Jean shows off about her daughter in London, with her big house and her successful husband whose hands are so precious that he has never once held a hammer in his life.

'So how are you going to get up to the hospital?'

'I was thinking of catching the bus.'

He tells her she needs the number 7 and says if she's in the hospital car park around six he can give her a lift home, though he has to swing by his sister-in-law's to pick up the girls. He drives a BMW estate with a roof rack. 'It's black and a bit of a pig sty,' he adds.

The nursery is at the back of a church. There is something about the proliferation of buggies that makes Anne feel nostalgic. Once upon a time she was as young as these mothers; her days were full of Spot the Dog books and teething rings. She has been here and done this, but she feels like an outsider. She is so old she could pass for a grandmother. She misses her little boys. Once upon a time, another century ago, Nat and Jools went to a rather smart little private nursery in the Village where they wore navy checked smocks and sang nursery rhymes in French.

Drew pushes opens the door to the nursery and Anne realises that it doesn't really matter where they go, what you pay or what they wear, all nursery schools smell the same, that mixture of sour milk, urine and rubber mats.

The noise level is extraordinary and the girls have pegs at different ends of the cloakroom. Amber leads Anne to hers; she has a sticker of a mouse next to her name. For some reason all Anne wants to do is lie on the floor and weep. Where did all those years go? Bits of it are flooding back so vividly that she can see the teeth marks on the red plastic beaker that Jools used to throw as hard as he could across the kitchen. She can hear the skeetering sound as it bounced across the lino. Of course this was back before they had the Yorkstone fitted, when they were still doing the house up and she had to fry fish fingers on an old free-standing gas cooker in the corner.

Without saying goodbye to Drew, Anne extricates herself from

Jumping Beans Nursery and continues down the road to Morrisons. Half an hour later she is surprised to find herself at the checkout, watching the woman on the till swipe a Peppa Pig colouring book and a Dora the Explorer jigsaw puzzle. What on earth could she be she thinking?

Jean

The Terrible Night

It was only as they were getting into the ambulance that they remembered Anne. She wasn't allowed to come with them, the ambulance men said it was against the rules. Jean was past caring, she'd have just locked the girl in the house and hoped for the best, but Jim was beside himself. 'We'll have to leave her with someone, we need a responsible adult.'

But who?

Mrs Kane next door was away visiting relatives in Hull and anyway, you couldn't exactly call her a responsible adult. Jean had seen her pocket a tin of Bird's custard powder in Pemberton's a couple of months ago! As for running the sleepy Anne round to Marie Boothroyd's, there wasn't the time. In desperation Jim found himself pounding on the door of number 115, Mrs Gaga's house.

Old ladies never go out, he reasoned, and he was right. She answered in a plaid dressing gown, her long grey hair roped down her back in a single steel-cable plait. He had Anne in his arms wrapped in a blanket and almost threw her into the hallway. 'Can you keep an eye on our Anne? We have to go to the hospital, the baby's poorly.'

Then he turned, ran and jumped like an Olympic hurdler into the back of the ambulance and the door was barely shut before the siren started its terrible wail.

Jean doesn't realise that her own trip here to the hospital just a couple of days ago followed almost the same route as that ambulance did forty-something years ago.

All she can remember is how she felt. She was in such a terrible state she was wearing odd shoes. She remembers sitting on a plastic chair in a corridor and looking down to see a brown suede shoe on one foot and a navy patent on the other. What would Shirley Lovell have to say about that?

There have been times when she has refused to think about that night, but there are other times when it replays itself over and over again. She can't help it, that night has always been ready to roll out on to the screen of her memory. It's the most-watched film in her head.

She can remember the nightie that little girl was wearing, feel the fabric, she'd made it herself in lemon winceyette. It was cold, it was winter, she should have been more careful, she should never have gone to work in that stupid clothes shop.

They took the nightie off her. She was such a little thing, all covered in wires. The men in the white masks wouldn't let her stay in the room, they said it wouldn't help.

So they sat, her and Jim, in the corridor with the green and black lino and she decided then and there that if Jess didn't come home then neither would she. She would leave Jim, run away and never come back. She would change her identity and dye her hair magenta; she would never want anyone to know that she had ever been a mother; she would go abroad and start a new life.

Anne would be happy with Jim, but she wouldn't be. It was simple: if Jess died then Jean would scarper. Hawaii, Madagascar, Canada, she went through all the countries that she knew absolutely nothing about, there was plenty of choice. There were lots of places she could go where no one would even think of looking for her.

Jim just walked up and down, smoking. Once he said, 'I hope Anne's all right,' and she nearly hit him. It was gone two o'clock in the morning when the doctor appeared and said that Jess was going to live. He said that she was still a very poorly girl and would need to stay in hospital for another five days or so, but that she was out of danger and as long as she was well looked after, especially during the cold winter months, she would be fine, although he added sternly, 'She will always have weak lungs. Let's just say she'll never be a great swimmer.'

That's the line that Jean found herself repeating over and over when recounting the story of how her youngest so very nearly died. 'She'll always have weak lungs. Let's just say she'll never be a great swimmer.' And she wasn't, though Jim insisted she learnt – 'It might just save her life one day' – and Jean surprised herself by agreeing.

They got a taxi home. It was nearly four when the driver dropped them off. Jean wanted to let Anne sleep the night at Mrs Gaga's. 'What's the point in waking them up at this hour?' she whispered to Jim and he was too tired to argue.

He was very easy-going really. As wives go she was lucky, but as he put the key in the door and they both tumbled exhausted into the house she was suddenly struck by the fact that this was her life. From now on there was never going to be any running away. The other Jean, the one she'd imagined for a few seconds down that hospital corridor, a red-haired Jean who for some reason she pictured in a circus outfit complete with a feather plume sticking out of her bum, had disappeared for ever.

She'd made a pact: if Jess had died, she'd have been free, but Jess hadn't died and so she must stay. It was like God had been listening. He had given her Jess and in return she had to stay with Jim and Anne.

Of course years later she'd given herself a copper rinse, so actually the red-haired Jean didn't totally disappear. There was always another me, thinks Jean, lying in her hospital bed all grey-haired and broken for the third day running.

Jim had fetched Anne back almost as soon as it got light. She was very quiet and very tired and the blanket she was wrapped in was covered in cat hairs. 'There are lots of cats next door,' she said and then she showed them the pompom Mrs Gaga had taught her to make. 'Mrs Gaga's house is full of cats and pompoms, and the biscuits taste funny' is all she would ever say about that night, but when Jim told her how Jess was going to be all right, she cried big fat hot silent tears and even Jean wanted to give her a cuddle.

'Come here lamb chop,' she said to her daughter, but when she did get on her mother's knee Jean couldn't help thinking how heavy she was and how you could smell next door's stinky old tabby on her.

Jean resigned from Shirley Lovell's as soon as it opened that morning. She simply phoned them up and said, 'I shan't be coming back. I've a poorly child in Blackpool Vic and my place is by her side.'

Jim thought maybe she'd been a bit rash, but she just looked him square in the face and said, 'I will never go out to work again, Jim Collins. From now on my daughters are my priority (she meant Jess really) and those toffee-nosed women in Shirley Lovell's who need someone to zip them into their frocks because they're too fat and idle to do it themselves can find someone else to be their lackey. If I'm to work again it'll be from home.'

Jim looked confused at that. 'But what will you do?'

'I shall make clothes and do alterations. I've a sewing machine and a kitchen table, there's not much I can't make from under this roof. I'll put a card up at E. R. Pemberton's and . . . well, we shall just have to wait and see.'

Every evening they took it in turns to go and see Jess, and after she'd dropped Anne at school Jean went every morning too. The child still looked a bit purple round the edges, as if her skin was too thin and you could see the dark blood lying just beneath the surface. But on the Wednesday she had perked up no end, and just as Jean was about to leave she sat bolt upright and asked for a boiled egg.

They got her home on the Friday. Not a week had gone by but life had changed in so many ways. The doctors had given Jean a talk about being vigilant for any chest infections, while not being over-protective. They said fresh air would do her good but that she should be 'wrapped up warm at all times and be allowed to nap should she tire'. Jean wrote all this down in her diary. 'We've to be vigilant,' she told Jim.

'Yes,' he replied, 'but we've to let her get on with her life, Jean. We can't just wrap her in cotton wool and keep her on the sofa.'

That was the tricky part, not hovering over her. Jean found her hand constantly straying to the child's forehead – was she not a bit hot?

She got Jim to phone Marie Boothroyd to tell her they'd no longer be requiring her services. Jim said she sounded a bit teary and a week later Marie turned up outside the gates of Pickering Street Primary. She had the stupid Alsatian with her, but at least she'd not brought the parrot.

Marie was upset, she said she blamed herself. She'd really not thought there was anything wrong with Jess; she'd have contacted Jean immediately if she had. Jean said she didn't blame her and she didn't: Marie Boothroyd was a decent woman but she wasn't a mother, she didn't have the instinct.

What was odd about the whole thing was that Marie was so upset at the prospect of not looking after Anne any more – 'She's such a good girl' – and Jean had to promise that any time she got too busy with her new business then she was to drop Anne off at the Boothroyds', she was always welcome.

In return, Jean made Marie promise that she'd tell all her friends about her bespoke tailoring service, and the next thing Jean knew Marie was dropping off a friend's very nice Harris tweed coat with a ripped lining. Jean replaced it with bottle-green satin, which cost the same as boring black but was just that touch more sophisticated.

Marie's friend was delighted, and that friend had another

friend with a mackintosh that needed shortening and a twisted zip in an evening gown, and that lady knew someone going on a cruise who'd lost ever so much weight and could Jean take in seventeen summer frocks?

They never really ate at the kitchen table again, apart from on special occasions such as birthdays and Christmas Day. It was always covered in patterns and pins and fabric. Still, it was a small price to pay. I was happy, remembers Jean, and this time she slips back into the black feeling perfectly content.

Anne

Ellen Falls Off the Window Sill

Ellen Armitage should be packing for the London train, but for some reason when she'd caught sight of the spare bedroom curtains from the landing she decided they needed taking down for a clean.

She should have fetched the little aluminium step-ladder from under the stairs but she was fine on the chair – until she stepped off it on to the window sill, misjudged the distance and fell.

'Well what a damn silly thing to do,' she gasps, finding herself in a crumpled heap on the Axminster.

She gets up as quickly as she can. She's not the kind of woman that goes in for lying on the floor: it's such a bad look, especially at her age. So reminiscent of those depressing adverts in the back of the colour supplements, the ones featuring a helpless old lady lying prostrate on a cheap carpet, clawing at her neck for an emergency alarm button that will no doubt alert a warden to her plight.

I'm not that sort of woman, thinks Ellen. I'm a long way from sheltered accommodation. She has, however, sprained her ankle quite badly.

Ellen tries to get up and walk, but the pain is blade-like in its intensity. 'Well, what a bally nuisance.'

There is no way she will be catching the midday train from Salisbury now. She should call Paul, but then again why should she spoil his plans? Her son works very hard, slicing through sinew and tumour. He deserves this break in the sun with his golfing chums. Surely her grandsons are more than capable of looking after themselves for the weekend?

For heaven's sake, Nat is eighteen! Young men his age were being shot down in fighter planes during the war. And Jools is sixteen, which is plenty old enough to make a bacon sandwich. What can possibly go wrong?

She will let the boys know that they're going to be on their own for the next few days, but as soon as she's fit she'll jump on a train.

Ellen has to go downstairs on her bottom. The telephone is in the hall, of course it is. Ellen is a stickler for tradition, she doesn't really approve of telephones being anywhere else. Hers is on a table next to a polished copper bowl, which, according to the season, contains bulbs (hyacinths are Ellen's favourites), a miniature rose bush, an arrangement of dried chrysanthemums or a poinsettia (Christmas). Next to the copper bowl is a tooled-leather address book in which the phone numbers of friends and family are alphabetically filed. Some of these names and numbers have been crossed out over the years; people do seem to keep dying.

'P for Paul – mobile'. All those digits for that tiny little phone, thinks Ellen. She's decided she's not going to bother him. She dials 'Paul and Anne – home' and leaves a cheerful but resigned message for the boys.

'Hello Nat and Jools, it's Grandma Ellen here. Sorry chaps, was so excited about seeing you but I've bust my blasted ankle and there's no way I'll be up for the foreseeable. Ghastly bad luck, was looking forward to having lots of granny fun but we'll have to wait. I tell you it's a good job I'm not a horse: any vet worth his salt would take me out and shoot me, hahaha.'

Ellen laughs her tinkling laugh that once upon a time rang

147

merrily across all the best drawing rooms in London and Wiltshire. It sounds a bit echoey and mad here in the hallway.

Limping into the kitchen, she manages to extricate a bag of frozen peas from the freezer compartment in the fridge and decides to spend the rest of the morning on the sofa watching that dreadful *This Morning*. Ellen spends an inordinate amount of time these days watching television programmes she utterly despises.

Ninety-eight miles away, Nat runs around the sitting room with his T-shirt over his head footballer-style. He has just heard his grandmother's message: the old bat can't come, he and his kid brother have the house to themselves and, with any luck, it'll be theirs for the entire weekend. It's PAAAAAAARTY time.

To kick off the celebrations Nat pours himself a small glass of sherry and sits down to watch *This Morning*. That Holly Willoughby has the best tits on the telly.

Two hundred miles north, Anne is on the sofa too. Well there's a lot of rubbish on the box, she thinks. Still, it's nice to have a sit down and a coffee and that funny little Italian chap sometimes has some interesting recipes. Not that she'll be doing much cooking up here. She stocked up on quite a lot of convenience foods in Morrisons: beans, bacon, sliced brown bread, cheese. It's a bit miserable cooking for one but she did buy some chicken. She thought she maybe she could make a casserole and share it with Drew next door: those little girls could probably do with something home-cooked. If she goes easy on the herbs there's no reason why they wouldn't like it, and then she won't feel guilty about accepting an offer of a lift home from the hospital.

Anne believes in a neighbourhood community and it makes sense for her and Drew to help each other out: he has a car, she can cook, and anyway, she might as well do something useful while she's here, even though her mother's kitchen utensils are going to be a bit of a challenge.

It feels strange not having access to a computer. Normally by now she'd have checked in as her Facebook alter ego, Star van Hoff, in order to snoop on her sons, but with her BlackBerry dead and her mother not being one of the nation's silver surfers, there's not much to do but watch telly, eat biscuits and try not to go wandering down memory lane.

Nat alerts Jools by text: 'Gma ellen fucked ankle not cuming YES cmon my son'.

Jools reads the text at lunchtime. The College is ridiculously strict about mobile phones; soon they'll be hiding them up their arses. He casually strolls out of school. He's got triple history this afternoon but he has something more pressing to sort out at home: he and Nat have a party to organise. If anyone stops him he'll tell them he's just been for a crap and there's blood in his stools. It's worked before, but on this occasion no one even notices him leave.

Anne cuts the chicken into chunks small enough for tiny mouths. It's good to be doing something with her hands, it takes her mind off everything else. Paul will be heading for the airport, Ellen will be on her way to London, Nat will be having his breakfast and Jools will be at school. She knows his timetable off by heart: lunch followed by triple history; it would be nice if he decided to read history, it's a good degree to have.

Personally, she has a 2.1 in English and French from Edinburgh. The flair for languages had been an unexpected bonus. Of course as a little girl she'd been keen on everything: English, maths, colouring-in. She remembers sitting at this very kitchen table, head bent over the pale blue Formica doing complicated sums that her father had made up. She's still good at mental arithmetic, she can still recite her times tables, even the eights and the sevens, which everyone knows are the trickiest.

She'd tried so hard with the boys. She bought brightly coloured educational posters and Blu-tacked them to the nursery walls, dragged them round the Dulwich Picture Gallery, played tapes of Spike Milligan's poetry in the car, anything to fire them up. Maybe Jools is interested in history because she potty-trained him in front of a massive kings and queens of England timeline. She'd like to think she'd done something right; so much of being a mother seems to be taking the blame for getting it wrong.

Paul just cruises through it all. He refuses to get overly concerned, he thinks they both need to find their own way, but Anne worries that their own way might be the wrong way, and once children start going down the wrong path some of them find it impossible to turn back. Once you're lost it's very easy to stay lost. She knows this more than most.

Though I never had a rebellious streak, she admits to herself. I never wanted to get into trouble. Nat and Jools don't seem to care, they find it as easy to break rules as they do to break wind or glasses or the ice dispenser on the fridge door. They are careless of other people's feelings. Nat seems almost to enjoy upsetting her, while Jools doesn't even notice. She's not sure which is worse.

Paul is at Heathrow. Some of the gang have already taken up residence in Harry Ramsden's, and are drinking lager. How refreshing, thinks Paul, who is far too posh to realise that ordering cod and chips and drinking Budweiser before getting on a plane to the Algarve is really rather common.

Paul, for all his medical know-how, surgical skills and Latin declensions, can be quite unworldly, which is why he doesn't notice that, five seconds after he puts his phone down on the table, it has gone. In fact, he doesn't notice that his phone has been stolen until he's on the plane and is trying to find it to turn it off.

Oh well, Ellen is in charge of the boys and if anything happens to Jean then Anne will tell his mother. When he calls to check up on things – probably on Sunday – she can fill him in. He is supposed to be on holiday, after all.

Jean

Working from Home

The work came in fits and starts. Sometimes Jean was rushed off her feet and at other times she'd be prowling round the house, wondering whether to ring Peroxide Mary and beg for a couple of cleaning shifts at E. R. Pemberton's. But deep down she knew she never would.

She'd only seen Ernest Pemberton a couple of times since he'd married that woman. His new bright gold wedding ring looked tight on his fleshy third finger, but he'd been ever so kind and refused to take payment for putting the card in the window.

'Bespoke tailoring service, discreet, local and reasonable'. She'd checked all the spellings with Jim and illustrated the card with a hand-painted cotton reel, needle and button.

'No job too big or too small – contact Jean Collins on 794216.'

'Jean, you're one of the Pemberton family,' he said. 'I wouldn't dream of charging. I wish you every success in your new business venture and if my wife Mary has any articles of clothing that need attention I shall insist she calls on you.'

Fat chance, thought Jean, and just to prove to the stuck-up cow how well she was doing, she bought a couple of fillet steaks from the meat counter.

'Is it my birthday?' asked Jim.

She needed to butter him up as she wanted to enrol Jessica at the local dancing school. She was three now and Jean knew that if she was to be any good in the future, now was the time to start.

'You never sent Anne' was Jim's argument.

'She wouldn't have enjoyed it' was hers back.

'How do you know if you never bothered to send her?'

Honestly, he could be that pedantic. Jean had to explain to him: 'Our daughters are very different, Jim. Anne is an academic. I'm not sure Jessica is, but what I do know is that she has grace, Jim, she's light on her feet and she's bendy, and now that she's properly well we need to make sure we keep her fit and strong.'

He still looked doubtful – he'd be thinking about how much it was going to cost – but Jean wasn't going to give up that easily.

'Now it wouldn't surprise me,' she went on, 'if Anne grew up to be a teacher, Jim, she's bright enough and she's bossy with it, but Jess might not be that way inclined and I think it's important that we explore other avenues.'

'But she's only three!'

Jean knew she'd won. She'd swung the argument by telling him how clever Anne was. Jim's only proviso was that Anne could have dancing classes as well, if she wanted to.

She didn't.

Jean took the bus right into the middle of Blackpool. Under the shadow of the tower, tucked into a back alley, was Prima, an Aladdin's cave of a shop that sold all the necessary equipment: a little pink leotard, a wrap-around pink cardi and a pair of satin ballet slippers.

She could have knitted the cardi herself but she didn't want Jess to feel different from anyone else when she started. It was important that she blended in right from the beginning.

Jean loved that shop. Even now she can feel herself having to budge the stiff wooden door open with her shoulder, she can see the curly gold writing on the glass door – 'Prima – Professional Dancewear' – hear the bell as the door opened, chang-a-lang-a-lang. This was a shop of dreams, of pointe shoes in glass boxes, racks of Leichner's stage make-up, pots of biscuit-coloured foundations and vivid sticks of greasepaint ranging from shimmering pale silver to deep peacock green, lipsticks darker than blood and boxes of stick-on lashes complete with tiny doll's house tubes of glue.

Prima catered for ice skaters too, with rows of spangled outfits and net skirts. The place was ablaze with sequins and promise. It made Jean want to part her hair down the middle, scrape it into a bun and walk with her feet pointing out like a duck. She wanted to be one of them but it was too late. Too late for her, but not for Jess.

The dancing school was at the local institute, a hefty cream and pink brick building built at the turn of the century and oddly positioned in an area that seemed surprised to have such a thing on its doorstep.

Heavily chandeliered and with a general air of Victorian pomposity, the institute was slightly too grand for its own good and the locals were at odds as to who and what it was for.

By the late sixties it had naturally divided itself into different zones. At the very top of the elaborate marble staircase was an entire floor dedicated to snooker, an overwhelmingly male domain where the curtains were permanently drawn and row after row of green baize tables hunkered down in a nicotine gloom.

The snooker club had a self-contained members-only bar that occasionally got rowdy on a Friday night when men who were old enough to know better would smack each other over the head with snooker cues.

In the smaller function suites on the first floor local societies would gather for slide shows and lectures. A couple of years ago the Ornithological Society invited a man from the radio to come along and perform bird impressions, which went down a storm.

On the ground floor the grand hall, with its wooden stage, trapdoor and velvet curtains, was home to the WI, various charity dinner dances, any number of local amateur dramatic productions and of course the biannual dancing displays from Miss Carr's Cygnet School of Dance for Young Ladies, where Jess had successfully been enrolled.

The school was in the basement, next to the kitchens and the boiler. The boiler was at the heart of the building, and it was an incredibly temperamental piece of Victorian plumbing. People tended to talk about it in whispers in case it overheard, took umbrage and exploded. Depending on the whim of the boiler, the temperature of the institute was either tropical or arctic.

She can remember Jess shivering with excitement like a damp puppy the first time she tried all her ballet things on. She remembers her flitting round the house, doing her dancing, and Anne scowling, already bored of the whole thing. 'I'm trying to read, why does she need to show off all the time?'

Audrey Carr ran Cygnets. She'd been a dancer herself but had developed gland problems and as a result was enormously fat. Audrey Carr must have been fifteen stone but she could still do the splits; when Audrey danced you forgot that she was a mountain of flesh and no one even thought to laugh. Audrey taught the older girls and Miss Evangeline taught the littlies. Her real name was Angela, but Evangeline sounded more 'ballet'. She was as thin as Miss Carr was fat, a celery stick of a woman with adenoid problems and the secret weapon of terrible breath. Children did what Miss Evangeline told them to do, because if they didn't she would come and breathe over them until they obeyed.

Jean can't remember the name of the boy who played the piano. He was gay – you could tell: he lived with his mother and talked of a fiancée that no one had ever clapped eyes on.

Every Tuesday, at four-thirty in the afternoon, Jess hopped, skipped and pretended to be every element going until three years later she moved up to the exam class. From then on it was Wednesdays for ballet and tap on Saturday mornings.

If Jim was working it was a battle to make Anne come with them. Wednesdays were bad enough, but twice a week was just too much to ask. Anne was ten and getting quite bullish: 'I'm old enough to be left in the house for a couple of hours.'

Jim didn't think she was, but Jean disagreed and the tap classes were that much more enjoyable when she didn't have Anne sitting beside her looking like a wet weekend.

'You'll not answer the door and you'll not go wandering off,' Jean warned her elder daughter, but she never did. What Anne did do was eat. Sometimes Jean would come home and half a loaf would have just vanished, along with a big chunk of butter and the best part of a jar of jam.

Jean never mentioned it. Anne always tidied up after herself so well it was obvious she didn't want anyone to know. Anne was binge eating before it was fashionable; mind you, it was increasingly obvious to anyone with eyes in their head that she was over-eating. The girl was increasingly stout for her age.

Oh well, Jean could always buy a yard of cheap and run her up a new skirt with an elasticated waist. It was just next year, when she went to big school and had to have a uniform, that Jean didn't want her growing out of everything every two seconds.

Jim was adamant that she should go to the girls' grammar in St Annes. 'It's a good school,' he said, 'she'll be with nice girls from good homes.'

Funny how he was such a snob about such things, especially considering his own background. Jim had cut off all contact with his family in recent years. In fact, he only knew that his brother Vincent had been cautioned for exposing himself in Stanley Park when they read about it in the papers: Local Man's Park Shame. Jim's face had gone that red, she thought he was having another fit.

'It's like I'm tainted,' he said to Jean that night. 'It's like my family have got some dirt in their blood and sometimes I think it's in me too.'

Jean said he was talking rubbish. Personally she wasn't fussed if Anne ended up going to the local comprehensive, it was brand spanking new and just a five-minute walk away. Anyway, as she told Jim, it wasn't up to them. Anne would sit the eleven plus next year, just like every other child in the borough, and then it was up to the markers.

To be honest, it wasn't Anne they needed to worry about. Jessica had been at Pickering Street Primary for over a year now and she was struggling with her letters. Jean was called in to talk about her younger daughter having special reading and writing classes. Her teacher explained that there were a couple of them in the same boat and a lady who was specially trained in these matters could come in and give them extra help.

So three times a week Jess and a chalk-faced boy called Alan sat out in the corridor at a special desk while a woman from Garstang gave them extra tuition.

Jess has got the same problem as me, Jean confided in herself, and to be honest the problem had never really gone away. Even though she was a grown woman she still approached books with caution. Sometimes the letters would slide around the page and trick you, a g would look like a d or a p. It was all very confusing and you just had to learn to take your time.

Unlike Anne, Jess liked Jean's made-up tales more than books. Books made her nervous. Her father was always trying to make her read along with him. She liked it best when her mum invented stories especially for her; she'd always start with 'Once upon a time there was a beautiful little girl called Jessica' and if Anne was listening she would snort, which would result in Jess calling her older sister 'a mean fat pig'.

Which occasionally, Jean thought privately, the elder sibling was quite capable of being.

Anne was jealous, of course she was, only it was more complicated than that. Anne was jealous of Jessica for exactly the same reasons that she despised her, but she also loved her sister with a ferocity that surprised even Jean. The only time Anne ever got into trouble in her entire time at Pickering Street was when a boy in her class, Richard Lonsdale, had called Jess a 'spaz' because she couldn't read properly and Anne marched right up to him and punched him in the face.

Jean was so proud of her that she took them up to E. R. Pemberton's after school and bought vanilla slices all round. From that day on, whenever something happened that deserved celebrating it was referred to as a vanilla-slice day.

Anne

Taking the Number 7 Bus

Paul will be boarding the plane now, thinks Anne as she steps on to the number 7 bus. In Portugal the temperature will be somewhere in the high eighties; here on the Fylde coast it is fifty-six degrees and wet.

It seems ironic to be catching the number 7. It's the same bus she used to catch to school, but in the opposite direction. Today she's heading towards the hospital in Blackpool; her alma mater is in St Annes.

She takes a front seat on the upper deck: old habits die hard. Rain blurs the local landmarks. Some are so familiar they barely register, a few she can't ever remember seeing before. She should have got herself into town earlier, tried to find a battery charger for her phone, but what with making the chicken casserole and *Loose Women*, there just wasn't the time. Anyway, it's too miserable to be out in this weather.

The institute looms up on the left. If the curtains were open you'd be able to look in and see the snooker tables, thinks Anne without even wanting to. The mind is a terrible honeycomb: just when you think you have managed to hide something in a little cranny right at the back it resurfaces somewhere else.

She wishes she had a book, even that dreary *The Thousand Autumns of Jacob de Zoet* would be preferable to sitting here on this damp bus with the words 'my sister, my sister, my sister' going round and round in her head.

It's the institute. How many times did she sit in that basement while a homosexual with trotters for hands plonked out Elgar and a tangle of small girls pretended to be crocuses, earnestly pushing through the frozen earth, slowly unfurling their leaf arms and turning their petal faces to the sun?

Not that she ever watched. She kept her nose firmly in a book, only a book she was interested in reading and not something Linda Mayer has chosen just to look clever.

Anne forces herself to think about her book club. The next meeting is on Wednesday – will she be back by then? How long can her mother be in limbo like this? She has a horrible feeling they might all be gathering at hers, and she may have promised them her famous baba ganoush. Oh sod it, sod the book club.

Her mind keeps straying. One of the reasons why she is glad she had boys is that she never had to do the whole girlie pink dance thing. Obviously she would have done had they expressed any interest, even though Paul would have thrown a fit, probably insisting that homosexuality, like dyslexia, is a stranger to his side of the family.

Back home in Dulwich Village, there's a church hall and every Friday afternoon a gaggle of girls clad in the same pink as they have been for ever skip down the street and disappear through the doors, as if led by an invisible pied piper. She has learnt to take them for granted, but sometimes when she sees a particularly small one, a blonde one with her hair pulled right back and pointed elbows, her heart turns over.

Yes, it's a good job she had boys. She's not sure she could have coped with fairy wings and all that tripe.

The bus stops at some lights; the illuminated green cross of a pharmacy flickers through the window. She hopes Paul has taken some sun tan lotion – he does burn so easily – and a bottle of Gaviscon. She doesn't think they've ever had a holiday when he didn't have an upset tummy, weeks spent in hotels with the en suite a no-go area.

Of course she never went abroad as a child, but then not everyone did, so it didn't seem particularly strange. There were a couple of caravan holidays in Wales but her father was always nervous about being taken ill and so they never strayed far. All she can remember are endless games of Monopoly, the sound of dice skidding across Park Lane and rain drumming on a metal roof.

Then came the shows, the endless bloody shows that stopped them from going anywhere. There will be a box of photos somewhere; obviously she's not going to look, but there will be cuttings and flyers and snap after snap and medals on brightly coloured ribbons and once upon a time there was a row of silver cups. They've all been put away now, hidden from view. It's for the best.

She should have brought one of her mother's magazines, even a wordsearch would have been preferable to this. Her memory has been very leaky today, the past has been slopping about all over the place. What she really needs to do is get all these old recollections and put them in a really good-quality plastic storage container (from the Lakeland catalogue), label it Upsetting and shove the thing on a shelf that is too high to reach even with a ladder. She checks her watch: she has been dwelling on the past for almost an hour. She needs to limit herself. If only she had something to distract herself. She promises not to do this journey again without a sudoku at the very least.

Anne gets off at the next stop. The rain is beating down now, puddles of the stuff splashing her ankles as she tries to out-jog the downpour. Of course, she remembers now, the weather is another reason why she had to get away from this place.

By the time Anne reaches her mother's bedside her linen trousers are soaked from the hems right up to the knee and she is freezing. Back in London what she is wearing would be eminently suitable for October. Forget the phone charger: if she's going shopping it's for a rainproof jacket and wellingtons.

Jean still looks like she's been in a boxing ring with a psychopath.

'Hello Mum, it's Anne.' She feels silly introducing herself. 'Your daughter Anne.'

Does she know any other Annes?

Her mother's social life is a mystery. Apart from the postcard from Marie Boothroyd, Anne has no idea who her mother communicates with any more. There's Drew, of course; he's given the impression that Jean is forever popping over. Suddenly Anne realises that the half-knitted blue and yellow SpongeBob SquarePants jumper in the living room is for little Coral next door. It makes her feel strange, her mother knitting sweaters for children that really have nothing to do with her. Why isn't she knitting for Nat and Jools? Even as she is forming the question she is answering it: because they would sneer. Whatever Jean made would be wrong. Both of them are designer-label boys, though while Jools twists his with a bit of vintage, Nat is a purist, he likes Abercrombie and Fitch and Ralph Lauren. It's a boarding-school thing, apparently.

Anne thinks back to her teenage wardrobe, the Laura Ashley rip-offs that Jean knocked up for her, the corduroy flares and puff-sleeved blouses. Her mother wanted her to take an interest in fashion, but the truth was she didn't know what suited her then and she still doesn't have a clue.

Jesus, these wet trousers are going to give her a chill. Fortunately the radiator in her mother's room is warm, so Anne quickly removes the soggy trousers and drapes them over the pipes – it's not as if her mother's going to notice – and then she launches into the latest instalment of her bedside monologues.

'Well Mum, I have to say you're not missing much with the weather, it's frightful out there. Mind you, I'm very cosy at yours. I've been to Morrisons and stocked up . . .' and she witters on about her day, taking Amber and Coral to nursery, cooking the casserole, her husband setting off to play golf. Words spill out of her mouth and her mother pays about as much attention as Paul and the boys do when she talks about her day at home.

Well, thinks Anne, pausing for breath for a second, here I am, sitting in my knickers talking to my mother who is in a coma. And suddenly she wishes that she did have someone to share this with, someone who could just nip out and get her a coffee or a doughnut. It's not as if her mother's got a fruit bowl bursting with grapes and bananas. She should have brought that packet of dried apricots.

'I'm peckish,' she says out loud. 'And lonely.'

But in the same breath she realises she isn't missing anyone, certainly not the boys. It's time she had a break from them, Paul included. She sometimes feels like she is an ivy desperately clinging to the foundations of her house, covering the cracks, trying to protect it, doing all the work. It's the ingratitude she can't bear, the casual acceptance of everything. It's their fault, of course, hers and Paul's: the children have always had everything on a plate, they have no idea what it is to want something and have to wait, to save up. Neither have they any idea how it feels to lose something. Apart from Galaxy, she mentally corrects herself, and to be honest it was at least three days before either of them noticed. Poor Galaxy, she'd been an unwanted gift for Nat's seventh birthday. 'I was hoping for a snake,' the boy had sulked. She could have hit him.

Anne looks out of the window. The weather reminds her of the paper round she had when she was twelve. Her sons have never had to get out of bed to cycle heavy sacks of newspapers round the neighbourhood. In fact, she can't think of either of them ever having to do anything they didn't really want to do.

Even on holiday, when she and Paul wanted to visit a museum or an archaeological site, they would drag their heels and pick fights with each other until it was easier to just get in the car and drive back to the pool. To do what they wanted to do. The constant giving-in to ice creams and video games.

It's strange, thinks Anne, how angry she can feel about her sons without them actually being present.

'The boys send their love,' she lies to her mother. 'I talked to them this morning.'

She didn't, they don't. The last thing they are thinking about is either Jean or Anne. Jools and Nat are plotting. Nat has played Grandma Ellen's message three times, they have high-fived each other on each occasion and opened a bottle of fine red wine to celebrate. Some of the fine red wine has spilt on the fine yellow carpet that Anne had installed just last year. Oh well, they can always move the sofa and cover the stain. Right now they have more pressing matters: it's time to get on with planning the party.

'Not tonight,' ventures Jools. 'We really need time to get this thing sorted – borrow some decks, make sure we have a really cool sound system. We don't want it to be a crap party, we need to get organised.'

'You thinking of making sandwiches and fairy cakes, you spaz?' jeers Nat, knowing full well that if Anne were here she would insist on party food and proper invitations and some mental rule about allocating the spare bedroom for coats. Their mother lives in another world, a world free from drugs and casual sex, of firm handshakes and thank-you letters, and knowing what people's parents do for a living. She belongs in the past.

'Nat and Jools really hope you get better soon,' says Anne, her voice trailing away. God this is exhausting.

Jean

Mrs Grainger Carmichael Calling

She had been right about Jessica: Audrey Carr told her in person, undulating up to her when Jess had been attending Cygnets for less than six months. Jean could feel her warm currant-bun breath on her cheek – Audrey often smelt of Eccles cakes. 'Nice turn-out,' she'd whispered. 'I hope there's no history of a bosom in the family.'

Jean hadn't known what to say; it was only later that she'd realised the significance of the question. Miss Evangeline had explained it to her: 'Your daughter shows promise, she has a natural flexibility, but obviously things can change as girls develop. Your other daughter is fairly chunky?'

'They've always been very different,' Jean had responded. 'Chalk and cheese.'

But she stopped making so many puddings and encouraged Jessica to eat an apple rather than a bag of crisps.

Regarding the bosoms, well, that was up to Mother Nature. Her own were on the small side, but her mother's had been vast, constrained only by yards of Elastoplast-coloured corsetry. As for the other side of the family? She dreaded to think and she didn't like to ask Jim. They would just have to wait and see.

Even when a mother is in a coma she cannot help her children growing up. Jean is finding that, however deeply she rummages in the recesses of her mind, eventually the memories of when her girls were really young start to run out and even though she is looking back she is forced to move forward.

Of course she could always stop herself remembering anything at all, but while she is lying here unable to even knit, there's really nothing else to do.

She wonders what day it is. It might be a Monday.

On a Tuesday she goes to the institute and does a pensioners' bums and tums class. Of course it's not like it used to be, they've a new silent boiler, the changing rooms have showers and hairdryers and the tray of chalk that the older ballet girls used to dip their pointe shoes into has disappeared, but sometimes on a Tuesday morning when she's chatting to Noreen and Pat she can still catch a whiff of it, and instantly she is back in the Cygnet School of Dance with fat Audrey and Miss Evangeline, and the gay boy on the piano is banging out some Brahms.

Of course, once she found out Jean could sew Audrey Carr was all over her like measles. 'We have a team of wardrobe ladies,' she wheezed, meaning volunteers, 'and a vast collection of costumes from previous productions, but we're always looking for an extra pair of hands to sew on the odd sequin or stitch a burst gusset.' Audrey had what looked like crumbs from a sausage roll at the corner of her mouth.

Jean didn't mind, even though she was up to her eyeballs in real work. Word had spread. Jean Collins was the woman to go to if you had anything nice that needed fixing properly. She'd also branched out into what she called remoding: taking something that looked a bit last season and bringing it up to date. She sourced fancy buttons for jackets, trimmed a tweed coat with a fur stole, split a pair of cigarette pants and inserted a yard of floral material for an extravagant flare. There wasn't much she couldn't do. In fact, she'd started to turn jobs down, redirecting

165

fallen hems and broken zips to the dry cleaner's. 'I'm a little more *bespoke*,' she would explain to potential clients.

When the phone rang at 113 Marton Edge Road it was usually for her, and she adopted a slightly refined voice when she answered. 'Jean Collins speaking,' she trilled, and she'd parrot clients' names and numbers for Anne to write down on a blue Basildon Bond unlined notepad. She never trusted herself to get them right.

'That's Mrs Grainger Carmichael,' she said, nodding furiously at Anne, '72694928, Weeping Willows, Brady Avenue.'

'Brady Avenue,' she repeated, almost choking on her excitement. Anne remained unfazed; she was used to being her mother's secretary. She was ten years old and waiting for the results of her eleven plus. Nothing else really mattered.

Jean put the phone down and announced theatrically, 'Marvellous news everyone, I have an appointment with a Mrs Penelope Grainger Carmichael, Weeping Willows, Brady Avenue, at three o'clock on Saturday afternoon.'

Jess did a celebratory lap of somersaults round the sitting room, finishing off with a handstand that arched into a backward crab.

'Very posh,' muttered Jim, pronouncing the word 'posh' to rhyme with gauche, which he often was.

Brady Avenue was the epitome of bespoke, an architectural pot-pourri of individually designed houses, ranging from fifties Californian-style ranches to seven-bedroom Tudorbethan pastiches. All had double garages, some had tennis courts and there was even rumour that the cream Neo-Georgian number with the colonnades had an indoor pool.

Brady Avenue was as close as St Annes got to Hollywood, despite being just minutes from the town crematorium. It was a must-see destination and sometimes grieving relatives would take themselves on a ten-minute gawping detour to distract themselves from the business of death.

This was where the bank managers and bigwigs lived. There was even a TV personality, a roly-poly funny man, Les Dawson, that was his name. Jean chuckles but her ribs don't move a millimetre. He was funny when he used to do that sketch dressed up as a woman.

Brady Avenue ribboned extravagantly round in a large grass-bordered U shape, a cul-de-sac but with houses on both sides of the road. Back then the gravel drives were full of polished chrome, a Bentley here, a Jag there. If you lived on Brady Avenue you did so with a sigh of relief. You'd made it.

Of course getting there wasn't easy. It was going to take Jean two buses and if Jim was working then it meant taking the girls, or leaving Jess with Anne.

'Apparently she needs help with a wedding,' Jean informed her family. Anne rolled her eyes, Jess gasped dreamily and Jim mentally said goodbye to the kitchen table. Weddings meant yards of white fabric that couldn't be moved or touched. They meant hastily thrown-together suppers, Toast Toppers eaten on laps while Jean crouched over the sewing machine till midnight.

All in all it was a memorable week, not that she knew then just how memorable it would turn out to be.

If she'd known what was going to happen she'd never have picked up the phone, but the fact is she did. However hard she tries she will always hear that phone call, she will always see her hand picking up the cream Bakelite receiver and hear her own voice answering, 'Hello, Jean Collins speaking . . .'

The letter stamped with the blue ink crest of the local council arrived the very next day. Jean opened it. 'We are pleased to inform you that Anne Collins has . . .' The words started to bounce around the page. 'What does it mean?' asked Jean.

'She's done it,' Jim answered. 'She's only gone and done it. She's passed her eleven plus, she'll be going to the grammar.'

The last time she'd seen Jim that chuffed was when Blackpool had beaten Southport three years ago. He looked as smug as if he'd been handed the keys to a house on Brady Avenue.

They celebrated that night with a Vesta chow mein. Jess didn't like it so Jean did her spaghetti hoops. 'You spoil her,' said Jim.

As it happened Jim wasn't working on Saturday, so he could keep an eye on the girls while Jean dolled herself up for her meeting. She'd jazzed up a plain navy coat with some jaunty white rickrack braid on the lapels and she teamed her good grey woollen skirt with a coral-coloured pussy-bow blouse that she'd got on discount from Shirley Lovell's.

'You look a right bobby dazzler,' said Jim as she ran a tangerine-coloured lipstick around her mouth. Upstairs she could hear the girls arguing. 'Put it down, it's mine.' Anne was very possessive about her things, she really didn't like sharing. She didn't like Jess going into her bedroom and touching anything, which was precisely why Jess did it. 'Try not to let them kill each other,' she instructed Jim. She didn't like the idea of trouble escalating while she was out. Jess was a terrible face scratcher, but then Anne did goad her.

Jean sashayed down the road with her sketch pad in her brown suede shoulder bag. She had a little pencil case containing a selection of sharpened pencils and some coloured crayons. It was always easier to draw things than to try to explain them.

Weeping Willows was a third of the way down Brady Avenue on the right-hand side. The aforementioned willow wept dramatically over the front lawn, its tears a small pond complete with a stone cherub blowing a dribbling water horn. Jean loved a water feature.

The house itself was more California than seventies Lancashire, a low-slung two-storey number with a vast balcony running the length of the building. Jean's very first thought was that it must cost a fortune in window cleaning.

'It's mostly glass,' she told Jim later. 'Glass and big broken bits of slate set into concrete, and all the wooden bits, the garage doors and the window frames, are pale lemon.'

Penelope Grainger Carmichael wasn't anything like Jean was expecting. She was a little bent woman in a pinny.

'Hello Mrs Grainger Carmichael,' said Jean in her best telephone voice.

'She's in the sun lounge,' the little gnome woman replied. 'I'll let her know you're here.'

'Ooh Jim, I've never seen a room with so much light, and a leather suite, Jim, imagine, in mushroom, and they've this unit all built in. Teak, I think, with a fancy record player and leather-bound books all lined up and not a speck of dust. That's because she has a char, Jim, a Mrs Glinn, all bent up from doing the hoovering.'

'Call me Penelope' Grainger Carmichael was a short woman doing her best to retain some kind of shape. Jean recognised the type, she'd seen plenty enough of them at Shirley Lovell's. Women for whom good foundation garments were vital. Mentally Jean weighed and measured her: five foot two, twelve stone three, 36DD brassière, a fleshy size 16 packed into clothes that were a too-tight size 14.

Mrs Grainger Carmichael's camel slacks squeaked at the seams while her chocolate-coloured silk blouse was the spit of Jean's. That was a good start! 'What a lovely blouse,' enthused Jean.

'Oh this old thing?' Penelope said dismissively. 'I was thinking of giving it to Oxfam.' Jean blushed and decided not to take her coat off.

'Coffee?'

'Please.'

Mrs Glinn brought it in on a tray, in a proper pot with cream and a plate of fancy biscuits.

'I shan't be eating the biscuits,' protested Penelope, lighting a Peter Stuyvesant. 'I'm on a diet. I'm mostly eating grapefruit and boiled eggs.'

She went on to explain what she needed. 'My elder daughter, Helen, is getting married. Late July, in fact.

'Anyway,' she continued, the ash on her cigarette growing tremulously long, 'the bride's dress is being created by a designer in London, but considering the bridesmaids are little girls of four and five they could have all sorts of growth spurts and it would be best if their dresses are made locally. I myself will be buying an outfit from Harrods, but what with my diet and Lord only knows how much weight I might lose, it might be nice to have you to hand should any last-minute alterations be required. Of course, the biggest problem is Belinda.'

'Is she one of the little bridesmaids?' enquired Jean.

'Unfortunately not. She is Helen's younger sister and difficult. She's seventeen, still at school – Queen Margaret's, you may have heard of it.'

'Oh yes,' ventured Jean. 'My eldest has just got in there.'

Penelope looked momentarily surprised. 'Well, it's very good. In fact I'm sure we have a redundant hockey stick somewhere. Anyway, they've tried their best but she can be quite wayward. Basically I need you to come up with something that will complement the bride and suit all three bridesmaids.'

Somehow over the next fifty minutes Penelope managed not only to eat the entire plate of fancy biscuits but also to employ Jean's design and sewing skills without ever mentioning money.

'How much?' asked Jim.

'Oh don't be so vulgar, Jim. Penelope is just the type of client I want to be working for.'

'Can't see the point if they're not going to stump up,' he responded.

He could be very working-class at times.

Jean decided to buy herself a coffee pot, a stainless steel one with a wooden handle just like Mrs Grainger Carmichael's. 'It's Scandinavian,' she told Jim.

'It's a waste of money,' said Jim. 'Neither of us really like coffee.'

Anne

A Night in with a Neighbour

Anne hovers in the car park, looking for a black BMW. She can always get the bus or a cab but a lift would be a luxury. The wind is cold after the incubator heat of the hospital, her trousers are crumpled, her hair is frizzy; she feels like an unmade bed.

'I need a bath,' she mutters. 'I need to have an early night. I need to moisturise my legs, they are dry and scaly, my shins are dandruffy. As for my bikini line, I have pubic hair down to my knees.' Anne isn't necessarily hard on herself, she's just honest.

A car toots its horn, it's Drew, he's seen her. Well thank goodness for that.

She lumbers over, wishing she could trot elegantly, but unfortunately she is flat-footed and overweight. Besides, anything beyond a steady walk and her bosoms take on a life of their own.

He was right about the state of the car. The passenger footwell is littered with burger wrappers and empty Coke cans. 'I'm a pig,' admits Drew cheerily, green paint on the bridge of his nose.

Anne has to adjust the seat belt to accommodate her bust. Sally, even when pregnant, must be quite small. Once she's strapped in she glances over her shoulder. Two hulking baby seats occupy most of the back of the car; how on earth are they going to squeeze in a third? The seats are thick with the paste of a thousand squashed biscuits, there's a chewed-up picture book in one seat and a Barbie torso in the other. The whole car smells as if it's fermenting. It's not unpleasant, it's like being trapped in a fruit smoothie bottle.

'How's your mother?' he asks, checking the wing mirror and turning down the stereo. Anne vaguely recognises the track, she thinks it might be by a band called Armpit or Elbow or something. She's glad he's a good driver. She relaxes; it's nice for someone else to be in charge for a change.

'She's the same really. I won't know much until I speak to the consultant tomorrow. Of course, her face is a mess, there's a lot of bruising. She doesn't really look like my mother, she looks like a picture in a newspaper. It's incredibly upsetting.' Tears well, she is on the verge of telling him more than he needs to know. She feels like she's about to spill the beans, a confession in her throat that might just be too big to swallow. What if she blurted it all out, what if she just said?

'I have been a dreadful daughter. I turned my back, I walked away. No, I didn't walk, I ran, I ran as far away as I could and it has been many years since my mother and I were able to look each other in the eye. I have shoved her to the back of my mind. I have dismissed her, I have tried to pretend that time is a great healer and that raking over the past is no help to anyone.'

But she doesn't, she swallows hard and changes the subject. She asks, 'And your wife, how is she?'

'Fed up to the back teeth,' he replies and for the next three miles he talks about Sally, about how amazing she is and how without her he is nothing. 'I can't cope with the girls,' he admits. 'I think both of them might be a bit mad, like witches or cuckoos. I can't tell what they are thinking but Sally can, she always knows. I think she is better at family than me, I think she's just got a better idea of how it's all meant to work. She's amazing really.'

Anne is quiet for a second. She wonders if Paul has ever described her as amazing. She doubts it. He would probably say that she was big-boned and good at making pastry.

'Children are hard work,' she tells Drew and despises herself for the cliché. At least she doesn't compound it by adding 'but they're worth it'. Because, deep down, she's not sure if they are. Most of the unhappiness that people experience is due to their offspring. Once you have children you can never really breathe easily again; from the moment they are born there is always a sense that something terrible might happen. Parenthood is painful, like indigestion. She retreats to the safer ground of small talk.

'And what are the doctors saying?'

Drew's hands tense on the wheel. 'They say that every minute the baby stays inside is a bonus. We just have to keep our fingers crossed.'

She's glad he doesn't talk about praying. She knows from experience that prayers don't work: she went through a phase of being rather fervent when she was a child and it never got her anywhere. She hasn't set foot in a church since her wedding, apart from when they're abroad, of course. Sometimes it's nice to pop into a chilly grey church just to get out of the heat.

He reminds her that they have to make a detour to pick up the girls. He says he hopes they are tired – he's tired. He says he dreads bath time: 'They're like mad dogs in the bath, water goes everywhere and sometimes they pinch each other. I never had siblings, I don't really understand the love/hate thing. I never knew small children could have so much emotion, they're like tiny jealous women: they laugh, they cry, they sulk, they want chocolate and attention and if I tickle Coral's feet then I have to tickle Amber's feet and it just goes on.'

She could say, 'I know, my sister and I, me and my sister . . .' But instead she fills the silence by blurting, 'I've got a chicken casserole, would you like to share it? I can give the girls a bath, you can heat up the casserole. There's plenty for everyone.'

She can feel him thinking; maybe the offer is a bit over the top. Maybe he thinks she's going to offer to rinse his underpants next.

But he's tired and he's hungry and he hasn't had a home-cooked meal in a week. He's sick of eating out of garages, he can't face another Ginsters, and once he's got the girls home it's not like he can just nip out down the road to the chippy. He can't leave them for a second, they'd set fire to each other.

'Go on then, you're on.'

'Good,' says Anne. 'Do you know if it's a boy or a girl?'

Drew shakes his head. 'I'm secretly hoping for a boy, but Sally doesn't want to know, she likes surprises. To be honest, I don't think it's going to be much of a surprise if it's another girl. She'll be as mad as the other two and I'll have to take refuge on the roof.'

Anne responds with yet another cliché – 'All children are different' – but privately she wonders if they really are. In some respects they're all the same: they're all self-obsessed and selfish; they all think they're the centre of the universe; they all want their own way; and 99.9 per cent of them would rather eat pizza than courgettes.

She sighs, but Drew is concentrating on the road. It's raining again, a cyclist is weaving, accidents are waiting to happen everywhere, lives on the brink of being ruined at any given second.

Five minutes later they pull up outside an ugly pebble-dashed terrace. This must be Sally's sister's house. Anne waits in the car and five minutes later Drew emerges holding a wriggly Amber, while a dumpy, rather slovenly-looking woman whom Anne would describe to her Dulwich cronies as 'a bit *Jeremy Kyle Show*' follows with a slumped Coral asleep in her arms.

Anne jumps out to open the back door. The fat blonde eyes her suspiciously. 'I'm Anne Armitage,' announces Anne, sounding like royalty on a walkabout of the northern slums. She has buried her Lancashire accent so deep that when she needs it she can't find it. She has a feeling she left it tucked down the back of her mother's sofa.

'This is Sally's sister Mandy,' indicates Drew with a nod of his head. 'Mandy, this is Anne, Jean from next door's daughter.' Mandy is tipping Coral into her seat, trying not to wake her as she fumbles around with the fastening.

'All right?' says Mandy, friendlier now that she's realised Anne can't be any possible threat to her sister. 'They've had their tea, I did them potato faces and beans.' Amber still has a baked-bean beard and is arching her back, making it difficult for her father to get her into her seat. 'Please, Amber?' he begs.

Anne takes over. 'Come on young lady, let's not have any nonsense!' To which Amber responds by arching almost double and screaming like a kettle.

Amber screams until she is in the bath. Anne scrabbles for the paracetamol in her bag. She really shouldn't have bothered – she could have had a nice quiet night – but now the screaming has stopped there is something about young children in the bath, a pinkness and sweetness that she cannot resist. She grabs a selection of books from a pile at the top of the stairs, stories she doesn't know, it's good to read new stories. She shows off a bit, she uses funny voices and the little girls look at her with round blue eyes and Coral sucks on a flannel.

They are heavy-lidded with tiredness, all they need now is to be tricked into bed. As long as they don't realise what is happening she will have them tucked up and asleep before they know it.

Getting children into bed is a military operation. If things go smoothly there will be no more fighting until the morning. Anne is calm and determined, the girls are befuddled and docile. They are scooped out of the bath, patted dry and rolled out of towels straight into nighties. Seconds later they are tucked under duvets, thumbs are in mouths, teddies are positioned and the bedside light set comfortingly low.

Yes, thinks Anne, tiptoeing out of the room, job done. It's only as she walks downstairs that she remembers she didn't clean their teeth. She's losing her touch.

Drew has set the table in the kitchen, even though the

casserole needs another thirty minutes. He has poured himself a lager but he offers Anne a glass of wine. It's sweet and German, she guesses, but she pretends to like it. She knows he would rather be slumped alone in front of the telly, but he has the manners to be grateful. 'I don't usually get them off to sleep till around ten, and then there's always one of them coming down wanting a drink or a poo.'

'You just have to be firm,' she tells him. Ha, that's a joke: since when has she been firm with hers? She has a horrible feeling that both her sons are capable of simply tuning out the sound of her voice. Her pleas for them to help, to do something, to get up, to take some responsibility, are reduced to a vague, annoying buzz. She is nothing more than tinnitus.

'Cheers.' She's surprised by how relaxed she feels. She's never really had any male friends before, not proper ones. You don't if you went to an all-girls school, you're never quite sure how to talk to them, even the ones you're married to.

For a moment she thinks about Paul and she has to recall a photograph of him before she can really remember his face. I have been married for twenty-five years, she thinks, but I still have no idea what makes my husband tick. But equally, she adds, he has been married to me for a quarter of a century and he has no idea who I really am either.

Paul is drinking gin and tonic in the bar with the boys. The boys (those who haven't gone bald) have grey hair and a couple of them are as paunchy as Humpty Dumpty, but on this first night of their holiday you can see in their faces the little lads they used to be. No one ever grows up completely, and although the evening will end with port and cigars on the balcony it won't really be over until Greg Taylor, who is fifty-three and a big cheese in the City, has apple-pied Justin Entwhistle's bed.

Paul should really borrow a phone and call home, but he's too drunk to care.

Jean

Wedding Ding Dong

'I can't remember you getting into such a tizz when we got married.' Jim was fed up with the Grainger Carmichael wedding. It had taken over Jean's life, all 'Penelope says this, Penelope says that'.

She'd still not met Mr Grainger Carmichael. All she knew was that he drove a powder blue Jaguar with leather seats the colour of butterscotch. There was a yellow Mini in the drive too. 'It's mine,' said Penelope, 'but the girls borrow it. Not that Belinda's passed her test.' Whenever Penelope mentioned Belinda her face would tighten. 'Helen's never been any trouble,' she would add, 'she'll make such a lovely bride.'

Jean nodded obediently, though privately she thought Helen would make a very average bride. She was a rather beige girl with an unfortunate mole in the crook of her nose. Not that the mole was evident in any of the silver-framed Helens on display in the sitting room. It seemed that the girl had been trained from a very early age to present her mole-free side to the camera.

She also looked better when her sister wasn't in the same frame. Belinda wasn't conventionally pretty but she had a spark to her. 'She can argue the back leg off a donkey, that one,' Penelope would mutter darkly. Belinda didn't approve of the wedding, she said the groom-to-be was a bully and a psychopath.

'Stuff and nonsense,' said Mrs Grainger Carmichael. 'I'm quite sure he's never laid so much as a finger on Helen.'

Roy, that was his name, a big beefy rugby-playing lad who worked in the same firm of solicitors as Mr Grainger Carmichael.

'I'm not interested,' said Jim when Jean insisted on imparting all this information.

Neither was Anne, but Jess was.

'How many bridesmaids again, Mum?'

'Three: two little ones and a big one, the bride's sister.'

'When I get married I'm going to have ten bridesmaids and none of them will be Anne.'

She had to take them once, both of them. Jim had a fixture at the bowls club and he wasn't prepared to fob it off. 'I've got a job too,' he told Jean.

Jean was furious – it meant Jess missing her Saturday afternoon dance class – but Penelope had been quite adamant: it had to be this Saturday afternoon, no ifs or buts.

'Helen wants a consultation,' she explained. 'She's worried that she might get a nasty shock when she comes down the aisle. It's not that she doesn't trust you,' she added a little lamely, 'it's just she'd like you to talk her through your design ideas and maybe you could bring some fabric swatches. We're still thinking purple, aren't we?'

'Shell pink,' Jean corrected and Penelope looked a bit doubtful.

'Well maybe you should show her a sample. It is her wedding after all.'

Actually I've always been good with colour, thinks Jean, lying in her hospital bed utterly drained of any.

She'd decided on raw silk for the bridesmaids, pale pink the colour of a baby's fingernail with lavender sashes – ballet length – like something out of a painting by that French fellow, the one that was forever doing dancers bending over and tying up their shoes, whatsis face? Degas, that was the chap.

She decided not to phone in advance, she'd rather just arrive with her daughters in tow. That way their presence would look like an unavoidable emergency. They bickered all the way over, pausing only to change buses. By the time they arrived Jean was so tense it physically hurt to smile.

Penelope had answered the door. As soon as she saw the girls one eyebrow disappeared into her newly dyed mahogany hairline.

'I'm ever so sorry to inconvenience you, Mrs Grainger Carmichael. I've had to bring my daughters because my husband has been called in to work.' She'd like to make out that Jim did something to merit all this fuss, but she didn't want to lie. She couldn't exactly pretend he was a kidney surgeon.

She wondered perhaps if Penelope imagined Jim to be an electrician or a plumber, a big handy cheerful chap in navy overalls who went around whistling with a pencil behind his ear. But then again she knew Penelope couldn't care less what Jim did, she was oblivious to everything and anything that didn't directly concern her.

Anne and Jess trudged in behind her. 'Pooh, what's that terrible smell?' piped Mrs Grainger Carmichael. They hadn't even made it to the kitchen. 'Someone has brought a woopsie into my house,' she squealed.

It was Anne, of course it was. They all had to turn to the wall and show Mrs Grainger Carmichael the undersides of their shoes. A dark orange turd was squashed beneath the heel of Anne's Start-rite lace-up.

Jean can feel herself burn with shame. Forty years on she can still feel the heat in her cheeks as she recalls Mrs Grainger Carmichael running around fetching newspaper and detergent. 'Take it off, for God's sake take that shoe off this instant. Open the door, open the door, that shoe is going outside this minute.'

After the drama with the shoe and the dog poo the children were confined to the kitchen to drink orange squash and eat custard creams while Jean, Helen and Penelope had their consultation.

'What about Belinda?' enquired Jean. 'I thought she might want to be involved.'

'She's out,' replied Mrs Grainger Carmichael, just a split-second before Helen said, 'She's not well.'

Jean found it hard to talk to Helen without staring at her mole. Fortunately the girl was too distracted by Jean's colour swatches and sketches to notice.

She was very complimentary. 'What lovely drawings,' she said. 'I wish I had been good at art, I was hopeless.'

'Yes, but you're clever,' her mother reminded her. 'And now you've done the cleverest thing a girl can do, you've found yourself a handsome young man with prospects. You don't get much cleverer than that.' Penelope visibly preened before helping herself to a large piece of shortbread. 'I know I shouldn't,' she tittered, and Jean made a mental note to cut Penelope's bolero a little more generously than she had previously intended.

'I did go to university,' Helen told Jean. The powder on the bride-to-be's face had worn off and she was all shiny. It was warm in the sun lounge and Helen started to take her cardigan off, but changed her mind. She shrugged it back on to her shoulders, but not before Jean saw the dark blue band of bruises around the girl's upper arm.

A floorboard creaked in the room above them and both Helen and her mother cast anxious glances to the ceiling.

I should have said something, if I'd said something about the bruising then surely Penelope would have stopped the wedding. There was still time, three months before the knot was to be tied. Eventually Helen would have found someone else, the same events would have happened but in a different order. But she kept her mouth shut and the first domino fell over. That's how she sees it now, a chain of events, one domino knocking over the next, right up to the last.

★   ★   ★

180

While Jean demonstrated her fabric swatches in the sun lounge the girls sat on high stools at the breakfast bar. Anne was just wearing one shoe, Jess still wore both; her shoes were clean but she needed a wee, badly. She was squirming on her seat, trying to squish the entrance to the wee hole so that the wee wouldn't come out, but it was coming and it would come soon, she couldn't hold on.

'I need to go to the toilet,' she told her sister.

Anne just shook her head. 'You can't, we just have to sit here and be good.'

Jess couldn't think what was good about leaving a puddle of wee under her stool. They'd already brought poo in, what kind of children would Mrs Grainger Carmichael think they were?

She slid off her stool and tiptoed out of the kitchen, one hand clutching at her front bottom and pressing hard to stop the flood. She needed to find a toilet and she needed to find one fast.

The Grainger Carmichaels had a downstairs cloakroom, of course (in burnt umber with imported Spanish tiles), but Jess was only used to bathrooms being upstairs so she headed for a wide set of uncarpeted steps. They weren't like the ones at home, they had holes between them, gaps you could slip through if you were young, like a baby. They were slippery too, because the wood was all shiny. The hallway still smelt of poo and washing-up liquid, but as she reached the landing she could smell something that reminded her of honey mixed in with perfume. It made the house smell like you could lick it.

The carpet on the landing was a shade of green that Jess hadn't seen before – Penelope would have described it as 'moss'. It melted as she stepped across it. For a second, as she glanced over her shoulder, she could see the trail of her footsteps; she could feel her heart beating in her chest and she could hear the tiny whistling noise that sometimes accompanied her breathing.

All the doors on the landing were shut. There were six of them, all wooden like the stairs, with shiny silver handles. There was a china plaque on one door, with pink roses and the name

Helen painted on it in curly writing. Another matching plaque, with little blue flowers on it and the name Belinda, hung from another door, only this one was cracked right across the middle. Jess wanted a plaque like Helen's, with pink roses and her name written all fancy. Anne could have a horrid broken one.

She opened a door without a plaque and bounced across Penelope Grainger Carmichael's new cream shagpile carpet. At the window was a dressing table, its three mirrors reflecting her face from different angles. She was the second prettiest girl in the class: only Sharon Kinnock was a bit prettier than her and last week she had been crying because she was going to have to wear glasses. Good.

Jess's mum didn't have a dressing table like this, she just had a hairbrush and a pink plastic mirror on a stand on top of a chest of drawers. This was much better. When I grow up, Jess thought to herself, I'm going to have silver brushes and all different perfumes with fancy labels.

She sat herself down on a stool with a pink and gold striped seat. The wee could wait. She opened a little pot of white cream and a voice behind her said, 'She'll kill you if she catches you touching her stuff.'

She was a big girl, bigger than Anne even, and she was wearing a dressing gown, a pale blue quilted one.

'I'm Belinda.'

'I just wanted the toilet.'

The big girl pointed and Jess stumbled from the dressing table into a cool green cave of a room with a shower in the corner. 'Green onyx,' Penelope would have told her. She dropped her pants before it was too late. The wee was hot and a lot, a lot of hot wee: she almost laughed. 'Are you OK?' the big girl asked.

'Yes thanks,' answered Jess. To the side of the sink unit was a gold lion's face. He held a ring in his mouth and a pale green hand towel was looped through this ring. It was the most beautiful thing Jessica had ever seen. This is the way to live, she thought, in this toilet with its walls made from hard striped green waves and its golden lion.

By the time she emerged from the bedroom the big girl was on the landing. 'Are you ill?' asked Jess. The only time she was in her dressing gown in the afternoon was when the tubes in her chest got all soggy and she had to lie on the sofa until it was time for another steam. Steaming was when you put your head over a bowl of hot water and your mum put brown stuff in it. That made the water go yellow, like witches' sick.

'Yes darling, I'm hungover and I feel like shit. That'll teach me to drink Campari. Fucking hell, this house stinks of shit,' she said, and then disappeared behind the door with the cracked 'Belinda' sign.

Anne was still in the kitchen. She'd eaten all the custard creams; she was like that, was Anne, once she started eating she never really stopped.

She didn't bother looking up, she was reading a book. She liked reading. Jess didn't; it was hard work, she could do one word at a time but long sentences were tricky and chapter books were a nightmare. Anne just read books like they were custard creams, one after the other. That's why she thought she knew everything, because of all the stuff she read in books, but she didn't know everything. She didn't know Jess had met Belinda and she certainly wasn't going to tell her either. Jess sat there grinning. The secret was inside her tummy, as warm as cocoa.

Anne

Making Pompoms with Mrs Gaga

Nat and Jools have come to a decision: they will have the party on Saturday night, but they won't advertise the fact on Facebook. Neither of them is that stupid, they have both been to gatherings that have got out of hand. Solid Victorian houses left quivering on their foundations, sixteen-year-old girls with blotchy faces sobbing hysterically in hallways as gate crashers piss in umbrella stands, wardrobes are ransacked for designer handbags and ecstasy is dropped in tropical-fish tanks.

Attending a party where the police have had to be called is a badge of honour among the privately educated sons and daughters of South London. Sirens are cool, arrests de rigueur and anyway, what they haven't actually seen for themselves they have heard about second hand.

Nat and Jools try to trump each other's stories of parties gone wrong.

Jools almost went to one in Sydenham last year where 'this guy drove the lawn mower into the pool'; however Nat tops this with a tale of a party he was meant to go to where the birthday girl 'choked to death on her own sick in the sauna cabin'.

They decide thirty guests is probably around the right number, with totty outnumbering blokes at a ratio of two to one. They will start texting the chosen few at lunchtime tomorrow: spontaneity is the key. Jools reckons that if he invites twenty people thirty will turn up.

Nat would like to be able to summon as many guests but very few of his boarding-school mates live close enough to make the trek over to Dulwich. After all, it's not exactly Notting Hill.

As Hetty van Oss said to him once, 'Oh yah, Dulwich, that's like near Croydon, yah?' Nat could have said, 'Actually it's nearer Brixton and Peckham,' but that would only have made matters worse.

At Nat's boarding school, living in an unfashionable postcode with a surgeon and a teacher for parents scored very few points.

The Armitages are wealthy but not stinking rich. Where are the polo ponies, the private helicopters and the ski chalet in Klosters? Why aren't his parents in fashion or the film industry?

Really, fumes Nat, when you think about it, Anne and Paul are a bit crap.

He scrapes the bottle-opener down the side of the coffee table. Some teenagers cut themselves; whenever Nat feels the pressure of family life he takes it out on the house. There are thirty-seven cigarette burns in various carpets and curtains, and a long blue biro scribble all along the landing. 'Where the hell did that come from?' shrieked Anne when she discovered it.

Anne thinks her sons are heavy on the house; she has no idea that the mysterious scratches and marks are in any way deliberate acts of vandalism, but they are. Take the scuff marks on the doors: there is something about his mother that makes Nat want to kick a door shut rather than close it.

It wouldn't bother him so much if either of his parents were in any way glamorous, but Anne is the antithesis of the MILFs who used to turn up at his school with great tits and high heels. Women who looked good in convertibles. Of course they were usually second or even third wives. Nat knows plenty of boys in his year whose birth mothers are tucked away somewhere discreet in the country, women who were as dumpy and embar-rassing as his own mother, but at least had the grace to stay away.

Not Anne. Possibly the biggest relief of leaving school is that he will no longer have to suffer the indignity of his fat-bottomed mother with her foghorn voice letting him down on Founder's Day, insisting on marching around the school bellowing stupid questions like, 'Have you got any of your art work on the wall, Nat? You used to be so good at colouring-in.' Fuck's sake, just the thought of Anne makes Nat's teeth grate.

It's easier for Jools, lots of boys in his year have embarrassing mothers. Earnest Dulwich Village types marching around in horrible dog-walking shoes, book club women obsessed with UCAS forms and league tables.

The truth of the matter, thinks Nat, is that the more academic the establishment, the easier it is to appear cool. No wonder Jools is so popular, he's an Adonis in a sea of maths geeks and Latin freaks, some of whom are bussed in from downtown Streatham.

Nat, on the other hand, has spent the past five years competing not academically (they were all there because they were thick) but socially with the heirs of Greek oil tycoons and diamond merchants. It's not that any of them was particularly better-looking than him, it's just hard to be a big fish in a pond full of gold-plated sharks. Deep down Nat knows his life would be easier if he had a family crest.

'Leave me to do the pimping, my son,' sniggers Jools. 'I'll get us a nice mix of posh and slutty. Now what are we thinking drugs-wise?'

While her sons discuss the various merits of ketamine versus MDMA, Anne is relaxing with her third glass of sweet white wine. 'I've been in this house before,' she tells Drew. He is wiping a slice of white bread round his plate, mopping up the juices of her chicken casserole. Paul would never do that; a well-bred man leaves his plate pooled with gravy.

'A very old woman lived here when I was a little girl; she had a lot of cats and she taught me how to make pompoms, I could do pompom-making with your girls, though they're a bit young. It's quite fiddly and I'd have to do the cutting bit for them.' She is rambling, she shouldn't drink.

'Anyway, as I was saying, the house stank. She was terrifying, cats hanging off her like scarves, tiny kittens stuck to her cardigan like brooches, pockets full of them.'

Drew looks up from the paper and interrupts her. 'Actually Sal and I bought the house from an old man. His wife had just died. I don't think there were any cats.'

'No,' says Anne, determined not to slur, 'they were the couple who bought the house off the Parkers, who moved in after Mrs Gaga passed away. My dad had to call the police. Milk bottles on the doorstep: when she hadn't taken them in for three days it was obvious something was wrong. What with the cats, she was milk mad, three pints a day, all crowded on the front step they were, half of them turned to cheese. It was summer, my dad shouted through the letterbox, he said all you could hear were bluebottles and cats.'

'Do you mind if I watch *Have I Got News for You?*'

He's ever so polite, thinks Anne, and she nods. 'Of course, don't mind me, I'm just rabbiting on.'

He doesn't want to be dragged down memory lane, she tells herself, and for the next thirty minutes she laughs when he does as oh-so-clever comedians skewer the news, but she hasn't got a clue what's going on. She's miles away. She's thinking of a terrible time long ago when she spent an entire night in this house.

She's never told anyone about what happened, not properly. To be honest, no one had ever asked. She'd been looked after and that was the main thing. Only she wasn't, she wouldn't have let her own boys be looked after by a creature like that. You don't just fob your kids off on a stinky madwoman who's more cat hair than sense.

'Taken your sister to the hospital, have they? Well you won't see her again.'

That's what Mrs Gaga had said. 'Oh no, the only way that one will be coming home will be in a box. Pretty thing as well, your mother will miss her, I'd say. Mothers like a pretty girl and you're no oil painting are you dear?'

Hours she'd sat there, with her hands outstretched while Mrs Gaga wound loose skeins of wool into tight round balls.

'I had two of my own you know, two little boys. Nice boys, no trouble, they went to hospital and they never came out alive. Diphtheria, dear, it's a terrible thing. They'd be big boys now but they didn't live. I've got a photo of them somewhere.'

And she dug a biscuit tin out from under a pile of newspapers. Inside there were lots of black-and-white photos, all faded and freckled with brown spots around the edges. 'This one's Michael and this one's Patrick, or is it the other way around? They've been dead in the ground for fifty years, dear, and my eyes aren't what they used to be.'

Mrs Gaga's irises behind her big tortoiseshell glasses were a milky blue while the whites were threaded with red veins.

'Michael's ears stuck out,' she went on, 'and Patrick liked a good laugh. Thing is, when I look at these photos both of them have got sticky-out ears and I can't for the life of me remember how that laugh used to sound.'

A large black cat purred around her ankles. 'That's Jemima,' she said, 'I can tell without even looking. Now I've had a good idea: why don't you and me make Jemima a pompom?'

They made five pompoms that night, including a giant one made out of three different colours of wool, pale green, white and lemon. 'It'll help you take your mind off your poor sister,' said Mrs Gaga, only it didn't. Anne found she could make pompoms and think about Jessica at the same time. She wondered if maybe she was to blame. Had she brought a germ into the house on her cardigan, had she touched her sister without washing her hands? If Jessica died, would it be her fault?

Mrs Gaga didn't do things like bath time or teeth cleaning, she just gave Anne some lemon squash and a Peek Frean and said she could make herself comfortable on the sofa and that she'd see her in the morning.

'I suppose the funeral will be some time next week,' she muttered, turning off the lights.

It was twenty-past eleven when Anne woke up; she was slumped in the armchair, a dark patch of dribble staining the pale pink cushion beneath her cheek.

Drew was hovering over her. 'I didn't want to wake you, but I'm knackered.'

'She wouldn't let me take the giant pompom, I wanted it for Jess but she said it was Jemima's.'

Drew cocked his head. 'I'm not sure what you're talking about. It's late, you'll be wanting to get back next door.'

She'd woken to the smell of fish. Mrs Gaga got scraps from the fishmonger's and boiled them up for her cats. 'You've to be careful of the bones,' she told Anne. 'You don't want your babies choking to death, not like Patrick and Michael.'

Her father had rung the bell. She remembers the knot in her stomach, the invisible hand that squeezed her heart and made it hard to breathe. 'Ah this will be it,' said Mrs Gaga. 'Tell your mother I'm sorry for her loss and tell her to get a kitty, a nice little kitty.'

The door opened; the light outside was blinding, all she could see was her father's silhouette. She ran at his legs.

'It's all right pet, she's all right, your sister's all right.'

And behind her she heard the door shut.

Jean

A Plague on this Wedding

The day of the wedding was drawing closer. Over the intervening months Mrs Grainger Carmichael had grown rather fond of Jean, and would tell anyone who would listen that the 'little woman' was 'worth her weight in gold'.

Jean found Penelope hard to say no to. One night she found herself dragging a massive suitcase full of chintz all the way home on the bus.

'I'm just shortening some curtains for Penny,' she explained to Jim.

'But you don't do curtains,' snapped Jim. She didn't, not as a rule, but as Jim said, it was one rule for the Grainger Carmichaels and another rule for everyone else.

Anyway, it wasn't just curtains. Now that Helen trusted her, Jean was making the bride-to-be a few bits for her honeymoon, including an ivory satin negligée with a matching kimono-style wrap.

'They're off to Sorrento in Italy,' she informed Jim. 'Mrs Grainger Carmichael has bought Helen some beautiful matching luggage and when they come back they're moving into a lovely old cottage in Wrea Green. Roy's uncle, who's a builder, has been doing it up for them. Apparently the kitchen's got all mod cons.'

Jim didn't know why he should be interested in any of this guff. 'Who's Roy when he's at home?'

Jean got very upset at this and recalls almost stamping her foot. (Ah, to be able to do that now!)

'You know, Roy's the groom. Honestly Jim, just because these people aren't sitting drinking brown ale in their vests you think they're from another planet.'

'They might as well be,' muttered Jim. Spending time at Weeping Willows was turning his wife into a terrible snob. The other day he'd found pâté sandwiches in his lunchbox!

'Can I not just have cheese and pickle?' he begged. She'd bought olives too, black and briny, but Anne was the only one who liked them.

'Her's a whole wol ou there,' breathed Jean. She meant 'There's a whole world out there', but she had taken to putting on an Anne French face mask once a week. Mrs Grainger Carmichael swore by them. Jean lay down carefully on top of the counter-pane with a slice of cucumber over each eye.

'What a waste of cucumber,' grumbled Jim. 'I could have had that in a sandwich.' Jean pretended not to hear.

The call came on the Tuesday morning, four days before the wedding. When she first picked up the phone Jean thought she had a dirty old man on the other end of the line: 'Honestly Jim, I nearly put the phone down.' But it wasn't a nuisance call, it was Mrs Grainger Carmichael and she was hyperventilating. 'God's honour, Jim, she sounded like a creature from *Dr Who*.'

Jean couldn't fathom out what on earth the woman was trying to say. 'Just take a deep breath, Penelope,' she hazarded. She didn't often tell her clients how to breathe.

Eventually the woman calmed down enough to relay the story, the gist of which went as follows:

'Oh my God, Jean, you'll never guess. It's all too awful, I can't bear it. I've vomited with the stress, Jean, vomited. That brat of a bridesmaid, Roy's side of the family, you know the one, five but big for her age, that one, the one meant to be fulfilling the role of flower girl to the happy couple? Well she's only gone and contracted chicken pox, the selfish child! I've seen her, Jean, what a mess, absolutely covered in weeping sores. Her face is positively oozing. There's no earthly way that child can be in the photos, the day would be ruined. It's a catastrophe.' Penelope paused. Jean could hear her shuddering as she drew breath. 'So I was wondering . . .?'

'Don't be so daft,' spluttered Jim. 'Why would they want our Jessica to be the bridesmaid? She's not family. I've not heard anything so silly in my life.'

'She's the same size, give or take half an inch,' Jean argued. 'I'm going to be there on the day to help with the veil and the train so I can keep an eye on her. Anyway, it's not just being a bridesmaid: they want her to skip down the aisle scattering rose petals. She'd be a flower girl as well as a bridesmaid, and God knows our Jessica can skip. She can skip better than that lummox of a cousin.'

He didn't stand a chance, not when Jess got to hear of it. She was spinning with excitement, clapping her hands and shrieking, 'It's like a dream come true.'

Anne buried her head in her hands. 'Can you not shut her up, Mum, she's giving me a headache.'

Honestly, sometimes having Anne around was like sharing the house with a middle-aged woman!

Jean hasn't let herself think of the wedding in such a long time that it's all jumbled up, flakes of prawn vol-au-vent here, a blizzard of confetti there.

There are bits of it she'd like to leave in the back of a locked drawer but she knows she can't; what's happened has happened and hiding it away doesn't un-happen it.

They popped round to Weeping Willows after school the next day. They left Anne at home: her father would be back by five. It was only for an hour, she was a sensible girl and there was plenty of pâté and some olives in the fridge.

The bridesmaid's dress was a tiny bit big for Jess. 'Better too big than too small,' gushed Penelope Grainger Carmichael, 'and she's a lot prettier than that Caroline. Don't get me wrong, I'm not blaming Roy, he's a nice-looking fellow and he'll make a handsome groom.'

'If you like gorillas in morning suits,' sneered Belinda, wandering into the sun lounge wearing her tennis whites. 'Hello kiddo,' she winked at Jess, 'joining us on the big day then?'

Jess went peony pink and whispered a barely audible 'Yes please.' Belinda picked up a magazine and sashayed out. She had grass stains on the backside of her otherwise pristine shorts.

'At least I can rely on one bridesmaid not to let us down,' huffed Penelope.

The plan was that Jess should skip down the aisle prettily strewing red rose petals – 'Real ones, none of your dried rubbish' – followed by the bride, who would of course be accompanied by her father. The flower girl should then stand or sit (as required during the service) to one side until the ceremony was over, when she would repeat the whole operation, this time with a basket of white petals.

'Isn't it an adorable idea, Jean?' Jean agreed. Penelope went on to explain that Belinda would take care of the four-year-old bridesmaid, but that Jess would be unchaperoned.

'Do you think she's up to it?' enquired the mother of the bride, looking even more like an anxious pug than she normally did.

'Yes,' said Jean, sounding more confident than she felt. Deep down she was a bit worried: Jess's concentration wasn't like Anne's, she was easily distracted and following the service would be tricky, what with her reading being that bit behind.

'Of course the most important thing between now and Saturday is that she doesn't catch chicken pox,' laughed Mrs Grainger Carmichael, but behind the laughter lurked a tiny threat of violence.

Jean decided to keep Jess off school for the next couple of days, just to be on the safe side.

Jim was furious: 'How is she ever meant to catch up if you stop her from going all the time?'

'It doesn't matter, it's the end of term anyway.' But he was right, she was being ridiculous, though to be honest she didn't care.

Books and reading weren't going to figure large in Jessica's future, Jean was sure of this. Call it a mother's instinct: her youngest daughter was going to be a dancer and skipping down the aisle at the biggest wedding in Lytham St Annes' recent history was just a start.

The next two days were nerve-racking. Not only did Jean have to worry about Anne getting to and from school by herself, but she had to stop herself from checking Jess for chicken-pox blisters every five minutes. She gave her a manicure on the Thursday night. 'You're never painting her nails,' gasped Jim.

'It's only clear polish,' Jean snapped back. Jess, quivering with excitement, looked a bit flushed. 'Anne, fetch the thermometer, would you?'

On Friday morning Jean awoke to coughing from down the landing and her heart froze. Jess had been so well for so long now, the nightmare emergency was almost a distant memory, but what if . . . what if? After all, there are worse things for a little girl to come down with than chicken pox. 'Please God, don't let lightning strike the same delicate chest twice,' prayed Jean.

Fortunately it was just Anne. She did have a tendency to be a little phlegmy first thing in the morning, but by the time she set off to school she was fine. She couldn't be ill, look what she'd eaten for breakfast: two bowls of cereal and a slice of toast. She had the constitution of a carthorse, that one.

Just twenty-four hours to go, thought Jean.

Yes, remembers her twenty-first-century self, in twenty-four hours it would be D Day, or rather W Day. Time ticks by, it always has and it always will. Scientists have invented just about everything else, but they cannot turn back time. Time on earth is like gravity, you cannot stop it from happening. Nothing is more reliable than time. Good things and bad things happen and neither last for ever, everything is over in the end.

The ward is almost silent, all the patients are asleep or in comas. The only sound comes from the rustling of sweet wrappers in reception. Two nurses are squabbling over a tin of Quality Street.

'Have you just swiped the last purple one, you fat cow?'

'Shhhh.'

Anne

The ND Puzzle

Anne opens her eyes and for a moment she cannot remember where she is. It takes a second for everything to slot into place. It's Saturday morning, she is in her mother's bed, her mother is in hospital, her husband is in Portugal and her sons are in London with their paternal grandmother, the one that can still walk, talk and, with any luck, clean silver.

It's time she spoke to her mother-in-law. It's eight o'clock, so Ellen will be up, pottering around the kitchen in her Liberty paisley-print dressing gown, making herself Earl Grey tea (black, no sugar, slice of lemon).

She dials her own number only to hear her own voice. No wonder the boys don't listen to her, she does sound incredibly annoying.

She tries not to feel panicky. Don't be silly, Anne, if there had been a fire it would be on the news. If anything dreadful had happened the police would track you down. They must be having a lie-in. She leaves herself a cheery message.

'It's me! Anne, Mum. Hello Ellen, I just wanted to check you're all OK. Call me back, I'm using my mother's landline, forgot my charger. I'll try to get one today. I hope the boys are behaving. I'll be at the hospital this afternoon, but I'll be here tonight. I'll try again later.'

All sorts of alarm bells are ringing in her head. No one really checks the answer phone these days, not now everyone communicates via mobile. She just needs to sort herself out a charger. As soon as her BlackBerry is juiced up there will doubtless be a whole heap of messages and texts waiting for her, and anyway Paul has no doubt managed to talk to his mother. Surely he'd have called her if he was worried. He must have her mother's number in his phone.

Hasn't he?

All of a sudden a wave of fury washes through her. Fucking hell, they are all such selfish cunts. Here she is dealing with a dying mother and if none of them can be bothered to contact her to see if she is all right, then they can fend for themselves until she gets back.

Anyway, why does she have to take responsibility for everything? Just because she is a middle-aged woman, why does everything have to land on her plate?

For the next hour she lies back on her mother's pillows and thinks about her life and how she came to be who and what she is.

This is something she rarely does; there's never the time. Maybe it's being here? Back where she began, back in a place where once upon a time she knew nothing of what was going to happen, good or bad.

She wonders if her husband is being faithful. She thinks he probably is: he's not the catch he used to be, his extra-curricular bonking days are over. She has turned a blind eye three times during their marriage, sat it out, let the affairs run their course.

Maybe she should have made more of a fuss, rocked the boat, but when you have a lovely thirties Dulwich Village boat sometimes it's best just to cling to the sides and weather the storms.

None of Paul's affairs was a serious threat: two medical secretaries and a barmaid. The barmaid was a surprise; she worked at Dulwich Golf Club, a very young widow with a five-year-old son. Anne had to wait nine months for that one to go off the boil.

He stopped messing about as soon as his sons became sexually active; it was as if he was passing on some kind of baton to the next generation.

These days he likes his golf, motor racing on the television and talking about buying a handmade bicycle so that he can take advantage of the local velodrome.

We have been together for twenty-five years, she notes, and apart from what is going on in my mind there is very little that he doesn't know about me.

She was always very honest with him. After all, they were seeing each other when it happened, but he has filed her past away for her and if she mentioned her sister now she has a horrible feeling he would struggle to remember her name.

Jessica, Auntie Jess, the boys found out about her before they'd officially decided to tell them.

Oddly enough, it was the last time she talked about it openly, years ago when they were in Majorca with the Robinsons. She'd had too much to drink, one of those long barbecue nights when Nat was about eight. Melanie Robinson had been going on about how awful her sister was, so she'd just waded in with 'At least you've got a sister,' and the whole story came flooding out.

'I don't believe it,' Melanie kept repeating. 'Why haven't you told me this before?'

Later Paul told her he thought her outburst had been attention-seeking and in poor taste, that it was the kind of story that could upset children. She remembers defending herself: 'They were out of earshot, Paul,' and she really thought they were. She thought they were all playing swingball right at the bottom of the garden.

Only Hannah wasn't. The boys didn't want to play with her so she was hiding under the table, her great flappy ears sticking out of her frizzy hair. She would have been about six, that loose front tooth of hers hanging on by a thread. Later that night she must have told the boys. Anne can imagine her all puffed up with her big secret, desperate to spill it. She can hear her needy little voice: 'I know something that you don't know.'

Nat mentioned it in the car the next day. They were on their way to Palma to look at the cathedral.

'Hannah says that you had a sister, Mummy, and that she would be called Auntie Jess.'

Paul had shot her a warning look, one that meant 'Leave this to me.' She had a hangover anyway, she couldn't form proper words so it was best he explained it.

So he did. One of Paul's great skills, realises Anne, is that he is boring. She recalls listening almost in awe as he managed to make even the most extraordinary and terrible of stories sound too dull to bother thinking about again.

And so it was that the memory of Auntie Jess had been conveniently cleared up and tidied away. Within minutes they were playing the number-plate game. By mid-afternoon the only one who still seemed remotely affected by the story was Hannah.

It was around three o'clock by the time they wandered into the cool of Palma Cathedral and they let the children experience being 'a bit Catholic' by lighting candles and kneeling down to say a prayer. It was at this point that Anne heard Hannah lisp, 'Dear God, I pray you magic back my friends' Auntie Jess.' Meanwhile, kneeling on the other side of her, she could hear her eldest son fervently praying for a Tamagotchi.

That's the difference between girls and boys, concludes Anne. Girls, on the whole, are more sensitive. As a child herself, a lost aunt would have been a dreadful tragedy, something to weep over at night, but to the boys an aunt who bought neither birthday nor Christmas gifts (or Easter eggs for that matter) was literally not worth a candle.

By the time Anne has done all this remembering it is twenty-past nine and she is starving. At home she could nip down the road to the deli and buy some delicious pains au chocolat, however the cake shop over the road is more iced bun than patisserie. She will boil herself an egg.

Anne traipses downstairs in her nightie. It's even colder than it was yesterday; she wishes she'd brought her dressing gown. The one hanging on the back of her mother's door is minute. Trying to squeeze into it would only depress her.

She searches in her mother's cupboard for an egg cup. The old ones are long gone: hers was a chunky pink elephant, her sister had the chick. There was never any question of doing a swap. Her father had the pig and her mother had the sheep, it was how things were.

Her sister wasn't a good eater when she was a little girl, but if she finished her egg her mother would turn it upside down and draw a face on the empty shell in felt-tip pen, a ring master with curly moustaches, a princess or a clown. Once the drawing was done her sister was allowed to smash the fragile egg head with her teaspoon.

Her mother was good at drawing, so it was something she expected one of her boys to inherit. It didn't seem fair that Nat had copped her mother's dyslexia but none of her creativity. She used to pore over his pictures looking for signs of an artistic nature, but it simply wasn't there.

Her mother has a calendar in the kitchen. Anne buys her one every Christmas: she goes to the shop at Tate Britain (less crowded than Tate Modern) and tries to remember what she bought the previous year so that she can pick something different. This year it's William Morris prints. The picture for October is 'Golden Lily' and some of the numbered boxes below the picture have been written on in biro. Her mother's handwriting belongs to another era, small and cramped with lots of loops. There is a memo on the 10th to pay the gas bill and next Tuesday her mother has an eleven o'clock B and T appointment. Her mother has a habit of abbreviating words, it's a way of avoiding her spelling issues. Apart from the cryptic B and T the letters N and D are scribbled in the top left-hand corner of every other square.

The phone rings. Anne snatches it . . . At last. 'Hello.'

'Hello Jean.'

Whoever it is sounds like Betty Turpin from *Coronation Street*, not that Anne watches it.

'No, it's not Jean, it's Anne, her daughter.'

'Oh, I've heard all about you.' For some reason this sounds like a rebuke. 'Is your mother in? It's Pat.'

Anne explains the situation to whoever Pat might be. The old woman responds with silence, then says, 'Oh, only I bought a lot of haddock from the wet fish van in Ansdell yesterday and I put half of it in the freezer. I was just seeing if she fancied it.'

'Not at the moment.'

Anne puts the phone down. Bad news affects people differently; it takes a while for it to sink in sometimes.

Two minutes later, the phone rings again.

'Hello, is that Jean's daughter Anne?'

'It is.'

'I'm Noreen. Pat's just told me. We'll be visiting later. Your mother's a very good friend: we do bums and tums together at the institute.'

'On a Tuesday?' Anne chips in. Funny how things start to fit into place.

She puts the phone down. She's glad her mother has friends, it makes the hospital bundle a little less sad, though why she should feel the need to exercise is beyond Anne. Her mother has never had much of a bum or a tum, she belongs to that exasperating band of women, the naturally petite.

Come to think of it, muses Anne, all my life I have felt bigger than my mother, even when I physically can't have been.

She should do bums and tums too. When she gets back she'll renew her membership at the local gym, it's time she sorted herself out. She needs to do something aerobic, lose some weight. No wonder her family treat her with such disdain.

What on earth does ND stand for?

The egg is boiled. She makes some toast and sits down properly at the table. He mother has salt and white pepper, no black. How quaint, thinks Anne, wishing she'd brought a small black-pepper grinder as well as her dressing gown. Once the egg is finished she turns it over and on the empty shell she draws a girl's face. She uses a biro and the lines are all wobbly, it's not very good. She picks up her teaspoon and caves in the girl's head.

Then she feels guilty. Her mother's head has been smashed like this, blood and goo running like yolk into the road. The accident is under investigation; the police have yet to apprehend the motorcyclist but according to several eyewitnesses it wasn't entirely his fault, the old woman had apparently just stepped off the pavement. But why? What had Jean been thinking, what on earth does ND mean and why had her mother been covered in cake?

Jean

The Big Day

It's time to remember the wedding. Jean hopes she has the energy to get through the events of the whole day without drifting off. It keeps happening, the sorting out of the past is as exhausting as being up, conscious and spring-cleaning the entire house.

The trouble with the wedding day is that it has some good parts and some terrible parts. To some extent it is one of the defining days of her whole life. This was the day when everything changed, a day that started so well and ended so dreadfully. What's odd is that even though she knows the outcome she can't help feeling excited by the prospect of reliving the events.

'So,' she says silently to herself, 'don't rush things, take it slowly, enjoy the nice bits,' and even though she has a tube down her throat and has not eaten solid food for days, once again she can taste the sweetness of wedding-cake icing melting on her tongue and smell the lily-of-the-valley of a long-withered bridal bouquet.

It's the 28th of July 1973, David Bowie is Aladdin Sane, Edward Heath is Britain's blue-blazered Prime Minister and Roger Moore is the latest and smoothest James Bond.

Jean has woken up with butterflies in her stomach. The weather has been unreliable all week, thick grey clouds scudding over dishwater skies. What if it's raining?

But the sun is already peering around a crack in the curtains and the bedroom is bathed in a honey-coloured glow. She knows before she pulls back the velvet drapes that the sky is going to be the blue of forget-me-nots.

She bathed the girl last night, her silky hair is washed, she will leave her to sleep while she gets herself sorted. Jim is snoring gently, his face waxy in the light. Look how yellow he is.

She'd asked if he wanted to come. 'There'll be quite a crowd on the pavement outside, we won't be able to talk to you but we could give you a wave.'

'Why would I want to go and see two people I've never met in my life get wed?' he'd asked, genuinely perplexed.

She didn't understand how he could possibly stay away. 'Well if you're at a loose end and Anne fancies it, we're at St Anne's Parish Church at half-past twelve. Now, you'll have to sort your dinner out. Jess and I have been invited to the do after the church at the Grand Hotel. Don't worry about us getting home, Mr Grainger Carmichael is insisting we get a cab. I can't imagine we shall be late, after all I shan't know anyone, but I think it's good for Jess to get used to mingling with these types.'

Jim rolled his eyes. 'She's a kid.'

To make up for not being around later to make Jim or Anne's dinner or tea, she decided to make bacon sandwiches for breakfast. It was important to line the stomach on a big day.

Jess didn't want bacon, she wanted an egg, so Jean boiled her one and placed it in the yellow chick-shaped cup. She timed it just right, the white firm but the yolk still runny.

She usually made her daughters get up and dressed before breakfast but today she wanted to make sure everything was put on clean right at the last moment. The girls liked having breakfast in their nighties, it was a novelty.

'Can we go to the library, Dad?'

Trust her, trust Anne to choose a mouldy old library over a

big society wedding on this, the most glorious summer day of the year. Typical.

Jean got hold of Jess's empty egg, turned it upside down and on to the delicate freckled shell she drew Anne's miserable-looking face, complete with her unflattering National Health specs. Jess laughed at the sight of Egg Anne and then smashed her felt-tip sister's head in with her silver teaspoon, and Jean laughed too.

She wishes she hadn't now. What's that word Pat always says? Karma, that's the one. Basically, if you do something nasty then something nasty will happen to you. Pat knows this to be true because when she was slagging off her daughter-in-law to Noreen a great big pigeon flew by and did a shit on her head.

'Nothing *lucky* about that if you ask me,' said Pat.

After breakfast she helped Jess into her second-best dress, the one she used to wear for parties last year but due to a Ribena stain had been demoted. It was a just a little yellow sundress with some smocking on the front, it would fold up easily into a carrier bag. Jean wasn't sure if Jess would be wearing her bridesmaid's dress home or if the Grainger Carmichaels would claim it back straight after the reception.

She'd bought her daughter a new set of underwear, Ladybird 100 per cent cotton. Jess tucked the vest into the knickers; they were a bit baggy even though they were for ages four to five years.

She'd bought her new socks too: white ankle socks, two pairs just in case. Jess was due to get changed into her bridesmaid's dress at Weeping Willows with the other bridesmaids. It was all arranged, they were being fetched at nine o'clock. 'On the dot,' shrieked Penelope, who had become so shrill as the wedding approached that Jean was surprised all the windows at Weeping Willows hadn't shattered.

Belinda arrived to pick them up in the Mini. Jean was sure she'd heard Penelope say the girl hadn't passed her test but she didn't dare raise the matter now. What if she said, 'No, I'm still a learner,' and Jim overheard and put his foot down about them getting in the car? No, best keep her trap shut. The girl had got here in one piece and with any luck she'd get them back in one piece. Anyway, there was no time to start faffing around with buses.

'Ready to roll?' Belinda was wearing a pair of denim pedal-pushers and a pink floral shirt. She hadn't done the buttons up properly on the shirt and she looked like she'd slept in last night's make-up. 'Let's go. I stink like a polecat and I need a shower. Bye Mr Collins, bye Anne.'

Jean glanced at Anne. She'd arranged herself on the sofa casually reading a book, a study of disinterest, but she couldn't help but look thrilled when Belinda remembered her name.

'Drive safely,' said Jim as they followed Belinda to the car, and Jean remembers thinking, If we crash, I hope I die.

Jess hopped in the back and Jean, her stomach in a knot as hard as a fist, sat next to Belinda in the front. The words 'Oh God, oh God, oh God' echoed around her head, but Belinda seemed to be quite a good driver. At least, she managed to pull out, turn the radio on and light a cigarette without incident.

Jean was glad Belinda opened the window: you don't want a flower girl stinking of ciggies. Belinda smoked and sang along to the Rolling Stones' 'Jumpin' Jack Flash' and Jean surprised herself by joining in with the chorus while Jess laughed her head off in the back.

'It's a gas, gas, gas,' they yelled, and for the first time in ages Jean felt too young to be a married mother of two growing girls.

The gravel driveway at Weeping Willows overflowed with unfamiliar cars. Belinda parked the Mini further up the road. 'The silver Merc belongs to Uncle Norman and Auntie Vi,' she informed Jean. 'They'll be taking you to the church, while you, Miss Monkey, will be in the posh car with me.'

Jess squealed, of course she did. It was all Jean could do not to squeal too.

Weeping Willows was a hub of activity. Mrs Glinn let them in and Jean followed Belinda up to her bedroom. Helen's bedroom door was shut. 'Mum's in there with the hairdresser, make-up girl, Uncle Tom Cobley and all,' whispered Belinda. 'Talk about tense.' Belinda's bedroom was uncharacteristically tidy. Three walls were painted in three different shades of purple while the fourth wall featured a psychedelic wallpaper that made Jean's eyes go all funny.

In the corner of the room was a built-in vanity unit with a plum-coloured hand basin and a mirror above it. It wasn't just Jean's eyes that had gone all funny: Jess's were practically standing out on stalks.

The other little bridesmaid was sitting on the bed while her mother brushed her hair. 'Ow, you're pulling me!' Charlotte was a four-year-old piggy-faced brunette. The mother was a similarly piggy-faced thirty-something woman called Carol.

'Stop wriggling then,' snapped Carol.

Belinda sniffed under her armpits. 'I'm just going to jump in the shower. I'll ask Mrs Glinn to bring up some drinks and stuff.' And off she went.

'They look very nice,' said Carol, nodding in the general direction of the bridesmaids' dresses, which hung from the back of the bedroom door.

'Thank you,' said Jean, wondering if she should risk creasing her pink linen shift dress by sitting on one of Belinda's beanbags. She fancied getting a couple for the girls, but Jim didn't like them.

She wasn't sure how chatty she should be with Carol so she opted for safe topics. 'Have you had to come far?'

'Fairhaven.'

'We live in Marton, near the mushroom farm,' said Jess.

'Gosh,' replied Carol and then no one seemed to know what to say.

There was an awkward silence for a couple of minutes before Mrs Glinn came in with a jug of orange squash and some chocolate fingers. Jean felt her blood pressure soar. Chocolate and orange, just think of the stains!

Fortunately Carol was of the same mind. The girls were given carefully poured juice and a biscuit, and then thoroughly damp-flannelled all over.

Belinda came in from the bathroom all hot and pink with her hair soaking wet. Jean felt her heart palpitate. What was she going to do with it?

The girl dropped her towel and, stark naked, rifled through her underwear drawer for some knickers and a bra. Jean was dumbfounded, she'd never seen anyone strip off so casually before. She tried not to stare but she couldn't help it.

'I refuse to wear tights, it's a hundred bloody degrees.'

'Language, Belinda, there are littlies present,' admonished Carol. Belinda winked at Jess and Jess winked back.

Jean felt her breakfast repeat on her; she could do with a Rennie. It was only once the dresses were finally on that she could relax slightly, though her fingers still shook as she did Jess's buttons up. It was a good job only a handful of them were real and the rest purely decorative.

Belinda tipped herself upside down and dried her hair with a hairdryer, the curls billowing around her head. If she put her hair in a bun the dress wouldn't look quite as . . . well . . . sexy, Jean fretted.

But nonetheless she was pleased. The fabric of the older girl's dress matched Jess and Charlotte's but while theirs flared from the waist Belinda's followed the curve of her body right down to the knee, where it dramatically fishtailed out.

Maybe the girl shouldn't have put so much eyeliner on and maybe the dark pink lipstick was a little attention-seeking, but you had to hand it to her: Belinda looked what Jim would call 'knockout'.

All they had to do now was put their shoes on and they were ready. Suddenly Jean felt sick again. The shoes were still in their boxes, pale pink leather bar shoes with a buckle fastening for Jess and Charlotte, and cream patent court shoes for Belinda.

Only they weren't Jess's shoes, they were Emily's shoes, the chicken-pox girl, the girl who was five but big for her age apart from her feet.

Jean knew as soon as she opened the box they were at least a size too small. 'Just scrunch your toes up, there's a good girl,' she whispered to Jess. 'Please, darling, just try.'

She managed to fasten the buckle on the last hole available, but you could almost see Jess's big toe pushing through the soft leather.

Mrs Glinn poked her head around the door. 'Jean, the Chamberlains are ready to give you a lift to the church,' and with that there was no time to do anything more than give Jess a quick kiss and wish them all luck.

'Good luck, darling.'

Ah luck, thinks Jean, immobile in her hospital bed. We all need luck and the thing about it is that often you don't know how lucky you are until your luck runs out.

Jean is tired now: the picture of that day keeps shifting out of focus. She will save the rest of the wedding for tomorrow. It's like a big dinner, she can't manage it all in one go. She'll leave some for later.

Anne

Steps Back in Time

Anne has decided to give herself a break from playing the dutiful daughter. It can't all be hospital, hospital, hospital. Before she visits her mother this afternoon she's going to catch a bus and check out a few old haunts.

Anyway, it's good to get out of the house. Staying indoors might lead to snooping. All middle-aged women have snooping tendencies and hers are acute, so it's best she removes herself from temptation.

Back in London her snooping is frequently out of control. Apart from her regular Facebook sojourns as Star van Hoff, she is a terrible one for sneaking into her sons' rooms when they are out and checking under beds, in drawers and right to the back of the wardrobe, searching for – what?

Boys don't write diaries, but they do leave evidence: unwashed socks they have masturbated into; obscene magazines featuring young girls and their hairless labia punctured by centrefold staples; little rabbit droppings of dope wrapped in cellophane. Once, in the back pocket of Jools's Diesel jeans, she found a bloodied tampon.

Do fathers ever snoop, she wonders, unable to picture her

own father having the nerve to open anything other than his own underwear drawer.

When she thinks about it, it was a good job her father died when he did, he missed all the unpleasantness. He wouldn't have been very good at it, but she still misses him. He was the one that had understood and encouraged her, it's because of him that she went to university. She sometimes struggles to remember his face, but the one thing she will never forget is how proud he was of her. He really didn't mind about her wearing glasses or knocking things over; all the things that made her mother wince just really didn't bother her dad.

Suddenly she is struck by a memory. She is about eleven and she is watching *Ask the Family* with Robert Robinson. She remembers how jealous she was of all those clever families with their correct answers and how, lying on her belly like a caterpillar in front of the black-and-white screen, she'd come to the conclusion that she and her dad would probably be OK on the programme, but that her mum and Jess would be a liability.

Funny the things you remember while you're brushing your teeth. The odd thing about being in this unchanged bathroom is seeing her almost-fifty-year-old face in a mirror that must be as surprised as she is to see how she has aged.

'You're getting whimsical now, Anne,' she tells herself, trying not to mind how yellow her teeth are. She gathers her bag and requisite keys. No point taking the phone, it's as dead as a dodo.

She steps out of the front door, relieved that for once it's not raining, though once again she is reminded how badly she packed for this trip. She really needs to buy herself some socks. Standing at bus stops is a chilly business.

''Twas ever thus,' she mutters. How many mornings has she stood and shivered on this particular square of pavement? Not usually on a Saturday, though: she wasn't one to have to turn up at school on a Saturday. That what the sporty types did.

Anyway, it's not a school any more. Her mother sent her a cutting some time ago, about her alma mater being turned into luxury flats, and an idle flick through last week's local paper after breakfast had spurred her into action.

Apparently Phase 1 of the rebuild was complete and site visiting was encouraged. 'Why not come and have a look?'

She just wants to see what they've done with it. Queen Margaret's was such a big part of her life: in some respects it set her free. The day the envelope came through the letterbox, offering her a place at the grammar, was like getting a train ticket for a journey that she's been on ever since. A journey that made all the usual stops along the way: O levels, A levels, university, career, marriage, children, big house, bigger house.

Obviously the journey hasn't been as simple as all that. There have been some terrible incidents, some grinding halts, some agonising waits. There have been the boring bits and the frightening bits, but it seemed that there was always a way out. She had a direction. She could always get back on the train.

Only now she is on a bus. No more tortured metaphors, she warns herself, and checks her watch. The journey used to take three-quarters of an hour.

Forty-five minutes of finishing bits of prep, polishing her French verbs, getting ahead with her Evelyn Waugh and checking her maths.

Some girls came in on designated school buses but she didn't. It was another thing that set her apart: she didn't belong to any particular group, not the school bus gang, or the cycling lot, or the girls who lived close enough to walk. She came in from a different direction.

It didn't really bother her; it meant she arrived without any baggage. The only other girl from her primary class who'd been offered a place at the grammar had moved to Guildford during the summer holidays, the rest had gone to the shiny new comprehensive. She was on her own.

Anne Collins. Her name had always been high up on the school register and she tries to remember the names of the girls who were called before her. There were three: Susan Abrahams,

Brenda Bains and Karen Burns – her memory has always been good.

She can remember her first day, everything stiff and new, shirt, skirt, satchel, her father insisting on coming with her, 'Just to be on the safe side.' The memory is so vivid she can almost see the inside of her new pencil case, the sharp end of her compass firmly stuck into her pristine new rubber: she was always sensible.

In some respects she'd been sensible to the point of boring, but it had been an easy role for her to fulfil. Reliable Anne, the girl you could turn to for help with your homework; kind Anne, who was never part of the glamorous bitchy group; ordinary Anne, who didn't make you feel any worse about yourself than you already did.

The girls divided then, as they do now, thinks Anne. The pretty, cool gang, the weirdos, the swots, the sneaks and the liars.

She herself had floated on the perimeter of the swots and the weirdos, occasionally being asked by a pretty bitchy type whether Anne thought her hair looked better 'like this, or . . . like this?'

She made herself useful: a shoulder to cry on, a keeper of secrets and a reliable translator of French into English and vice versa.

As the years went by, her confidence in being a nice bright willing student increased and her circle of friends widened. Her trick, she realised, was that she posed no threat. She didn't betray confidences or gossip in the toilets, she never flew off the handle like Marcie Grainger and she wasn't the type who'd try and get off with your boyfriend like Simone Evans.

By the time she was in the Lower Fifth the friendship groups in her year had settled down and Anne found herself in a comfortable tripod arrangement with Angela Metcalf and Grace Long, both of whom lived close enough to the school to walk. Anne envied them this, as she envied them lots of things: Grace's only-child status and bookish parents, and Angela's large house and slightly bohemian family; Mrs Metcalf was a potter and an adventurous cook. While Jean was still ripping open Vesta meals, Mrs Metcalf was experimenting with her own paella pan.

Angela was the prettiest of the three of them, then Anne, then Grace, who was really rather plain and played the flute.

She wishes she'd kept in touch better. The last time she'd seen Grace was at her wedding; as for Angela, she was living in Canada with a great big bear of a husband and four rugged sons, all tremendously sporty and vying for places on the Olympic bobsleigh team. Well bully for them!

Angela had turned into the type of woman that sent enthusiastic round robins every Christmas.

I can't do that, thinks Anne, I'm too honest. My seasonal round robins would be rather bleak: still teaching, still married to Paul (just), still mothering two ungrateful lumps and still no nearer to finding out what happened to my sister.

That was another reason why she enjoyed Queen Margaret's: she didn't have to play the part of Jess's big sister. It was a relief, she was an independent unit and only had to look out for herself. She could be whoever she wanted to be.

The bus comes to another lurching halt and Anne realises it's her stop. For the past half an hour she has been back in the seventies. She can always pop back; the past is at least more reliable than the future.

Queen Margaret's looks the same as it did thirty years ago, an impressive red-brick façade, just two storeys high and set far back from the road. In her day, the grounds in front of the school had featured grass to be kept off and well-tended borders stuffed during the summer months with the flower of the school emblem, the marigold.

The grounds in front of the building are now littered with site offices. A bright yellow prefab unit offers Information and Tours.

Anne would rather just wander round unaccompanied, but this is not to be. Twenty minutes later My name's Hilary is marching her into the show flat where everything is taupe and grey.

'Very tasteful,' Anne murmurs, thinking that this was Miss Calvert's office, this was where the headmistress sat and issued orders. Outside this room girls dropped their voices and tiptoed across the parquet.

Hilary drones on about parking spaces and a real sense of community while Anne thinks about the old science labs above her head. She wonders what happened to the jars of pickled mice and the embryonic baby. If she broke away and ran up the stairs would she still catch a whiff of formaldehyde and rotten egg?

She sits down on the show sofa and pretends to read the literature. Literature, my arse, thinks Anne, it's a brochure, but it's useful for burying her head while the compass of her brain gets its bearings.

Thirty years ago, if you turned right outside of this room and walked to the far end of the corridor you'd come to the toilets and the library. Outside the library were the bike sheds and the entrance to the modern block, where Anne took her maths classes with a teacher whose moustache was stained dark yellow by tobacco.

'Would you like a coffee?'

'Yes please.'

But of course if you turned left out of this room and walked in the opposite direction you'd pass the secretaries' office, lost property, the vast recess of metal pegs where the girls hung their coats and through the double doors and into the art rooms.

'I used to come to this school.'

'When was that then?'

'1973 to 1980.'

'Before my time.'

As if reminded, Anne glances at her watch. It's later than she thinks. 'I have to go.'

She doesn't even make a pretence of taking the literature, just leaves it on the taupe sofa

'I was really happy here,' she admits rather weakly.

'Really?' replies Hilary. 'I fucking hated my school. I went to the comprehensive.'

Hilary is well preserved, but beneath the acrylic nails and the St Tropez she's pushing forty. If things were normal Anne would just ask, she would just drop it into the conversation. 'Oh really? Then you may have known my sister.'

But obviously she doesn't.

The name Jess Collins might not mean a great deal to the world at large, but round here there are still those who remember.

She decides to walk from the school to St Annes. She can't deal with lunch at the hospital so she'll treat herself to something nice in the parade around the town square, buy some socks and then hop on a bus up to see her mum.

The walk takes her past the bungalow where Grace Long practised her flute under the doting eyes of her aged parents. She liked going to Grace's house. Mr and Mrs Long didn't approve of television; instead they listened to concerts or comedies on the radio, though never at meal times. At meal times you talked while Mrs Long dished out vegetarian meals that seemed to consist mostly of cheese and macaroni.

Come to think of it, Grace's parents taught her many things that came in very useful when she went to university. Thanks to them she knew her Haydn from her Handel and could play a mean game of chess.

This is when I learnt to be a sponge, thinks Anne. Thanks to Queen Margaret's and the girls she hung out with she learnt how to be more middle-class than she actually was.

Her mother might have had social aspirations – she was certainly very drawn to the glamour of showbusiness – but she never read a book if a magazine was available, refused to understand the rules of draughts, never mind chess, and given the choice would rather watch *Coronation Street* than listen to classical music.

As for her father, he was bright but badly educated, a victim of a northern working-class background, but more than that he was not a man born to be lucky.

Angela had lived with her family in a side street off the main road nearer to the town centre. Theirs was a sprawling Victorian pile containing a rabbit warren of rooms where Metcalfs of every age seemed to burrow. Angela was the quietest one of her family, the second-eldest of four and the only girl.

Anne had an enormous crush on Angela's older brother Peter who, as far as she knew, was unaware of her existence, despite the fact that she often stayed the night and was a frequent visitor at meal times. Angela's younger brothers, an interchangeable set of freckle-faced auburn-haired practical jokers, spent all their time trying to annoy Angela, who spent all her time trying to ignore them.

From the Metcalfs Anne learnt how to eat spaghetti that wasn't out of a tin and how not to die of shame when you sit on a whoopie cushion in front of the person you are in love with. She also learnt that the bohemian northern middle classes liked to smoke, drink and swear, but that their smoking, drinking and swearing were very different from the smoking, drinking and swearing the lower classes did.

So, thanks to the Longs and the Metcalfs, and of course Queen Margaret's, she eventually went off to university with four grade-A A levels, an inter-schools chess tournament cup and the ability to say bloody hell without sounding like a navvy.

Her personal Phase 1, a bit like the alterations to the school, had been completed.

Jean

The Big Day Continues

She really wishes she'd not eaten that bacon sandwich now. Something's not agreed with her, her stomach rumbles like a badly plumbed bathroom. She hopes the couple sitting in the front of the car can't hear.

Vi and Norman Chamberlain, Belinda said their names were, they didn't introduce themselves. She can sense they don't really want to be taking her: that Norman fellow made a nasty joke as she got in the car; he muttered, 'I'm surprised they don't want us to take the char as well.'

Vi Chamberlain had elbowed him and hissed, 'Behave yourself Norman, apparently she's a gifted seamstress.'

He barely spoke for the rest of the journey. She could see his face in the rear-view mirror but she looked down rather than catch his eye. The back of his neck was very red and his hair was silver and bristly above the collar where it had recently been shaved.

Vi was inclined to be chatty. 'Well, I bet you never thought you'd be fortunate enough to actually be attending the ceremony,' she gushed.

'Actually, Mrs Grainger Carmichael had already invited me,' Jean replied in her best telephone manner.

'She's all heart, is Penny,' the older woman responded and Jean heard herself agreeing.

'Penny told me you used to work at Shirley Lovell's? I got my hat there,' continued Vi.

'And very nice it is too.' Jean's previous customer-relations experience came in handy. She could feel Vi preen in the front seat.

'I think it's going to be quite a big turnout,' the be-hatted Vi prattled. 'Of course both families are very prominent locally, they've both done very well for themselves. Penny just needs to get Belinda off her hands and then she and Kenneth can have some time to themselves.'

'Another wedding?' interjected the scarlet-necked Norman. 'Are you mad, woman, why would he want another wedding? This one's cost him an arm and a leg. I thank my lucky stars, I really do.'

'We've just got the one son,' Vi explained to Jean. 'He's working in Dallas, in oil, not married yet but I keep expecting to hear some happy news soon.'

'Hmmph,' responded Norman.

There was an awkward silence.

'I've got two daughters,' Jean chipped in. She had to say something, her stomach was growling like that teddy bear Jess had when she was small.

'But Jess is only six and Anne is eleven, so it'll be a good while till I'm worrying about weddings – that's if I can find anyone who'll have them.' It was meant to sound like a joke but somehow it didn't. Anyway no one laughed and there was another silence.

Fortunately, before Jean's stomach could make another alarming gurgle the church loomed into view, a solid dark red-brick edifice, and Norman pulled over to park.

'I don't want to park all the way back here,' complained Vi.

'Oh put a sock in it, woman, the exercise will do you good.' Jean followed the Chamberlains out of the car. She suddenly felt a bit lost: were they going to give her a lift to the reception after? Did she dare ask?

She lost them in the throng outside the church, a sea of women in pastel shades and brightly coloured hats and men looking sweaty in suits that were too tight.

Suddenly the top-hatted ushers in white magicians' gloves were directing people into the church. There was a bit of a bottleneck so Jean hung back. She'd be on the bride's side at the rear of the church. It was a good position really, she'd barely have to crane her neck to get the first glimpse of the bride.

The ushers were the groom's brothers, one older, one younger, both with necks the circumference of an elephant's thigh. Rugby boys, their shoulders filling their jackets like tightly upholstered sofas.

Jean waited until she was the last one in, taking her seat just as the mother of the bride made her entrance. Penelope Grainger Carmichael was playing her part to the hilt, making her way down the aisle to the front of the church waving and nodding like the Queen Mum.

All of a sudden the congregation stood up, the organ boomed into action, heads swivelled like sunflowers in the direction of the door and in came Jess, her graceful little arms strewing red rose petals as she skipped down the aisle like a sprite. The reaction was a communal 'Ahhhh'. Jean gulped. A gull's-egg-sized lump had arrived in her throat and no matter how hard she swallowed she couldn't shift it. Her little girl skipping so lightly in her bare feet. Her bare feet? Of course, she must have slipped the tiny Cinderella slippers off in the car, they were too tight for skipping. Who said she was thick?

The music swelled again and all eyes turned this time to the arrival of the bride. Jean's first thought was that Helen should always wear a veil. She looked beautiful and who would guess that under all that white net was the face of a pleasant but very ordinary-looking girl with a rather ugly nose?

Behind her came the bridesmaids, Belinda holding Charlotte's hand. Again there was a gasp: was it for the bride or for the bride's sister? Really, fretted Jean, if she'd known Belinda was going to wear a push-up bra she wouldn't have cut the dress so low! Mind you, you could put Belinda in a sack and she'd still be sexy. Naughty Belinda was enjoying the attention, accentuating the wiggle in her walk as she followed behind her virginal older sister.

Jean cannot be bothered to recall the rest of the service. She edits out the vows and the signing of the register and skips straight to the bit where the bells peal and Jess skips once more down the scarlet carpet, flinging rose petals – white ones this time – into the air.

She expects her daughter to catch her eye as she exits the church, but she doesn't. Jess is so caught up in the moment that she has forgotten her poor old mum.

Oh well, never mind, she will seek her out after the photos are taken and give her her school sandals to change into.

It's at that moment Jean realises that the sandals are still at Weeping Willows along with the second-best yellow dress, all neatly folded up in an old Shirley Lovell's carrier bag.

'Bugger.' She doesn't swear often, but sometimes other words just won't do.

The photos are taken on the daisy-studded lawn outside the church. The sunshine blazes as the photographer summons different groups: 'Just the bride and groom' – *click, click* – 'and the bridesmaids.' Here comes barefoot Jess flying across the lawn, leaping into the air, *click, click, click.*

The Chamberlains had indeed forgotten all about her, and Jean ended up walking to the Grand. It didn't matter, it was only ten minutes and it was a glorious day.

By the time she got to the hotel it was buzzing. Jean stood in a corner of the function suite and eavesdropped for a while.

'Well they really pushed the boat out . . . It's proper champagne, none of your cheap fizz . . . That's right, a cottage in Wrea Green . . . Penelope looks like the cat that got the cream

'. . . Dallas my foot, he's living down south with a Spanish bloke – flamenco dancer. Norman just won't have it.'

It was a sit-down luncheon for two hundred. On an easel in the corner of the room was a map of the tables indicating where everyone should sit. The name Charlotte Robins had been crossed out and Jessica Collins inked beside it. She was on the top table, right at the end but nonetheless, Jess was on the top table!

She herself was near the back, by the ladies' loos, which was a relief. If it all got too much she could just lock herself in a cubicle and wait until it was polite to leave.

Still, she quite fancied the meal: melon to start, followed by salmon in a cream and dill sauce with Jersey Royals and asparagus, she'd never had asparagus; pudding was summer trifle or profiteroles. Jean hoped Mrs Grainger Carmichael wasn't going to attempt both: that frock of hers would simply burst.

She managed to catch Jess for a quick natter before the meal was called. 'Did you enjoy it?'

'Yes.'

'Are you having a nice time?'

'Yes Mum.'

Of course she was, she was having the time of her life. Lots of attention and a small gang of kiddies her own age to run around with.

Suddenly a man all dressed up in a scarlet coat banged a hammer and told them to take their seats. 'Ooh, a master of ceremonies,' someone whispered.

She really wasn't thinking of staying that long, but every time she looked at her watch another couple of hours had sped by. She was having fun! Jean didn't normally drink much, but the champagne flowed and after a couple of glasses she felt quite chatty. In fact, by the time pudding was served she found it was easier to tell a long funny story about an amusing incident at Shirley Lovell's than navigate the dessert spoon into her mouth. Eventually her little pile of untouched profiteroles collapsed in an exhausted heap.

There was dancing after the meal, traditional rather than disco. A five-piece jazz band in dickie bows sat on little gold chairs in the corner, trumpets and saxophones all polished and poised for action. The dance floor filled up, people were jiving and twisting, and, oddly enough, Norman and Vi were doing a foxtrot.

She'd always liked to dance; they hadn't been since the girls, but she'd always had rhythm. She danced with a man called Neil and an old fellow by the name of Bernard who held a cigar in one hand and twirled her round the floor with the other.

She was a bit breathless after that. She looked at her watch: it was eight o'clock, how could that possibly be? Jim would be worried sick. She needed to get herself a taxi, that's what Mr Grainger Carmichael had said: 'I'll pay.'

Only at that moment the bride and groom were leaving and she got swept up in waving them off and laughing when Belinda dodged as her sister threw the bouquet in her direction.

Suddenly it was quarter to nine.

If she hadn't had six glasses of champagne she wouldn't have done it, but she found herself tapping Mr Grainger Carmichael on the shoulder. 'I think it's time me and the flower girl went home. Could you help get us a taxi?'

He was a bit unsteady on his feet. A lot of the men were drinking brandy now, balloon-shaped glasses littered the tables. She could smell it on his breath.

'Ah yes, taxi, follow me. I don't seem to have change for the payphone so . . . I know, come with me.'

She just followed him, she didn't have her bag but she didn't think anyone would pinch it. This was a posh do, full of posh nice people.

She simply followed him down the patterned carpet, that vivid swirl of red and blue paisley, all the way to the shiny chrome lift. 'Come on Jean, follow me.' She wasn't steady, her legs felt loose at the hip, as if they weren't properly attached. The lift was mirrored. She could see a hundred hers and a hundred hims reflected in the glass.

They stumbled into each other as they exited the lift. He took her by the arm. 'It's just down here, there's a phone and everything.'

He had a key in his pocket on a big metal fob. The door opened on to a suite, lots of yellow, yellow wallpaper and a yellow silk bedspread. Oh she was tired.

'Helen and Roy got changed into their going-away outfits in here,' he gestured. She hiccupped.

'Sit down, let me get you a glass of water.'

She was so very tired.

She must have just rested her head for a second while he was getting her the water, because she woke up to find him taking off her tights.

'There's a good girl.' She thought for a moment it was Mr Pemberton, Mr Pemberton touching her breast that time, making her feel all tingly and wet. She closed her eyes. He had his fingers inside her, expertly coaxing her, finding a place Jim had never found, but it wasn't Jim and it wasn't Mr Pemberton, this was another man, a big man smelling of brandy, pushing her back, not hurting her, just making her do what he thought best. The zip down the back of her dress had come undone, his big hands were kneading her breasts, hard. 'There's a good girl,' he breathed into her. She couldn't reply, she couldn't ask what on earth he thought he was doing.

His full weight was on top of her, squashing her flat against the bed. He shifted his weight for a second, fiddling at the belt around his waist. She tried to roll away but he pinned her down by her throat.

'Now let's not play games, Jean.' She felt her eyes bulge. If he didn't move his hand she was going to be sick. She gagged, a mixture of fish, sick and champagne in her mouth. He released his grip, she gasped and he rolled her over, burying her face deep in a pillow. A heavy hand held her head, she could only breathe through one nostril. Why was he doing this? Didn't he like the work that she'd done?

'Come on Jean, it's only a bit of fun. Open your legs, there's a good girl. There now Jean, that's not so bad, is it?'

He was inside her. She'd never done it this way before, she didn't know it could be done this way round. She was frozen, his hand was still on the back of her head, her hair bunched in his fist. His other hand reached around and pinched at her nipples. 'Come on, you fucking slag, might as well enjoy it, eh?' His breath was uneven and rasping now, he was gasping like a man pushing a car up a hill. She shut her eyes, she wasn't even here, she was safe in her own bed and somewhere outside in the sunshine a fat middle-aged man was pushing a car up a hill.

'Ungh, ungh, unghhhh . . .'

She felt him slither out of her. 'Good girl, that was very nice.' He stood above her now, tucking his shirt in and zipping up his flies.

'Now let's just keep this between you and me, Jean, because I think you'll find that my word counts for more than yours. But because you've been such a good girl I'm going to give you the number of the taxi company and your fare.' He propped a business card up by the phone. In red letters she made out the words 'Whitesides Taxis'.

He then dropped five twenty-pound notes on to the bed.

'I've spent enough money today, but at least that'll pay for something I've enjoyed. Now come on Jean, how's about a little kiss?'

She pretended to be dead. She lay where he'd left her and didn't move a muscle.

'Just leave the key at reception,' he told her, and with that he left the room.

If Jean were capable of crying she would cry now. She would cry and cry and cry. She would cry until they had to change the sheets and the nurses would wonder how on earth they got so wet.

Anne

Soup and Socks

Anne has walked all the way to the town square. She can get a bus from here directly to the hospital, but first she must eat and buy socks. Sometimes being a middle-aged woman is a relief: prioritising one's needs is simpler as one gets older, food and warmth being so much more important than hair or the approval of one's peers.

St Annes is both the same and completely different from how it used to be. She doesn't recognise a lot of the shops: some of the individual boutiques from the seventies offering unisex gear and mod modes have long disappeared, replaced by the usual American coffee chains. Since when did we need to drink so much coffee, and why do they encourage you to buy it in bucket-sized containers? No one's got a bladder that big.

I'm like a dinosaur come back to earth, she thinks, bewildered by the strange metal sculptures that are dotted around the wide pavements.

Oh well, T. J. Naylor's, the department store, is still on the corner. Once upon a time it housed the first branch of Danish Kitchen in the area and women came from miles around to eat open sandwiches on pumpernickel and exotic pastries oozing with confectioner's custard.

Back then her mother used to buy her sewing materials from the indoor market directly behind Naylor's. She can suddenly picture her, a blunt square of blue tailor's chalk in one hand, tracing around flimsy paper patterns pinned to cloth. She can hear the crunch of scissors.

I didn't even bother to ask her to teach me. I can barely sew a button on, she reminds herself, though once at school she completed an apron.

The socks cost slightly more than she would normally pay but she is tired now and she needs to sit down. She takes a lift to the third floor and is surprised, when the door opens, not to be transported back into the shiny varnished pine of the seventies.

The café offers lite bites, which infuriates her. In fact, she'd walk out in protest at the Americanisation of the word 'light', but she's too hungry. She'll have the roast butternut squash soup and a Greek salad.

Anne glances round. Her mother used to love coming here; it was one of the few places where they would come together, without Jess. Why was that, why was it just her and her mother? Where was her sister?

It was because of her short sightedness, of course! The optician's was just a few doors along and a couple of times a year she would have her eyes tested and meet her mother here for a Danish pastry after. Her mother always came laden with haberdashery from the market, shimmering gauzes, layers of pink nylon netting and strings of silver sequins. Jess had started doing a lot of dancing shows and her mother was roped in to do the costumes.

Her father used to complain: 'There's no money in it, Jean, you're working yourself to the bone for nothing.' Mind you, he was the one who was all skin and bone. Her mother was petite and she often forgot to eat, but she thrived on work. Anne

227

remembers sitting in this very window and her mother pointing out Shirley Lovell's across the road and telling her stories of when she was a shop assistant.

It's a shame her mother hadn't been more financially astute, she let people take her for a ride. She got in a muddle over bills and was too embarrassed to take a stand when people didn't pay up.

Like that wedding, the one everyone made such a fuss over which ended in tears and non-payment. 'You've been diddled, Jean.'

But her mother had refused to go back. 'It's his word against mine,' she kept saying, 'and he's a very influential lawyer.'

Of course her father hadn't been able to do anything about it. It wasn't as if he could storm round to Brady Avenue on Jean's behalf and demand payment. He wasn't a well man; in fact the day of the wedding was the day he had his first heart attack.

The waitress brings the soup. It's very hot, she should have known. The first mouthful burns her chest, makes her gasp. Is that how her father felt?

They were in the library. It was a boiling hot day but neither she nor her father was particularly good in the sun. It was nice to be in the dusty cool of the library, like a church but with better books.

She'd just brought back *The Day of the Triffids* and was taking her time, wondering if she should choose another John Wyndham, when the commotion began. The commotion was her father. He was staggering around in the military history section, clutching his chest as if he were re-enacting a battle. At first she thought it might be his epilepsy but it wasn't. His lips were turning blue and he was crashing into the periodicals.

Someone shouted, 'Get an ambulance' and immediately someone else responded with a 'Shhhh'.

Anne's favourite librarian, Mrs Rogers, was loosening his tie. 'Put him in the recovery position,' a stranger instructed and Anne remembers Mrs Rogers taking off her green cardigan and placing it ever so gently under her father's head and that's when she started to cry.

It was only when she was sitting in the ambulance that she realised she was still clutching a copy of *Heidi* that she hadn't had stamped, therefore it was stolen. When they got to the hospital she accidentally on purpose left it under the seat.

It was a heart attack. Her father was a poorly man. Was there anyone who could come and pick her up? Where was her mummy? How old was she?

She told them she was twelve and they believed her because she was big for her age and mature. Of course she could get home safely, her mother would be back soon. She was just at a wedding with her little sister, she said she would be home around tea time, she promised.

She had her pocket money and she knew which bus to get. She wasn't a ninny, it just felt strange, sitting on her own on the bus without a parent. In some respects, if it hadn't been such an awful day she'd have enjoyed it.

The soup is cool enough to eat now. She's as ravenous as she had been that day: her stomach rumbles at the memory.

It had been lunchtime when her father had been taken ill and it was five o'clock when she set off home. With any luck her mother would already be back, as she hadn't got a front-door key. The key was in her father's trouser pocket; she hadn't liked to ask. Oh well, she can sit on the step and wait, it's a nice day, only she's ever so hungry and now she wishes she'd kept the stolen book, it's boring being on a bus with nothing to read. Anne smiles at the memory. She never did get round to reading *Heidi*.

Both doors were locked, so she sat on the step. It was all right apart from being hungry and needing a wee. In the end she went round to the back garden and did a wee in the yard. Her mother had thrown half a bacon sandwich out for the birds; she was so hungry she nearly picked it off the scrubby bit of grass and ate it, but she was scared of germs.

After sitting on the step for a bit more she crossed the busy main road, even though she wasn't really allowed to, and spent the rest of her pocket money on a packet of fig rolls. Then she went back and sat down on her step again. It was seven o'clock and it wasn't hot any more; she didn't have a cardigan and the fig rolls made her want a poo.

Mrs Parker from next door saw her when she was on the way to the pub with Mr Parker. 'Are you all right pet?'

'Yes, I'm just waiting for my mum and my sister,' she replied.

An hour later the Parkers walked by on the way home from the pub. Mrs Parker was a bit wobbly. As Jean always said, 'She likes a sherry or three.'

'Are you still there pet? Come and sit on our settee, you'll get piles on that step.'

It was cold on the step now, and even though the last thing she wanted to do was set foot inside the house where Mrs Gaga had fed her stale biscuits and nightmares she reasoned the Parkers would have a toilet to poo in, so she agreed to go with them.

They watched the television in a room that was the same shape as it had been in Mrs Gaga's day, but looked and smelt completely different. Nicotine, Anne decided, was preferable to the stench of sour milk and cat piss.

Eventually, when she really couldn't wait any longer, she crept upstairs and used the lavatory, her heart almost stopping with embarrassment at the sound of the flush. What if they knew what she'd been doing?

The Parkers were actually very kind. When she said she'd not had her tea Mrs Parker made her a jam sandwich and Mr Parker offered her a game of dominoes. But all she wanted to do was stare out of the window, while Mrs Parker repeated, 'A watched kettle never boils,' not that she put the kettle on. Mr Parker drank two cans of beer while Mrs Parker drank vermouth after vermouth.

In the end Mrs Parker wrote her mother a note. 'We've got your Anne on our sofa, your Jim is up Blackpool Vic.' And she went wobbling out on her slingbacks to shove it through the letterbox. 'I don't know what that woman thinks she's playing at,' she said when she wobbled back and poured herself another vermouth.

They'd all nodded off by the time Jean rang the doorbell. Her mother looked dreadful, her make-up all smudged. She just grabbed Anne by the arm and started dragging her out. 'I'm ever so sorry to inconvenience you, Elaine, if there's anything I can do to return the favour, please just ask.'

She was trying to sound all posh, only it didn't sound right. She sounded like she was about to cry and she did. As soon as she got Anne back in the house she cried buckets. She kept saying, 'Poor Jim, he doesn't deserve it, he's such a good man,' and Anne had to stroke her hair and say, 'Hush Mum, it'll be all right.'

She remembers her mother phoning the hospital but she kept getting the number wrong. Her mother was incoherent; Anne had only just learnt that word but she was glad she had, it described Jean exactly. She was incoherent, hysterical and insensible. Thinking of clever grown-up words to describe her mother's behaviour kept Anne calm.

That night she put her mother to bed and when she tucked her in she noticed that her mother's throat was all smudged, which was odd. Her mother was very boring about Jess and Anne washing their necks, so how come hers was so dirty?

In the morning she couldn't tell whether her mother had given her a grubby neck a good scrub with the loofah because she had a red chiffon scarf tied 'just so' around it.

The soup and salad were just what she needed. Her ankles are much warmer in the socks. Anne breathes deeply; she is just about ready to face the hospital again. Who'd have thought that visiting someone in a coma could be quite so exhausting?

Jean

Recrimination

Jess fell asleep in the taxi, Jean can remember that. The child was barefoot and her feet were filthy, she'd been dancing, dancing all night long. She hadn't noticed her mother's disappearing act. She fell asleep mid-sentence, as if someone had turned off a switch.

She couldn't understand why there were no lights on in the house. She asked the driver to wait, the keys were in her handbag and her hands were shaking. She'd been shaking all the way home, she was cold and she wanted to be sick. The note was on the mat and as soon as she read it she was sick, she only just made it upstairs and into the bathroom. As she vomited she heard the taxi driver blow his horn. She'd left her daughter in the back of a strange man's car, what kind of mother was she? What kind of wife was she? In the toilet bowl in front of her, the wedding breakfast reappeared in reverse order. She flushed and rinsed her mouth, ran back down the stairs and paid the driver – 'I'm sorry, there's been an emergency' – but she knew she smelt of sick and the driver just looked at her as if to say, 'I know what you are.'

She carried Jess into the house and put her into bed. One

night sleeping in a bridesmaid's dress wouldn't do her any harm. Jess didn't wake, not even for a second. She just lay there, her lovely face on the pillow. She was smiling but it looked a bit like a smirk, and for a split-second Jean didn't like her.

Anne! She had to get Anne back from next door. At least this time she'd not been stuck with that stinking old lady with the cats. At least Elaine Parker only stank of booze, and who was she to talk? If she hadn't had all that champagne, if she hadn't been such a stupid show-off, if she'd just come home when she said she would.

But she hadn't and no one would ever know. No one, because from now on she was never going to think about it again, she wouldn't ever see any of them again. If Mrs Grainger Carmichael ever telephoned her again she'd just say she was busy, that she had too much on. Obviously it was a shame about Jess's dress and shoes, but Jim needn't know about those either.

Jim, poor Jim. He'd not been looking well lately and she'd had no time to look after him. Well from now on she would, as soon as he was out of that hospital she was going to take care of him, she was going to be a proper loving wife and mother, and with that decision made she went next door and fetched her elder daughter.

He never did know either. If there is one thing she is grateful for it's that her husband never knew. No one did, it was too shameful to ever talk about to anyone.

Not even Noreen or Pat, and they were her best friends now. Nice to have friends when you're an old woman, thinks Jean, who, if only she could open her eyes, if only she could see or hear or feel, would know that they are both here in this very room.

'Well it doesn't look like you'll be coming to bums and tums on Tuesday, lady,' says Pat, and Noreen looks at the bad side of Jean's face and sighs, 'Ooh you have been in the wars.'

They have come with sandwiches and fruit and wine gums, determined to stay for as long as they're allowed. They've heard that folk with severe head injuries respond to stimulation so they have come to talk their friend out of this silly coma.

'Your daughter Anne's here,' says Noreen. 'She'll be popping by in a while, but for now you'll just have to make do with me and Pat.'

They know about Jess, of course they do, but there's no way they will mention her name now. Noreen and Pat will stick to safe topics, they will talk about things that are real and true, like the awful weather and the fish that Pat has in her freezer, waiting for when Jean decides she wants to wake up. They will talk about what's in the news but they won't stray near anything that might upset her. They will steer clear of missing girls and unsolved mysteries.

'Ooh Jean, it's like December out there.'

'The wind, it's like a knife.'

'You missed ever such a good *Emmerdale* last night, Jean.'

'Pat's on a diet, she's not to eat any carbohydrates.'

And on they yatter, fat Pat and skinny Noreen, Jean's best friends. Grey-haired ladies in sensible anoraks with carrier bags and pictures of their grandchildren tucked away in their purses, women who've had their fair share of hard times and family troubles but never anything like what poor Jean's been through.

And they only know the half of it, they only know the Jess bit. What they don't know is the bit that happened before, the other shocking thing. She's not let herself think about it for years, but she has a feeling that now is a good time to go over it. There is a reason for this but she can't remember what it is, she will get muddled if she mixes up the running order. By the time she fetched Anne back from Elaine next door, the dreadful thing had already happened, it was just that she wouldn't realise it for a while.

One crisis at a time, Jean reminds herself.

She telephoned the hospital as soon as she got back with Anne. She got the feeling that the nurse had been waiting for her to call. Yes, Mr Collins was in intensive care. No, children

234

were not permitted to visit. No, he wasn't in any imminent danger, there was no need to make a midnight dash, but it might be a good idea for her to come along between two o'clock and four o'clock the following afternoon.

The next morning she went on to automatic pilot, it was the only thing she could do. She was hungover and guilty, but she needed to get on. The girls got up, she fed them breakfast and asked Anne to tell them precisely what happened. When Anne finished Jess said, 'It's my turn now,' and started to tell Anne about how *amazing* it had been to be a bridesmaid. But Anne just put up her hand like a policeman and said, 'I don't want to hear, Jess, I am not interested. Dad is in hospital, he could die, and all you want to do is talk about some stupid wedding.'

They both started crying then, Anne because she genuinely thought Jim might pass away and Jess because she was furious that Anne wasn't the slightest bit interested in the four-tiered cake or the dancing or the photographer or the limousines or anything. How could it be?

She had to be strict, she needed to go and see Jim and she needed Anne to hold the fort. She told her, 'I'm trusting you,' and she did trust her. If she told Anne to be good for her father's sake, then she would be. Jess needed to be bribed with the promise of a new pair of shoes: 'Tomorrow, on my life, but only if you're good.'

He looked dreadful, did Jim, not that she could see much of him. He had a great big oxygen mask over his face and was all wired up to different machines. The noise the machines made reminded Jean of going to the fair and hearing the generators round the back of the rides.

She just sat for an hour stroking his left hand. 'I'm here, Jim, it's going to be all right, I promise.'

And it was, sort of. He didn't die, which made her think that God didn't think what happened in the hotel had been all her fault. Surely if God had blamed her he would have punished her by taking Jim, but he didn't. Jim came home. He weighed about eight stone in his pyjamas and he had a beard, he was too weak to shave himself so she had to learn how to do it for him.

She didn't mind, it was like she was being taught a lesson. This was no less than she deserved. Looking after an invalid would put an end to her slutty ways, not that she was a slut, not really. She hadn't wanted to do what Mr Grainger Carmichael did to her, but had she fought hard enough?

Should she have kicked and screamed, should she have gone running down the corridor yelling blue murder after he'd left her? Why hadn't she called the police?

It was too late now to do any of those things, she just had to swallow back the guilt and live with the consequences, and anyway, looking after an invalid was a full-time occupation. She didn't have time to dwell on that night, she was forever traipsing up and down the stairs with cups of tea and bowls of soup. He was still having to lean on her when he went to the toilet.

The bowls club was very good, they put him on six weeks' sick pay and they said they'd wait for him to get better. His job was secure, he was popular with everyone, she mustn't worry.

But she did. It gnawed away at her. It wouldn't have been so bad if she'd been paid up front for the wedding but as it was she was out of pocket and Anne needed her uniform buying.

She sold the bits of jewellery her mother had left her, the pearl earrings and a gold wristwatch. The sewing machine lay idle. She put its plastic cover on, she couldn't face the idea of that needle going up and down, up and down, up and bloody down. Not yet. In a bit, maybe.

The first time Jim got up, got dressed and went out was to accompany Anne to the grammar school on her first day: 'I promised,' he said. His clothes hung off him and when he got home he went back to bed and didn't move for three days.

They got back to normal in the end. Jim returned to work and they just let him sit and do the bookings, and sometimes if things were quiet he'd polish all the cups and shields in the display cabinet.

Anne loved her new school. She was terribly self-important about her homework, forever asking her parents to test her on her French vocabulary and chuckling at their inability to pronounce the words properly. As for the Latin!

Jean got a handwritten card some time in September from a Mrs Roy Pickering. She couldn't think who Mrs Pickering was until the photo fell out of the envelope. She would have liked it framed, but he was in it. Of course he was; after all, he was the father of the bride. She ripped it up into little shreds and hid the bits in an empty tomato-soup can, which she then dropped in the pedal bin.

The photo didn't matter; the best one had appeared in the local paper a week after the wedding itself. It was a funny choice, if you thought about it. The bride and groom in the background while in front of them a fairy girl leapt scattering rose petals in mid-flight.

She'd been out and bought ten copies.

'I got you some haddock,' says Pat. 'I had mine last night, made ever such a nice fish pie. Homemade white sauce and topped it off with a big dollop of creamy mash.'

'I though you weren't eating carbs,' says Noreen and they laugh, knowing Jean would laugh too, if she could.

Jess

The Wedding

It was the best day of her life. When she woke up in the morning still wearing the beautiful dress she felt like Sleeping Beauty. If she had her way, she would never take the dress off ever again.

She imagined herself wearing it for school. Everyone would be so jealous that the fact she hadn't been on a summer holiday wouldn't matter, not a jot, because she would have the wedding to write about in her 'What I did in the summer holidays' composition and it wouldn't matter if her spelling was very bad because she would draw really good pictures and because she would be wearing the dress. The teacher would invite her to come to the front of the class and talk about her exciting experience. Just like she had when David Borsley had gone to London for his mum's birthday and seen the Crown Jewels.

She had it all planned in her head, whole sentences that she could say, about meeting a grown-up girl called Belinda who was the chief bridesmaid and the happy bride called Helen and how she had skipped down the carpet in the church, toes pointed, knees high, just like Miss Evangeline had taught her at her dancing school, and maybe at that point Miss Shelby would ask

Jess to demonstrate the skipping bit and everyone in the class would clap, even Tina Heygate who was so mean to her.

Yes, thought Jess, wishing she could have some more of that trifle right now, for breakfast. Being a bridesmaid was better than going to boring Spain.

But it was all spoilt by her dad. Trust her boring dad, he was getting very old and ugly and he didn't even have a car and now he was in 'tensive care', which meant tiptoeing round the house and not upsetting Anne, who kept bursting into tears.

Jess tried to be nice. She fetched her sister some toilet roll so she could blow her nose and she suggested all sorts of games they could play together while their mum was at the hospital, but Anne didn't want to play wedding discos or Sindy goes on honeymoon and she refused to let Jess talk about the wedding at all, not even about how she'd secretly taken the tiny pink shoes off in the big limousine and skipped down the aisle bare-foot. Every time she tried to say something about yesterday her sister simply shut her eyes, put her hands over her ears and sang 'Lalalala' really loudly and out of tune.

It was only after a horrible lunch when all they'd had to eat was Jacob's crackers and meat paste and they were playing Mousetrap that Anne finally relented. 'So,' she asked, 'what did you have to eat?'

After that they'd tried to make a trifle, only they didn't have any cake sponge so Anne decided to use bread all splodged with lemon curd and then she poured hot custard made from a tin of powder all over the ripped-up bread and actually it was very nice and so Jess sang, 'Three cheers for Anne the champion trifle maker,' which made Anne laugh until she started to cry again.

Anne

Friends and Relatives

It was perturbing to walk into her mother's room and find that she already had visitors.

'We're Pat and Noreen,' announced a short fat woman rather proudly, as if Victoria Wood had cast them in a sketch featuring two elderly women from Lancashire who spend their days randomly visiting hospitals.

'I'm Noreen,' said the thinner one.

'We spoke on the phone,' they chorused.

Anne thought she could feel another headache coming on. Oh well, at least they had wine gums.

'I'll go and fetch another chair,' chirruped Noreen.

'You're not much like your mother,' added Pat. It felt like an accusation.

'No, I take after my paternal grandfather. Apparently he was a great ox of a man.'

Pat blinked as slowly as a pigeon behind her thick National Health glasses. 'Now don't put yourself down love. You're not an ox, you're a fine figure of a big strong girl.'

'Hmmm, I shall take that as a compliment,' she responded. She'd been too long out of the north. It still came as a shock, the calling a spade a spade thing, the bluntness that bordered on rudeness.

Noreen came back in with a third chair and they arranged themselves in a semi–circle around Jean. She looked like an Egyptian mummy that had been partially unwrapped.

'So you've come all the way from London?' asked Noreen.

Pat answered for her: 'Of course she's come up, it's her mother lying there. Honestly Anne, we can't imagine what happened. She's not gaga, your mother, it's not like her to go running out into the middle of the road.'

Anne suddenly realises that these women know her mother better than she does.

'I've got two daughters,' interjects Noreen. 'It's much easier when there's two of you. Of course, if things had been different . . .'

Instantly Anne realises they know about Jess, but what do they know? What has her mother told them?

'It's not easy,' she admits. 'Sometimes I feel it would be nice to be able to share this with someone,' and all of a sudden she thinks of herself some time in the future, old and frail. Will her sons visit her, would they do this? Would they travel the length of the country to keep a vigil over her in an NHS hospital bed?

She doubts it. In fact, she can imagine Jools offering her a plane ticket to Switzerland. 'It's for the best, Ma, we're only thinking of you.'

'Well my son's very good to me,' Pat remarks, as if commenting on the conversation in Anne's head. 'He's a driving instructor, always popping by. It's not just daughters who are good to their mums.' She and Noreen exchange looks. This is obviously a well-worn topic.

When does it end? wonders Anne privately, the one–upmanship of parenthood? She herself has opted out: her sons are good-looking but not particularly nice and neither has an unblemished school record, but of course Pat, Noreen and her mother (for that matter) don't need to know the messy details of her disappointing home life. She attempts to stick up for her sons.

'My sons would be here but my eldest has just got his first job as a landscape gardener and my younger boy is studying for his A levels.'

'My granddaughter got three As. She's just gone off to Leeds to study history,' smirks the thin one. It's all Anne can do not to say, 'Well bully for her.'

'Noreen's lot are academic,' explains Pat. 'Mine are more practical. Your mother always said you were the brainbox of the family, very proud of you she is.'

Anne feels the prickle of tears. Ridiculous, of course her mother would have told these women she is proud of her. What else was she going to say, the truth? Imagine that . . . 'Anne's nice enough, but she was never much fun. No, it was my other daughter who was the life and soul.'

Because that was the truth of it: she and her mother had very little in common and as the years went by the gulf between them yawned ever wider.

It hadn't helped, marrying Paul. As soon as she signed the register she took herself another step further from her roots. Anne Armitage sounds like what she has become, a fully paid-up Aga-owning member of the middle classes.

My mother is slightly common, Anne admits silently to herself, and she has always found me a little bit dull because I didn't like watching the same TV programmes and I wasn't interested in clothes. She would have liked a dressier daughter, a groomed, perma-tanned, sports-car-driving blonde, preferably married to a local big cheese with a time-share in Marbella. Wasn't that supposed to be Jess's destiny, local girl made good?

Jean's dream for Jess would have been for her to have stayed close by (but in a big flash house) and maybe, once it was time to hang up her spangled tights, she could run her own children's dance school, the Jessica Collins Academy of Dance.

242

She's not sure where she's dredged this assumption from. She has never talked to her mother about the great 'what if'.

But it's here, the elephant in the room, or rather not in the room. The truth is, Jess should be here but she isn't.

And I am the one who is here, the wrong daughter, admits Anne, but only to herself.

'Well this won't buy the baby a new bonnet,' states Pat, getting up and instantly bustling. 'Come on Noreen, let's leave these two together. There's a cardigan in Marks I've got my eye on. We can pop in there before we go home.'

'Ooh yes,' replies Noreen. 'They've got a meal deal on.'

'Main, side, dessert and a bottle of wine, all for a tenner,' they chorus and off they go, grey-haired women with carrier bags, laughing.

Anne waits until she is sure they aren't listening at the door before she starts to speak. 'They seem good fun, Mum, your friends,' and then she launches into a monologue about what she got up to this morning, snooping round the flats in her old school, the walk into St Annes, Grace and Angela. 'Do you remember them, Mum, they were my Pat and Noreen?'

She doesn't think Jean would remember them, not really. Anne went to their houses, she didn't invite them back to hers. 113 was too small and too far away, there was nothing to do, her mother wasn't interested in cooking, her sister was a silly show-off and her father was either in the process of dying or dead.

Her mother only saw her school friends when she came to Queen Margaret's for concerts and Christmas carols. Anne was in the choir. She remembers one occasion quite vividly, sitting on the stage cross-legged at the front because she was in the first year and spotting her mother in the sea of parents' faces. Jean was sitting on the end of an aisle, wearing her best coat. Suddenly all the pupils who weren't in the choir streamed in to the assembly hall and as the girls poured in she saw one of the sixth-formers try to catch her mother's attention. It was Belinda Grainger Carmichael, waving and winking, but her mother just ignored her, looked straight through her as if they'd never met. How odd.

Her sister didn't attend Queen Margaret's, she didn't pass the eleven plus. No one expected her to, she wasn't academic, she was a dancer, all her brains were in her legs. Instead Jess went to the comprehensive and to three dance classes a week. She was the star of the Cygnet School of Dance, Audrey Carr's pet. She was Thoroughly Modern Millie and the Sugar Plum Fairy; she did ballet, jazz and tap; she had different-coloured leotards and won medals on candy-striped ribbons; at Christmas she was especially chosen to be one of the child dancers in the Grand Theatre's annual pantomime: 'A professional engagement,' her mother had cooed, and once again there were vanilla slices all round.

Should she remind her mother of that first panto? What if the memory stirred her out of this sleep, like Snow White herself? What if she did sit up, only to have forgotten everything? What if she had to be told all over again?

Anne decides not to mention the panto. She is too tired to talk any more and so many of the memories are too sad to revisit. That show at the Grand, was that the last Christmas her father had been alive? All the dates are getting jumbled up. She leans forward in the chair and rests her head on her mother's bed. She just needs to close her eyes, just for a moment.

Anne sleeps, she sleeps and dreams. She is sitting in the stalls of the Grand Theatre; they have come by taxi. Her mother is giving evil stares to people with rustling bags of Maltesers, her father is trying not to cough. Grace and Angela are there; Grace is reading a book of poetry, her father is trying not to cough. The lights go down and the little girl ballerinas come on, the audience sigh a communal 'Ah' but her mother is looking agitated. She seems to be counting the woodland creatures: one is missing, the squirrel is missing. Her mother made that costume, a red squirrel costume with the most enormous bushy tail. Her mother stands up in the stalls of the Grand Theatre and screams, 'Where is she? Where is my Jessica?'

Anne wakes up with a start and remembers what really happened. Of course Jess had been there, she had skipped on in her red squirrel outfit and her mother had clapped and her father had tried not to cough, while she herself had tried not to feel both bored and jealous at the same time.

She's never been a fan of pantos. The boys have never been: she has taken them to the theatre, of course, last year she managed to drag them along to see *War Horse* at the National, but that's different. No one can deny that she has tried with her sons. Maybe she tried too hard, maybe she needs to learn to back off.

A woman pushes a trolley into her mother's room. She's a decade or so older than Anne, with a mole in the crook of her nose. 'Hello dear, I'm a trolley volunteer. I realise your mother's not in any fit state for papers or sweeties, but maybe you'd like a little something? A treat to keep you going? Visiting a loved one in hospital can be ever such hard work.'

Anne doesn't know why but this casual piece of kindness is the thing that pushes her over the edge. She shakes her head and manages to keep herself together until the woman backs her treat trolley out of the little room, then she puts her head in her hands and sobs.

Outside in the corridor the Friend of Blackpool Victoria Hospital, volunteer Helen Pickering, pauses. The trolley is cumbersome, weighed down with chocolate bars, magazines, newspapers, sweeties and a small selection of grooming items – combs, tissues etc.

She wonders whether she should go back in to try to comfort the big woman who is crying her heart out, but she decides against it. People like to grieve differently, and if the big crying lady is anything like herself she might want to keep things private.

Of course, not everything can be kept private. She knows that and sometimes it's good to be able to talk; some secrets aren't worth keeping anyway. Helen knows this for a fact. When she was very young she kept quiet about how her husband beat her. She couldn't tell her sister because she'd have said, 'I told you so' and she couldn't tell her mother, not after what her mother went through. So she kept her mouth firmly shut until he beat her so badly she ended up in here, three broken ribs, two black eyes and a fractured cheekbone.

No one could really believe it. She could almost hear the gossip from her hospital bed: 'But he's such a respectable man, a solicitor, that lovely house in Wrea Green. Poor girl, and after what happened to her father, he was a solicitor too. What was his name? Kenneth, that's it, Kenneth Grainger Carmichael, terrible business.'

Helen wheels her trolley on, the wheels squeaking alarmingly. For once she's glad: the dreadful noise drowns out both the whispers and the sobbing.

Jean

Third Time Unlucky

Jean wonders if she's going to be in this place for ever. It's like being left in a waiting room with no magazines, not even a raggedy old *People's Friend* like in the dentist's. Not that it matters, reading has always been a chore and anyway, she has this massive story in her head to get straight. Still, it would be nice to see a friendly face, she misses her friends. Hopefully she'll feel like bums and tums on Tuesday, whenever that is.

Of course back then, when the first worst thing happened, she didn't know Pat and Noreen. Maybe it would have been easier if she had, maybe one of them would have guessed.

Jim never did, which was the main thing. What would she have done if Jim had ever found out?

The strangest thing was how different it was from before. She wasn't sick, for starters, and she barely put on any weight. Mind you, she didn't have any appetite. She might not have been physically sick but she was sick with worry.

She kept thinking it might not stick, bought bottles of gin in secret and drank them in boiling hot baths, afterwards cleaning her teeth until her gums bled, hiding the empty bottles in the airing cupboard, trying not to be drunk but waking up in the morning not remembering how she'd got to bed the previous night.

A couple of times she attempted to throw herself down the stairs but the house wasn't very big and she doubted she'd be able to do much damage. Anyway, what if the baby stayed put and Jean damaged her spine? Crippled and pregnant, that would never do.

She got quite fat around Christmas time. Jim mentioned that she and the Christmas pudding were the same shape and they all laughed, which was a nice moment, even though she was dying inside.

Thinking back now, she wasn't the only one dying inside. Jim's health hadn't been good since that little heart attack in July. He was back at work but he tired easily. In some respects it was a relief: the fact he went up to bed before she did meant she managed to arrange things so that he never saw her naked.

As for claiming his conjugal rights, he'd developed this cough and any exertion made it worse, so they more or less stopped bothering.

At night, when she finally crept into bed next to her sleeping husband, she lay on her front, squashing the lump into the mattress.

Of course if she hadn't been so concerned for herself she'd have had more time to worry about him, but when spring came and his cough got worse she used it as an excuse to sleep on the sofa. 'I miss you Jean,' he said, and the look in his eyes reminded her of a condemned dog.

Whatever was curled up inside her was getting restless. It was a good job that the first three months of the year were bitingly cold. She swaddled herself in woollen layers and literally buried herself in her work while the shape inside her rolled and kicked, half fish, half horse.

A small hotel in Blackpool had commissioned her to make curtains for eleven bedrooms. She didn't like doing soft furnishings – she was more interested in fashion – but at least the job meant that she could hide behind her sewing machine, the yards of pink chintz on her lap covering up any tell-tale bulges.

She avoided certain people too. Once she hid down a back alley when she saw Marie Boothroyd approach with the Alsatian and that little lad she'd adopted.

When she went to watch Jess do her classes at the institute she kept her coat on, blaming the cold on the boiler, and all of a sudden she hadn't the time for cuddles, even telling her beloved Jess to 'get off me, you're too big for all this silliness'.

Sometimes it felt like she was carrying a bomb: at some point her body was going to detonate. She had given birth before, she knew the score, she knew how it started, the twinges, those tiny little alarm bells that only ever got louder.

Drrr, drrrr, it was the phone. Automatically she picked it up; she hadn't a clue who to expect but half the time she thought it might be the hospital. Jim really did look dreadful. Easter was looming, she hadn't got long.

'Hello, Penny Grainger Carmichael speaking. Is that Mrs Collins?'

She almost dropped the receiver. 'It is,' she whispered.

Penny began to gabble. They were going away for Easter, a cruise, even Belinda had been persuaded to join them, would Jean be available to run up a couple of sun frocks, maybe a kaftan, they were all the rage after all, also one of the fancy buttons had fallen off her wedding bolero, would Jean have a spare?

'When are you going away?' asked Jean.

'Two weeks on Saturday,' trilled Penny.

'I'm very sorry, Mrs Grainger Carmichael, but due to other work commitments I shan't be able to help on this occasion.' Would Penny detect the wobble in her voice?

'Oh!' Her ex-client sounded shocked. 'Are you sure?'

'Quite sure, Mrs Grainger Carmichael. I'm very sorry but I cannot help on this occasion.' And with that she put down the phone and trembled for a good ten minutes, which is hopeless when you're trying to sew six feet of straight seam up a bedroom curtain.

She half expected to see Penny on the doorstep, but she never did. She never clapped eyes on her again, at least not in the flesh.

But she did go back to Weeping Willows. After all, she had nowhere else to go.

The plan only gelled the day she knew the baby was coming. It was April and Jim was at work, but Anne and Jess were at home on their Easter holidays.

'I have to go to St Annes, I'm all out of thread,' she lied to them.

It was a Thursday. By the time she caught the bus she was contracting regularly and by the time she got off at the stop round the corner from Brady Avenue she was finding it hard to walk.

She knew where they hid the spare key to the garage's side door but it was still a relief to upend the plant pot round the back of the house and actually find it lying there, a silver Yale with a Cornish pixie hanging from the fob. Maybe the pixie would bring her luck.

Once she was in the garage she just had to squeeze round the front of the Mini and reach for the Chubb key that would open the connecting door into the kitchen. It hung from a hook to the left of the door; this was how Mrs Glinn gained access when there was no one home to let her in.

Jean froze at the thought of Mrs Glinn. What if she was in the house?

'Then the door would be open, wouldn't it, silly.

'Christ.' She'd started talking to herself, she needed to calm down, she needed to decide where in this house she should give birth to her third child.

As if on cue her waters broke. Better here, she thought, on the easily wiped kitchen linoleum than all over the sherbet lemon carpet in the lounge.

Things were moving fast now and she needed to make

decisions. A sheet, she needed a large double sheet and they probably wouldn't miss a couple of towels either.

Before the next contraction could knock her off her feet she climbed the stairs. How many times had she seen Mrs Glinn iron the bed linen before folding it neatly into an oak-panelled chest on the landing?

As for the towels, she knew they were in the airing cupboard. She chose a plain white sheet and three salmon-coloured towels, large, medium and small, a set that she had once heard Mrs Grainger Carmichael describe as a mistake.

'Ow!' That one caught her unawares.

She made her way crablike down the stairs, clinging on to the banister as her uterus gave agonising squeeze after agonising squeeze.

This baby was coming, by nature, by gravity, by hook or by crook, there was no doubt about it, this baby was coming.

By the time she lay down in the kitchen she had a horrible feeling that had she dared put her hand down there, she could have felt the baby's head. Thursday, which day did the window cleaners do Brady Avenue?

She pulled herself up using the kitchen units. She needed to close the Venetian blinds and get her knickers off.

Thursday's child has far to go . . . arghhhh . . .

The pain was intense. Without knowing quite why she grabbed a wooden spoon from the ceramic jar on top of the sink that contained various kitchen utensils and bit down hard on it.

She had no hand to hold, she was just going to have to do this on her own and if it killed her then it would serve that bastard Kenneth Grainger Carmichael right. What a treat it would be to see his face when he walked into his kitchen after a three-week Caribbean cruise to find her split open, bloodied and dead on the floor.

But what about the baby?

If she died the baby would die. Until this moment she hadn't dared imagine the baby as something real, living, breathing and independent of her, but in that split-second she knew that while she didn't want this child, she didn't want it to die either.

Instinctively she positioned herself on all fours on the large towel. It made sense to give birth this way: why had the hospital always insisted on putting her on her back and tethering her to the bed with metal stirrups? She folded the medium-sized towel beneath her bottom, so that the baby's fall would be cushioned. After all, it was likely to come out head first and the last thing she wanted was the hurt the poor little mite any more than she already had. What with barely eating and all that gin, who knew what damage she had already wreaked?

'Sorry,' she whispered through wooden spoon and clenched teeth.

She just had to hope that the baby would know what to do. They had no choice but to trust each other. With any luck it would be clever like Anne and physically able like Jess, in which case it would find its way out.

She had to keep calm, she knew that. With both her daughters, once the head had emerged the rest of the little human arrived quite quickly. She knew babies were a funny colour, she knew it would need rubbing down and she wondered how long it would be before she heard its little animal cry.

What if there was no cry?

The baby seemed to sense that she needed to resolve this situation. She felt herself bearing down, she breathed hard as suddenly, with an accompanying explosion of pain, a massive contraction pushed the baby's head out of the birth canal and into the world.

She couldn't look back, she just had to push. With her face contorted in a silent scream she forced every molecule of air that she had in her body into the place where the baby was and, as she pushed down with skin-splitting force, for the third time in her life she felt the slither of a tiny set of limbs leaving her own body.

The instant it was over she started to shiver. If she was cold then the baby would be too. She turned to face the child she had delivered, a face both familiar and alien, a gaping mouth registering shock, ready to scream but not yet able.

She swaddled the baby in the sheet and rubbed its body until the gaping mouth emitted a high-pitched wail, and then she remembered. Babies don't just come out, they are born with baggage. They come trailing blood and tubing and the thing no one ever talks about, the placenta. She and the baby were still connected, a fleshy worm of gelatinous sinew tied the two of them together. It was called the umbilical cord, she knew that, and she knew in hospital it had been cut, but how and when?

She froze, but the cord pulsed as if it contained a separate heart. What if she cut it and the baby stopped breathing? Anyway, what would she cut it with?

The bacon scissors in the utensil pot, of course.

But how would she tie the cord?

With the string in the cupboard under the sink, next to the first aid tin!

Mrs Grainger Carmichael was very organised.

Suddenly she felt the urge to push again. Please God, not twins. Surely it couldn't be possible, she'd put on less than a stone in weight; laying the baby beneath her she repositioned herself on all fours and delivered what felt like a great pile of wet tripe while staring into the dark blue eyes of her newborn child.

The placenta was hideous, a trembling heap of purple jelly, but she noticed that now it was free the cord had stopped pulsing and the baby was definitely breathing on his or her own.

She hadn't even checked. Maybe she shouldn't, maybe it was best she never knew.

It could then remain it, but she knew she couldn't resist. She glimpsed beneath the umbilical cord and saw, for the first time in her life, a tiny set of male genitalia. A boy, she was the mother of a son.

She kissed the child quickly on the brow and rocked him against her heart. If only they could stay like this, but she knew she had to move fast.

Gently she laid the baby down and on quivering legs she hauled herself upright and put the kettle on. Those bacon scissors needed sterilising before she cut the cord.

Then she found a crêpe bandage under the sink and cut herself a long narrow strip before she sterilised the scissors again, to be on the safe side.

The cord was chewy like cheap meat, but she managed to sever it around six inches from the baby's little pot belly. Then, with all the expertise of a woman who had spent years dealing in thread, she secured the bandage around it in a neat, tight double knot.

She started talking to the baby now. Suddenly it was vital that he should know what was going to happen next.

'I'm going to put all this nasty in a plastic bag, darling,' she told him, and dug a bin liner out of the kitchen drawer.

The bin men came on a Friday. If she triple-bagged the towels, sheet and the afterbirth then it would be on the back of a lorry within twenty-four hours. Good, any longer and it might start to smell.

A plan was forming in her head and the quicker she got on with it the sooner it would be over.

'Right, young man,' she told her crumple-faced son, 'you're coming with me,' and despite the place between the top of her legs feeling as if it might be on fire, she carried her newborn baby up to Belinda's bedroom.

Mrs Glinn had obviously had a good tidy while the girl was away, but you could still sense Belinda in the room: the heady, musky scent of patchouli oil, the overcrowded dressing table. Jean laid the baby down on the freshly made bed.

She found what she was looking for in the wardrobe, a pair of navy needlecord jeans, a white school shirt and a grubby pair of tennis shoes. She dug further back and found a denim jacket complete with a half-empty packet of Number 6 cigarettes in the pocket.

But before she got changed she lay down on Belinda's bed with her son and cuddled him while she explained what she needed to do. 'You see, it's very important no one knows who I am. I'm married and I have two daughters. I'm sorry, we just don't have very much choice in the matter.'

Gingerly, she then pulled on her disguise. Belinda was much curvier than Jean, much broader round the hips, so pulling up the jeans and fastening the zip wasn't too much of a struggle, although she did leave the top button undone.

Back down in the kitchen she helped herself to three aspirin from the first aid box. Walking was agony but she really had no choice. She gently laid the sheet-swaddled baby in a Schweppes tonic water box and, despite feeling as though someone had bored the very essence of her with a burning poker, she left the house via the same route she'd entered.

The phone box was a thirty-second walk away, but it seemed to take for ever to reach as she could only take small, excruciating steps. However, she saw no one and no one saw her. It wasn't the most original place to leave a baby but that was the point, babies who got left in phone boxes usually got found.

She refused to look at him again. She placed the box on the floor and dialled the emergency services. She put on a French accent, it wasn't very good and she had to repeat herself several times before the operator understood what she meant.

'Zere iss a babee in zis phone box, need help now, pliss.'

And then she put the phone down and limped back to Weeping Willows as she had some tidying up to do. She also needed to help herself to some sanitary towels: she could feel herself leaking. She needed to get out of these jeans, she needed a bath, please God, she couldn't manage without a bath, she needed to be in water, she needed the comfort of a warm bath, she needed to wash the evidence of her baby away, she needed some crying time.

Three hours later, with a handbag full of stolen Dr Whites, she found herself putting a key into her own front door. She cannot remember the journey home, but she can remember thinking if she just kept feeding herself aspirin she would get through it.

Once she'd cooked her daughters' tea she could pretend to have a migraine and go to bed.

'Fish fingers, girls?' she heard herself say.

Anne

Time for the Truth

Anne has cried herself out. Her mother's hospital sheets are damp with her tears and she doesn't need a mirror to know that her face is blotchy and raw.

There is so much about her life that her mother doesn't know, so much that has been left unsaid. Some of it should perhaps be left unsaid, but there is a feeling in her chest as if a paving slab is crushing her heart and the only way she can lift it is to talk.

I need to get something off my chest, she thinks, and hysteria courses through her. Oh God, but where does she begin, which year or event? But suddenly it dawns on her and she begins where she knows the truth really starts.

'I was so jealous of her, Mum, of Jess, I was jealous from the moment she was born to the moment I last saw her.'

Even now she can't actually say the words, 'until she disappeared, until she went missing, my sister is missing, I've lost my sister'.

How can you lose a sister? You can lose your car keys, you can leave your umbrella on the bus, you can mislay your slippers, but how on earth can you ever explain the fact that once upon a time you had a sister, a living breathing sister, and this sister vanished, just vanished into the night?

'And it was my fault, Mum, I wasn't wearing my glasses. If I'd been wearing my glasses I would have seen something, I could have told them, I could have helped with their enquiries, but I couldn't, Mum, and I'm so, so sorry.'

The paving slab feels a little lighter but it's still there, pressing down, making it difficult to breathe, so she keeps going. 'She was so pretty, lots of little girls are pretty aren't they, Mum? And I pretended I didn't mind because I knew I was clever and that was one thing Jess could never have. I used to think, Well when I'm older I can have plastic surgery, I can pay for a better face, but she can't pay for a better brain, and as long as Dad was around it was OK. There was him on my side and you on Jess's side and I know you shouldn't really take sides but it didn't really bother me, it felt like we were in different teams but still playing the same game. But when Dad died it got a bit lopsided, Mum, and I know it must have been hard for you because I think you did love me, it was just you liked Jess more. I'm glad I don't have a favourite with my boys, though to be honest I don't like either of them much at the moment. It just varies which one I dislike the least, according to which one has been shittiest.

'I just think sometimes you were a bit blinkered, like you knew she had faults but you just refused to see them. But no kid is perfect, Mum, she was sly and you know it, and she was a liar and a thief and I might have been priggish and superior and a snobby little cow but—' Anne stops. She was going to say something that wasn't true, that she'd never been dishonest, but she was, she had been.

A long time ago she did a terrible thing and she is not sure, even though it happened years ago, whether she can ever admit it out loud.

It wasn't her fault, it was Jess's really, she had started it and Anne had finished it. A simple tit-for-tat thing and anyway it wasn't anything she actually did, it was just something she pretended to forget to do. And does it really matter where the blame lies? The consequence was far worse than anyone ever deserved.

It was thirty years ago, that long hot summer of A levels and being eighteen and knowing that soon she would be leaving everything behind, and she couldn't wait.

She couldn't wait to walk out of that claustrophobic little house, to turn her back on her widowed mother and annoying little sister. 'Soon,' she would whisper to herself. Soon she would take her place at Edinburgh University, where she would peel off the skin she was bored of and become a much more interesting Anne.

That summer the Parkers next door had a nephew staying. He was about to join the army, a big, strong dark-haired boy with a slow smile and white teeth. He would sit on the party wall and tease both Anne and Jess, sometimes jumping down into their garden to demonstrate his northern soul dance moves. Every Saturday night he'd go to the Wigan Casino, only returning, sweat-soaked and done in, at Sunday lunchtime.

Sometimes he would drink beer or even cherry brandy. 'You'll not be allowed to do that when you're in the army,' Anne told him and he mimicked her, his voice all high and self-righteous.

Jess giggled with the new giggle she'd recently affected.

'Oh come on, Annie, girl, let your hair down.' And he'd offered her the bottle of cherry brandy, the rim wet from where his lips had been. Anne swigged some back, the sticky, sour cherry brandy all mixed in with his tobacco-scented saliva.

Jess wanted some too, but as she was only thirteen Anne insisted she couldn't, it wasn't legal. The boy had laughed and passed Jess the bottle. With one hand on her hip she raised the glass neck to her lips and, as she threw her head back to sink the dregs, her newly formed breasts pushed against her white school shirt. Anne had felt both powerless and furious.

★　★　★

259

That summer, when she left school, she got a job working in a hotel in Blackpool. She had to wear a black knee-length skirt, a black shirt, American tan tights and sensible low-heeled black shoes. She looked prematurely middle-aged and felt it too.

Every time she came home, sweaty and smelling of roast dinner, Jess would be mucking about in the garden in her shorts, showing off for the boy sitting on the wall. Walking on her hands and pretending to be embarrassed when her T-shirt rode over her head, squealing as he sprayed her with a garden hose, giggling while Anne watched as sourly as a little Greek widow.

Not that he ever ignored her. He told Anne she was the only person he could really talk to, he trusted her, he told her that he was excited about joining the army but that he was scared of going to Northern Ireland. He told her that he missed his mum but her new boyfriend made it impossible for him to even visit, he said it made him sad but hopefully in the future they could build some bridges.

She felt like an adult when he talked to her like this. She liked it when he was quiet and serious, but she liked it best when he sniffed her shirt and tried to guess what she'd been serving for dinner. 'Pork and apple sauce?' he would hazard, his nose nudging her breast. 'Stop it!' she would protest, but when he'd gone back next door or disappeared off to the pub 'to see a man about a dog' she would lock herself in the bathroom and pull at her breasts and finger herself into oblivion.

He told her once that he'd seen her in the bathroom. He said he could see her silhouette through the cream-coloured roller blind as she stepped out of the bath – 'May I say, Anne, you have a mighty fine pair' – and she'd blushed to her roots but sometimes, when she couldn't sleep and she heard his back gate open, she would dash to the bathroom, pull down the blind and take off her nightie. Then, not being sure what to do, she would stretch and yawn, her breasts moving of their own accord. Or sometimes she would simply clean her teeth, never really knowing if he was watching. He must have caught her a couple of times though, because one afternoon he whispered into her ear, 'I like a girl who realises the importance of giving her teeth a good clean,' and then he'd winked and quite casually rubbed at the bulge between his legs.

She doesn't tell her mother this. Jean might be in a coma but Anne still cannot say the word 'masturbate' in front of her.

She gives her mother a PG version of the truth.

'I know you thought I wasn't that interested in boys,' she admits and, thinking back, she hadn't been.

Apart from the crush she'd had on Angela Metcalf's brother there hadn't really been the time. She'd been studying, first O levels then A levels, and since she was sixteen she'd always had part-time jobs, working on the till at the newsagent's across the road or as a chambermaid up in town.

'I was a bit self-conscious,' she continues. 'I knew I wasn't particularly attractive.'

Of course now, looking back, she'd been perfectly presentable. A bit lumpy and her glasses hadn't done much for her, but she wasn't hideous. It was just that next to her younger sister she'd faded to plain.

Jess had always been a pretty little thing, but around the age of twelve she blossomed. Unlike most pubescent girls whose hormones conspire against them, she emerged from childhood into her teenage years without a blemish. Overnight her little straight up and down body resculpted itself into a series of small curves: her waist narrowed, her hips, although slight, began to sashay and her breasts bloomed magically from a pancake 28A to a pert 32B.

'And all I could do was watch,' Anne sighs. 'She really was a looker wasn't she, Mum? A right bobby dazzler, and for a while she had no idea.'

By the time Jess was thirteen she was being whistled at by scaffolders on building sites. Once when walking home from school she'd been followed by a man in a mac who had exposed himself to her and Jean had insisted on calling the police. A constable in his forties had paid a visit and advised Jess to avoid dark alleyways and talking to strangers. 'There's lot of strange blokes out there,' he'd warned before asking Jean for her phone number as she saw him out.

'Do you remember PC Tony?' Anne asks her mother. He'd taken Jean out for dinner a couple of times, but then she'd found out he was married and refused to ever see him again.

Only they had seen him again, four years later. He was a detective by then, it was ironic really.

Anyway, she mustn't keep getting side-tracked, she needs to confess something to her mother, something that happened that summer.

The summer of the audition. 'Do you remember, Mum, when the man from London came to Jess's dance class?'

Of course she would remember. At first it had been a casual thing, a talent scout in a camel coat standing right at the back of the class with a black leather notebook in his hand.

'Just having a general recce,' Audrey Carr told Jean.

Only one evening, when Anne had got back from the Sandy Shore Hotel (yes really), Jean and Jess were waiting with vanilla slices. Anne hadn't really fancied a vanilla slice, she'd been picking at work (roast beef with all the trimmings), but even if she didn't want one she knew they meant something.

As soon as she'd walked through the door her mother and sister had started babbling. It took a while for Anne to under-stand what had happened.

Jess had been chosen to audition for a film, a proper cinema film about a girl whose dancing career is ruined by a drunk driver and whose father is intent on revenge.

'I'll be in a wheelchair,' screeched Jess, 'because my legs are paralysed!'

'So why do you need to be able to dance?' Anne had asked. The sight of the cakes made her feel sick, the yellow confectioner's custard reminding her of a spot on her chin she'd squeezed that morning.

'Flashbacks, there's going to be loads of what they call flash-backs to when this girl was a ballerina.' And to demonstrate why she was the ideal candidate for the role Jess jetéd from one side of the room to the other.

They had to go to Manchester for the day. The audition was going to be held at the Opera House, they would have to take the train.

Apart from Jess, only one other girl from Cygnets had been chosen to go. But as Jean had whispered conspiratorially to anyone who would listen, 'Between you, me and the gatepost, that Abigail Moran has no chance of getting the part. Not with all that red hair and a million freckles, not even if she is double-jointed.'

Though she did add that Miss Carr had warned them there'd be stiff competition from all the other dance schools in the north-west and that none of them could take anything for granted.

'It's a nationwide search,' whooped Jess.

'We will just have to go and try our best,' beamed Jean, and Anne was suddenly struck by how pretty her mother was when she was happy.

Jean

Baby Neville and Other Headlines

The memories are looking nice and tidy now, a good deal of her past has been put in the correct place. Unfortunately there are still some messy bits to go through, things that should never happen to anyone.

She remembers leaving the baby in the telephone box and she knows for certain that she has thought about him every day since.

He was found, of course: a young lad out on his bike had a puncture and went into the phone box to call his dad. He should have called the police really, but as the lad said to the local newspaper, 'My dad always knows what to do.'

The father called the police and they all arrived together, the police with their sirens and the dad with a puncture repair kit.

They took the baby to hospital and a senior staff nurse in the maternity ward asked the officer carrying the infant what his name was. 'Neville,' the officer replied, and so the baby was named Neville, for a while anyway, until he was adopted and then . . .

It was no business of hers, but for years she had guessed: Richard, John, Peter, Simon? She liked the name Simon. She'd have called him Simon, only he wasn't hers to call anything.

Sometimes, over the years, it was hard not to mention him in conversation, her secret son Simon, but she never did.

There was an appeal of course: 'Where is baby Neville's mummy?'

The general consensus was that the mother was very young, possibly still a schoolgirl, probably from a nice home, given where the baby was found. Mothers, could your daughter be baby Neville's missing mum?

No doubt there were some anxious moments up and down Brady Avenue, parents looking closely at their daughters for changes in their behaviour and possible emotional outbursts, but no one was forthcoming and anyway, within a matter of weeks there was a bigger scandal to knock baby Neville right off the front page.

She remembers feeling sick at the sight of the grainy image. Jim was reading the paper, but because he'd turned straight to the back page she was faced with the headlines over her corn-flakes.

Local Lawyer in Suicide Horror.

It was him, Kenneth Grainger Carmichael, grinning with a cigar in his hand as he stood next to the Mayor. 'Shock as daughter finds father hanging in garage.'

She waited until Jim went to work; she needed to be alone to read it properly. Finally, after faffing around for what seemed like hours, Jim left the house, cycle clips around his ankles.

'Goodbye dear.'

'Goodbye.'

As soon as he'd wobbled off on his bicycle she snatched up the paper and collapsed on to the sofa to read the story. Her eyes darted from paragraph to paragraph, picking out random fragments: 'youngest daughter . . . luxury cruise . . . well liked and respected . . . out of the blue . . . Penelope Grainger Carmichael . . . society wedding of the season . . .'

Eventually, after reading the story several times over, Jean was able to piece together what had actually happened.

Belinda had found him. Poor Belinda, Jean was very fond of that girl, it wasn't her fault her father was a monster. The Grainger Carmichaels, apart from newlywed elder daughter Helen, had recently returned from a luxury cruise to their elegant Brady Avenue ranch-style home.

Belinda had been at school and was returning her bicycle to the garage, only to find her father hanging from a metal beam.

Attempts by the ambulance service to resuscitate Mr Grainger Carmichael were unsuccessful and he was pronounced dead on arrival at hospital.

The family are said to be devastated and the bereaved Mrs Grainger Carmichael is reported to have said she 'knew of no earthly reason why her darling husband Kenneth Grainger Carmichael should take his own life'.

Only there was a reason, of course there was. It all came out in the end: for the past eighteen months Kenneth had been embezzling funds at the law firm where he had worked for thirty years. Apparently, underneath the respectable exterior, the Rotary Club charity fundraising smile and golf club bonhomie, Kenneth had a chronic gambling problem and his daughter's wedding had put him under considerable financial pressure.

The whistle was about to be blown and Kenneth knew it. He took the coward's way out. Rumour had it that his son-in-law had played a part in his downfall, but nothing was ever proved and eventually, just like baby Neville, the Grainger Carmichael news became stale.

Weeping Willows went on the market for a phenomenal sum of money, although because of the tragedy it eventually sold for several thousand pounds less than the asking price.

Penelope and Belinda moved to Malta: Jean found this out from the horse's mouth, or rather from Mrs Glinn, whom she bumped into in St Annes indoor market. 'Poor Penelope, I've never seen her so thin, skin and bone she was by the time they left,' ghouled Mrs Glinn. 'And of course it completely messed up Belinda doing her exams. Between you, me and the gatepost,

I blame that husband of Helen's, that Roy Pickering. Mark my words, he's a nasty piece of work.'

Jean didn't disagree. She wasn't a fan of Roy Pickering but she didn't hate him like she hated Kenneth Grainger Carmichael. She was glad he was dead.

'They've repainted the house,' Mrs Glinn added, 'the new people, it's a sort of olive now. I can't bear to even walk past, I don't think I could ever go down Brady Avenue again if I live to be a hundred.'

Which she didn't. She died when she was seventy-six, Jean knows this for a fact: she read about it in the paper. For some reason she always checks the births, marriages and deaths. 'Let's face it,' she once joked to Noreen and Pat, 'you get to an age when you have to check the obituaries just to make sure you're not in them yourself.'

Of course Jim died too young, not that he was ever going to make old bones. She remembers looking at him on their wedding day and thinking, He looks peaky.

It was a shame he never saw Anne married, he would have liked that and he would have approved of her husband, a doctor no less. Oh yes, there was no doubt about it, Anne did very well for herself.

She has to stop herself for a moment. She's racing ahead again, grabbing memories from a different time, missing out great chunks in the middle. Even if there are things that would be easier to forget she has to be more careful.

She should go back to Jim dying, that was the next big thing. Obviously lots of little things happened between Kenneth killing himself and Jim keeling over at the bowls club, but you'd go mad if you tried to remember everything.

It was another heart attack; he was only forty-three. They did what they could – the bar manager at the club even attempted to give him the kiss of life – but he passed away in the ambulance.

Anne was beside herself. She didn't say much but Jean would hear her weeping at night and for months she wore a black elasticated hairband around her wrist and Jean knew it was in memory of her father.

Jess was upset about her daddy dying too, but she was even more upset that Jean wouldn't buy her a pair of shoes with a heel for the funeral. 'Why not? she demanded, stamping her stockinged foot in the middle of Stead and Simpson.

'Because you can't wear heels for school.'

'But everyone else does,' the girl snapped back. In some respects she was right: the local comp was a lot more lax about the school uniform than Queen Margaret's.

In the end they compromised: Jess got a medium-sized heel that she could wear for both school and parties.

'And funerals,' Jess added, smiling sweetly at the shop assistant.

Jean was convinced that not many people would turn up for Jim's funeral, but he was surprisingly popular. 'He was ever such a nice man, your husband,' people kept telling her. In the end she wanted to scream, 'I know, I know, he was a nice man, that's why I married him. Do you think I am stupid?'

But she didn't, she was very dignified. She had to be, she was a widow with two young daughters, not to mention an abandoned son. She really wasn't sure how she was going to manage.

But you did, she reminds herself, and right up until it all went horrible you did a good job. You couldn't help what happened in the end, it wasn't your fault.

But there is a tiny barb in her heart, like a splinter that has never worked its way out. A nagging doubt that wonders if, in a roundabout way, she was to blame.

Maybe I made her feel too special, is that possible? Can you encourage a child too much? She means Jess, of course, she barely had to intervene with Anne about anything. Anne was what they called self-motivated, she was a model pupil and when she said she was at school you could bet your bottom dollar she was at school.

Jess, on the other hand, sometimes you couldn't really trust her to tell the truth. It wasn't her fault, she didn't really like school and with every passing year it seemed to get harder. She struggled with the work because of her reading problem and by the time she was in the third year some of the girls were being horrible to her because she was so pretty.

That's why it was important for her to keep up the dance classes to take her mind off the nasty bullies, and anyway she was talented, everyone said so, though Audrey did complain about her not working hard enough.

She discussed it with Jean: 'I see it all the time, they're keen as mustard when they're little but as soon as boys come into the picture they get all gooey and silly and they don't put in the hours.'

'She's only fourteen,' Jean had protested.

'And she's getting a bit busty too,' Audrey had added.

Jean bit her lip. She couldn't deny that Jess had developed, it was obvious for everyone to see. That's why she got so much attention on the street.

Fortunately, just as Jess was starting to moan about spending 'half my life at that bloody place' she got the audition for the film and Jean had never known her work so hard. For the two weeks between being chosen and going up to Manchester she practised and practised and practised – in the house, in the garden, she never stopped and I never tired of watching her admits Jean, she lit up my life.

And just before she drops off into the dark again she treats herself to a medley of Jess's greatest dances. She watches her tap, shuffle and hop, she watches her do her Grade Six ballet solo and she watches her turn a series of perfect flick-flacks right across a sunlit lawn. If only she could hear herself clap, but something has happened to her hands and she can't make them do anything, not even clap her own daughter. 'Bravo Jess,' she mouths to herself, 'bravo.'

Jess

Getting Ready for the Audition

Jess thought she might burst with excitement. She thought about the audition from the moment she woke up to the moment she fell asleep and even then she would dream about it. Sometimes these dreams turned into nightmares – a lost ballet shoe, a period seeping through her leotard mid-pirouette – but most nights the dreams were triumphant, her favourite being the one when she finished to a standing ovation, while her only local rival, Abigail Moran, was carted off to hospital having broken her leg in three different places.

For the first time since she broke up for the summer holidays she wished it was still term time. Then she could tell her schoolmates and watch the rumour spread. She could almost hear the whispering: 'That Jess Collins has got an audition for a film, in Manchester.'

'Never!'

'Yeah, cross my heart.'

Of course they'd all be really jealous. No doubt she'd come home with gob all down the back of her blazer; that's what they did at her school: if you stepped out of line you got spat at.

Maybe it was a good job it was the holidays after all.

She didn't need some great psycho bully giving her a shove

on the stairs or tripping her up down the corridor, she needed to be careful. She couldn't afford the slightest twist or sprain, there were some nutcases in that place and the girls were far worse than the boys.

Boys liked her, though some of them thought she was a bit stuck-up. She wasn't, it was just the lads in her class were idiots and anyway, she liked them a bit older.

She liked the boy next door, the boy who had come to stay with his auntie, the boy who was going to be a soldier. He was nineteen and dead fit.

She liked the way he watched her through his fringe when she did her dancing in the garden. She could feel his eyes on her breasts, the way they jiggled about when she moved. They were getting bigger, though not as big as Anne's. Anne's were massive and already a bit saggy; Jess's were just right. They bulged out of her training bras, she needed to go up a size but when she pointed this out to her mother Jean just got really upset. Honestly, sometimes she really didn't get her mum, it was like she wanted her to stay a little girl for ever. Well that just wasn't going to happen.

That's why she wanted to get this film so badly. She wanted to get away too, she couldn't bear it that Anne was going to escape first. She was going to go to university and leave Jess in this dump with her mum, who just wanted her to be nine years old and flat-chested again.

If she got the film she wouldn't have to go back to school where the lessons bored her and the bigger girls frightened her, the skinhead ones with their shaved eyebrows and non-regulation Crombie coats, girls with peroxide feather cuts who would get you in the playground if you didn't watch it.

This was what she had been waiting for all her life. Ever since she skipped down the aisle at that posh wedding she'd been waiting for something just as exciting to happen again. She'd waited long enough. What did her mother always tell her? She was special and very soon everyone and not just her mum would know just how special she was, and even Anne would be impressed. Even if she was at university she would have to own up, she would have to admit it, she would have to say the words, 'Yes, my sister is that film star, the dancing one. Yes, that's my sister, my famous sister.'

And all Anne's new university friends would go, 'Wow Anne, that's amazing, you're so lucky. Can we meet her?'

Only she'd be too busy living in Hollywood to meet Anne's boring brainy new friends, ha ha ha.

Anne

Getting Mad

Anne sits by her mother's bedside, an entire box's worth of tissues discarded in snotty balls at her feet. She has blown her nose so hard her sinuses are stinging, but she has started this story and her mother needs to be told how it ends.

'The day you went to Manchester for the audition was the day I got my A level results,' Anne reminds her mother. 'You and Jess had left the house before I even got up. I don't think any of us saw each other to actually say good luck, though you did say you'd ring at lunchtime to see how I'd got on.' Anne pauses. 'Only I didn't come home at lunchtime.'

Thirty years roll away in a matter of a seconds and Anne is once again craning her neck to look at the examination results pinned up on the board outside school.

Once she'd checked, double-checked, triple-checked and silently cheered her four grade-A results she'd gone back to Grace's house (two As and two Bs, her parents were a bit put out), then along with Angela Metcalf (three grade Bs) they joined the rest of the year for celebratory drinks in a big Victorian pub by the train station in St Annes.

She started on lager but switched to cherry brandy. It was

more sophisticated, only by three o'clock she was feeling poorly and by four o'clock she'd been sick three times.

Grace, who had stuck to Britvic orange because she genuinely didn't like the taste of alcohol, phoned her father and begged him to take Anne home. He didn't speak to her all the way back to Marton: he obviously thought four As were wasted on a drunk.

The boy from next door was sitting outside the house on a motorbike. He was talking to a friend, but when he saw Anne tripping up the garden path he leapt off the bike and helped her get her key in the door.

She was staggering, so he supported her up the stairs. Her legs kept giving way and she was a dead weight but he pulled and pushed her up to the landing. He knew what to do; she needed to get into bed. There was sick on her T-shirt, she needed to get out of her clothes.

He helped her get undressed and she was too drunk to be embarrassed. He was gentle; she slumped down on the bed and held her arms up like a child so that he could pull off her stinking top. She wished she was wearing a nicer bra, it was just a big white one gone grey in the wash. Her knickers were frayed too but he didn't say anything, he just pulled back the covers and tucked her in. She was embarrassed about her white mottled legs and the rolls of fat on her belly, she started to whimper and apologise. He shushed her and gave her a kiss on the top of her head, then said he'd see her later and perhaps when she was feeling better she'd like to clean her teeth for him again. And with that he reached beneath the sheet and squeezed the fleshy mound of her left tit.

If only she hadn't had to run to the bathroom that very second to be sick, maybe he would have kissed her on the lips.

She heard him leave as she puked.

'I really liked him, Mum. Even though he once told me he'd never read a book I still really liked him.'

By the time Jean and Jess got back from Manchester she was

dozing, but she got up to tell them about her results and lied about eating a dodgy pork pie that had made her sick.

'What a shame,' Jean tutted. 'We've had a fantastic day and Jess was a complete star. I should have bought some vanilla slices.'

'I'm glad you didn't, Mum,' Anne said, 'I'm not feeling too good. We can save the celebrations for another day.'

'Yes,' shrieked Jess, 'like when I get the part. Then we can buy cakes, when we've got something proper to celebrate and not just a bunch of mouldy exams.'

Anne sniffs for the umpteenth time. Her sister's words still rankle.

'I missed my father then, Mum, I missed him because he would have been so proud of me. I'm not getting at you, you were really pleased, but you weren't proud and I really wanted someone to be proud of me.'

Waking up the next day and feeling normal again had been an enormous relief. She hoped to see the boy next door, to say thank you for looking after her, but she kept missing him and she couldn't just hang around all day waiting for him to show up. She had to go to work.

It was almost a week before their paths crossed. It was dark when she got back from the hotel; she'd stayed late, clearing up after the evening meal before setting the tables for breakfast, then she missed a bus and she had to wait ages for another. It was after ten by the time she got back and as it was drizzling she cut through from the bus stop down the back alley, even though her mother had warned both her daughters not to, not after dark.

The back gate was open and as she walked on her sensible rubber soles into the garden she noticed the bathroom light was on. The blind was fully open and Jess was dancing at the window. She was swaying in her bra, running her hands through her thick blond hair. Suddenly she stopped dancing and reached round to unclasp her bra, peeling it off and then cupping her breasts as if struck by shyness, before fondling herself, one hand at her

275

breasts, the other out of sight. She was writhing, her hair masking her face until she suddenly shook it out of her eyes and raised both hands to her lips to blow kisses.

Anne heard a low moan from the other side of the wall. She smelt the familiar whiff of tobacco. She stood rooted to the path, frozen as if playing musical statues, then, like a robot set into reverse, she backed out of the gate and, pausing to take a deep breath, she re-entered, this time slamming the gate behind her. The light went out in the bathroom almost immediately.

'So you see, Mum, I was really angry.'

Jean

Comedown

The day after the audition Jean had bumped into Audrey Carr's emaciated sidekick Miss Evangeline outside the dentist on Clyde Road. 'How did it go, Mrs Collins?'

'One of the best days of my life,' Jean crowed.

Only it wasn't, not really.

For starters, she'd never seen so many girls around Jess's age all in one place, hundreds of them in their black leotards and white tights, their hair scraped back into uniform buns. Some of them, she had to admit, were very beautiful, seriously beautiful. As was Jess, of course she was, she was the prettiest girl at the Opera House, even if her leotard did look a little tight across her chest.

She danced like an angel, really it was obvious she was head and shoulders above most of them and Jean wasn't surprised at the end of the morning session when Jess's number was among those read out for a late-afternoon recall.

They went to Kendal Milne's, the department store, for a spot of lunch, but both of them were too nervous to enjoy their open sandwich – 'I'm not sure that I actually like smoked salmon,' Jess admitted, her stomach churning with the unfamiliar raw fish, while Jean had found her cottage cheese and pineapple combo 'a bit titchy', so on the way back to the Opera House they'd shared a Kit Kat.

Some of the other mothers were a little standoffish. One of them spoke just like Penelope Grainger Carmichael, which made Jean feel faint.

'Does your daughter have film experience?'

'No,' admitted Jean, 'but she's done a lot of shows and panto.'

'Oh panto, really, how sweet!'

It was nerves, they were all pretending that it didn't matter but the tension in the green room after lunch was palpable. Seven girls and seven mothers, although one girl referred to her companion as 'my chaperone'. Spoilt brat, thought Jean.

Jessica Collins was called first. Abigail Moran was already on the train back to Blackpool and Jean recalls smirking as she hovered in the wings waiting for Jess to do whatever was required for this next step of the process. Poor Abigail, poor Mrs Moran, she would be so bitterly disappointed.

She wishes now she hadn't been so cocky – pride comes before a fall and all that – because this time they didn't want to see Jess dance, they wanted her to read a scene from the film.

A man strode on to the stage and handed her a fat yellow script. 'If you can just start at the top of Scene Three.'

It was all Jean could do not to go marching out and snatch the script from Jess's quivering hands. Her daughter needed time, she couldn't sight read, she had a genetic problem, it wasn't her fault, it wasn't fair.

Jess tried her best but Jean could tell that her reading was stilted. She was stumbling over baby words, making no sense of any emotion that might lie behind the print. Her armpits prickled with embarrassment for her daughter.

'Thank you,' came a voice from the stalls, 'we'll be in touch. Please leave your telephone number with Clare in the green room. If we have any news we'll call you directly.'

Jess curtsied at the voice and, to give the girl credit, it was a curtsy fit for royalty.

They gave their number to Clare in the green room and Jean beamed as if to demonstrate to all the other mothers and daughters how wonderfully well it had gone.

It wasn't until they found their way out of the stage door that she realised: Jess had no idea, none whatsoever, quite how dreadful it had been.

The child was buzzing. 'Oh Mum, when do you think they'll call?'

All the way home her golden-haired daughter prattled on. Would they live in London while they were filming? What if they wanted to shoot it in America? After all, that's where most films were made. 'Oh Mum, just think, we could be living in LA.'

Fortunately Jess fell asleep just outside Bolton and Jean spent the rest of the journey crunching aspirin, trying to ease the headache that gnawed at her temples.

Maybe it hadn't been that bad.

Don't kid yourself Jean.

It was only as they got off the train in Blackpool that she realised she had forgotten to phone Anne. Her eldest daughter had gone to pick up her A level results and she had completely forgotten to be interested.

She wasn't worried, she was confident Anne would pass. She tried to recall what grades she needed for her place at Edinburgh but she couldn't remember if it was two Bs and a C or a B and two Cs.

She would make up some excuse as to why she hadn't called: she didn't have any change, there was chewing gum stuck in the coin slot, the phone rang and rang but no one answered.

She would try to make it up to Anne. They could have a little holiday, nothing too fancy but abroad would be nice, the three of them had never been anywhere hot. She would pick up some brochures next time she went into town.

They did get their passports done, she remembers that, but that's as far as the holiday went: all the way to Woolworths to sit in a photo booth!

Well what a very uncomfortable pack of memories, thinks Jean, not many laughs in that lot, and she decides to give it a rest for a while. The trouble with getting depressed when you're in a coma is that there's not a fat lot you can do about it. It's not like you can cheer yourself up by having a cake or going to the cinema. The only thing she can do is to let the darkness close in on her, wrap her up in starless black velvet. There is enormous comfort in just nothing, thinks Jean, nothing can go wrong when nothing is happening, and she sighs a tiny sigh, too small for even a machine to hear.

Anne

Revenge

No one knew how angry she was. She just seethed quietly, and in an odd way she quite enjoyed this feeling of hurt.

The summer stretched ahead, just an endless round of gravy-smeared plates and watching the telly. Grace and Angela had escaped on holiday with their parents, the Longs had gone to Greece to look at the ruins, while the Metcalfs decamped to a house in France. They went every year and every year Anne desperately wanted to be invited.

Her mother brought home some brochures and the three of them looked at shiny white hotels with tiny windows in Tenerife and Majorca. They even sent off for passports, but somehow nothing ever got booked.

They were waiting for the phone call. Cygnets was closed for the entire month of August; Audrey Carr was accustomed to spending time off with her brother on the Isle of Wight, returning every year sneering about the standard of the shows at Shanklin: 'Not a patch on our piers, Jean.'

'We can have a holiday right here,' Jean insisted. 'We live a couple of miles from some of the country's most glorious beaches, we've got the best rides in Europe and we can see the shows without the expense of hotel accommodation.'

Had the weather made even the slightest effort to be on their side it might have been bearable, but the skies reflected Anne's mood: surly and inclined to spit.

As for the shows, her mother and Jess might have enjoyed them but Anne found the comedy bewildering and she was sick of the sight of over-made-up women kicking up their legs and flashing their gussets while simultaneously trying to keep their headdresses on and the seams of their stockings straight. Had no one ever heard of feminism?

The seventies were over. On the promenade gangs of self-conscious punks paraded in their bin liners, scowling through clouds of candyfloss that clung to their piercings.

The world was changing and Jess was changing too. She didn't want to go to Blackpool with her mum, she wanted to hang out at the Pleasure Beach with her mates and scream when men with tattooed arms and golden earrings spun their waltzer carriage, faster and faster till their buttons came undone and they were breathless and giddy.

So Anne worked at the Sandy Shore, Jess met up with Nathalie and Gina, and Jean stayed at home waiting for the phone call and when the phone call didn't come she waited for Jess. She didn't like her being out after dark but Jess didn't care. Sometimes Anne would be home before her younger sister.

'Is that you Jess?'

'No, Mum, it's only me.'

Jean tried not to row with Jess when she eventually did come home, but sometimes Anne could hear them arguing down in the sitting room. Her sister was putting on weight too, all that hanging around on the seafront eating chips. Good.

The day the phone call came Jess had gone to Pontin's holiday camp. Jean hadn't wanted her to go but Jess had twisted and twisted her arm until she'd relented and given her the money for a day pass.

'How can it be dangerous? There's loads of families and

kiddies. Of course we won't go back to anyone's chalet, I'm not stupid.'

So Jess had set off in her shortest shorts and her tightest T-shirt and Jean had gone to do a measure for a job in Ansdell, which was further out than she really liked to travel but work was work so she'd probably have to take it even though it was a tricky upholstery job involving a lot of complicated mental arithmetic that terrified the living daylights out of her.

Anne was due in to work later that afternoon so she treated herself to a leisurely breakfast. It was nice having the house to herself. The boy next door had gone to Bovington for training; they probably wouldn't see him again: according to Mrs Parker, his mother had kicked her fancy man out so he'd probably be heading back there when he got leave.

She was on her fourth slice of toast when the phone rang. Maybe it was the police: with any luck her sister had fallen under a tram.

It was a woman called Clare from *Justice for Laura*.

'Sorry?'

'The film, *Justice for Laura*. Is that Mrs Collins?'

'No, it's her daughter.'

'Well congratulations Jess. It is Jess, isn't it? We'd like you to come to London for a screen test. Now isn't that exciting? Have you got a pen and a piece of paper?'

'Hang on a minute.' Anne grabbed a biro and the electricity bill.

'Your screen test is booked for next Tuesday, the nineteenth, at Ealing Studios.'

The biro didn't work.

It was fate.

She pretended to write down the address and telephone number. She assured Clare that she would indeed tell her mother and that yes, of course they could get there by three o'clock and thank you so much, yes she was very excited indeed.

She put the phone down. If she grabbed another pen quickly

she could scribble the address and phone number down from memory, Ealing 738957, it wasn't too late.

'But I didn't, Mum, I went back into the kitchen and put a fifth piece of bread into the toaster.'

Anne pauses for a second but Jean doesn't move a millimetre. In some respects she is relieved; if anything was going to stir her mother out of this coma it's the admission that Anne had purposefully sabotaged her sister's chance to be a film star.

Someone else got the part, the phone never rang to enquire as to why Jess hadn't turned up and when the summer finally came to a soggy and unsatisfactory end they all pretended to have forgotten about it.

'It wasn't any good anyway,' Anne informs Jean. 'The film, when it came out. *Justice for Laura*. I read the reviews when I was at university, a big thumbs-down from all the broad-sheets.'

She had got away by then. Edinburgh was a relief, a clean start, a reinvention. She spent the first term in halls, which was fine, but just before the Christmas break Rowena Mundie approached her over a canteen baked-potato lunch and offered her a room in a flat share on Dundas Street.

Rowena Mundie's family owned a big chunk of Aberdeenshire, complete with a whisky distillery. Miss Mundie might have been as thin as Olive Oyl, complete with an undiagnosed thyroid complaint that made her eyes bulge, but she was a very popular girl.

Anne was thrilled. She didn't even enquire as to the size of her room, which turned out to be the box room next to the bathroom. She didn't care, she was in the in crowd.

Ideally, Anne wouldn't have bothered going home that Christmas at all. As it was, her brief visit was fraught. Her mother, as usual, was up to her neck in sequins and tulle. The Cygnet School of Dance Christmas show was in full swing, only this year it was missing its star turn.

Jess had given up ballet. She'd given up tap as well. The only class she attended these days was modern jazz, which was just disco dancing really.

Her mother put a brave face on, a face Anne recognises sometimes when she looks at herself in the mirror.

She wishes she'd been more sympathetic, but to be honest she wasn't fussed. Her mother and her sister came very low on her list of priorities.

'I was a superior cow,' she admits. 'I was mixing with a different class of people, out of my depth but determined not to let it show.'

Even Angela and Grace noticed how her accent had become more refined. It was nice catching up with them, even if Angela's brother had a steady girlfriend who draped herself around him like a human flypaper.

She escaped as soon as she could, returning to Scotland for Hogmanay. Rowena had organised a dinner party for which everyone dressed up. The girls wore long dresses and the boys wore black tie. At midnight they trooped up the hill to Princes Street to watch the fireworks, crossed arms and sang 'Auld Lang Syne', then rolled home for a wee dram of the Mundie family's finest single malt.

That was the second time Anne was sick from drinking too much. It was an occupational hazard living at Dundas Street with Rowena and her chums.

She'd felt like an intruder for the first six months but as she came to the end of her first year Anne had learnt to blend in. She laughed more stridently, adopted Rowena's habit of eating a croissant instead of toast for breakfast and began smoking with her left hand. Just like her flatmate she wore piecrust-collar shirts and wine-coloured cords that did nothing for her bottom but gave the impression that she might be quite handy on a horse.

Rowena's family had a place in Bergerac, and at last Anne was invited away for the whole summer. She couldn't help feeling thrilled when the place turned out to be vastly superior to the Metcalfs' gîte.

Meanwhile, her sister had turned fifteen and nasty with it. She was still pretty, but when Anne finally managed a three-day visit before the autumn term started she was shocked by how much Jess had changed.

Her sister was no longer a skinny little will o' the wisp. This new Jess, since giving up two-thirds of her dance classes, was heavier all over. A languid sexiness oozed dangerously from newfound fleshiness; she was all cleavage, home-bleached streaks and heavy eyeliner.

A bit common really.

'Boy mad,' her mother said, pretending it was just a bit of teenage nonsense.

'Is that why she's on the pill then?' Anne shot back.

'She was having trouble with her periods,' her mother lied.

Really it was much easier not going home at all.

That Christmas, the Dundas Street gang went skiing. Anne was the only one who'd never been before, but what she lacked in experience she made up for in sheer bloody-minded determination.

By the end of the fortnight no one could tell that she wasn't a Klosters regular, or indeed that her salopettes were second-hand.

It was the first time she hadn't been home for Christmas, and what with the expense of the Klosters trip it made sense to stay in Edinburgh for New Year. Hopefully she'd make it back for Easter.

Whether or not she did, she can't actually remember.

She finished her second year at the same time as Jess sat her CSEs: unsuccessfully, as it turned out. When the results came out Anne was aghast, but Jess didn't care. She was going to do hairdressing at college, starting in September. Anyway, once she'd finished her exams Audrey Carr had offered her a job teaching contemporary dance to the littlies on a Saturday morning, but it was a nine o'clock class and more often than not she didn't make it. The third time she phoned up pretending to have tonsillitis, Audrey sacked her. 'The fucking cow,' fumed Jess.

Anne knew she should have gone home and tried to knock some sense into her sister, but it was August, the Edinburgh Festival was in full swing and she had a cushy little part-time job selling tickets at the Assembly Rooms on George Street; she was also seeing a fellow student who was performing at the festival with a close-harmony singing group. The Acapella Fellas garnered a three-star review from the *Scotsman*. 'Should have been four stars,' Anne told her boyfriend loyally.

Her mother rang her in Dundas Street. 'When are you coming home? Be nice to see you.'

'Your mum sounds ever so like my auntie's cleaner,' remarked her flatmate Charlotte. 'Is she a northern woman?'

The truth was she didn't like going home. She couldn't sleep in her old bed, she just lay there, the half-forgotten details of an Ealing address and phone number like grit under her eyelids.

Anne checks her watch. She will stay here until she gets slung out, this story isn't over yet.

She takes a sip of water. 'And anyway I was seeing Paul and the next time I came home, Mum, well, you know what happened.'

Anne swallows hard. Even though she knows the next part of the story is true, there is still something shockingly unbelievable about it.

Jean

For the Last Time

Jean forces herself out of the soft blackness. She needs to shake a leg, not that she can, but she has a feeling she needs to get a move on. Time is running out. Each time she falls into the blackness it's harder to pull herself out and anyway, who would blame her if she did simply roll back into oblivion? Why would any mother want to remember what happened next?

Now where had she got up to exactly . . .?

Anne had started university, a four-year joint honours course in English and French. She might as well have been studying Double Dutch for all it meant to Jean. What she did know was that her daughter seemed happier in Edinburgh than she was at home. University Anne was more confident, she dropped little bits of French into everyday conversation and waved her hands around a lot. Suddenly she started smoking foreign cigarettes and took to wearing a velvet Alice band.

Jean missed her more than she thought she would, especially as every time she did make the effort to pop back she'd changed that little bit more. Gradually her daughter was becoming a stranger and it dawned on Jean that she'd missed her chance for the two of them to ever be really close.

Thing is, Jean reminds herself, you put all your eggs in one basket.

She'd been so besotted by Jess that by the time Anne was eighteen she was so used to being pushed away that the distance between them, both physical and emotional, felt natural.

She never invited either Jean or Jess to the flat she shared on Dundas Street, but she did show Jean some photos. It looked very swish: the sitting room, which Anne referred to as the 'drawing room', had walls the colour of red wine; the hall was big enough for a baby grand piano (apparently Rowena could have been a professional); and there was even a dishwasher in the kitchen.

'But it's right at the top of one of those old tenements – millions of stairs, *très* knackering,' Anne had laughed, blowing Gitanes smoke rings.

If only she'd been able to confide in Anne, tell her how worried she was about Jess, how she felt she'd gone off the rails since she'd given up her dancing, how she thought not getting the film had knocked her confidence. After all, there's nothing worse than building up your hopes only to have them crumble to dust around your ankles. Better not to dream at all.

Jean can't decide who was more disappointed about the outcome of the audition, herself or Jess. They certainly never talked about it, but then Jess never wanted to talk about anything any more. She grunted, she shouted, she made demands, she lied, she wheedled and whined but she barely ever talked.

I wasn't prepared, thinks Jean, I never thought she'd go off like that. I thought she'd always be my Sugar Plum Fairy.

The worst thing about the whole sorry situation was that she still loved her younger daughter; she didn't like her very much because she was so nasty, but she missed her. She missed the old Jess; she was like a butterfly in reverse, a glorious creature turned ordinary and mean.

With Anne at university and Jess out all the time Jean often felt lonely. It was a good job she had her soaps and enough work to stop her from going mad.

She still helped out with the costumes for the Cygnet School of Dance, but she found the novelty of sewing a zillion sequins on to a satin bodice wore off a lot quicker when the leading lady's costume was not intended for her own daughter.

Abigail Moran was Audrey Carr's favourite now. 'Not an ounce of fat on her,' purred Audrey.

Sometimes she felt she was being punished. She had let her baby son go and now she was losing her other children too. First Anne to university and all her posh new friends, then Jess to . . . to a world she knew nothing about but one she suspected was dangerous.

She worried about Jess all the time. The worry was like a little mouse chewing on her guts. She worried about her taking drugs and getting pregnant, she worried about her getting drunk and falling into the road, but mostly she worried about her not really being very happy.

Strange the way things turn out. Who'd have thought that Anne would have been the one to get lucky? Not only did she have a flat with a piano and a dishwasher, all of a sudden she had a boyfriend.

Jean wasn't used to her eldest daughter talking about boyfriends. For a while she'd wondered whether she was a lesbian and imagined her living in a little cottage somewhere with a dungaree-clad companion and a lot of cats, but just before she embarked on her third year Anne met Paul and all of a sudden it was 'Paul and I . . . myself and Paul . . . Paul thinks . . . well I'll have to talk to Paul'.

He was a medical student, which was impressive, and he'd been to boarding school, which made him like something out of a story book. Of course she didn't imagine he'd be particularly good-looking and he wasn't. Anne showed her a photograph. 'That's Paul,' she said, pointing to a fuzzy blob with gold-rimmed spectacles and a mousy receding hairline.

Good luck to them. They got engaged the Christmas of Anne's third year in Edinburgh, so obviously she couldn't come home.

She and Paul had been summoned to Wiltshire to visit Paul's parents: for some reason it seemed more important for them to approve of Anne than for Jean to meet her prospective son-in-law.

'You do understand, Mum.'

Oh yes, she understood all right.

From then on it was almost impossible to detect a trace of Lancashire in the girl's accent. Anne just fluffed up her flat vowel sounds to match her new Lady Di hairdo.

They were to be married that summer – why wait until they graduated? It wasn't unheard of, they were adults after all. Only in the end they did have to wait. You couldn't go eating cake and celebrating, not so soon after the terrible night.

The terrible night, that awful moment, the dreadful time that never really ended.

Nearly thirty years ago now, another century. Anne had just turned twenty-one and was newly engaged. It should have been a happy time but Jean had been feeling anxious for months. She often couldn't eat because her intestines felt like knotted string; she mostly lived on milky tea and biscuits. Silly really, because recently things had taken a turn for the better.

Jess had left school the previous year and started a hairdressing course at the local tech. They encouraged her to get some work experience so she applied for a Saturday-girl position at a hair-dresser's in St Annes.

Michael St John's was part salon, part time warp. The clientele was ageing and tightly permed; pensioners sat under pink plastic capes heady and bad tempered from peroxide fumes.

Jess hated it. All she did all day was sweep up clumps of frizzy grey hair. She wanted to dance again; she went back to Cygnets and begged Audrey Carr to let her attend classes again.

Audrey agreed, but told her it would take time to get her back to anything like her previous form, and that she was too late to be in the Christmas show.

Jess gave up the college course and the Saturday job; she told them she had dermatitis, proffering red raw hands as proof.

Michael St John believed her, Jean didn't. She knew she'd been scratching at herself for effect.

Deep down she didn't mind – all she'd ever wanted was for Jess to dance – but she also knew it was too late. Jess didn't have the discipline, she was lazy and distracted, she had lovebites on her neck – you can't be a ballerina with lovebites on your neck! Not even if you did try to disguise them with toothpaste.

Anyway, she was too busty to be a ballerina any more. That particular dream was over, not that it bothered Jess. She was still going to be famous, she was still going to be a dancer, she would still travel the world. The kind of dancing she could do, you could do anywhere: on cruise ships, in nightclubs – especially in nightclubs – there was good money in it, good money for girls who could dance and had big tits.

She didn't tell Jean about the topless bit, of course, all that came out later.

Without moving a single muscle Jean braces herself. It's time to tackle that night. It needs tidying away. This is the last time she will ever have to think about it.

Strange really that Anne was home, she very rarely was. It was Easter, she was revising for her end-of-year exams and was rather self-important: 'I'm afraid I'll be studying in my room most of the time.'

She'd only really come home for Grace Long's twenty-first.

It was the first time they got to see her engagement ring: three diamonds in a row, the biggest one in the middle. 'It doesn't look real,' Jess commented bitchily.

But it was real. Jean had never seen her eldest daughter so content, she just walked around with a little smile on her face. By contrast, Jess was in a fury, constantly snappy and rude. There was a particularly horrible row over some laundry: Anne had taken a pair of Jess's knickers by mistake and had handed them back over the breakfast table. 'Sorry Jess, I thought they were mine. We're a very similar size these days.'

Well, Jess just went off like a Catherine wheel in Anne's face:

'How fucking dare you? I'm nowhere near your size, you great fat cow. Just go fuck yourself.'

Anne simply smirked and responded in French, which for some reason turned Jess into a madwoman, clawing and spitting at her sister. In the end Anne had to defend herself with the bread knife.

'And if you think I want you to be my bridesmaid, you've got another think coming.'

'Ha,' spat Jess, 'why would I even want to go to your stupid spazzy wedding? You must be joking. I'd rather die than be your fucking bridesmaid.'

Jean wishes she hadn't said that.

She went banging out of the house but came back ten minutes later because she was still in her dressing gown. Then she locked herself in the bathroom for an hour and had a bath. Jean thought she could hear her crying over the running of the taps.

She felt like she was in a war zone. Her little boy would be nine years old now, he would play with cars on the carpet and make motoring noises, that's what little boys did.

Strange how much you could miss someone whose face you could only imagine.

Work was a relief, the sewing machine drowned out most of the shouting and the door-slamming. Even now she can recall its reassuring hum.

Every machine she'd ever owned had its own distinctive sound, like a car engine, she supposed, not that she'd ever learnt to drive. She wishes she had now, a car would have come in handy.

April 1983: she was working on a bedroom suite in yards of glazed floral cotton, a slippery riot of pink and red roses. The client wanted a bedspread, valance, curtains, matching pelmet and new drapes for a kidney-shaped dressing table. Any scrap material was to be used for cushion covers – Jean reckoned she could squeeze out three.

She kept her head down and tried not to wish that things had turned out differently.

Anne was off to Grace Long's twenty-first. Mr and Mrs Long were taking Anne, Grace and Angela to a Chinese restaurant in St Annes. Jess was going to a disco in Blackpool.

She worked until nine and then went to bed. Her hands were seizing up, her fingers frozen into claws; it was happening more and more.

She heard Anne come home around eleven o'clock and then Jess about an hour later. She remembers looking at the clock on her bedside table, glad that they were both safely indoors and it was still a minute off midnight.

But then she thought she heard someone go out again, but why would anyone do that? No one comes home and then goes out again at midnight. Where would you go? The day is finished, you might as well go to bed and start a new day in the morning, that's how life works. One day, then the next, breakfast, dinner, tea, sleep, repeat, breakfast . . . No, she must have been mistaken, she was very tired after all. The last thing she heard before she fell asleep was the flushing of the lavatory.

Anne was alone in the kitchen in the morning.

'Did you have a good time, love?'

'Yes, it was very nice.'

'Did you have those duck pancake things with the jam?'

'Yes.'

Jess liked to sleep in, she wasn't a morning type of girl. Anne went upstairs to get on with her studying; Jean got on with her valance. She stopped at eleven for a coffee as she always did. She made a mug each for Anne and Jess, put the coffees on the tray with the wicker handles and added a biscuit on a side plate for Jess, a choc chip cookie, just the one. After all, she'd not had her breakfast.

Anne was studying at the desk Jim had bought her the Christmas after she passed her eleven plus. She had her books all heaped up around her; Jean balanced a coffee mug on top of the pile.

'*Merci*,' muttered Anne.

Jean backed out into the hallway and pushed the door open into Jess's room.

Jess wasn't in her room and she wasn't in the bathroom.

She called her.

'Jess?'

The tray trembled in her hands. She put it down on the floor in Jess's room. Her chest of drawers looked like it had been ransacked, clothes all over the place.

'Jess?'

She knocked on Anne's door. 'I can't find your sister.'

Anne looked guilty, just for a second.

'I heard her come in.'

'But did you hear her go out again?'

'I heard the gate. I looked out of the window; I thought it was her but I didn't have my specs on. I'd left them in the bathroom and by the time I'd fetched them she'd gone. She wasn't there, I just presumed she'd come back in.'

Only she hadn't.

Later Anne told a policeman that by the time she'd got her glasses on her sister had disappeared. All she could see when she looked out of the window were the tail lights of a lorry pulling away from the kerb.

Jean remembers butting in at this point. She was cold and sweating at the same time.

'Why didn't you tell me about the lorry?'

'I didn't want to frighten you.'

'Can you remember the registration number?' asked the policeman.

Anne's mouth opened . . .

Anne

Wrong Number

Ealing 738957. The numbers slip out now as easily as they had that April night.

The policeman had scratched his head. 'No love, you've got to have some letters. A registration plate has got letters as well as numbers. Close your eyes for a second and think.'

She tried, she shut her eyes, but all she could see was a blur. 'I didn't have my glasses on.'

Time and time again during the months and years that followed she would try to trick herself by suddenly screwing up her eyes, hoping that her subconscious, caught on the hop, would deliver an entire number plate.

Anne is holding her mother's papery hand, the one that isn't connected to the drip and tubes.

'I tried, Mum, I really tried, but every time I closed my eyes all I could see were the tail lights shrinking into tiny red pinpricks in the distance.'

She can recall in horrible detail how they searched for Jess that morning, as if the girl might be playing some kind of game. Silly really, the house was so small there was nowhere she could possibly hide, but even so they looked under the beds and behind the sofa. Anne found herself unlocking the drawer in her desk, as if her sister could fit in there!

Jean had wanted to phone the police immediately. Anne tried to keep her calm; she remembers promising her mother, 'She'll be back, just you wait and see. Any moment now she'll waltz through that door.'

Only the moments turned into minutes that stretched into hours and Jess failed to materialise. There was no scrape of a Yale key in the lock, the front door didn't magically swing open, there was nothing but waiting.

The phone rang once but it was the lady Jean was doing the curtains for. 'I'm sorry Mrs Dalgliesh, I'm not well today. I'll call you when I can.'

Then it rang again, but it was a wrong number.

Just after lunch (which neither of them ate) Jean called the local police station. She started crying as she uttered the word 'daughter' and Anne took over.

'My sister,' she said, trying not to garble into the olive-green receiver, 'my younger sister hasn't come home. Well, she did but then she didn't, she's not here, we don't know where she is.'

Twenty-four hours, they said, 'you can't be missing until you've been gone twenty-four hours, not when you're sixteen. A lot of sixteen-year-olds consider themselves adults, why don't you wait? Try not to worry, most teenagers turn up safe and well.'

Only Jess wasn't most teenagers.

Three decades on and Anne is finally confessing to the shape of her mother how her sister's disappearance made her feel.

'I remember thinking how bloody typical it was of her, that she'd run away for attention. I was furious, I thought, If I fail my exams it will be her fault. All this time I'm wasting staring out of the window when I should be revising.'

Her mother's hand has shrunk over the years. The one she holds now is freckled and knotted with blue veins, her fingers are twisted by arthritis and her nails need a trim.

Deep down, she'd known right from the moment her mother had called her sister's name that everything had gone wrong and the first emotion that swept through her wasn't sadness or fear, it was exhaustion. Jess wasn't yet officially missing but already Anne felt tired and a bit bored of the situation.

'I just had a feeling it wasn't going to resolve itself, that it was just going to go on,' she continues. 'Mind you, I never thought we'd still be waiting. I never dreamt that this would never be over.'

Her sister had to wait to be officially declared missing but once that declaration had been made it was Jean and Anne who had to wait, and they are still waiting. Twenty-seven years ago a sixteen-year-old girl went missing and no one ever set eyes on her ever again.

At first the police were blasé about the case. After all, she took a duffel bag and her passport; she was less likely to be missing than absent by choice.

The police started to put pieces of the jigsaw together. They made enquiries and came back with suggestions as to why she might have run away.

Did Jean know her daughter wanted to go to London? Did she not realise that Jess was bored, that she hated where she lived, that she dreamt of bigger things?

'Yes,' her mother told the policeman, 'of course I know that. Jess and I share the same dreams.'

Only they hadn't. Jean dreamt of Jess starring in West End musicals – it wouldn't matter if she started out as a chorus girl, she could work her way up – but it turned out Jess had other ideas. Dreams she hadn't shared with her mother.

It was her friends who spilt the beans, Nathalie and Gina. Jean had never liked them; who's to say it hadn't been their idea in the first place? Like the homemade tattoo under Jess's watch-strap, a scrappy little blue star, all wonky: that was Gina's doing, she'd actually done the inking herself. You couldn't trust either of them.

'A go-go dancer,' the policewoman had said, and as she formed the words she blushed bright pink, right to the tips of her ears. 'Did Jess ever talk to you about going to London and being an exotic dancer?'

Jean hadn't understood what she was saying, so Anne had to explain: 'There are clubs, Mum, mostly in London, and . . . well, men pay to watch girls dance and they pay extra if they take their tops off.'

Her mother had looked dazed. 'Why would you want to dance with your top off? Bosoms just get in the way of proper dancing. That's why Jess had given up ballet, because of the breasts.'

'But Mum,' her eldest daughter reasoned, 'that's the whole point of that kind of dancing.'

'Like the Folies Bergère?' her mother had hazarded. 'You get a fabulous costume, everyone says so, and they're very highly trained. Maybe she's gone to Paris. She needn't have bothered, mind, she could have just stayed here. Audrey Carr's got contacts on the pier.'

The doctor had given her mother some pills, just to help her sleep, but the pills made Jean so foggy she'd wake up forgetting what had happened and remembering all over again was almost too painful to bear.

Anne helped her mother sort out some photos. They sent the same woman constable to pick them up,

'Head and shoulders is probably best,' the woman suggested, 'and maybe not in a costume?'

But Jean ignored her, she was in another world. 'Here she is as Little Red Riding Hood. I made that cloak: red velvet, it was a bit hot, especially with the hood up. She was only twelve.'

'Do you have something more recent?' requested the WPC.

Different images were used in different papers. The local paper appealed for help finding Missing Local Dance Sensation along-side a picture of Jess doing the splits, but the nationals published her last school photo, a younger-looking Jess, all plaits and innocence.

Nathalie and Gina showed the police some other pictures, taken in a photo booth. The three of them had been drinking and stripped off for a dare. Nathalie and Gina looked embarrassed, but Jess didn't, she looked like she'd done it before.

The photos went to Scotland Yard. 'The London coppers will keep an eye out for her. They'll find her, love, don't you worry. Likely as not, she'll be in the Soho area.'

Jean wanted to go and search Soho for herself, but every time she set foot out of the front door she thought she was going to be sick or faint or both, and anyway, she reasoned, what if she comes back and I'm out?

The doctor gave her some more pills, to help with the panic attacks. It wasn't practical to stay indoors all the time, she needed to be able to get out to the shops. She couldn't keep relying on Anne, she needed to go back to university, she had exams.

'I did offer to stay though, do you remember, Mum?'

Did she really, honestly? Her mother is as silent as a waxwork.

'But you told me to go back.'

She knows now she should have stayed, but she couldn't wait to break free. There was nothing normal about being at home any more. The house was just a box of grief: her mother's stricken face, Jess's tights still in the laundry basket, the smell of her getting fainter by the day.

She caught the train north and every mile that further separated her from her mother was a relief.

Back in Scotland the story was of little interest. A girl was missing, but she wasn't Scottish. A body hadn't been found, she had obviously run away. Lots of girls did that, London was littered with them: some of them returned home, tails between their legs, and some didn't.

Jess didn't.

Anne decided to play it down; she couldn't bear people looking sorry for her. She told her flatmates that she thought Jess had been planning this for a while and that she would be lapping up the attention. 'It's typical, I'm afraid.'

Paul was slightly shocked by it all: 'My mother thinks it's slightly odd, Anne.' Years later Anne realised that, by odd, Ellen meant common. In the world according to Paul's mother, younger sisters stayed at home until they had passed the requisite exams to go to university. They did not hitch rides to London with lorry drivers in the middle of the night.

This was the conclusion that had been drawn, that Jess had come home from her night out in Blackpool, dashed indoors to fetch her passport and some clothes then nipped back out to cadge a lift to London. If only Anne could remember just a letter or a digit of that registration number. But she couldn't.

It was Paul's mother who decided they should postpone the wedding. Ellen thought people might think it a little quaint: after all, the bride-to-be's sister was still the subject of a police investigation. Might it not be more seemly if they waited a while?

There could be good news any day now. Only there wasn't, there wasn't any news at all, not good nor bad.

Bodies were found, but they weren't Jess. Teenagers turned up, but not Jess.

She had simply disappeared and no one knew where on earth to look next.

'I'm still looking, Mum, I promise.' Anne is exhausted now, the memories have wiped her out, but suddenly she knows that she needs to try harder. She must find her sister. Perhaps when she gets back to London she can hire a private detective. She can afford it: they're probably the same price as a personal trainer and Paul's always nagging at her to get one of those.

Jean

Mother's Little Helpers

The police stopped searching in the end, but Jean refused to give up. She was like a woman possessed: two of her children were out there somewhere, please God let her find at least one of them.

Not that she believed in God. The local vicar had paid a visit, a man as greasy as suet, smelling of cake and biscuits. It was no wonder he was so fat. She had nothing to say to him, apart from, 'Would you like another slice?'

There was talk of some counselling, to get over her 'grief', but as she said to the doctor, 'She's not dead, how can I grieve when she's not dead? I'm just waiting and everyone has to wait. It's just that waiting for a daughter is harder than waiting for a bus.'

As long as she had the little pills, the white ones and the yellow ones, she could get through the day. It helped to imagine Jess dancing, which is what she did when she couldn't sleep.

First she'd put her in a costume, a costume she'd made herself using fabric and trimmings she imagined herself choosing from the market, and then she would place her on a stage and watch her dance.

Sometimes she put her in a big feathered headdress and

imagined her leading the chorus on Central Pier. Other times she popped her in a yellow catsuit and watched her gyrate on the Saturday night variety shows on the telly: *The Generation Game, Russ Abbot's Madhouse,* Jess did them all. For a girl who'd not been seen for months she was all over the shop.

Once Jean found herself watching a holiday programme featuring Judith Chalmers on a cruise ship enthusing about the on-board entertainment. Behind Judith's elegant head, a dance troupe were throwing themselves into a Fosse number, something from *Sweet Charity.* It didn't take much for Jean to convince herself that the blonde second from the right was Jess.

The girl might have vanished into thin air but that didn't stop her from working. Indeed, eight months after she'd gone missing she turned up on the Royal Variety Performance.

Even though, deep down, she knew these Jesses weren't really Jess, the mirages (as she secretly called them) calmed Jean down. She could eat after she'd seen her, she could leave the house, she could go about her daily business.

Some people thought she was getting over it, coming to terms with her loss. She wasn't, she was just coping with the horror the only way she could.

Socially she found strangers easier than acquaintances: people she knew trod on eggshells around her, some crossed the road rather than look her in the eye. Men were the biggest cowards: lots of Jim's old bowls chums couldn't cope at all, although a few of their wives sent nice letters, well-meant but full of platitudes – 'We were so sorry to hear . . . Our thoughts are with you . . .' – but they just reminded her of the condolence cards her parents received when her brother was killed and for the first time in her life she understood how her mother managed to die of grief.

Dealing with clients was more straightforward, she could communicate with them on a purely professional level while any small talk was kept minuscule. She became a very quiet and conscientious worker, eyes down, needle flying.

Sometimes at the end of the day her hands would take a good half hour to uncurl, which was a worry but in the grand scheme of things not a worry she could be bothered to worry about.

Once she was on a bus visiting a client who lived way out in Fleetwood and she found herself talking to a woman who was a similar age to herself. The conversation turned to children, how many did Jean have?

'Three,' she replied, 'two girls and a boy,' and she talked about her children all the way to the docks, how her eldest was engaged to be married, while her younger daughter was a professional dancer in London, and as for her youngest, 'my boy', he was just a cheeky little monkey.

'Ah, but you love him,' the other woman acknowledged, nudging Jean in the ribs and offering her a Liquorice Allsort.

After that it was easier. If she wanted to get away from the real world she would catch a bus, position herself next to a middle-aged woman and swap mum stories.

'My eldest girl is getting married,' she told a Brummie woman who was up visiting her sister in Squires Gate, and indeed Anne was. She didn't always have to make everything up.

'In Wiltshire,' she added.

The Brummie woman raised an eyebrow. 'Would you not rather she got married in her home town?'

'Well yes,' Jean replied, but deep down she knew she couldn't have coped with the organisation that a wedding required.

For starters, the little pills made her far too muzzy in the head to sort out silver-edged invitations. As for choosing between a finger buffet and a sit-down three-course meal, she just couldn't. Lamb or beef, trifle or cheesecake, how did people make these decisions?

Come to think of it, weddings didn't hold very happy memories for Jean. It was best she kept herself out of the picture.

Which is why you can barely spot me in the wedding photos, she reminds herself, not that it wasn't a nice day. It was a splendid day, a real success, it was just that she never really felt part of it.

She was surrounded by strangers, even the girl in the white dress, whom she knew for a fact was her own flesh and blood, seemed unfamiliar.

The doctor suggested she cut down on her pills.

It took the best part of a decade, ten years of not really knowing what she was doing, of sleepwalking through her life, of not feeling anything. Ten years of muddled memories that she has no hope of ever getting into the correct order, a whole heap of stuff that just happened, vague recollections that will just have to be lumped together under Miscellaneous.

It didn't help that she'd started having a couple of drinks with Elaine Parker next door, there didn't seem any reason not to. Elaine would arrive with a bottle and when they finished that, they'd have another. Sweet white wine was her tipple. She didn't really like Elaine, she was a bit hard-faced, but after a couple of glasses of Liebfraumilch she softened.

'All kids are trouble,' Elaine would proclaim. 'They all let you down in the end.' She was glad she never had any; her sister's lad – her nephew – was bad enough. 'Remember him?' she asked Jean, and she vaguely recalled a nice-looking lad that used to sit on her garden wall on those summer days before . . .

Elaine called him a bad penny, never heard from him from one year to the next and then he'd breeze by, begging a loan, helping himself to the contents of the fridge, wanting a bed for the night. The army hadn't worked out, he was in and out the nick until he lost control of a car on an icy stretch of road just outside of Glasgow on the eve of the millennium, drunk at the wheel and not wearing a seat belt. Tragic, really.

Of course the Parkers had moved by this time and Jean couldn't tell by Elaine's letter if she was still boozing, but the handwriting suggested she probably was. Elaine said she'd never really forgiven him since they'd been on holiday and he'd pinched their car. 'Mark my words, Jean, they all let you down in the end.'

Only Anne never did. Anne was a good girl, happily married to her young doctor husband and safely settled in Herne Hill.

She didn't visit very often, but she did write and she phoned every Sunday. In fact, there were times Jean only knew it was a Sunday because Anne's voice was on the other end of the line.

She straightened herself out in the end, she had to. Her work was suffering, she was spending as much time unpicking as she was actually sewing. The hangovers were crippling, she was being sick in the mornings and she was too thin.

One day she caught sight of herself in Jess's bedroom mirror, the one that still had her younger daughter's lipsticks kisses all over it. She looked haggard and her top was stained. What if Jess was to walk back in right this minute, what would she think?

She stopped drinking, she weaned herself off the pills, and one day she took a cloth and some Mr Sheen to Jess's bedroom mirror and wiped off the lip prints. It was time to put her daughter away.

It made her cry, of course it did, she sobbed over every tiny thing: hair clips and bobbles, chocolate wrappers and little pots of make-up. She put everything in boxes and then stood on a chair on the landing, posting the boxes into the space under the eaves. If she fell off the chair she might fall down the stairs and break her neck and then it would all be over. But she didn't, the chair she was standing on didn't even wobble and she took that as a sign.

She got a painter in and he redecorated both the girls' rooms, pale blue for Anne's and primrose for Jess's, then Jean set about making them nice. She bought everything brand new, for once deciding not to make everything herself. She couldn't afford these rooms to be too personal, they were just rooms now, they were no longer her daughters' bedrooms. She went to buy new duvets from the market and to her amazement the fellow on the bedding stall asked her out.

His name was Mark and his wife was in a wheelchair – she'd dived into the wrong end of the swimming pool while they were on holiday, it was a tragedy. Mark told her that before the accident his wife had been a ballroom dancing champion. After she broke her neck he had to get rid of all her silver trophies and hide her dresses in the garage, where they got eaten by mice and fell to pieces.

She needed a lot of care, did his wife. He did his best but he was a man at the end of the day and Jean was a woman and they both needed a little bit of pleasure. He was kind and she was kind back.

Sometimes they did a little foxtrot round the front room, sometimes they just went to bed.

They weren't hurting anyone, only his daughter found out and she yelled at her father that if he ever saw 'that woman, that bitch' again he would never ever see his grandson again.

'No one is worth losing a child over,' Jean told him and she made him promise not to ring her. 'You'd only end up blaming me.'

So that was that and it was hard not to hit the Liebfraumilch, but she didn't, which was something to be proud of.

She decided to learn to swim instead, and that's where she met Pat and Noreen, down at the swimming pool. They looked like Laurel and Hardy in bathing-suit drag.

What would she have done without them?

They got her out of herself, took her to the cinema and the bingo. She even managed a couple of shows: not dancing, that would have been too much, but they took her to see the comic Tom O'Connor and she surprised herself by laughing out loud.

There were still bad days and even worse nights, nights when she'd dream that Jess was drowning and she thought she had saved her but every time she brought the girl's body up to the surface of the water it turned out to be Anne.

Anne didn't need saving, Anne was thriving. She was pregnant and pleased, it was planned, but that was Anne for you.

The baby was called Nathaniel. When Jean received an envelope full of photos she tried to look for clues in this strange baby's face, but there were none. He didn't look like anyone she knew.

Another baby came along a couple of years later and this one gave Jean a bit of a shock. There was something about his nose. Julian, this second baby was called. She was glad that neither of them are called Simon, that name belonged to another baby boy.

Being a grandma was a good thing: it meant she was part of the nanna club, which automatically gave her permission to bore strangers about her grandsons without ever really knowing them. Lots of women do it, thinks Jean.

At least she's actually met hers. Pat's sister has got three in Australia she's never clapped eyes on.

Nathaniel and Julian have even stayed in her house, a long time ago when they were little and easier to please, not that they were. In fact, it was a relief when they stopped coming.

Julian didn't like donkeys, he was phobic about them, so the beach was a no-no. As for cards? They didn't know the simplest of games, in fact they couldn't really play any game that didn't go beep-beep-beep on a daft little screen. To be honest, they were a bit stuck-up, heads too big for the jumpers she knitted them.

But deep down she was disappointed. It would have been nice to be closer to her grandsons. It upset her, it felt like part of the punishment.

You've got to stop that now Jean, she tells herself. The punishment is over. And she knows this to be true because there is a calm in her heart that she hasn't felt for years and although one of her children is still missing, at least she knows now where the other one is.

Anne

Last Wishes

At last a doctor has spoken to Anne. For a moment she didn't realise he was a doctor because he wasn't wearing a white coat. He looked like he'd just wandered in from the golf course.

He introduced himself as a consultant. 'So is my husband,' Anne chipped in. In her experience, once the medical profession knows you are one of them they tend to patronise less,

'Ear, nose and throat – London. St Thomas',' she barked. Being a member of the medical profession is a bit like being in the army but with speciality and hospital location replacing rank and regiment.

Mr Avidi nodded, he knew where she was coming from. 'Your mother,' he informed Anne, 'is a very sick woman and there is very little chance that she will see this weekend through.'

She wasn't sure how she was supposed to react. Was she meant to collapse weeping at his feet? She decided to play it stoic, like a twenty-first-century Celia Johnson, but with difficult hair.

'The head trauma is very great and your mother is frail,' he continued. 'We are also concerned about the amount of fluid on her lungs: there is an indication that pneumonia could be a problem. Obviously we are doing what we can, but we have to advise you that there is very little chance of recovery. I'm sorry.' And with that he backed out of the room, whether to attend more patients or resume his game of golf, Anne has no idea.

She is shocked but not surprised, sad but in some respects relieved. If her mother is definitely going to die she doesn't have to worry about what to do with her should she live and need round-the-clock care. Paul will be relieved, the children can just get on with their selfish lives unencumbered by a smelly old grandma and she won't have to worry about sorting out the spare bedroom.

Anne is slightly taken aback by her own callousness. Surely it's a bit hypocritical to be holding the hand of a loved one while simultaneously looking at your watch and thinking, Well when?

But then, she reasons, at least she knows her mother isn't going to suffer. Being in a coma is bad enough but it could be worse; no one wants an aged parent rotting away on shit-stained sheets. At least Jean has been spared a Mrs Gaga-style demise.

Basically, she concludes, what everyone wishes for his or her parent is a quick, efficient death, preferably nappy-free and with all their marbles, before a lifetime's savings get gobbled up by private nursing.

Not that her mother will have any savings. Poor Jean: arthritis put an end to her professional sewing days and, embarrassingly enough, she'd ended up as a cleaner before she retired. Anne still gets a little hot under the collar about this: having a seam-stress for a mother was one thing, but a cleaner!

Of course Jean lives on her pension now and (presumably) a bit of pin money from babysitting the children next door. Nathaniel and Jools probably have more in their savings accounts than Jean, not that her mother's finances are any of her business.

That said, she couldn't resist a snoop through her mother's purse once the nurse finally relented and handed over Jean's battered old handbag.

Three pounds, twenty pence and a receipt from the bakery. Maybe she was buying cakes for the little girls next door.

Drew has told Anne how good she is with them, how they make her laugh even when they are really naughty. 'She spoils them,' he said, and suddenly Anne realises that the keyring in her mother's handbag features Amber and Coral.

How odd, it's not as if they are blood relatives, but then if you think about it no one keeps pictures of hulking great teenage boys on their keyrings. Children stop being keyring-friendly once they leave primary school.

Anne decides she has sat with her dying mother for long enough. She has told the truth and perhaps her mother would rather not hear her voice or indeed ever sense her presence again.

Would a fully conscious Jean have forgiven her? Anne would like to think so, but she can't be too sure. Who knows how her mother would have reacted. Who knows if Anne would have had the guts to tell her if her mother hadn't been deeply unconscious. Could she have told her, face to blinking face, watched her expression change, seen the anger, disappointment, and upset on her face?

She's not sure what else she can do.

Mr Avidi has made it official: her mother's life can now be measured in days not years, hours not months, minutes not weeks. The consultant has signed the death sentence, the hospital will be expecting this bed back in forty-eight hours, tops.

Of course she will have to arrange a funeral, how peculiar. She will have to consult the double act that is Pat and Noreen. After all, Anne has no idea who should be notified.

She glances at her watch; it's ten to six and she is starving. With any luck Drew will be heading for the car park and she can cadge a lift. She kisses her mother on the cheek and suddenly it feels like she is the mother and her mother is the child. 'N-night,' she whispers, an echo from her childhood, 'sleep tight.'

For once it's not raining, but the wind blows hard. Debris skitters across the tarmac, fast food cartons mostly. Really, some people won't do anything to help themselves: every day on the steps of the hospital Anne sees morbidly obese people pushing burgers into their faces and tiny shrunken yellow people smoking in their wheelchairs. It's enough to make you buy the *Daily Mail*.

She only manages to catch him because there's a bit of a queue to get through the exit barrier. If she hadn't made a grab for the car door he'd have left without her. She feels a bit peeved; it's not as if he's even bothered to return her mother's casserole dish.

She heaves herself into the passenger seat.

'God Anne, I thought I was being carjacked for a second then.'

'Oh that's right, that's what middle-aged women go round doing in hospital car parks.'

Blimey, she wouldn't normally snap like that, not even at Paul.

'I'm sorry,' she apologises, 'I've just been in that place too long and of course there's no hope, my mother is dying. It's not even a matter of days.'

'Fucking hell,' he responds, 'that's awful.'

She decides not to contradict him. She doesn't want him to think she's a cow, but privately she doesn't think it's a bad way to go: a bang on the head and a short slide into oblivion. No slow decay, no doolalliness or incontinence, too late for regrets, too swift for deathbed apologies.

Not that Jean had anything to apologise for, not really. True, she had loved one daughter more than the other, but where had that got her?

It was Jess that she lost; punishment enough, surely?

Anne closes her eyes and leans back on the headrest. 'How's Sally?'

Drew bites his lip. 'They don't think they can keep the baby in for much longer, there's a danger of infection. It looks like it might be tomorrow. The kids have gone to Sally's mum and dad's, which is a relief. Means I've got a few hours to myself. I need to tidy the house.'

She hears herself say, 'I'll help.' Even though it's the last thing she wants to do.

The relief on his face is so palpable she's glad she offered.

'I'll go out for fish and chips,' he promises. 'And I'll buy you a bottle of that wine you like.'

'I'll buy the wine,' Anne insists. 'I really can't drink another glass of that German crap.'

He laughs and both of them are surprised by this easy, sudden friendship.

It's gone ten by the time they are sitting down at a pristine kitchen table. Anne doubts she has ever eaten anything as delicious as this portion of cod, chips and mushy peas: even the native lobster salad with royal beluga caviar and fresh figs that she ate at Hakkasan in Mayfair for her birthday last year pales by comparison.

'I'm going to go up into the roof,' Drew tells her, thumping the bottom of a brown-sauce bottle. Nat is the only other person Anne knows who likes brown sauce with fish and chips: everyone else likes ketchup.

'I think I could get planning permission for a small extension; we're going to need some more space and moving isn't an option.'

'Everyone does it in London,' replies Anne. 'There's not a Victorian house in a five-mile radius of where I live that hasn't been pushed up, sideways or back.'

'What will you do with your mum's place?'

'I haven't thought,' she lies. She has, but she has no idea whether her mother has left a will. For all she knows, Jean might have left 113 Marton Edge Road to a cat sanctuary, not that she ever particularly liked cats.

'It's in a shoebox under her bed,' he blurts.

'What?'

'Her will, she told me.'

'Did she tell you about Jess?'

'Yes,' he replies, and after a short pause he keeps going, but he doesn't look her in the eye. 'She said for years she thought

313

that she'd come back but when she stopped drinking she realised it wasn't going to happen.'

'I didn't even know she drank,' mumbled Anne, reaching for the chardonnay she'd bought earlier.

'Not any more.'

'What else do you know about my mother that I don't?'

'That she was here, before she was run over. She was meant to be tidying the house, doing a bit of laundry, but for some reason she just left everything, went running across the road, bought some vanilla slices and then, I don't know. Maybe she was coming back here and she just forgot to look and bang, she got knocked down. It just wasn't like her to leave the place in a state.'

'What sort of a state?'

'My laundry, a big heap of it on the floor. Odd.'

'She used to buy vanilla slices when we were little, whenever we had something to celebrate. I haven't been able to face one since my sister disappeared. I'm surprised she could either.'

Drew burps. 'Excuse me. Oh well, I don't suppose it really matters.'

Anne is suddenly exhausted. She needs to get back next door, have a bath and read her mother's will. Hopefully it won't be as confusing as David Mitchell's *Jacob de Zoet* thing.

Forty minutes later, fresh out of the bath and wrapped in one of her mother's worn towels, Anne reaches under her mother's bed. The shoebox contains old postcards and letters that date back to when a first-class stamp cost sevenpence. Anne glimpses her old university handwriting, envelopes postmarked Edinburgh. Every single letter she ever sent to her mother is here, a frayed yellow ribbon holding the bundle secure.

Right at the top of the pile lies a pale blue Basildon Bond envelope, unopened. In the corner of the envelope her mother has scrawled 'In the event of my death'. Her handwriting is barely legible, it slants this way and that as if, even in her seventies, she is still undecided as to which direction it should take.

314

The spelling is atrocious. The envelope is addressed to Anne; her name is spelt in capitals: TO ANNE ARMITAGE (KNEE COLLINS).

Anne slides her finger under the flap and withdraws a single sheet of note paper. Quickly she scans the letter:

Hello Anne, my reel will is with my bank, HSBC, the manager is a Mr Shaw.

As you probably know, I don't have much and with sircumstances being what they are, as in not knowing if your sister Jessica is alive or dead, I have been in a right old stew about what to do?

I have decided, the house should be sold and 50% of the proffits held in trust in the event that your sister should turn up.

I know this is unlikely but I've never quite given up, a long time ago, I was convinced she was alive, now so much time has passed, my flame of hope is a bit like the pilot light in the kitchen, I wouldn't be suprised if it went out at any moment.

I want Pat and Noreen to have any of my ornaments that they fancy as they've been true friends to me and there is a box of Jess's costumes that I'd like to go to my little ladies next door, to Coral and Amber because they've given me a lot of laughs in the past few years.

To Drew and Sally (Coral and Amber's Mum and Dad) I've got a few bob in the post office that I'd like them to have, I got lucky on the premium bonds and I never really knew what to do with it, so it just sat there, about five thousand pounds, I hope they have some fun with it.

Anyway, just so you know, I've left my body to medical science, there's an offishal letter with my doctor, I thought I might be more intresting on the inside than the outside. I have wondered for a long time whether my heart will look any differunt to the heart of a mother who knows where all her children are?

So the good news is you don't have to worry about a funeral, I'm sure I've been enough of a nuiscence already.

Sorry Anne, Love Mum.

The word 'love' is blurred, the ink has run. Anne blames it on her dripping wet hair, but as she bundles it turban-style into a threadbare pink towel tears continue to drip off her chin. She did say sorry after all.

Nat

Party Time

It's Saturday and Nat and Jools are counting down the hours to the Dulwich Village party of the decade. They have decided, in their current South London private-school patois, that it is going to be totes safe, sick, awesome, random and epic.

Obviously they would have liked to have pushed the boat out further on some of the finer details, a DJ for starters and some proper decks, but in the end they decide to make do with the iPhone dock that Jools got for his birthday.

Jesus, my parents are so tight, seethes Nat, what this dump of a house needs is some Bang and Olufsen gear. Not that his mum would know what Bang and Olufsen is, she probably thinks it's a shoe shop.

Ergh his mother's shoes, those ridiculous red clown Crocs, her horrible big feet with her hideous yellow ridged toenails. Why doesn't she paint them? She belongs in a farm or a zoo.

Maybe they should call her, if only to check she's not on her way back. Fuck, what if she should arrive home just when things are jumping? What if that little stick of a grandmother has kicked the bucket and Anne comes weeping up the drive?

Not that he reckons they're that close, his mum and

317

whatserface. It's not like she ever comes to stay, not like Ellen. To be honest, Nat doesn't think he's seen his mum's mum in the past five years. Why should he? No one goes to Blackpool, it's like really grim. It's not even the kind of place you go for a laugh and to shag some fat birds, you go to Magaluf to do that. If you're going to run the risk of catching an STD, you might as well get yourself a tan while you're at it.

They used to visit when they were kids and his Nanna, as she liked to call herself, always had new sweaters waiting for them, jumpers she'd knitted herself with holes that weren't big enough to squeeze their heads through. Always too tight and always too itchy, like a mosquito's fanny, a mosquito with thrush, sniggers Nat, muttering 'jokes' to himself.

She didn't even have a DVD player. There was never anything to do. If they hadn't taken their Game Boys up north him and Jools would have gone mad with boredom.

'Why don't we have a nice game of cards?'

'Yeah Nanna, that's exciting, let's play Happy Families.'

Silly cow. Still, if she's dead that house has got to be worth . . . what? A hundred and fifty grand, surely, even if it is in the middle of fuck knows where. It's a three-bedroom, one-bathroom terrace. Jesus, you'd get half a million for that down the road, easy. Some people buy their houses in really stupid places, decides Nat, wondering whether he should maybe go into real estate.

Still £150k, him and Jools should be in for a fair whack of that. After all, his mum doesn't need any money, she's got this great big fuck-off kitchen, what more does she want?

Money is wasted on his mother, Nat decides, whereas he and his brother have been, like, totally cleaned out by this party.

They've been to the offy in the Village at least five times today, deciding whether to buy plastic tumblers (yes) and crisps (no), and as a result there is now a pretty safe-looking bar on Anne's oh-so-precious granite kitchen island: five big bottles of vodka, ten bottles of red wine and ten bottles of white. The fridge is full of beer. As for anything non-alcoholic, if people don't want booze they can help themselves to water from the tap. Shame the ice maker is fucked, why the fuck hasn't his mother got the thing fixed? What is the point in having a fucked ice maker?

All the valuables and breakables, vases and shit, have been cleared out of the living room and they've opened the French windows. Hopefully people will smoke outside, but just to be on the safe side he and Jools dotted a few saucers around the house. It's a party, people will smoke wherever they want.

If only Anne hadn't gone for that stupid yellow carpet all over the place, that's just asking for trouble. Oh well, they can worry about spillages in the morning, there's a load of those little bottles under the sink, Stain Devils or some shit like that.

Fuck's sake, what is happening to him? He's eighteen and he's worrying about stains like a fucking middle-aged housewife. What's he meant to do? Ask people to drink red wine in the kitchen or garden and stick to white wine or vodka in the yellow-carpeted areas? Yeah, what kind of cunt asks his guests to do that?

Nonetheless, Nat locks his father's study. They've hidden their Xboxes and laptops in there, and their mother's jewellery box, not that she's got any jewels. She's not exactly P. Diddy when it comes to bling, but Paul's got a couple of watches that are probably best tucked out of sight.

Talking of nicking stuff, Nat knows for a fact that Jools has swiped that half-empty bottle of good brandy from the kitchen and taken it up to his room, complete with two balloon-shaped glasses. No doubt he's got a plan. Jools usually has, he targets his women whereas Nat snatches at whatever he can get. I'm the snatch snatcher, he sniggers to himself, determined that tonight he's going to get laid.

By rights, as the older brother, he should have first dibs at his parents' double bed, but the idea of trying to fuck someone on sheets that stink of his mum and dad turns Nat off and once more he is haunted by the recollection of his mother's pallid quivering arse disappearing up the stairs not quite fast enough.

He wonders if Zoe Carpenter might show her face, or rather her tits. Her face is a bit spotty, not that he's ever looked at it properly – that cleavage is a hell of a distraction. Ideally she'll arrive early, he can give her a quick one and then she'll fuck off and leave him free to pick up someone who's got everything, a nice face and great tits.

He's bought a selection of condoms, some ribbed, some plain, though with any luck he'll be able to persuade the lucky girl to ride bareback. Most girls these days are on the pill, and if they aren't he can always promise to pull out in time, which he can, mostly.

It's six o'clock, there's not much left to do. He's decided what he's going to wear: Diesel jeans, Calvin Klein underpants and his favourite Jack Wills green and navy checked shirt, which has been in the laundry basket since his mother left but fortunately smells OK.

Jools is getting a lot of texts: his phone beeps with the regularity of a heart monitor. Seems like there's a big house party in Clapham, so a lot of people will be coming to theirs after that, but then again some people are coming to theirs first and then going to Clapham after. 'And those that can't decide are going to just get pissed on the number 37 bus,' jokes Jools, but his face looks twitchy and his hair is refusing to flop in the right direction.

Nat is thinking he might have another shower. For some reason he smells a bit stale and maybe he should eat something, line his stomach, maybe a glass of milk and some toast? Christ, it's happening again, this inner wuss voice, the one that keeps reminding him about ashtrays and coasters. If he's not careful it will instruct him to cycle up to Sainsbury's and pick up some buffet snacks, a tray of cocktail sausages and some vol-au-vents.

At seven the doorbell rings. Trust his mother to have the naffest chime in London. Nat slouches into the hallway; seven o'clock is a seriously uncool time to show up for a party. With any luck it'll be that dealer mate of Jools's, who has promised a goodie bag of drugs or, as Jools described it, 'a fifty-pound selection box of the finest narcotics money can buy'.

Whoever is standing on the doorstep is rather short. In fact, there are two unidentifiable squat blobs distorted behind the stained-glass tulips. Nat opens the door.

'Oh hello Nathaniel, where's your mum?'

Nat gawps. If he were in a cartoon his eyes would go *BOINGGG* out of his head. What the fuck is that dog-faced Melanie Robinson doing here? And as if the sight of Melanie wasn't bad enough, standing beside her, all red and freckly, is Hannah. Sweaty-palmed Hannah Robinson, fifteen and lumpy with a nose full of blackheads, wearing something brown, wearing lots of brown, brown trousers, a white vest and a brown cardigan. Who the fuck wears that much brown?

'Mum's not in.'

Oh why doesn't he just tell them to fuck off and slam the door in their faces?

'Well never mind, I'm sure she'll be back soon.'

There's no point contradicting her. Melanie Robinson is clearly on a mission. She looks at her watch. 'Must dash, Christopher's waiting in the car. Your mother said she'd keep an eye on Hannah tonight, obviously she's old enough to be left home alone but our house does make some peculiar noises and it's not always Christopher's tummy!' At this point Melanie laughs very hard at her own joke and spittle flies from her mouth.

'Anyway, we're at a function at the Dulwich Picture Gallery up the road and we should be back around eleven to fetch her. We discussed it all the other night: your mother said what with Paul away she'd be glad of the company, so here she is!'

At this point Melanie shoves Hannah at Nat like a particularly unwanted gift.

'Byeee,' waves Melanie. 'Be a good girl, Hannah.'

Nat closes the door.

'I'm very sorry, Hannah, but you can't hang around here tonight.'

She looks like she might cry.

'Only we're having a party and, well, you're not on the guest list.'

'I haven't got anywhere else to go.'

'You must have some friends who live locally.'

'I haven't got any friends.'

Somehow he can believe that. Nat pushes the girl into the sitting room.

'Jools,' he shouts, 'Jools, come down here this minute, we've got a crisis.'

Bloody hell, he sounds like his mother when she's at her most menopausal.

Two hours later Hannah, Jools and Nat are hiding in what used to be the playroom at the top of the house, watching *Glee* DVDs.

They have turned off all the lights in the house and pinned a note to the front door saying that, due to unforeseen circumstances (family bereavement), the party has been cancelled.

As Jools commented, it might even be true. Northern Nanna can't hover on the brink of life and death for ever, she may well have carked it by now.

'Or popped her clogs,' sniggered Nat. 'Isn't that what old Lancashire biddies do?'

Despite the note and a flurry of texts and Facebook updates, the doorbell rings about seven times throughout the evening and every time Hannah gasps and wraps her brown cardi tightly around her rolls of puppy fat, as if for protection. 'Jeez,' mutters Jools, turning his phone onto silent, to think there are girls in her year who have sucked his cock.

Jean

ND

Jean is feeling a bit better, perkier. She's just about finished the memory tidying and it's all there on the shelves in her head, everything categorised and cross-referenced. There are memories labelled Jim and memories labelled Pickering Street Primary and big boxes containing the Cygnet School of Dance. All she needs to do is put the lid on the box labelled Vanilla-Slice Days and she's done.

In this box are all the days when they had something special to celebrate: the day Anne passed her eleven plus, the day Jess won her first dancing medal and even the time Jim's bowls club triumphed in the County Cup.

Of course once upon a time she would buy four vanilla slices, one each for Jim, the girls and herself. After Jim died it was just three cakes with their sticky white 'lick me' icing, and then after Jess disappeared there were none.

Not for years. There were things to celebrate, of course, like her eldest daughter getting married and the births of her grand-sons, but nothing she could bring herself to buy a vanilla slice for. To be honest, she went right off them.

These days when she goes out for a coffee and a cake with

the 'girls' (as Pat and Noreen insist on calling each other) she chooses a meringue or a wedge of chocolate gateau or a fancy macaroon to remind her of Mark from the market; he had a sweet tooth.

She's boxed him up too, in Lovers and The Ones Who Got Away. She put Mr Pemberton in that box too, she'd always had a soft spot for Ernest. Funny, there was a time when she thought they'd end up together. She used to fantasise about that wife of his dying and then she could have him all to herself.

No, Jean decides, it's been a long time since she's had reason to buy vanilla slices. Only she knows she bought some the other day. Now why on earth was that?

She really needs to remember, everything else is just about done. Come on Jean, think.

She is stepping off the pavement and she has a carton in her hands. She can feel the weight of the cakes, there are four of them. Why has she bought four vanilla slices? After all, it is just an ordinary day.

A bowl of cereal for breakfast, then she got that chop out of the freezer. Pork, she was going to do herself a little dish of apple sauce, but first she had to go somewhere. Where on earth was she going? She can see herself almost leave the house in her slippers but no, she remembers in the nick of time and she watches herself change into her slip-on leather shoes, button her coat, walk out and shut the door. She hovers for a second on the step, should she double lock it? No, she'll be back within the hour. After all, she's only going . . . Where?

Where is she going?

She needs to look at the kitchen calendar, that will jog her memory. Look in the little box, it's Wednesday, what does it say?

It says ND.

Of course! She is going next door, she goes ND quite frequently, they need her and she needs them. Drew and Sally, they've changed her life, like Noreen and Pat. She's not lonely any more, she has her friends, she has the family next door. She loves Coral and Amber, she keeps them with her always, look at the photo on her keyring – this one's Coral and that little minx is Amber.

The key for next door is on this ring too. They trust her, she's like their nanna and sometimes she pretends she is.

Sometimes she pretends they are Jess's children, but they aren't, not really. Their mum is called Sally. Poor Sally, she's in hospital. Now why on earth is that?

Jean tries to picture Sally and visualises a woman shaped like an Easter egg.

Of course! Because she is pregnant. Poor Sally is having her third baby and there are complications, that's why Jean has to go ND more than usual.

Drew can't really cope, bless him. He's the best dad in the world but they know how to wind him up, the little madams, and the mess they make!

Still, she can sort it out, she's done her fair share of cleaning. All those years ago when her hands curled up like dragons and she couldn't really see to sew, she didn't have much choice. She took off her thimble and put on her Marigolds. She'd rather be a char than idle.

She lets herself in ND. She can smell burnt toast; he'd obviously tried to boil some eggs, bits of shell and jelly whites splattered on plastic plates and all over the table. He'd not done them for long enough, little girls like a firm white and a runny yellow, all the better for sticking soldiers in.

Then when you finish your egg you can turn it over and draw a face, a funny face or even a sad one.

No more sad faces. Cheer up, let's get these dishes into the machine. She'll hoover the sitting room later, but first of all she needs to sort out this laundry.

She empties the contents of the drier into a green plastic basket, a crackling tangle of static and woollen tights, red and blue, little girls' tights, nothing really changes. She sorts the dried clothes into two piles, the girls' and Drew's. She carries these piles upstairs and deposits Amber and Coral's vests and knickers into the requisite drawers, all neat and tidy, she's good at folding. Then she spends a few minutes picking toys up off the floor, they've got more toys than Woolies those two, not that there is a Woolies any more.

Down the hallway and into Drew and Sally's bedroom now. She chucks the clothes on the floor so that she can open the chest of drawers. She's never done Drew's laundry before, it's all guesswork, but most men keep their socks and pants in the top right-hand drawer – it's just something she has noticed. She tugs at the handle and she's right, a pair of red socks and a pile of hankies spring from the confines of the drawer. No wonder it sticks, she needs to get everything out and fold it all properly.

Jean empties the drawer until the only thing left at the bottom is a picture frame, a plain wooden one, nothing fancy. Behind the glass lies a yellowing story cut from a newspaper. Baby Found in Telephone Box.

The picture features Police Constable Neville Banks cradling an abandoned infant.

Realisation hits her like a wave and the shock knocks her off her feet. For a while she just sits there, on top of her son's socks and pants. She has found her boy, he has never been a Simon, he is an Andrew. He is Drew and he lives next door. Her son is alive and well and handsome and good, and suddenly in that split-second of realising she has found her son she knows she will never see Jess again.

She will let that sink in later. She will weep over her daughter later. She has lost Jess but she has found her baby boy, the final pieces of the jigsaw of her life have slotted into place. She is a mother and a grandmother all over again, she is both the unluck-iest and the luckiest woman in the world.

Oh, but what on earth is she meant to do now?

Jean hauls herself up. There is only one way to deal with news like this and that is to buy cakes. She will buy four vanilla slices, one for herself, one for her son and one for each of her grand-daughters.

She feels a bit dizzy. If only she had one of her little white magic pills, but her supply ran out over a decade ago. She needs a bit of fresh air. She'll pop over the road and buy the cakes then she'll come back, put them in the fridge and get on with the cleaning.

She wobbles as she walks down the stairs, her balance has gone. It's anxiety, she recognises the symptoms: a racing heart, a feeling of light headedness. What if he's angry with her? What if he doesn't want a relationship? Her women's magazines are full of stories like this. 'Reunions Gone Wrong!'

Abandonment isn't easy to forgive, she sees it every day on the *Jeremy Kyle Show*, ugly faces purple with rage. 'What kind of mother are you?'

Surely she should have recognised him, her next-door neighbour, her son. A horn toots and someone shouts, 'Look where you're going you stupid fucking cow.'

She walks into the shop. Her feet feel like they are on the wrong legs, if she doesn't hold on to the counter she will just drop down on to the floor.

'Four vanilla slices please.'

From a distance a voice reaches the inside of her ear. 'Ooh very nice, is it a special occasion?'

She cannot hear her own response but she feels her lips move. She needs to get back over the road, have a cup of tea.

It's always tea for shock. She drank oceans of it when Jess went missing and suddenly it hits her. Jess and Simon, or rather Jess and Drew, they aren't going to meet. She has robbed them of each other and the thought is so upsetting that she forgets where she is, she forgets what she's doing. Her eyes blur with tears and she just steps off the pavement. She didn't do it on purpose but maybe it's for the best, maybe never knowing is better than finding out.

Jess

Leaving

Jess had been planning it for weeks. She was bored of being bored and now her sister was home it was time to go. She couldn't stand being under the same roof as that smug cow. The constant wink of her stupid engagement ring at the breakfast table, the way she kept singing snatches of pathetic songs in French. Who did she think she was?

Her mother was just as annoying, it was like she'd switched sides. It was all about Anne, Anne and Paul. She asked questions all the time: 'So he's going to be a doctor is he? He must be ever so clever.'

Christ, it was doing her head in. Paul this, Paul that. She'd seen a photo, he looked a right saddo, he was wearing a bow tie. What sort of freak wears a bow tie?

And he was nearly bald. He was disgusting, he'd be the kind of bloke that couldn't get your bra off, sweaty fingers fumbling around, yuk.

Actually she wouldn't be surprised if Anne was still a virgin. She was probably saving her hymen for her wedding night. Nice! Paul looked like the type to wait, he looked like he could be a Christian, or a Mormon. Ha, that would be funny if he turned out to be a Mormon and Anne had to share her idiot sweaty-fingered bald husband with a load of other stupid wives.

She told Gina and Nathalie that she was thinking of going. She thought they might want to come with her but both of them were too chicken. Anyway, Gina had just started seeing a bloke she was mad about, a garage mechanic from Cleveleys, and wouldn't leave him alone for a second. She was becoming a bit boring, was Gina.

Nathalie was still up for a laugh but she was lazy. She wouldn't stand on the side of the road with her thumb out for more than two minutes, wouldn't Nathalie. She'd want to sit down, go indoors, have a fag and anyway, she'd be rubbish in London, she couldn't do what Jess was going to do. She had crap tits, did Nathalie, they were like gnat bites on her chest. Sometimes when they went out, like tonight, she wore two padded bras, one on top of the other.

She wasn't sure when she was going to actually do it, but she'd had her bag packed for a week. She didn't need much, just the sexy lingerie she'd nicked from Miss Selfridge – matching red and black satin bra and knicker sets trimmed with frothy layers of lace, 34DD, the most beautiful undies she'd ever seen – a spare pair of jeans and a jumper, her make-up bag and her passport.

It still looked brand new, her passport; that pissed her off as well. Anne had already used hers, she'd been to France and to Switzerland, skiing with her posh mates. How bloody annoying was that? There's never an avalanche when you need one.

They hadn't had much of a night out, her and Nathalie. They'd set off for Cinderella's in Blackpool but Nat's brother's mate was on the door and he knew they were under eighteen. He said they could come in if Nat gave him a wank, but she wouldn't. Honestly, sometimes she was a bit wet! Jess would have offered had the bloke not looked like a giant pig with dandruff. They went to the Eden Club instead but it was full of old blokes in suits and signet rings, and women who looked better in dark corners, women with mean eyes who threw Jess and Nat dirty looks in the ladies' toilets, jealous cows.

Then Nathalie got a bellyache and said she wanted to go home, which was really annoying. She kept going on about appendicitis and how you could die from a burst appendix so they jumped a bus and it was barely midnight by the time she got home.

She just decided on the spur of the moment: why not? She might as well go tonight as any other night. The duffel bag was squashed under her bed; she dragged it out. If it was raining she wouldn't bother, but it wasn't raining so she went.

She crept downstairs and out of the front door and crossed the road. There wasn't much traffic and when a car did come along, she forgot to stick her thumb out until it was too late. The next one, she promised herself. The next one will stop.

She put her hand on her hip and stuck out her chest. A lorry seemed to slow down, but when she caught the driver's eye he looked away and drove off. The next car didn't stop, or the one after, and before the next one came along he was there.

He looked older, but then so did she. He was still smoking, he offered her a cigarette out of a crumpled packet of Embassy. He was a bit pissed: he swayed and his eyes kept losing focus apart from when he noticed her tits.

He had a kit bag with him, he was in the army after all. He said it was just a flying visit, his auntie wasn't expecting him, and Jess told him they were away, the Parkers were on holiday. He said he must have forgotten, he said he had a key. Why didn't she come in for a drink? She could run away later, it wasn't like she was catching a train, time wasn't important, nothing was important. As she followed him into the house she noticed the lorry that hadn't quite stopped earlier had returned and pulled up across the road. The driver must have gone round the block; the brakes groaned and hissed as it pulled away. Oh well.

'Come on Jess, me and you have got some catching up to do. Come on Jess,' and he looked at her through his fringe like he did when she was younger and more than anything she wanted to show him just how grown up she was.

How grown up and daring and not scared of anything, so when he suggested they take the Parkers' car out for a spin she couldn't see why not, it sounded like a laugh. Before they left she swiped a bottle of brandy from the drinks cabinet. Elaine Parker liked a drink: there were bottles and bottles of the stuff, gin, vodka, vermouth, but she knew he liked brandy, sweet, sticky cherry brandy.

Maybe she didn't need to run away any more. She could always come home; he would bring her home, she was only having a laugh.

Only he went a bit funny in the car. He told her some things that she didn't want to hear, he told her she was just a silly girl, that she had nothing to run away from, not like him. He was running away properly, he was running away from the army, he was AWOL. But she didn't know what that meant and he told her she really was fucking stupid. He told her both she and the army had shit for brains and if either of them thought he was going to Northern Ireland, they could fuck off, no chance.

She tried to take his mind off it. It was better when they were just kissing, when she could just close her eyes and forget his angry face. She thought she could make him feel better, but it went wrong. The kissing was all right but he couldn't do what both of them were expecting to do. She didn't know what to say, it had never happened to her before. His penis was as soft and as small as a curled-up mouse in her hand. She was nervous, she laughed, she shouldn't have laughed.

She tried to grab her duffel bag, she tried to get out of the car, but he wouldn't let her, he just wouldn't let her.

Anne

Saying Hello and Saying Goodbye

Anne gets the call just after nine in the morning. It's the ward nurse.

'Maybe you'd like to come to the hospital.'

She doesn't need to ask why. Oddly she feels the same as she used to before an exam, nervous but slightly exhilarated. Why on earth would that be?

She decides to get a cab, there's no point mucking about with buses on a deathday, especially when your mother's deathday is a Sunday. Public transport is awful on Sundays.

She dresses a little more carefully than usual. She puts on a skirt and attempts to do something with her hair. Her mother would like her to make an effort.

She decides to have a bacon sandwich; who knows how long the bedside vigil will last? Just before the cab is due she has one last attempt at phoning home.

Nat answers. 'Hi.' She is so shocked she almost drops the receiver.

'It's me, your mother. I'm still here, but I'll be back soon. Are you OK? How's Jools?'

'He's fine, we're fine.'

'How about Grandma Ellen?'

'I'll get her to call you back, shall I, Mum?'

He is stalling for time, he has excuses a mile long tucked up his sleeve.

'No it's OK, I'm going to be at the hospital. It's not good here.'

'Oh, I'm sorry to hear that.'

In Dulwich Nat quivers at his own charm.

A minicab toots from the kerb outside. Anne lifts her mother's net curtain and waves at the driver.

'I've got to go.'

She puts down the phone, gathers up her bag, the David Mitchell book, a copy of *Woman's Own* with a picture of Julie Walters on the front, and a banana.

It's raining again, which Anne decides is perfectly fitting, and she trots to the minicab thinking, I'll be home soon, I'll be back at work, things will get back to normal, Nat will sort himself out, Jools will grow up.

She promises herself she will be more patient when she gets back, she has to be.

The driver is the one that took her to the hospital from the train station all those days ago.

'Off to see your mum?'

'Yes, thank you.'

'Is she on the mend?'

'No, she's not, she's dying'

'Oh dear. Would you like a Werther's?'

'Thank you.'

They don't speak again. He listens to a sports channel on the radio but at least has the grace to keep the volume respectfully low.

'I lost my mum on Friday,' he says as she gets out of the car.

'I'm sorry,' mumbles Anne, handing over ten pounds for the fare.

'Oh don't be, I found her in British Home Stores.'

Anne waits for her change. He's not getting a tip now.

★　★　★

Jean looks the same as she looked yesterday. The bruising is still livid and whatever they've been putting into her veins hasn't exactly fattened her up.

Anne sits down and picks up her mother's hand from where she more or less left it yesterday.

'I've read your letter, Mum, the one in the shoebox. It all makes sense. I'll sort everything out, you mustn't worry, and maybe she is out there somewhere, Mum. She took her passport after all, she could be anywhere, she could be dancing anywhere in the world.'

She doesn't believe it, not really, but it's nice to think it might be possible, and for a split-second she imagines her sister dancing on a beach, a black silhouette against a blood-orange sunset.

At around midday a female doctor explains to Anne that they want to remove Jean's breathing apparatus, that there is no hope of a recovery and perhaps it is time to let her mother go. The doctor is hesitant, slightly embarrassed. She puts a box of tissues within Anne's reach, she says how sorry she is.

Anne looks at the tissues; she blows her nose because it might make her think straight. This is it, this woman is telling her that her mother is about to die. Everything Anne has ever shared with her mother and her sister is about to disappear. She alone will be the custodian of their past, the keeper of the memories, there is no one else left. They have all gone, her father, her sister and now her mother. Her first thought is that she will be lonely, but then she remembers how she has another life to go back to. She has friends, her work, she might even buy a new dog. Paul can't say no: it will help her get over all this, a puppy. She is suddenly desperate for the warm fur of a living, breathing, wriggling puppy. Her past is a book that she has finished. She might pick it up now and again and flick through a few chapters, she might try to explain some of the contents to her sons, but they won't really listen, they aren't interested, it's over.

Anne stops blowing her nose; her sinuses are agony. The doctor suggests she goes and gets a drink while they make Jean comfortable. Anne walks down the now-familiar corridors in a daze, past the chapel, turn left at the picture of 'Germs'. In Costa she orders a cup of tea and spoons a sachet of sugar into it. It's meant to be good for shock. It tastes disgusting.

By the time she returns, twenty minutes later, her mother is wire and tube free, there is nothing plastic going into anywhere and the room is a lot quieter without the gasp of the respirator.

'It shouldn't be long,' they tell her and she nods. It would be rude to ask 'When?'

She sits and attempts to reads some *Jacob de Zoet* but she can't remember who any of the characters are, so she flicks though the *Woman's Own* article about Julie Walters's happy *Mamma Mia* memories and wishes she'd brought something to do with her hands.

For the first time in her life she wishes she could knit. If she could knit she could sit here and finish off that jumper Jean was knitting for Coral, the SpongeBob SquarePants one. Maybe her mother would find the click of the needles soothing. They say that your hearing is the last of the senses to go.

After all the revelations of yesterday her mother would probably rather hear the soothing click of knitting needles than yet more home truths. 'Don't worry Mum, all the skeletons are out of the cupboard,' whispers Anne, and her mother's face seems to twist into a tiny smile.

She yawns too, as if she is bored of waiting, and Anne calls the nurse. Is it normal for a dying woman to yawn like that?

The nurse tries to explain that Jean is relaxing into death, that her muscles are letting go. Like a nicely cooked steak, thinks Anne. We're all just meat.

For a while Anne snoozes. When she wakes up she's starving so she nips out to the canteen for yet another dreadful cheese-based panini. She decides she can't take the toastie back into the ward as snacking by her mother's bedside would be inappropriate, so she eats it as quickly as she can, burning her mouth on molten mozzarella, anxious not to miss her mother's final breath.

But she hasn't missed anything. Her mother is hanging on. Over the next few hours various nurses and the odd orderly pop their heads around the door. 'Still here?'

'Afraid so, hahaha.'

Dear God, why is she apologising and why is she aping Paul's socially awkward tittering?

At five o'clock, just as she is getting bored and hungry again, there is a knock on the door. It's Drew and he is carrying a baby, a brand-new raw-skinned rabbit of a baby.

Drew is grinning.

'He's much bigger than they expected. He's strong, Anne, he doesn't need any help: he's five pounds of pure muscle,' and he holds the swaddled baby right up to Jean's face, so close she can probably smell the amniotic fluid behind his ears.

'This is Simon, Jean, he wants to say hello.'

Jean smiles, a wide smile, a happy smile, and five minutes later she is officially pronounced dead.

Jean

Letting Go

The memories are like slides now, flickering on a screen. Someone's slotted them into the projector the wrong way round, everything's going backwards. First up is her new grandson, which makes three grandsons and two granddaughters, that's a good hand: she can trump a lot of grannies on the bus with that.

His name is Simon, a brand-new baby Simon. Simon the second because she also has the original Simon, her son Simon who is actually Drew, he's here with his half-sister Anne. She's not a bad girl, we all make mistakes. She's not keen on what Anne is wearing, it looks a bit shapeless. It's a shame she never had any dress sense, and you can disguise a lot of weight problems with a good foundation garment.

Ah, somebody's waving, it's Phillip Schofield saying, 'See you tomorrow.'

'Bye Phillip, goodbye.' Hello now to Pat and Noreen, getting changed into their bathing suits, red for Pat and blue for Noreen.

It would be nice to have a last swim with her friends but she's not got her costume and anyway, she hasn't the time. She's

337

just going to nip into the covered market and give Mark a wave. She'll make sure he doesn't see her, she doesn't want to cause any trouble with that daughter of his.

Daughters, eh, where would we be without them? She's home on the sofa now, knitting for Coral and Amber, the monkeys. She strokes their faces and sniffs their sweaty bad-tempered heads. 'Ta ta my darlings, be good for your dad.'

She feels like she's spinning, the pictures start to flash randomly. Snapshots of cleaning jobs she never really enjoyed, she's pulling off her Marigolds and putting on a thimble, watch her run up a pair of curtains, the machine going so fast it might just take off, you can actually see the table vibrating, *drrrrrrrr*, foot down Jean, look at her go.

She's on the promenade now, walking into the wind with that red rinse that Jim never liked. Oh well, it's time she went home and made him and the girls some dinner. He's no trouble, Jim, she can just fry him some Spam. He was a nice bloke but not sexy like Ernest, ah Ernest, he's winking at her now is Mr Pemberton and she's dancing in her special silver shoes. She can hear a piano and some trumpets in the distance.

She's young again, her waist is tiny, there's not been a single baby to weigh her down, not yet. She's wearing a kilt and bending over a keyboard and she's typing nonsense. 'Is this a joke, Jean, the quack brown focs? I've never known a fox to go quack.'

Everyone is laughing. She is playing hopscotch in the school playground, wobbling on one leg, and now she's out playing in the back garden with her brother. 'Come indoors, your tea's ready.' Her mother is smiling, Brian's chasing her and she's screaming with laughter. Even her dad's there. It's hotpot with red cabbage and after her tea she'll feed the rabbit, the big soft white rabbit that she holds in her arms, warm and heavy. She can feel it breathing, the thump of its heart beating in time with hers, boom, boom, boom, and then it stops.

Anne

After

Drew gives Anne a lift home. He is buzzing with the adrenalin of watching a new life come into the world; Anne is exhausted by watching her mother leave.

'I'm glad she met him, I'm glad your mother knows he arrived safely, that Simon is here.'

Anne hopes he is right, she hopes that her mother was aware of the baby, but who knows what has permeated the coma? Maybe the whole trip has been a waste of time. Should she even have bothered? She could have stayed at home. Has it all been for nothing?

But she knows deep down that it has done her good, that she has faced up to some of the lies she buried long ago and she feels better for having told the truth. All she needs now is to find someone to forgive her, but that would have to be Jess. There's no one else left in the story.

Drew keeps talking, 'Honestly Anne, I never thought I'd have a son. He's great, isn't he?'

She keeps quiet, he might be great, he might be a fine cricket-playing boy with sturdy limbs and a sweet smile or possibly an arty poet with bony wrists strumming a guitar or he might turn out to be a little shit.

Babies are like parcelled-up books, you know what they are because of their shape but you have no idea what lies inside. Her own babies have emerged from their infant wrappings into difficult teenagers; they have shifted their shapes and changed their personalities. Their feet are unrecognisable, their sweet tiny pink toes grown hairy and long, but they can change again. No one stays the same for ever and she thinks about all the Annes that she has been: the sour jealous Anne; the clever conscientious schoolgirl Anne; the priggish virgin Anne; the copycat wannabe Edinburgh University Anne; the smug young wife and middle-class mum Anne; the anxious peri-menopausal Anne, dumpy and worried.

Suddenly it strikes her that whichever Anne she might be, she is no longer my daughter or my sister Anne. Her mother is dead and her sister has been gone too long.

Drew is still talking but he's stopped driving.

'I will see you again?'

They're home, and as if on cue the sky rips herself open and tips rain out of her skirts like dishwater.

'Oh yes,' Anne replies, 'I'll have to come up and organise the house.'

'That's exactly what I'm going to do,' he responds, his unshaven jaw poking with determination. 'I'm going to sort the house out. I'm going to get up into that attic pronto. First thing in the morning.'

He tells her the girls will stay with their grandparents until Sally and Simon come home. He says he's going out tonight, that he's meeting all his mates to wet the baby's head. He thanks her, he tells her she's been a diamond and that he will miss her and he will miss her mum.

She tries not to grunt as she gets out of the car and she kisses him on the cheek before they walk up their separate garden paths. He puts his key into the door where, once upon a time, Mrs Gaga lived with all her dead-boy memories and live tangle of cats and then, a few years later, the Parkers with that naughty nephew, the northern soul dancing soldier, killed in a car crash ten years ago.

Anne stands in the hallway of the house she grew up in and just for a moment she thinks she can hear the sound of a sewing machine. She walks on automatic pilot into the kitchen and glances at the calendar; her mother's handwriting makes her feel sad to the marrow. Jean wasn't old enough to die, there were many more bums and tums classes in her, she could have come to London, she should have made her more welcome. Fuck Paul and his snobbery, fuck the boys and their selfishness, she should have been kinder to her mother, she could have taken her to the theatre and out for dinner. Guilt and embarrassment kept them apart. If only they could have been more honest, but the damage was too deep.

She sits down at the table, wishing her mother kept a bottle of whisky for occasions such as this, but then remembering her mother didn't drink and wondering if maybe she should give up too, just for a while. It would help her lose weight and maybe she could deal with her sons better if she stops anaesthetising the disappointment.

Anne picks at some cheese from the fridge and toys with the idea of boiling an egg, but the memory of four animal eggcups long broken makes her feel weak. Instead she fills a hot water bottle and lies fully clothed but shivering under her mother's duvet. How many nights did her mother lie like this, waiting and wondering and hoping?

At least her sons are home and safe, at least she has a husband who will return from his golfing holiday with his receding hairline bright pink and peeling. She has a lot to be grateful for, including a really lovely kitchen, which, thanks to Ellen, will be absolutely spotless when she returns tomorrow.

If only she could sleep, if only she didn't keep thinking of Jess, baby Jess in a yellow blanket, 'Don't touch the baby, Anne.' Toddler Jess laughing and running away, her pink leather reins straining. Jess holding her big sister's hand to cross the road to

341

school, Jess doing handstands in her baggy knickers, Jess on the front row of the Cygnet School of Dance annual show, Jess in the local paper as a leaping bridesmaid and then again on the front page as a Missing Girl.

The photograph depicting a younger more innocent Jess, a girl who had already disappeared.

She refuses to think of Jess as she'd last seen her, the badly dyed peroxide hair, the sexy but sulky mouth, the slammed doors and recriminations, runaway Jess with her blue duffel bag stuffed with things she thought she'd need in London and beyond. She took her passport, she could be anywhere, she could be in India or the Philippines. Perhaps she's in Vegas.

But she isn't and she never will be. Poor Anne, she is physically and emotionally drained but somehow sleep eludes her and for what seems like hours she tosses about on pillows that refuse to get comfortable beneath her head.

If only she knew, if only she knew that the clue to whatever happened to Jess lies almost within her grasp. She could almost reach out and touch it, for just yards from where she tries to sleep, behind a chipboard partition in the loft next door, lies the blue duffel bag with a white plastic trim. In a matter of days Drew will find this bag and he will know what it is before his hand reaches inside and gropes the edge of a long-expired passport. He will know what it is before he tips the faded satin scraps and the rusty-zippered make-up bag on to the kitchen table and before he opens the passport to stare at a black-and-white picture of a girl wearing too much eyeliner. He will know who it is.

But all this will happen later, for now Anne is fretful but oblivious and anyway, answers don't always help.

At last Anne sleeps, she sleeps and dreams of finding her sister. In her dream she is back in Dulwich, she is in Sainsbury's, she has only popped in for a few bits and bobs but the trolley she is pushing is already brimming. She is going to make Diana

Henry's cheesy pork dish and she just needs some green beans, but as she turns the corner into the frozen veg aisle she bumps into Jess.

You wouldn't really know it was Jess, she is just another middle-aged woman, but the legwarmers give it away. 'Hello Jess,' says Anne. 'Hello Anne,' says Jess, and the two women embrace.

Under the duvet Anne is finally warm.

BRAND NEW TOUR

JENNY ECLAIR

ECLAIRIOUS

"RUTHLESSLY FUNNY"
THE TIMES

VISIT
WWW.JENNYECLAIR.COM
FOR FULL LIVE DATES